TERROR TALES
OF WALES

TERROR TALES
OF WALES

Edited by Paul Finch

TERROR TALES OF WALES

First published in 2014 by Gray Friar Press.
9 Abbey Terrace, Whitby,
North Yorkshire, YO21 3HQ, England.
Email: gary.fry@virgin.net
www.grayfriarpress.com

Typesetting and design by Paul Finch and Gary Fry

ISBN: 978-1-906331-45-0

TABLE OF CONTENTS

UNDER THE WINDINGS OF THE SEA
Ray Cluley

When I was younger I came out here with my friends to do the Three Peaks Challenge," Eddie told his son. He glanced away from the road for just a moment to see if his comment had registered but Dylan was still playing with his phone. He couldn't tell if the boy was texting or playing a game. "You have to climb three mountains, that's why it's called Three Peaks. There's Ben Nevis in Scotland, Scafell in England and Snowdon in Wales."

Dylan made a noise, some sort of grunt, but Eddie didn't know if it was encouragement to continue or a response to whatever he was doing on the phone.

"Anyway, we came out here for a practice walk, you know, a bit of training. And do you know what the place was called?"

"Fanny Big," Dylan said, with no trace of a smile. "You've told me already."

"Have I?"

Eddie had hoped the name would make his son laugh. Fan-Y-Big.

"How much further is it?" Dylan asked. "I need to take a p … I need to pee."

"There's a services coming up."

The road trip had been Beth's idea. "Weekends at yours aren't enough, especially when all he does is play the X-Box while you work on some new project," she'd said. "You two need to bond, especially now."

Eddie had said nothing. The 'especially now' didn't sound as temporary as they'd agreed the split would be.

"Why don't you take him to Wales? Show Dylan the country where you grew up, and you've got that book thing so it could be research."

Eddie didn't need to do any research – he was only writing the introduction for the awfully titled *Writers of Wales* – but he agreed that the idea of visiting his old haunts was an attractive one. *Hen wlad fy nhadau*, 'the land of my fathers', that was Wales. It would be a good place to take Dylan.

"I could take him to Aberdyfi."

"Yeah, good. That's it. And that place with the underwater city you used to go on about."

"That is Aberdyfi."

1

"Well okay then."

"It means 'mouth of the dark one', because of the …"

"He'll love it."

And so here they were.

It hadn't been a great trip so far. Eddie loved Wales in the rain, particularly this kind of fine drizzle that seemed to just hang in the air, casting a mystical sheen over the landscape. The weather made it easy to imagine one of Arthur's knights stepping out from behind a ruin, or the ancient Merlin emerging from behind standing stones as grey as the sky behind them. But this was summer, and he couldn't help but feel slightly disappointed for Dylan's sake.

Dylan, quiet at the best of times, had shifted his mood to sullen ever since they'd crossed the border. He'd seemed quietly impressed by the bridge for all of five seconds, judging by how he turned his attention from phone to window for once, looking down at the sea as they crossed it, but ever since then he'd been uncommunicative save for the occasional syllable. "I'm not going to talk about Mum," was the most he'd said all the trip, and he'd said that getting into the car as a kind of caveat for his company.

A sign flashed by announcing the services again and Eddie began to change lanes, ready to leave the road behind for a bit.

"How about a burger as well, eh?"

The boy grunted.

"Dylan?"

"Yeah, alright."

Jesus.

It had been a long three days. So far they'd been to Hay-on-Wye (a bad start; what teenage boy liked books?) and they'd seen the standing stones, and they'd stopped at Pen-coed, where Eddie had lived briefly as a lad. They had just one more stop before Aberdyfi.

"You know, you're named after Dylan Thomas," Eddie said. "The guy whose house we're going to."

"I've really gotta pee, Dad."

Eddie already knew his son didn't care for poetry, but it had been worth a try. Maybe he'd like stories better. He'd like the one about the drowned city.

"Dad, we just passed it."

"What?"

"The turn off. We missed the exit."

"*Cachu.*"

Eddie glanced around as if he could somehow turn them off the road anyway, but it was too late.

"You'll have to hold on a bit longer," he said.

Dylan tutted and looked out of his window. "Don't blame me if I wet myself," he said.

One night, when Eddie was young, younger than Dylan, he'd heard a noise downstairs in their new house. He wasn't sure what the noise had been, only that it had woken him. Part of him knew it was probably just the sounds of a place he wasn't used to yet, settling down, but another part, a stronger part, remembered the stories his father told him about ghosts and monsters. He lay clutching the bedclothes, listening, hearing only the soft hush of the blood in his ears. And then a bang at the front door. He nearly wet the bed in surprise, his bladder full to bursting, and now he couldn't get up to go, no way. An unformed voice, a moan that rose in volume, came to him from downstairs.

"It's all right, Eddie," said his mother, making her way past his room and down the hall, and Eddie wondered where his father was, why he wasn't the one investigating. Another succession of banging at the front door downstairs startled him again and again he nearly wet the bed. There came with the banging a cry of "Carry" and he thought 'carry what?' before understanding it was Cari, short for Ceridwen, the name of the woman Eddie only called Mum.

"Ca*rriiii*..."

"All right, I'm coming." And, because she was angry, "*Lesu Grist.*"

Eddie found the courage to venture from his room.

"Get back to bed," his mother told him, tying her dressing gown closed at the foot of the stairs.

"I need the toilet."

She reached for the door as the letterbox banged-banged-banged. "All *right*!" And for Eddie she gave a hasty wave of permission so he scampered away to the bathroom. Locked the door.

As the flush receded he heard the tail end of a scream from downstairs. It wasn't the serious kind, but it wasn't quite playful either, and the deep dull tone of his father's voice came after.

Eddie looked down the stairs as he passed them on his way back to his room, expecting to see his parents in some argument or playful fight, but what he saw made him cry out and a remaining trickle of pee escaped him, wetting the front of his pyjamas.

His mother was trying to pull herself free from the grip of some skull-headed monster. Eddie saw a curve of white and then it was turning his way and a long white beak pointed up the stairs at him, his father's face beneath, mouth open in a dark O.

"Eddie, my boy," he said, "Don't be scared."

3

He wore the skull like a hat. It was like a horse skull, like the ones for Mari Lwyd, only longer and narrow like a bird's.

Eddie's father tutted. "He's pissed himself."

He hadn't, not really. It was only a little bit.

"He was going to the toilet."

"I did," Eddie said. "I did go to the toilet."

"Come here, Eddie," his father said, squatting at the foot of the stairs. He raised the skull from his head and for a terrifying moment Eddie thought he'd see brains underneath but it was just hair stuck down with sweat or maybe rain. "Look." He held the skull out but Eddie did not want to touch it. It was what Death left behind and he did not want it. "It's just a skull. From a dolphin."

The skull was round like a ball at one end. Eddie could see a hole in the top, the blowhole where it would have breathed when alive. The eye sockets were vacant curves at the sides. An elongated length, sloping from the ball and becoming flat, was the upper part of the jaw. Eddie could see lots of little teeth.

"It's weird," Eddie said. What he'd wanted to say was, "It's wrong."

"Yeah. Weird." With that his father put it back on and made a few quick nods to make the dolphin playful, trying to imitate a dolphin sound. To Eddie it sounded more like that noise Popeye made in the old cartoons, *huh-guh-guh-guh*. Then he held his arms out like a sleepwalker, groaning and reaching for Eddie's mother. "*Driiink*," he said, like a zombie doing Mari Lwyd.

"No, you've had enough."

So had Eddie. He returned to his room, changed his pyjama bottoms, and went back to bed where he dreamed men with dolphin heads chased him out to sea.

*

"Would you want to live here?" Eddie asked Dylan.

Dylan pushed a handful of French fries into his mouth. "Burger King? Hell yeah."

It was the closest they'd come to joking, though the boy didn't smile.

"Wales, I mean."

"Way-yels," Dylan said. And, "What's occurring?", which had been a favourite for the last couple of days. Then finally, "No thanks."

"I loved it here."

"Why did you move then?"

"Your mum wanted to live in London."

Dylan wiped his mouth. "She doesn't anymore."

4

"Did she say that?"

Dylan realised he'd broken his own rule and became overly interested in which part of the burger to bite next.

"Does she want to move? Where to?"

Dylan shrugged. "Abroad somewhere."

Shit.

"We're going to sort things out, you know," Eddie said.

That shrug again.

"I know this isn't brilliant but – "

"It's fine. You were always working anyway." Beth's words from their boy's mouth.

Eddie thought of his own father. Always working.

"I wish you could have met your grandfather," Eddie said.

Dylan slid a pickle out from his burger, licked away the ketchup, and dropped it to the wrapper.

"He used to tell me all these stories. Scared the shit out of me."

That got a reaction, Dylan momentarily delighted by the swear word.

"One of them was about dead people living in the sea, ringing bells."

His father told him lots of scary stories, about ghosts and devils and witches, but his favourites to tell were ones about the sea. And then he would go back out fishing for days at a time, leaving Eddie with nightmares.

"Did you ever read *The Grey King*?" Eddie asked. He didn't want to tell Dylan the bells story yet. "It's a book by Susan Cooper?"

Dylan shook his head.

"How about *The Silver* –"

"Can I play in the arcade while you finish that?"

Somehow Dylan had finished his burger and his fries in the time it had taken Eddie to take a few bites.

"Fine," Eddie said. He'd wanted to ask about Lloyd Alexander as well, and Arthur Machen, and a whole load of others, but it was probably pointless. "Okay." He tried to smile, to show it was all right, really.

"Can I have some money?"

Eddie handed over the change from their meal and Dylan ran to the machines that blasted their sounds and colours a few metres away. These were the heavy blocks Dylan's generation worshipped, ones with screens and buttons and bright lights. What had Eddie been thinking, taking him to a bunch of rocks in wet and windy South Glamorgan?

"People say that if you sleep here on a certain night," Eddie had told Dylan, "you will either die, go mad, or become a poet." It had always amused him, that combination of apparent dangers.

"Why don't you sleep here then?" Dylan had asked. Eddie knew the insult had been accidental because of how Dylan's face had flushed and how quickly he'd added, "So you can be a proper poet I mean," which hurt even more. Dylan probably saw some of that, too, but didn't realise how he'd managed to make things worse, didn't realise the power of that one word; as every 'proper' poet would tell you, a single word can make all the difference.

"Was this made by the same people as Stonehenge?" Dylan had asked, his hand on one of the standing stones. And that had been enough for Eddie. That was Dylan still trying to make amends.

"Doubtful," he'd said. "But the stones that make Stonehenge came from Wales, did you know that?"

His apology made and accepted, Dylan was back to minimal responses, but that was all right, too. They had a week to get past that.

Eddie dropped the rest of his burger, calculating what was left of that week, and looked at where Dylan was shooting zombies or aliens or terrorists. It made him sad to see it was the happiest Dylan had been so far. He gathered what was left of his food into the mess of wrappers and binned the lot on his way over to his son.

"Come on," he said, "Let's go."

"I'm nearly dead."

Eddie nodded and waited, his hands in his pockets.

*

"Dylan!"

He was yelling it before he was completely out of the Boathouse, ignoring the views of the Tof estuary and searching the cliffs for his son.

A visitor coming out of the tearoom said, "He's long gone," and Eddie knew he was joking, knew he meant the other Dylan, the one who'd lived and worked here, but it still sent a cold thrill through him.

He'd been distracted by everything inside. Dylan Thomas had written *Do Not Go Gentle* and *Under Milkwood* here, this was where he'd *lived*. Eddie had just watched a short film in the exhibition area and then Dylan was gone. He had searched the few rooms for him all the time imagining he could hear the poet's voice whispering from the walls, telling him to rage, rage.

"Dylan!"

6

He ran to the corner of the building and there was Dylan, there was his boy, looking out to sea. The hood of his jumper was down for once and the wind blew his heavy fringe back. There was something serene in his expression and it angered Eddie almost as much as his wandering off.

Eddie grabbed his shoulder and turned him round. "Jesus, Dylan."

The boy pulled away, "What?" and Eddie grabbed for him again, this time because of how close he was to the edge. Again, Dylan shook himself free. "There's a barrier, Dad, I'm fine."

"Where did you go?"

The answer was obvious, he was here, but he said, "I wanted to see the sea."

"I was calling you."

"It's windy," Dylan said. "I only heard the sea."

"Don't wander off, remember? I said –"

"You were taking ages." Dylan glanced at the house behind them as if to wonder what could possibly be so interesting about it.

"Dylan Thomas lived here once," Eddie said.

His son's nod was as dismissive as a shrug and he turned away from the building. Below them, waves curled in and broke apart without urgency.

"You're named after him."

"Yeah."

"He was one of the best," Eddie said. "One of my favourites."

"We do poetry at school."

"Yeah?"

"It's all about dying."

"'And death shall have no dominion'," Eddie said.

"What?"

"It's a poem. About how death isn't the end." He was ready to recite the entire thing, it was one he had memorised, but Dylan's attention was on the ground.

"You can go back in if you want," Dylan said. He picked up a stone and threw, trying to reach the sea. "I won't go anywhere."

Eddie looked at the building. What had Dylan Thomas thought, leaving it for a country from which he'd never return? Had he thought of home as he lay dying, poisoned with alcohol? Or did he think of his poetry? T.S. Eliot had called him a poet of considerable importance. Toynbee had called him the greatest living poet in the English language. Eddie thought he'd quote both in his introduction. He wouldn't mention the alcoholism. The man needed to be remembered for his words.

"Dad?"

"Hmm?"

Dylan was frowning at him, stone unthrown in his hand.

"Hey," Eddie said, recovering, "do you fancy a milkshake in the tearoom? Maybe some *bara brith*?" He wanted Dylan to ask what it was – fruit bread made with tea and spices – but the boy only turned to cast his rock at the sea.

"No thanks. But you can. I'll wait."

"No," Eddie said, casting one last look at the building. "We can go."

But they both stood staring as the sea swept further and further out.

*

"It's where the dead live," Eddie's father told him once, talking of the sea.

"Davey!"

"What? He's old enough to know these things."

Eddie had looked from father to mother and back again, quiet.

"Where the sea is now, all that out there, it used to be fields and towns and trees," Eddie's father said, pointing and then sweeping his hand to encompass all they saw before them. Behind them, to the east towards Snowdonia, the sky was merely grey with cloud, but out over Cardigan Bay, where his father pointed, the grey was nearly black and the sea was darkening. "All that out there used to be a place called Cantre'r Gwaelod. Then one day the sea came in and everyone who lived there died. Drowned, or swept against rocks and buildings."

"Davey, really."

"It's all right, Mum."

"See?"

Eddie's comment earned him a hair ruffle and a smile.

"Why didn't they run away?" Eddie asked. He was thinking of how he used to stand by the sea and flee each wave that came in to wet his feet.

"It was too quick. Like a tidal wave, see? There used to be walls protecting them, but the man who was supposed to look after them didn't pay attention."

"Seithenin the Drunkard," Eddie's mother said. Eddie saw the scowl his father aimed at her, but she didn't. She was hugging herself against the sea breeze and looking out to where a fisherman was casting line.

"Yes, Seithenin. He was supposed to take care of the walls but he didn't and one day the sea came in and knocked them down or washed over them."

Eddie thought that must have been horrible. Not just everyone dying but knowing it was your fault.

"Why didn't he take care of the walls?"

"He was always drunk," Eddie's mother said, but it didn't sound like she was really answering his question. It sounded like she was talking about something else.

"He wasn't paying attention," Eddie's father said. "But in another story it wasn't the sea at all. There was a woman who was supposed to look after the well and she didn't and the water came up and up and up and drowned everyone. She hadn't been paying attention either."

"Right, and which one seems more likely?" Eddie's mother asked. She was still looking at the bay, the grey waves small but coming in quickly.

"The first one," Eddie said, thinking the question had been for him.

"Exactly," his mother said.

"But they're just stories," Eddie said. He didn't really believe either version.

"Oh really?" his father said. "Well, when the tide is out I'll show you. Sometimes you can still see the trees."

"Really? Is that true, Mum?"

She'd turned back to them then and finally smiled. "Yes," she said. She even smiled at Eddie's father. "And sometimes you can still hear the bells of the church out there." She tilted her head to the sea. "Under the water. Faint chimes from the bells, quietly tolling beneath the waves."

Suddenly Eddie believed it, believed all of it. Because his father said there were trees and his mother said there bells.

"But you don't want to hear them," Eddie's father said.

"Why not?"

Eddie's father looked out to sea and said, "Because the bells call the dead."

Eddie looked at the sea as well. It was the same dark colour as the sky. It looked like it was everywhere ahead of them.

Eddie's mother tutted but said nothing, which Eddie thought meant it was true.

"Taffy heard the bells once," Eddie's father said. Eddie didn't know who Taffy was but he didn't want to ask; his father was concentrating, his voice quiet, and although he was looking out to sea, Eddie didn't think he was really seeing it. "He kept looking at the water, you know, over the sides. Could barely concentrate on what he was doing. Said he kept hearing a chiming in his ears. In the end, Tom sent him below, just to get him out of the way, and he

9

never came back. We couldn't find him anywhere. We had to report him overboard."

Eddie's father nodded as if agreeing with something the sea was telling him, then he looked at Eddie and said, "That can happen, if you don't pay attention."

Eddie was pulled in close to his mother suddenly and she squeezed him to her body with one arm. "*Cwtch*," she said, announcing the cuddle. She said, "There's a beautiful song about the bells," and then she sang. She sang for him in Welsh, hushed and gentle, "*Os wyt ti yn bur i mi, fel rwyf fi yn bur i ti...*" and she was right, it was beautiful.

"What does it mean?"

"It means I love you," she said, and kissed the top of his head.

"Do you have to be a fisherman?" Eddie asked his father.

"Until I can find another job."

Eddie looked at his mother but she had nothing to add. She just tried to smile at him.

"Come on," Eddie's father said, setting off towards the beach. "Let's go for a swim, eh?"

It was far too cold for that, so they laughed. Not that Eddie wanted to swim in the sea ever again; a dead hand might grab his ankle and pull him to a town where corpses walked on the ocean floor, ringing bells only certain people could hear.

"If you hear the bells just cover your ears," Eddie's father said, putting fingers in his as they walked.

"Or sing," Eddie's mother said, and on their way to the sea she taught him *Clychau Aberdyfi*.

The Bells of Aberdovey.

*

They arrived in Aberdyfi late from Laugharne. It was the perfect Welsh town, Eddie thought, with its steep green hills, the river, its long stretch of beach. Not that he could see any of that now from their window; just the dotted lights of a boat in the dark. Finding a hotel with a vacancy had been tricky, having not booked in advance, and finding one with a sea view nearly impossible. But only nearly.

"*Mae'r clychau dan y mor*," Eddie said. He wrote it down to see what it looked like, then compared it to 'The bells under the sea'. He was trying to write a section for the book but the television was on, annoying him. It had been fine while scribbling notes but now that he was trying to write ...

"The first mention of the drowned city is in a poem from the *Black Book of Carmarthen*," he read aloud. "The song, though, was written by Charles Dibdin in 1785. No, John Hughes in the 1800s. Shit."

The news came on, distracting him with its headlines and the punctuation of Big Ben. Christ, ten o'clock already.

"Dylan, can you turn it down?"

Still the television.

Eddie turned in his chair. "Dylan –"

A man stood leaning over Eddie's son. He wore a dolphin's skull for a head and his clothes were soaking wet. Water ran from the dolphin's bony bottle-nose beak to drip onto Dylan's face. Dylan lay with his mouth open and his eyes closed. The man reached for him with wrinkled hands as grey as dolphin skin and the sea ran out from his heavy sleeves.

Eddie opened his mouth to say, "No," and though he wasn't sure the word had come out he saw the man stop reaching. The dolphin head turned suddenly, the man raising it to look out through open skeletal jaws, but Eddie looked away. A heavy book of verse lay open, facedown, and he grabbed it. Slammed it closed. Raised his arm to throw it, turning with a cry that never left his throat.

The man was gone.

Dylan was still sleeping. One of his arms hung over the edge of the bed. His head was tilted to one side. Though his hair was damp, it was only sweat. The puddle on the pillow beside his open mouth was only drool. He looked like the child he once was, rather than the teenager he was becoming.

Eddie went and sat beside his sleeping son and stroked the hair back from his eyes. The boy stirred, wiped at the saliva on his cheek and closed his mouth, fidgeting back into sleep.

Eddie's mother used to read to him before bed. When other children were getting fairy tales, Eddie's mother gave him poetry or she'd sing. Ceridwen, Blessed Song, living up to her name. He'd always found the soft lilt of her language soothing, gentling him into sleep with all those ls.

It was Eddie's father who told him the stories. Some from *The Mabinogion* but mostly made up ones, always about Wales and always frightening; Eddie had loved them and he had hated them, too.

He muted the television by remote, rearranged the covers over Dylan, and recited for him some words by his namesake. He whispered of men in the wind and the west moon, lovers who were lost and love that was not. He considered phoning Beth, but his phone was in the pocket of his jacket on the door. His brick, as Dylan called it. Not that Beth answered his calls. She responded to his texts, eventually, but his calls went unanswered. She thought it would be better if they didn't talk for a while so they could try the

11

separation properly but Eddie thought there'd been enough of that already. He could probably call her on Dylan's phone, but that was bound to be in the boy's hoody pocket and he didn't want to disturb him now that he was asleep.

Eddie leant over, kissed him good night, "*Noson dda*," and returned to his work, trying to ignore the salty tang that seemed to linger in the room.

*

"You're doing it again."

Eddie had been looking out to sea at a small boat passing back and forth across the bay. He was watching its wake and thinking that skulls and bones were death's wake, the sign of its passing, and he thought of funeral wakes, thinking he could get a poem out of the boat's churned up waters. "What, Dylan?" Churned up waters, yes, spreading wide before they dissipated. "What did you say?"

"You were talking to yourself."

Dylan was scraping a stone against the pavement with his foot. It made a harsh sound but left little trace; if he was trying to write something he'd be disappointed.

"Was I?"

Still looking at the ground, dragging his shoe with sharp scrapes, Dylan said, "You were going on about naked men rising again or something. It was a bit gay."

"It's from a –"

"Poem, yeah, I know."

Eddie nodded. "Your grandfather used to tell me ghost stories about this bit of water."

"Yeah?" Dylan lifted his foot and inspected what little mark he'd left. He looked at Eddie. "What kind of ghosts?"

"Yeah, he was always telling stories. I used to hate them because they frightened me but when he died I missed them more than anything."

"How did granddad die?"

"He drowned," Eddie said. "He was a fisherman."

He had fallen asleep on the beach after a heavy drinking session, or passed out more likely, but Eddie didn't want to tell his son that. Not yet, anyway. He hadn't lied, though.

"And the ghosts?"

Eddie didn't know if Dylan was asking about his granddad still or the stories. He told him about the bells that called the dead.

"And sometimes, at night, you can see them standing in the shallows, unable to come ashore."

Dylan looked but saw only tourists like themselves.

12

"The ghosts," Eddie explained. "Or you saw someone walking out to be with them. Walking, and never stopping."

"That's not scary," Dylan said. He resumed scratching stone against stone with hard kicks of his foot.

"Imagine all that water rushing in here," Eddie said. "Hills made of seawater swelling inland, a huge wall of water coming right at us."

"Like a tsunami?"

"Exactly. That would be pretty scary."

Dylan shrugged.

"That's what some people think happened out there. Thousands died. And if you hear the bells ringing, it means *you'll* be next."

"There'll be another tsunami?"

Eddie was telling it all wrong.

"Come on, I want to show you something." He picked up the pace so Dylan would have to follow. "Did I tell you the story about Taliesin?"

Dylan made a noise.

"Well, there was this sorceress, Ceridwen, and a drunk, Gwion Bach, and they had a kid called Taliesin, a legendary poet. Sixth century. Anyway, the sorceress cast him into the sea and he washed up at a place called Borth, near here."

"She got rid of him?"

"Hmm? Yeah. And he washed up here. It was okay, he was taken in by the king of Cantre'r Gwaelod." He'd point out where Cantre'r Gwaelod was meant to be when they reached the jetty. There was a bell beneath it that rang at high tide. If he timed it right, with the story still fresh, maybe that would do the trick when he told him about the flooded kingdom and the dead, calling.

"You hear it?" he said.

"What?"

The bell chimed clear enough but he'd mixed the stories up too much or taken too long telling them or something. Dylan had already forgotten them.

"There's a bell underneath the jetty," Eddie said. There was no point in pretending otherwise now. "The Time and Tide bell. There's an inscription on it, 'below the awesome tide' or something like that. From a –"

"Poem?"

There was no point answering that, either. "Anyway, it rings when the tide comes in."

"Cool."

"Yeah?" Eddie hadn't thought that would impress the boy, but then he saw what Dylan had seen. "Idiots," he said.

13

A group of boys in their early teens were playing on the jetty. One of the lads launched himself into the air, held his knees to his chest, and made his own explosion of sea spray. His friends cheered. The tide was high, all right, and the boys were fearless, but Eddie knew there were dangers hidden in those waters. Maybe not ghosts or dolphin-headed men, okay, but the discarded debris of shopping trolleys and stolen 'for sale' signs, perhaps. And what if a particularly strong wave came in to dash you against the supports of the very jetty you leapt from?

"Can I play with them for a while?" Dylan looked like he knew the answer already, but it didn't completely extinguish the hope from his face, a hope that brightened when he thought to add, "You could work on your book in peace."

"No. Absolutely not."

Eddie tried to explain some of the dangers as he saw them but all Dylan heard was no.

"I'll be careful."

"It's too cold."

Surely he was too old now to join any random group of friends? That was the pure privilege of the very young, wasn't it? Toddlers in the park and play areas.

"Dad –"

"No."

His ruling was made all the more harsh by another splash and whoop of cheers.

"Are we ever going to go in the sea?"

A boy was climbing up the ladder, dripping, waiting to watch a friend fly and splash.

"There are dolphins out there," Eddie said.

"Can we see them? Get a boat or something?"

"Maybe."

"That means no."

"Dylan."

"What?"

Eddie sighed. He saw a chippy and pointed, suggesting lunch, eager to get away from this argument before it could really begin. Eager, too, for the sharp tang of salt mixed with vinegar. "We'll go for a swim later," he promised, knowing he could delay another hour after eating.

Dylan said nothing. He scuffed his feet and kicked at everything he found in front of them.

Eddie tried to ignore it, just as he tried to ignore the laughter of the other children and the persistent toll of the jetty's bell.

*

14

Eddie worked in the hotel's lounge. He'd found the poem, *Araith Seithenyn*, the one with the 'awesome tide' line, but a 'rejoice' reference made him think of the children playing on the jetty, jumping and cheering. He hoped Dylan wasn't too disappointed, wandering the shops and arcades. He'd annoyed Eddie with persistent questions and cajoling about the jetty, and the more Eddie said no, the more he wanted to do it. Eddie had sent him away with some money.

It was quiet in the lounge, the small bar serving only a half dozen people, but still he couldn't concentrate. The window he'd sat beside was old and rattled in its wooden frame whenever a gust came in from the sea, the cries of children playing on the beach coming in with it. Some of the breeze found a way in through the cracks and bigger gaps around the panes of glass, occasionally lifting his papers. It chilled his skin.

"Somebody buy me a drink!"

Eddie glanced up from his notes and gasped at what he saw; his father standing in the doorway of the hotel lounge. He wore a dolphin's skull tipped forward so the long beak, nose, whatever the hell it was, hid his face, but it was definitely him. He raised it to better see the customers in the bar, hoping someone would answer his command.

It wasn't his father. Obviously, it wasn't his father. And it wasn't a dolphin skull. It was a grubby baseball cap that had once been white. There was some kind of logo on the front. It looked nothing like a dolphin skull at all, not really.

Another man came in, slapping the first on the back and calling, "Who's going to buy us a drink, eh?" He carried something like a toolbox, only it was made of wood. He held it up as if it explained their request, just as another man joined them, and another, until the bar had suddenly doubled in customers, the newcomers clearly already drunk. They kept calling for drinks.

One of the men had managed to persuade someone sitting at the bar to buy him one. The others were dispersing amongst the customers to try their luck.

Eddie returned to his work and tried to look busy. Tried to *be* busy.

The man with the grubby cap put the heavy box on the table. It stank of the sea, and some of Eddie's nearest papers began to soak, the ink blurring. He moved them away quickly.

"What you writing?"

"A book about Wales," he said. It was easier than explaining it was a book about Welsh writers and that he was only doing the introduction.

The man sat, but on the edge of the seat as if just for a moment, which was good. "The place or the animal?"

"The place."

"What, like its history? The customs and things?"

"Sort of."

The man grinned and Eddie felt like he'd stumbled into a trap. "You heard of Hunting the Wren?" the man asked.

"No."

"It's a custom, see," said the man, "a wassail." He paused, then spelt it out for him so Eddie could write it down. "A ritual for luck. And the wren represents winter, like a bad winter, yeah, only we catch it and carry it around the town and everyone who pays a tribute with a drink gets to escape a bad winter."

Eddie said, "It's summer."

"It is," said the man, "yeah. But this isn't Hunting the Wren, it's just a bit like it." He played with some coils of fishing line that had been tied around the box's handle.

"What's in the box?"

"Buy me a drink and I'll show you."

The man's persistence annoyed Eddie, reminded him of Dylan's whining. Eddie grabbed the box and pulled it open. The top of it parted into shelves like a tool box and a stench wafted out from inside the main storage well.

"It's a fish," Eddie said. He had no idea what kind. It was big. It glistened. Its one eye stared.

"Yeah, a fish. Now mine's a Buckley, *diolch ffrind*. Just a half."

"It's dead."

He wondered if it was already dead when they put it in the box, or whether it had flopped around inside and suffocated, drowning without water.

"Well it is *now*."

As if Eddie opening the box had somehow killed it. Like he'd let the water out or the air in. Eddie thought of Schrödinger's cat and began to laugh. Schrödinger's *fish*. Schrödinger's *cat*fish. Neither alive or dead and somehow both at the same time. It reminded him of his marriage.

"What's so funny?"

"Nothing," Eddie said, calming himself easily because it was true. He slipped his papers into the middle of the book he'd been copying from. "I've got to find my boy."

"What about that beer?"

Eddie said, "Sorry, I don't drink. Excuse me," and hurried out of the hotel.

*

16

Eddie looked for a coffee shop where he could finish his work but keep an eye out for Dylan. He glanced at his watch: it was just gone four. Actually, Dylan should've been back by now. He tucked his book and papers under his arm and retrieved his mobile.

No answer. Seemed it wasn't only Beth ignoring his calls.

Thanks to the curve of the bay, Eddie had a pretty good view but despite the poor weather there were still plenty of people about. He'd have to look for Dylan among them, but first he'd get his jacket; he was only wearing a shirt, and the breeze coming in off the sea was cold. He'd go up to the room, dump the book and his notes, grab his coat, and find Dylan.

He was probably in the room anyway by now. Television blaring, stretched out across the bed with his shoes still on.

But he wasn't in the room. It looked like he had been, though; the hoody he always wore was slung over the chair with his jeans.

"Dylan?"

Eddie tried phoning again.

From beneath the clothes came the vibrations of Dylan's mobile, followed by a repetitive melody the boy had downloaded as his ring tone.

Why would he have left his phone?

Eddie went to the window, phone still pressed to his ear as if Dylan might answer his at any moment even though he could hear it ringing behind him. The tide had come in. There was only a narrow strip of beach out there.

Eddie cancelled his call, tossed the phone, and grabbed Dylan's. He thought her number had been deleted at first, then remembered she'd be Mum, not Beth.

She answered right away. "Hi honey, everything okay?"

Honey. It should have made him smile, and it did, but it twisted in him too. "Beth."

"Oh. Where's Dylan?"

"Good question."

Was that someone else? A voice in the background?

"What do you mean, 'good question'? Where is he, Eddie?"

Yes, there was someone else there, asking what was wrong. Trying to comfort her.

"*Eddie.*"

"Who's that with you?"

He stared out the window, trying to focus on something else. People were still on the beach, despite the weather and early evening air. Some were even playing in the shallows, a couple actually swimming.

She ignored his question and repeated her own, "Where is he?"

"It doesn't matter," Eddie said quietly.

"Eddie, put Dylan on the phone."

"I'll just get him."

He hung up and pocketed the phone, watching the people in the sea. He knew where Dylan would be.

He remembered his jacket again only as he left the hotel and the sea-breeze settled on his skin. It didn't matter. He'd soon warm up, walking quickly, though he wondered how Dylan was managing. He'd be in just his swimming shorts and wet by now, shivering on the jetty as the sun struggled to shine and he waited for his turn to jump.

"Damn it, Dylan."

Eddie walked with his head down, eyes on the pavement, trying not to think of the voice he'd heard, the male voice in the background, trying to plan how to reprimand Dylan but thinking of the voice he'd heard, the male voice in the background, until, looking up, he realised he'd passed the jetty. He turned and headed back for it, though he could already see it was empty. No one played there.

"*Cachu.*"

Eddie grabbed his phone again, remembered it was Dylan's, and pushed it back into his pocket. "*Shit!*"

He looked out to sea as he walked. He could feel it on his skin, occasional gusts whipping up a light spray. There was supposed to be a whole town out there. Under the water. He imagined what might live there now, swimming out of broken homes, weaving around trees of stone. He imagined them walking the wet sands and swatting at dolphins that swam too close. He imagined what it would be like to walk out there and join them, walk until too exhausted to return, to fight against the tide …

The bell wasn't ringing.

Although Dylan clearly wasn't on the jetty, Eddie hurried along its length to where the kids had been jumping. There was a circular grille set into the boards so you could look down at the bell but there was too much darkness down there and the sea was too close. He tried to look beneath the jetty but had to resort to his hands and knees to really see and even then his view was limited. A ladder descended into the water. He climbed down the first few rungs.

"Dylan?"

The bell looked more like two stuck together, one upside down atop the other. Angles of cable supported the bronze construction so that it hung suspended beneath the jetty. Its lower half had a paddle for a clapper, the motion of the sea moving it to lever the tongue in the top bell. Only it wasn't doing this because …

Dylan's legs stuck out from beneath the bell. For a moment Eddie thought he was tampering with it, "*Dylan!*" But the way his shins moved, lazy with the tide rather than kicking, feet limp ...

"Dylan!"

Eddie let go of the ladder and dropped into the sea. It grabbed him entirely and held him cold but Eddie kicked and with one broad stroke he was at the bell. He grabbed Dylan's ankles and pulled. A rush of bubbles instead of a yell burst from his mouth at what he saw. His boy. His little boy.

Eddie hugged him close and kicked to the surface. He spoke his son's name before taking breath and it came out of him empty. Ghost-like. Faded.

The boy was pale. Eddie put his mouth to Eddie's open one, the boy's cold lips telling him it was futile but doing it anyway. He tried to give him breath but had nothing yet to give. He turned his head, gulped at precious air, and gave it to his boy.

"Come on son, come on."

He knew he'd never get back up the ladder with Dylan so he leaned back and draped an arm around him, kicking for them both, sweeping one arm back in the water to carry them to land. When the shore pressed against his back he turned and dragged Dylan up the beach. He pumped at his chest, copying moves he'd only ever seen on television. He tilted Dylan's head to one side only to tilt it back almost immediately afterwards so he could try breathing life back into him again.

"Dylan, come on, I'm sorry, come on." He pushed his boy's chest, pushed, pushed. "I'm here now." Pushed.

Behind him the bells were chiming.

*

Eddie carried Dylan back to the hotel. He could feel people staring but he didn't see them; he was staring into the eyes of his son. Eyes he couldn't close. Bright blue eyes that had somehow turned grey.

"We'll call your mother," Eddie said. "Put you to bed and call your mum, she'll know what to do." His feet squelched in his shoes with each step and the pair of them left a wake of wet carpet behind them in the lobby. He took Dylan up the grand stairs, carried him as he had once carried the boy's mother.

The key was oversized and easy to find in his pocket, easy to hold even with a child in your arms; they really thought of everything.

Inside, he lowered Dylan to the bed. Folded the quilt over him to keep him warm, patted him with it to dry his clothes and skin.

"Okay," he said. "Okay."

19

He still had Dylan's phone but it was soaked and refused to work. It's not dead, Eddie thought. It just needs to dry out. He tucked it into the quilt with his son and saw his own discarded phone on the pillow.

Hers was the first number.

With the phone pressed to his ear he couldn't bear to look at Dylan, as if looking at him and saying what had happened at the same time would make it true. He turned to face the window.

The wide curve of the bay where the dead went. He thought of the houses out there under the sea, the trees, all that the sea had reclaimed, and he imagined the waters rising up for him as well. A tidal wave building and rushing towards the coast, the hotel, to swallow him up and take him away, sweep him out and away. Churn him up and dissipate. Wake, he thought. Wake.

"Though they sink through the sea," he said. "Though they sink through the sea." He couldn't remember the rest.

The phone at his ear, like a broken conch shell, gave him nothing of the sea. Only a ceaseless ringing that called and called and waited to be answered.

LEGIONS OF GHOSTS

The whole history of the British Isles is stained by rivers of blood spilled during countless wars of conquest, rebellion and repression. Wales is by far the smallest of the three countries forming mainland Britain, and given its soaring mountains, rugged coasts and countless river-valleys, probably the most difficult in terms of pure military logistics, and yet it has suffered appallingly in the storm of conflict. Much of this stems from the concerted Welsh campaigns launched by the Anglo/Norman state throughout the medieval period, but there was carnage earlier on during the Roman occupation and later when the English Civil War embroiled all the nations of these islands.

The upshot is that many of Wales's fairest hills and meadows are reputedly the haunt of ghosts, either mournful or vengeful, but all bemoaning a savage demise.

In AD 60, the massed Roman armies of Gaius Suetonius Paulinus crossed the Menai Strait and struck the Isle of Anglesey, centre of the druid religion in Britain. The druids fought back, but ultimately were massacred. Thousands upon thousands were slain, the Romans seeking to tear the heart out of the Celtic belief system that had proved so resistant to their rule. The only evidence today is the occasional clatter of Roman armour still allegedly heard on the Anglesey beaches, and the eerie chanting of voices deep inland where oak groves sacred to the druids once grew in abundance.

In 1136, Kidwelly Castle in Carmarthenshire was the scene of horrible violence when Gwenllian, wife of Gruffyd ap Rhys ap Twdr, Prince of Deheubarth, led a rebel force against its Norman garrison. The rebels were slaughtered and Gwenllian decapitated in the chaos. On foggy nights, her headless spectre is still said to roam the gloomy hillside.

In 1165 at Chirk, near Wrexham, the forces of Henry II were stopped in their tracks by the Welsh army of Owain Gwynedd at the battle of Grogen. For centuries afterwards the field remained unploughed, locals believing any disturbance of the warriors' bones lying under the surface would unleash phantoms across the district.

In 1175, at Abergavenny, the Norman baron, William de Braose, in a scene reminiscent of the terrifying Red Wedding in George R.R. Martin's novel, Game Of Thrones, invited a number of Welsh chieftains to a lavish banquet, and when it was over, had them butchered where they sat. These days, the castle is an ominous *ruin where disembodied voices can supposedly be heard pleading and shrieking.*

In 1295, Welsh blood was shed again when the forces of Madog ap Llewellyn were met by the army of the Earl of Warwick at Maes Moydog in Powys, and died almost to a man. Mist forms are still sighted, drifting unnaturally across the battlefield.

In 1402, the boot was on the other foot, when legendary Welsh patriot, Owain Glyndwr, waylaid an English army at Pilleth, inflicting a gory defeat. A commemorative church now occupies the site, but this too has seen ghostly activity.

Wales's innumerable magnificent castles also play their part in these haunting tales. During the 1460s, at the height of the Wars of the Roses, Harlech Castle and its Lancastrian garrison endured an apocalyptic seven-year siege, the longest in British history, and at one point, in his frustrated anger, Yorkist leader Edward IV sacked and killed widely across the surrounding district. The result: bereft ghosts are said to infest the ancient, atmospheric structure. Meanwhile, Pembroke Castle, a strategic strongpoint in Wales for two millennia, was besieged on many occasions during the Anglo-Welsh wars, but most brutally in 1648, during the English Civil War, when Oliver Cromwell launched a seven-week assault, which finally broke its defences. Again, many died or were executed afterwards. As recently as 2006, a ghost-hunting group camping in one of the castle's lower levels recorded an eerie and inexplicable wailing, which they later posted online, where it can still be heard as the 'Pembroke Voice'.

If supernatural forces are stirred by the actions of the living, it can hardly be surprising that battles and wars feature high in the list of probable causes. The mayhem and terror of close combat must surely release immense psychic energies. When a preponderance of lives are taken swiftly and violently all in the same place, it has to be a breeding ground for the entities we call ghosts. Little wonder that Wales, with its long history of struggle and oppression, is apparently overrun by them.

OLD AS THE HILLS
Steve Duffy

If you ever visit Llanberis in North Wales, there's a café called *Pete's Eats*. All the local climbers use it, and you may as well follow suit – only don't ask for the large coffee unless you're comfortable with volumes significantly over the pint and heading inexorably towards the quart. Seriously lots of coffee, mainliner caffeine; a jolt back to life on those dead suspended days when the weather digs in and Snowdonia lives up to the first syllable of its name.

It was on just such a day, a hard January sleet lashing up the slate-grey lake, that I was last at Pete's, hunkered down in a corner hearing this tale first-hand from Rafi. I've written it up in accordance with his wishes, and broadly speaking he approves of the treatment you're about to read, though he raised a few eyebrows here and there on reading it through. He says it was all weirder, somehow, more mysterious, but when I press him he says never mind, stick with what you've got. It's not exactly a vote of confidence in his own storytelling, let alone in mine, but that can't be helped. He did ask me to change all the names, and as many of the locations as I could; this I've done.

Otherwise, this is what happened:

Rafi is one of those guys you can't help but like, no matter that you suspect they're altogether better adapted to the world than you, and you're sure they're much better looking. Well into his fifties, Rafi still cuts the mustard, the looks of an earthier Frank Langella or a smoother Sly Stallone. He's the son of a former Italian prisoner-of-war and an ex-land girl from Preston (lots of POWs were set to agricultural duties in North Wales during the war, and numerous private armistices seem to have been concluded down on the farms thereabouts). At the time of these events he was just thirty. It was the winter of 1981-82, and he was making then, as now, a decent living as a specialist woodworker and restorer. He'd just split with a girlfriend and rented a flat in Bangor. Things must have been hectic, because the girlfriend hadn't yet been replaced.

He came downstairs one dark December morning to find a letter on the doormat; a woman, Eleri Pritchard Evans, asking whether he might look over the staircase and the oak panelling in her family's house and quote them a price for some renovation work. The address meant little to Rafi, who'd lived most of his life in municipal touristy Rhyl, and like many people in that thoroughly Anglicised locale considered the farther reaches of the Llyn peninsula foreign territory. As if anticipating this response, Miss Pritchard Evans had included brief directions: Plas Glyn-y-Cysgod was hardly on the beaten track, but everything about the phrasing of the letter and the quality of the stationery said *money*, loud and clear to Rafi's keen ear. It would, he decided, be worth a trip out to see the lie of the land, given that in-tray and bank balance alike were looking worryingly empty with the year's end at hand. Drop by for a chat any time before Christmas, said the letter. Rafi rang the number on the letterhead and confirmed a date a fortnight ahead.

The day he set off was bright and breezy-cold, in Bangor at least. There had been sunshine first thing, but one thing and another held him up, and by the time he was revving up his rackety Scimitar round midday, thick heavy-laden clouds were piling in off the Irish Sea. A good look at the skyline might have persuaded a more experienced traveller to stay put. The first flakes of snow were falling before he cleared the end of his road; when he cut off along the A487 the fields all around were white, and the road just beginning to sift over. Still he drove on, south past Nebo and Nasareth, Glandwyfach and Rhoslan, tiny towns with deserted streets and close-curtained windows. All the time it snowed, and the roads, already quiet, emptied till before long there was just Rafi in his Scimitar, heading west.

He hit the coast again at Llanystumdwy on the southern side of the peninsula, and by the time he reached Pwllheli the snow was whirling through the streets, turbid and flurrying. The road out of town forked beyond Llanbedrog pretty much where he expected it to, with the side-track following the course of a small stream up a thickly wooded hillside. The trees sheltered the road and kept it clear, but on breasting the hill Rafi found himself on a rocky plain, bare and undulating, with the snowstorm coming straight at him.

Up on the plain there were drifts, already well formed, covering in some places the low stone walls at the side of the road. Not for the first time, Rafi seriously considered turning back. But again there was the question: was going back the sensible thing to do? Judging by the atlas, he could follow this B-road through to Glyn-y-Cysgod and then strike off for the A497, which would bring him to the coast on the far northern side of the peninsula, near Morfa Nefyn. From there the drive home would surely be easier ... always assuming he could make the northern coast, that was. With very little real choice in the matter, Rafi drove on.

Visibility was now severely reduced in the face of the swift blizzard, and the road itself was for the most part completely covered over. Snow must have fallen here days, weeks before, half

24

melted, then refrozen into treacherous sheets of black ice on the un-cleared, untreated B-roads. Now fresh snow was settling over it, feet deep.

In some places, Rafi had no choice but to follow the line of the telegraph poles, negotiating dips and inclines on little more than faith. In others, the shearing crosswinds conspired with the slippery surface to send him lurching perilously off-line, wheels spinning uselessly on glassy-smooth ice beneath the snow, frozen run-off from the fields. Knowing no better, Rafi kept dabbing at his brakes when the car started to slide, rather than keeping his left foot tucked safely under the seat as he should have. There was another vehicle up ahead, just visible on the longer, straighter stretches, and as he drove on Rafi came to invest an almost talismanic significance in this outrider. He steered into its tracks, reassuring himself that if *it* could get through, then so could *he* ... His good fortune lasted another couple of miles before the inevitable happened.

Coming out of a blind bend in the tracks of the trailblazer, revs racing heedlessly, his heart plummeted with the road that dropped away between low hedges down into a vicious declination. Before he could correct his line or moderate his speed he was already launched into an irresistible downhill skid. Wrestling with the steering wheel, jamming on the brakes (do you steer into a skid, or against it? Does it make any difference if you're going downhill? He couldn't remember) he was peripherally aware of various disconnected images, away off down the slope: a building, four-square and solitary, at the side of the road; a car parked up alongside a telegraph pole; some animals, black sheep perhaps, scattering into the shelter of the hedge. But all this was for later, because now he was starting to panic.

As the car gained momentum, his manoeuvres became more frantic, though no more effective. More time, and he might have thought his way out of it; less, and instinct might have come to his aid. As it was, he had just long enough to anticipate disaster, and that was the least use of all.

Inevitably, by the bottom of the hill he'd lost control totally. The Scimitar sideswiped the hedge, half-hidden behind drifted snow, on the right and rebounded in a sickly wobbling arc. More scared than he'd ever been behind the wheel, Rafi felt his back end shimmying round to overtake the front, and with a last desperate wrench at the wheel he sought to straighten out the car. In doing so, he abandoned whatever chance he might have had of steering his way out of the skid; directly in his path, dead ahead on the left, was the vehicle he'd glimpsed from above. Only now, in the last moments before the collision, he saw that it wasn't parked up after all. It had rammed into the telegraph pole, just as *he* was going to ram into *it* –

Fortune was on his side, though, favouring as it often seems to the Rafis of this world, the good-looking innocents. The back end drift momentum carried through just enough to bring him back over to the left hand side of the road, where the rear wheel socked into a deep ditch plugged with drifted snow. Immediately the car was slowed down; a loud grating noise suggested that the transmission was taking a ruinous scraping, but the overall effect was to brake the Scimitar to no more than ten miles an hour when it ran into the back of the crashed car in front.

Any faster and Rafi might not have been so lucky. As it was, the Scimitar's bonnet crumpled a little, and the rust-loosened bumper came away entirely, but the chassis held together, and his seatbelt took the strain. The collision, though unnerving enough, was nothing like as bad as it might have been. A minute or so of deep breathing, and he was ready to take stock of his circumstances.

Inside the car it was very quiet, with the snow outside damping down all sounds and Rafi slightly shocked still in the aftermath of the impact. The windows were steamed over with his heavy breathing. He wiped the windshield clear, running a cold condensation-wetted hand across his lips to moisten them. But snow had already settled across the outside of the glass, and to see anything at all he had to get out of the Scimitar.

He was stuck, so far as he could determine, pretty much for good, or at least until something bigger and better equipped came along to haul him out. A snow-plough, he suspected, would be necessary in the end, because the blizzard was unrelenting still. And then the services of a garage, and still more expense, and time and trouble and general pains in the arse ... Shaking his head at his own stupidity, he straightened up, gave the driver side tyre a kick and looked around.

Ahead of him the hilly terrain settled into a shallow bowl perhaps a mile across, low stone walls and bare December hedges. Descending to the left was a valley, thickly treed. There was an abstraction of high chimneys barely visible beyond the treetops in the flurrying snow; Rafi guessed Plas Glyn-y-Cysgod. Much closer, only four or five hundred yards further along the road, were several tiny slate cottages in a terrace, hugging the roadside as if apprehensive of the hills in their wintry desolation. Nearest of all, up on the left, was a chapel with lights showing in the windows. Remembering all the miles he'd travelled that day through wild and uninhabited mountain stretches, Rafi fumbled his St Christopher keyring in appreciation of his luck in this respect at least, then turned his attention in the sharpening cold to the more immediate scene of his collision.

The car ahead was a black Variant-E Volkswagen estate. It had rammed into the telegraph pole, canting it over at a slight angle; as in Rafi's case, though, the damage to the vehicle itself was comparatively light. For one thing the engine was still running, ticking over with a rusty clattering purr that was the only sound on that bleak and wintry plain besides the slashing north wind.

Rafi buttoned his coat tight and trudged the few steps to the driver's side of the Volkswagen. Squinting against the driving snow, he peered in at the side window. The driver was slumped forward over the steering wheel, and reacted to neither knocks nor shouts. Rafi opened the car door, releasing a vanishing breath of warm air and a sharp stink of engine fumes—the exhaust, he supposed, must have fractured somewhere underneath. Again he shouted. Receiving no response, he gently shook the shoulder of the driver. The man simply shifted sideways, all of a piece, and Rafi had to grab with both hands to support his weight.

The driver of the Volkswagen was breathing, just. With the engine turned off and his ear pressed close to the other's mouth and nostrils, Rafi picked up a shallow yet regular passage of breath. There was blood all across his face, though, and his lips were an unhealthy purplish-blue. He was white-haired, somewhere in his seventies, bundled tight against the cold with a heavy black overcoat over his charcoal suit. Around his neck was a clerical collar. There was a deep, ragged cut all the way across his wrinkled, liver-spotted forehead, and blood had already started to congeal around the orbit of his left eye, giving him a ghastly pirate's patch. With the glove he'd removed to check the old man's thready pulse, Rafi wiped the blood away, wondering as he did so what might have caused the cut. The windshield was intact; the steering wheel padded with a faux-leather grip sleeve. Even in these extreme circumstances, the question drew his curiosity.

An abrupt, almost furtive movement round the back of the Volkswagen brought him back to his immediate surroundings. Steadying his grip on the old man – he'd nearly let him fall in pure surprise – Rafi craned round to see what had made the scraping, rustling noise. There was something behind the car, scrabbling in the ditch; an impression of blackness, of legs and flailing, tripping feet ... and then there came a harsh throaty baaing noise, repeated with brainless insistence from out in the snowy fields.

In the general course of things Rafi didn't do sheep, and under these extraordinary circumstances he felt he had enough to deal with without turning stockman. Let the stupid bloody thing find its own way back. With a deep breath he hoisted the old man clear of the vehicle and up in a fireman's lift.

"Mint-sauce," he shouted, and raised a single finger to the baaing from beyond the hedge.

Afternoon was fast winding down to dusk as Rafi tramped the few hundred yards along to the chapel, the old man a dead weight on his shoulder. The weak lights in the narrow high windows seemed barely a welcome at all, but the gate stood open, and the front doors beneath the painted legend HINNOM yielded to his barging shoulder.

Into the poky vestibule clattered Rafi and his casualty. Panting from the exertion, he leaned against the wall for a second, checking to see that the old man was still breathing before pushing open the interior door with his foot. This opened on to a cramped and lowering space, the chapel proper. Tiny glass-shaded ceiling lamps strained against the gloom; plain boxy stalls and heavy panelling gave something of the impression of an indoor cattle market, at least to Rafi, more used to the Italianate marble and gilt of his childhood church of the Sacred Heart.

Five people were standing down at the front, beneath the pulpit. As they turned at the noise of his entrance, Rafi saw what they had been standing around: a coffin, bearing a single wreath of colourless dried flowers. Like the panelling, like the stalls and the pews and the pulpit, the drab dull-varnished casket seemed to draw in all the meagre light and swallow it, returning not the faintest gleam. For a moment, Rafi had the fantastical impression that it might have grown out of the very substance of the chapel itself, that the dark-stained wood of the coffin was some dismal *lignum vitae* sprung up to enclose its hapless occupant.

This moment of fancy was dispelled grotesquely enough. A high, querulous voice rang out to the damp knocked-back echo, "Excuse me – is that a dead person? I'm sorry, but you'll have to try elsewhere; we've already got one, you see …"

*

As luck would have it, Rafi's misadventures had led him straight to his prospective employers: the Pritchard Evanses of Plas Glyn-y-Cysgod, all three of them. The man who had spoken first, a comical little butterball cocooned inside a shabby blue duffel-coat, was Hari Pritchard Evans, brother to Eleri, a gaunt intense-looking woman in her early forties. The third, their father Huw, had been the centre of attention up until Rafi's arrival; he was the occupant of the coffin.

To hear the sexton tell it – the sexton being Bob Jenkins, another of the mourners by the side of the coffin – Huw Pritchard Evans had been no stranger to the public eye throughout most of his long and dignified life. As master of Plas Glyn-y-Cysgod he had

28

held the rents of all the farms thereabouts; as lay preacher at Capel Hinnom, the very chapel in which his remains now awaited their final disposal, he had thrown open his doors to the farmers and their sins twice every Sunday, morning and evening, for the last forty years. Now, at the age of seventy-eight he had been called to his Maker, and the Reverend Idwal Harris from Abersoch had received the slightly less momentous summons to come and evangelise over the body – the same Idwal Harris whom Rafi had dragged from the Volkswagen into the chapel, and had just deposited in one of the pews for whatever medical attention might be available.

Wasn't it rather a small turnout for the funeral, then? asked Rafi, quietly so that the immediate family might not hear him. What with the old man being the local bigwig and all? They were standing aside from the others, who had transferred their attentions from the late Mr Pritchard Evans to the ailing Mr Harris.

"Oh, no," whispered Mr Jenkins, looking scandalised, "*tomorrow* is the funeral, do you see? Not today; no, indeed not. Prayers this evening over the body, here in the chapel; prayers all through the night, then the funeral tomorrow lunchtime, and a reception after at Plas. It's how *he* – " a bow, almost a genuflection, in the direction of the coffin, "it's how *he* wanted it."

Which, of course, would have been enough for all present; though perhaps not for Eleri Pritchard Evans, the daughter. It was her turn to take Rafi aside, once Mr Jenkins had rejoined the little knot around the ailing minister. She introduced herself, explaining, more concisely and with altogether less reverence than the sexton, the peculiar circumstances in which they found themselves. For his part, Rafi gave his own side of the story, what there was to tell.

When he expressed his condolences, there was something about the manner of her acceptance – brief, almost dismissive – that struck him as significant. He sensed it again in the way Eleri laid a hand on his arm and apologised for not having rung to cancel their appointment, thus bringing him so far out into the sticks on a wild goose chase.

"And this terrible turn in the weather, too," she said, her keen grey eyes searching his own, "I doubt whether you'll be able to make it as far as Pwllheli, even, let alone back to Bangor. We shall have to find somewhere to put you up for the night." Alerted by her tone of voice, the predator in Rafi twitched awake and started taking notice.

Perhaps it's something particular to Rafi and his ilk, the stone cold ladykillers – some wild talent of perception, an attentiveness to nuance insufficiently developed in the rest of us. Perhaps these scenarios arise only with the Rafis, and not with the likes of you and me. Whichever: even as Eleri spoke, Rafi was appraising the slim, elfin body beneath the thick fur coat and the charcoal suit, the rich copper cast of her brushed-back hair, the freckled paleness of her complexion, the edginess, recklessness almost, in those serious eyes … he saw all these things and already he knew what was going to happen, sooner or later, between the two of them; probably sooner, rather than later – if not now, in fact, then quite possibly never, and certainly never again, once the first headless rush of it was over. But it would end in sex, he knew it. Very likely, that same night.

He knew this for a fact. Funerals do take some people that way; it's a grotesque yet undeniable fact, with perhaps even a shred of biological sense to it, something to do with the persistence of the life-force and the shameful dog-like relief of those spared. So certain was Rafi of what was in prospect if he stayed – so certain was he of the way things would inevitably fall into place – that he even had time momentarily to consider how such a development might affect any job of work he might still be hired to do at Plas Glyn-y-Cysgod. Meet the odd-job man, he helps out around the place. Upstairs, downstairs, and in my lady's chamber. Pros and cons, plan A, plan B, complications and contingencies … all this before he spoke, mind made up on the spot:

"Would you? That would be nice. I could squeeze in anywhere you like, if you're sure that's not a problem." Let her make what she wanted of that.

"Oh, I'm sure we can find you a place," said the mistress of the house, her hand still resting on his arm, just that little while longer than was strictly necessary.

"What are you talking to that man about?" The voice was adult, not to say refined in timbre, yet oddly school-boyish in cadence and inflection. It was like listening to a vicar reading aloud a story for children.

Colour came into Eleri Pritchard Evans' face for a moment, high on her thoroughbred cheekbones. After slightly too long, she looked away from Rafi's face, down to her patent-leather shoes.

"Grown-up things," she said, her voice raised with a long-suffering yet still unruffled firmness. "Nothing for you to trouble yourself over, Hari Longnose." She glanced once more at Rafi, apologetically it seemed, and turned round. "Hari, this is the man who's come about the woodwork – on the stairs, remember, and the panelling in the banqueting hall? Dad and I told you about him, remember?"

Hari Pritchard Evans looked bemused. "Yes, I remember. Don't shout, 'Leri *fach*. He's not going to do the stairs today, is he? Or has he come for the party? He's early – it's not till tomorrow."

"It's not a *party*, Hari. Don't say that."

"There's going to be sandwiches," said Hari, and his round face brightened. "Paste sandwiches. You said."

"Pate," said Eleri briefly, and with a glancing excuse-me in the near vicinity of Rafi, she led Hari away towards the vestibule.

At this point, things started to go a little fuzzy round the edges for Rafi. Everything seemed to be happening *to* him, rather than him participating in any meaningful way, and this was just as well, because he desperately needed a sit down and a rest. Aftermath of the crash, he supposed, and the shock of finding the old feller, and then barging in on a funeral – and *now*, a flimsily veiled proposition to boot. *Iesu grist*. He subsided into a pew and tried to put behind him the accumulated craziness of the last half-hour. When had he last felt wholly in control?

He shifted sideways on the supremely uncomfortable bench seat until his head was propped against the pew-end. Aware that his heart was still racing, he took several deep breaths and tried to think calm thoughts. Instead, there came into his mind the image of Eleri Pritchard Evans standing in front of him in a sumptuous oak-panelled bedroom, stepping out of the silken puddle of her slip like Lady Chatterley ...

Try to think of nothing, says Lord Buddha, who probably didn't find himself in these sort of situations with any great regularity. Rafi yawned, and let his gaze drift up into the gloomy reach of the ceiling. The professional in him spotted several damp patches in the flaky distempered plaster, where the slate tiles outside on the gable-ends must have come loose. Was that an actual gap there, just in the far corner? Or only cobwebs? Cobwebs for sure, and lots of 'em, but behind ... ? Just another damp patch, perhaps. It *was* damp inside the chapel, damp and clammy and cold, too – his feet were wedged directly up against the radiator, and only the faintest warmth was permeating through the soles of his heavy boots ...

A cough, together with a discreet nudge, roused Rafi from the verge of nodding off. Guiltily, he jerked his feet down from the bench and struggled upright, re-focussing upon the sepulchral figure of the sexton, a lugubrious horse-faced man with snow-white hair and a raw outdoors face that seemed scrubbed with pumice.

"Come with me now," he said, once Rafi looked capable of paying attention, "come along to the house. Tudur will stay and keep watch for the time being, till we organise something."

"Watch?" Rafi was puzzled.

"You let us worry about that. Now, are you strong enough to give a hand with the Reverend Mr Harris here?"

"Strong? I'm fine, but shouldn't we be thinking about getting him to a hospital?"

"The snow's much worse now," said Mr Jenkins, with finality. "We'd never get out of the valley, even. But we can't leave him here – he needs to be in the warm." *Don't we all*, thought Rafi.

The still unconscious preacher was easier to manage between two of them, with Hari helpfully opening the doors ahead. "Where are we going with him?" asked Rafi from the legs-end, as they passed through the vestibule.

"Just up to Mrs Morris's, there," said the sexton, and the last of the mourners, a shabby little bird of a woman in her late sixties, murmured from behind Rafi's back:

"It isn't far, and he'll be comfortable there. Tudur Morris will stay by the body meanwhile."

"Mr Morris will keep the *bwganod* away," amplified Hari, throwing open the front doors of the chapel and letting in a freezing blast of snow on a harsh thin wind.

For a single uncomfortable beat, everyone in the vestibule – Bob Jenkins, Eleri, Mrs Morris – looked at Hari; Rafi too, trying to work out what he'd just said. Then the sexton shuffled out into the snow, forcing Rafi to follow on with the Reverend Mr Harris between them.

In this manner they covered the few hundred yards between the chapel and the terraced cottages along the road: Bob Jenkins at the head, Rafi at the feet; Mrs Morris skipping and darting alongside, dabbing her handkerchief at the bone-pale face of the preacher lest the snow settle there; Eleri and her brother Hari in their train. In the teeth of the biting cold, struggling to keep his footing in the deep snow, Rafi still had time to appreciate the absurdity of their situation. To any onlooker, they must have seemed the world's most disorganised funeral procession. *Let's hope it doesn't come to that*, he thought.

"I'll get the gate!" Hari forged ahead and unlatched the picket gate outside the nearest of the four cottages. Up the little path they tramped, Mrs Morris hastening past them to open the door, holding it open (with Hari's wholly unnecessary assistance) as one by one they squeezed inside.

Even with just the Morrises at home the cottage must have seemed uncomfortably full; low ceilings, narrow stairways, tiny windows deep-set in their recesses in the thick stone walls. Getting Mr Harris upstairs and into the slope-ceilinged bedroom (there seemed to be just the one) was a ticklish undertaking, accomplished only at the expense of several wall-ornaments and knick-knacks.

Mrs Morris followed them upstairs, crying, "It doesn't matter!" and "No harm done!" at each fresh dislodgement.

Once the preacher was divested of his outer clothes and laid out on the bed with the covers over him, Rafi withdrew.

32

"I'll sit with him," said Bob Jenkins. "It'll be a comfort to him to see a familiar face when he wakes."

That's what you reckon, thought Rafi, mindful of what the sexton did for a living. Aloud, he said, "Fine."

Downstairs, he found Eleri sitting straight-backed on the cottage suite in the front room, like Royalty on a visit, and Hari squatting in front of the coal fire behind its steel mesh guard. Mrs Morris was making tea in the kitchen, as Hari lost no time in telling him.

"She said she might find some cake—*bara brith*, perhaps, or just scones."

"That'll be nice," said Rafi, trying to get a handle on Hari's – what would you call it? – his condition.

"I hope it's *bara brith*, with lots of butter. This is like an adventure, isn't it?" Hari's broad enraptured face, flushed from the fire, bore only the outward signs of ageing: grey at the temples, shiny bald on top; burst capillaries in the nose, across the apple-cheeks; little divots of hair nestled deep in each red rubber ear. None of the personal things, the difficult inmost things; no worry-lines of sorrow and disillusionment, no ineffaceable knowledge in the eyes. A greater contrast with his sister would be hard to imagine.

"Yes, it is a bit of an adventure, I suppose," agreed Rafi, squeezing in next to Eleri on the two-seater settee.

"And after we've had our tea, we'll take it in turns to watch over Dad, to make sure the *bwganod* don't get at him."

"Hari!" Eleri tried to cut across the conversation, but Hari chose to ignore her and answer Rafi.

"That's why the Reverend Harris was coming all the way up from Abersoch – it was for the vigil, to keep guard in case the *bwganod* came. Dad made him promise, when he was still alive. I promised too, but Dad said it was all right, I didn't have to. *Three* sugars for me, please!" This last to Mrs Morris, who entered the room bearing tea, cake and bad news.

"The phones are down already," she said, with the weary resignation of one for whom a turn for the worse in the weather generally means isolation for a day or two. "Usually the farmers have their snow-ploughs out as soon as it's stopped – *Tudur*?"

The front door banged open, and into the room came Mr Morris in a stamping flurry of snowflakes. By the time he had taken off his coat and gloves and black boots, Bob Jenkins the sexton had hurried down from upstairs.

"Tudur! Tudur, man, what the bloody hell are you doing here? There's no one at the chapel!"

Mr Morris, a frail little man with watery poached-egg eyes, looked up at the sexton with an unreadable expression. When the

33

other switched to Welsh, speaking at greater length but with the same undertone of query and alarm, he merely replied:

"Go yourself, then. I'm not stopping there by myself now it's dark." And those were his last words.

Swiftly Bob Jenkins threw on coat and cap, and laced his heavy boots on the stairs. At the door he rattled off a string of instructions to Mrs Morris, then, without a backward glance he was out. Through the window Rafi watched him march off back down the road towards the chapel, a blot against the pallid snow in the evening darkness.

The self-effacing Mr Morris, moving very gingerly as if in an attempt to render himself invisible, took up a seat by the fireside from which he was not to move for the remainder of the evening. His wife had gone upstairs to sit with Mr Harris: "He's still quite *comfortable*," she shouted down from time to time. Hari, meanwhile, had tucked into the cakes; Eleri was pouring tea for everyone, and under Rafi's questioning she expanded a little on the matter of the vigil being held over her dead father.

Eleri's great-grandfather, Jonathan Pritchard Evans, had built Hinnom chapel round about the turn of the century. He had died in 1918, upon which his son Rhodri, just returned from France, took up his duties as lay preacher. Eleri's father Huw, son of Rhodri, had been keen to keep up the family tradition in every respect, and so, since both his predecessors had spent the night before *their* burial in the chapel, prayed over by a handful of the faithful, he had left instructions for this to take place when he died.

Rafi nodded, wondering what was the point in praying over the dead anyway. Religious observance held no real interest for him, and one ritual seemed about as pointless as another. Look at Eleri, no wonder she was in need of some affection, a woman like her trapped in a life like that –

" *'Leri*! You missed out the best bit – the *bwganod*!"

"Oh, for goodness' sake!" Eleri's exasperation was clear, but her brother would not be put off.

"*Tell* him! It's the most important part of the story!"

Eleri sighed, as Rafi supposed she did often. "There was a story," she began, "back in great-grandfather Jonathan's day, that Glyn-y-Cysgod was a bad place to build a chapel, because there were supposed to be little hairy trolls or something. Yes, Hari, *bwganod* – little hairy men things who lived in caves hereabouts, and each night they would tear down the bricks the builders had laid the day before. So, great-grandfather had everyone out praying and keeping watch all the time the chapel was being built, day and night, and eventually they managed to finish it, and then all the *bwganod* could do was throw rocks at the windows and steal slates and what have you. This was during the Revival: people would believe anything the preacher told them. If he'd said it was Papists, or Martians, or whatever, they'd have believed him; he said *bwganod*, and they swallowed that."

"But the *bwganod* came back for him, didn't they?" Hari was nothing if not persistent. "When he was dead. They wanted to get him."

"No, Hari, they didn't." Eleri would not be swayed. "He's buried down the road there in the graveyard. No one *got* him."

"Only because they watched over him." Clearly stubbornness ran in the family. "That's why there's railings all around the graveyard, and spikes on top. It's why they only open up the chapel just before service, and lock the doors straight after. Otherwise they'd get in and wreck everything. And every time a Pritchard Evans dies, they come for him, and all the congregation have to stand guard to keep them off."

Eleri opened her mouth to answer him, then gave up. "And this is the congregation," she said, turning to Rafi instead, "the Morrises, Bob Jenkins, Hari and me. And you, of course; though you're excused participation in tonight's fol-de-rols." This last with patent scorn.

"I don't mind taking a turn," said Rafi helpfully. The narrow little cottage was already hemming him in, and Hari and the Morrises threatened to cramp his style; and he had an idea …

There followed one of those droll comedy-of-manners exchanges, in which Eleri's innate sense of protocol and decorum stood in the way of her grasping the larger picture concerning Rafi, herself and the possibilities of the moment. For his part, Rafi had already marked out an hour or two alone together in the chapel as his best chance of cutting Eleri out from the herd. True, the presence of Huw Pritchard Evans in his coffin might under normal circumstances have been considered something of a hindrance, but Rafi had been watching her closely, and he reckoned under the circumstances he might just get away with it.

He'd already picked up on the coolness in her voice and the more-than-coolness in her manner each time she spoke of her father. He was confident enough of his own powers of persuasion, and between one thing and another his hopes were high for the evening's developments. There might even, he thought in an optimistic spirit of rationalization, be a measure of closure in it for her, *vis-a-vis* the whole father-daughter issue … this was Rafi all over, convincing himself that what he wanted was what was best all round. Utterly incorrigible.

They argued back and forth politely for a while, but in the end it was decided. Rafi and Eleri would take the evening watch together once Bob Jenkins stood down. They would keep vigil through to midnight, after which Rafi would partner the sexton till three and then go and fetch the errant Tudur Morris.

"That's that settled, then," said Rafi. "Now ... " he cast around for some conversational gambit. Weather? Done that. Football? Probably not. A well-placed joke? He glanced around the room: nonconformist virtue and faded floral wallpaper stared him down. In desperation he turned to Hari. "So, tell me more about these troll things, then. The *bwganod*, yes, that's right." This, of course, was all the encouragement Hari needed.

They lived in caves, apparently, under the hills. They were like men, only smaller and hairy all over, with long thin legs and arms, and big heads with big staring eyes. If you saw one, you had to run away – only you had to cross your fingers and say the Lord's Prayer three times while you were running, otherwise they'd come back in the night and get you. They were from the old times, the times before men; they had always roamed the valley, and when men came and built their houses they went underground. They came up nowadays mostly to steal livestock, huddling up in a ball and pretending to go *baa* till the sheep came to see what the matter was, and then they would snatch them and take them underground to eat them up. Was there any more cake, Mr Morris? Or was Mrs Morris going to cook us dinner now?

"But why don't they like the Pritchard Evanses?" asked Rafi, prompting a dig in the ribs and a tut of exasperation from Eleri at his side.

"Because we built the chapel," said Hari, artlessly sticking a finger underneath his bow-tie and canting his head at an alarming angle to release the pressure on his podgy neck. "They don't want it there, and they kept trying to tear it down all the time. They still come round there now, pull slates off the roof and smash the windows like Eleri said, only it used to be much worse in Great-grandfather's day. Back then, they'd come around the house itself at night, hide in the orchards and the plantations round Plas Glyn-y-Cysgod, and poke their heads out in the moonlight and snarl like dogs and howl like wolves and flit from tree to tree in the shadows." There was a vivid uncomplicated relish to his recitation; Rafi imagined the story told and retold down the generations, growing more elaborate and far-fetched at each iteration. "And now Dad's gone they'll get their way at last – it's only a matter of time, now there's nobody left to preach on Sunday."

"I suppose they *will* close down the chapel now," said Eleri, reclaiming the conversation for the grown-ups. "Why keep it open for just half-a-dozen people, and no money coming in for repairs?"

36

"It'd be a shame, though," said Mrs Morris from behind them, coming down the stairs. "Wasn't that Bob Jenkins I saw just now from the upstairs window? Coming back down the road to his cottage, next door but one there? Did he stop by here and sort things out – arrange for one of you to go up to the chapel, sit with Mr Pritchard Evans, like?"

"No, no one's been here," said Eleri. She frowned. "Perhaps he got fed up." She glanced at Mr Morris, huddled between the broad wings of his deep armchair; he simply stared into the fire. For her part, Mrs Morris gazed expectantly at Eleri, waiting for her to take the initiative. "Well …"

"Well, I suppose we'd better wander over there," said Rafi, rising from the settee to seize the moment. "I'll nip back over in, let's see, an hour or so maybe, and you could put up some tea in a Thermos or something? Sandwich or two, something cooked, maybe? That'd be fine – no, Hari, that's all right, you can stay here. Mrs Morris might want some help getting the dinner ready." With a long unreadable look at him, Eleri got to her feet, shrugging back into her fur coat. The Machiavelli in Rafi's soul rubbed his hands together.

"I think it's strange, though, Mr Jenkins not stopping to tell you he was going home," said Mrs Morris nervously, edging behind the settee so as to avoid brushing up against Rafi and Eleri. "He was in a bit of a hurry, mind – almost fell over, he did, trying to run in the snow – but it still seems not right, like. I wonder …"

"We'll drop by his place on the way over," said Rafi, alert to the threat from his other flank, "find out what's up. Next door but one, you say?"

But when they got there, Mr Jenkins was not answering. The front gate was wide open; footsteps in the snow led up the narrow path, but the downstairs lights were out and the front door bolted shut. They took turns to hammer on the knocker and call him, but no response came from indoors. Eleri thought there might be a faint light burning in one of the upstairs windows, but the curtains were closed, and did not twitch even for Rafi's energetically flung snowballs. So they retraced their steps back to the road, and on past the Morrises' cottage up to the chapel, its sombre bulk standing out against the snowfields even in the dark.

Rafi remembered the torch in the glove compartment of his Scimitar, and told Eleri to wait by the chapel gate while he retrieved it. Snow had drifted all the way up the passenger side of the car, and inside it was pitch black and freezer-chest chilly. Heading back towards the chapel he paused by Mr Harris's Volkswagen. That stray sheep from before must have been sheltering in the lee of the car, because there were animal footprints all around and an eye-

37

watering feral stink. Flicking the torch on and off for a signal, he rejoined Eleri by the gate.

"What was that behind the car?" she wanted to know. "While you were looking at the ground. I saw it in the hedges."

"Sheep," Rafi assured her. "Hey, you're shivering." A protective arm wound round her. "Come on, let's get you inside." So they passed through the wrought-iron gate and on up to the solid double doors, left ajar by the retreating Bob Jenkins. "Just what we need," grumbled Rafi. "Letting all the heat out."

In the freezing vestibule there was no heat whatsoever; nor, with the front doors shut behind them, was there any light. Rafi flicked his torch around the confined space. The beam caught Eleri's face, white as the plaster on the walls. He shifted it to chest-level, so they were both lit from below.

"Don't worry," he said, and gripped her shoulder through the wet thickness of the snow-clogged fur. "Don't worry, it'll be all right." He paused, then drew her closer to him, his eyes never leaving hers. Obediently she came into his arms, and Objective One was accomplished.

A few minutes later, Rafi disengaged himself from the clinch, mindful of the batteries in the torch. "Come on," he said gently, "let's get inside. It'll be warmer there."

It wasn't, though, nor was it much lighter. The lights in the ceiling were out, and would not come on at the wall switch. With a sinking heart, Rafi realised that meant the power was probably down along with the phone lines. The only illumination in that dim and frigid place was from a storm lantern placed down near the front, close by the coffin. The radiators were stone cold; in the weak ellipse of lantern light Rafi saw a squat columnar paraffin heater, and made for it. Eleri followed him hesitantly, her heels clattering on the bare boards.

Rafi had the good sense to move both heater and lantern back down the aisle a little, as far away from the bier as seemed necessary. He guessed that the vigil required only their presence in the ballpark, so to speak; they didn't need to be squatting on top of the coffin. Job done, the two of them squeezed into a box-pew halfway back from the front and huddled together for warmth, or from some other equally primal imperative.

In the interests of propriety, I can only stand aside from the circumstances of the next half-hour or so. For one thing Rafi, chivalrous after his own fashion, wasn't forthcoming; for another, I find it as hard to visualise such a passage of events, in such a place, as to visualise … I don't know. Imagination fails me. The inessentials I can just about conjecture, I suppose: what he did, what she did, the obvious stuff. But I haven't got the fixity of purpose that Rafi and Eleri shared that evening, and instead my mind wanders, and I see the gloomy twilight void of the chapel, all draughts and creakings; the faintest glimmer at the high windows, the midnight blue reflection of the snow outside. The hissing of the paraffin stove, the ticking of the lantern, foregrounded in the damp dead snow-hush. And behind it all, waiting, omnipresent, the country silence, and the country dark, and all its hundred stories, old as the hills.

And against this weird backdrop, things took their course as expected – let's leave it at that. What Rafi wanted fell, as it always seemed to, bang into his lap.

A while later, in the slightly stunned aftermath, Eleri raised her head from Rafi's broad warm chest.

"Mmph?" he said, pulling stray strands of her hair from his mouth. "Wha?"

"Did you hear it?"

"Nnn . . . 'ear wha?"

"A noise." Eleri propped herself up on one arm, tensed and nervous along the whole length of her body. "Something over there."

"Where?"

"Over there, near the –" She choked on the word *coffin*. "Near the pulpit."

Rafi sighed, braced himself on an elbow, poked his head up above the pewback. "It's probably nothing. I wish it was old Bob what's-his-name, the sexton with that electric blanket. Not that it'd do him any good with the lecky off – "

"*Shush*! There it is again, over that way."

"I told you, it's probably just – "

Eleri gasped, grabbed at his shoulder. Rafi, who had been trying to find the torch inside all the folds and layers of their clothing, heard it too; a soft, brushing, scurrying sound from somewhere beyond the lantern's feeble glow.

The beam of light from Rafi's torch shot up at an angle into the darkness, danced there for a moment, then levelled out across the pews. Towards the back of the chapel there was movement, quick, surreptitious. By the time the torch beam reached there, it was gone.

Rafi raised himself into a sitting position, and the torchlight skewed all haywire around the walls. "Hello?" he called. "Mr Jenkins? Mr Morris? Hello? Is there anybody there?" The old, old question.

Then they both heard the noise again, only nearer this time – much, much nearer, only a pew or two behind them. Eleri gave a horrible low moan and clung to Rafi like a drowning woman.

39

Up on his feet, Rafi shouted "Who's there?" He ran the torchlight all along the length of the pews. The noise seemed to sink away into the shadows at floor-level, always ahead of the beam.

Disconcerted, Rafi swung the torch in a wide unsteady arc around him. *Rats*, he told himself, *bloody massive graveyard rats*. Out loud he was about to say "Mice", when the torch beam passed across the pulpit, down across the coffin ... where it came to an abrupt, wavering halt. The lid of the coffin, screwed down before, was off and to one side.

Eleri, clinging to Rafi's arm, saw the open coffin and gasped. What happened next set her to screaming. Stiffly, awkwardly, something rose from inside the casket. Mostly it was dark – a black suit, a births-weddings-and-funerals suit – but some of it was light, and the light parts were hands, and a face, a dead white face ... but that wasn't all.

Horrified beyond measure, Rafi thought for a second that the body had more than one head. There was the obvious one, the cadaverous fallen-in face, ghastly in the trembling torchlight, lolling clownishly to one side; but alongside it was another, darker mass, hard to make out in terms of its constituent features, even as it turned in their direction, drawn to Eleri's scream. All dark, this second head, coffin-snug against the other. A glint of teeth, snapping and clashing, a glint of eyes, unmoving, unblinking ... and then it surged upwards, outwards, fast and fearfully strong, and wiry arms flung the body of Huw Pritchard Evans aside.

Rafi dropped the torch in pure panic, and for a second there was only the faint backwash of the lantern light, and Eleri's screams ringing round the chapel. Then more shapes rose up out of the pews all around them, sly and silent, and settled on the lantern, dragging it down into the shadows, and Eleri screamed again as the darkness swallowed them up.

Down at floor level the torch was rolling on the dusty wooden boards beneath the pews. Rafi clutched after it, glimpsing without wanting to vague animal shapes scuttling in the torchlight, behind them, in front of them, every direction. Some went on two legs, some went on four; there were dozens of them, and they seemed to come from everywhere at once, above, below, and all around. The whole chapel was alive with pattering and scuffling and soft thuds, and everywhere a kind of hissing, panting sound, horribly wet somehow, and a clatter as of chattering teeth.

Eleri was moaning, over and over; Rafi admits to making some involuntary noise himself once, when in reaching for the dropped torch his fingers closed momentarily around a scrawny, leathery, hair-covered arm, a leg, whatever ... A hideous moist snarling came from just the other side of the pew, and Rafi snatched back his hand.

It brushed against the torch; Rafi grabbed at it, gave thanks it hadn't broken when he'd dropped it. He levelled the strong beam towards the open end of the pew. Shapes, now crouched down low, now leaping high, too agile for the ray of light to hold them; but the direction in which they were moving gave him the hope he'd hardly dared wish for. In a second or two, the last of them had passed by the bench-end. Rafi pulled Eleri tight up against him, got his free hand over her mouth.

"They're not looking for us," he hissed, never taking his eyes off the torch-lit gap at the end of the pew. "They're all going that way, down towards the front. Come on – if we just get into the side aisle, we can give 'em the slip, sneak around the back, make for the door."

It took three or four efforts to get her to move; what it took for either of them to do what they did next, to venture out on hands and knees into the side aisle, away from even the illusory safety of the pew, I can barely imagine. Only the space in the torchlight existed for them: in all the horror that ran through the shadows of the chapel, all that scurrying and thrashing under cover of the dark, the bright cone of torchlight remained blessedly clear, as it picked out their way towards the door.

Gaining the vestibule at last – only there did they dare rise to their feet, ready to make a run for it – Rafi turned for one last look into the chapel. Down near the pulpit, where the coffin of Huw Pritchard Evans lay half off its trestles, there was something like a hellish, nightmare rugby scrum, a writhing maul of piebald bodies round the toppled-over casket. A couple of the creatures turned around at the torch beam, and spat in their slavering hissing fashion. Rafi could stand it no longer. Hurling the torch in their direction, he dragged Eleri out into the freezing moonless night and slammed the door tight shut on the dreadful scenes inside.

He remembers one last detail from that awful denouement, with a clarity that came through in the retelling, years later. All around the chapel, he said, there were fields, and upon all the fields lay a deep and even blanket of snow. Only there were tracks scored deep into the snow-crust; animal tracks or man-tracks he couldn't say, but they were converging from every direction towards the chapel.

*

Back at the cottage after their stumbling sprint back down the snowy road, Eleri more or less passed out on the doorstep. Mrs Morris took her straight up to bed, and stayed with her all that night. Hari was fast asleep on the settee, snoring loudly and wetly in a way that gave Rafi the creeps. Mr Morris and Rafi shared an all night vigil; both men, knowing what they did, thought it best to stand watch till the morning came.

Through all that long night they hardly spoke at all, even to acknowledge the extreme unlikelihood of their situation.

Pretty much all the older man said was: "Did you see them, then?" To which Rafi could only answer:

"Yes," staring at the log fire in the grate that was the room's sole illumination.

Mr Morris nodded, and thought it over for a little while. After a minute or two, he said, almost to himself: "I heard them myself, up on the roof and down under the floorboards. That was enough for me, that was. If I get through however many years I've got left and don't get any nearer to 'em than that, you won't hear me complain. Bob Jenkins can say what he likes – I mean, he run off himself, didn't he? No room to talk, him, has he?"

Rafi nodded, and Mr Morris looked mildly gratified. After that they lapsed into silence again, taking turns to throw logs on the fire, keeping it banked high and strong till the first lead light of dawn.

Round about nine a snowplough came shouldering along outside, and not long afterwards a white-faced Mr Jenkins was rapping on the window. He did not ask what had happened, nor did he volunteer any explanation of his absence from the chapel the night before, or of his refusal to answer their knocking on his door.

All he said was, "I've dressed him again in some spare clothes of mine, and put him back in the coffin. If you two will just help me now, we can bury him before the children come and ask questions, or anyone from outside comes and sees the kind of state the chapel's in."

And so the only service Rafi ever performed for the Pritchard Evanses turned out to be that of stand-in sexton, unpaid. He shovelled snow out of the ready-dug plot in the graveyard, and waited, leaning on his spade, for Mr Jenkins and Mr Morris to wheel out the resealed coffin on its undertaker's trolley. Rafi could not bring himself to re-enter the chapel – it felt safer in the open air. A little while later, the three of them stood around the filled-in grave, and Mr Jenkins mumbled a few words under his breath that might have been a prayer. The sound of a tractor engine at the head of the hill broke the silence, and Rafi heard in it his chance of escape.

He got a lift with the farmer as far as Llanbedrog, where there were telephones and taxis to magic him back into the world, where life as he had always known it resumed its even course, give or take the odd shadow round the corners. These he continues to deal with, just as he deals with all such setbacks, giving them as little thought as possible, refusing to dwell on past negatives to the detriment of present positives. He had just a couple of regrets. In his haste to escape from the valley of Glyn-y-Cysgod, he had missed saying goodbye to Hari, who'd been waving from the Morrises' garden gate as the tractor bore him away. Eleri he missed altogether; nor did he ever see her again afterwards.

Once or twice in the months that followed his telephone would ring at odd hours of the night, but when he answered it the caller would always hang up. Best to leave it, he thought, and still thinks now. So, nothing after that day and night in 1980 ever took him back to Glyn-y-Cysgod: not curiosity, which he reckons to have finally mastered at this belated stage in his life; not even his car, which he arranged for the garage in Bangor to pick up from the scene of the accident.

"It was fine, really," he explained, more than eighteen years later, when he told me the tale of his adventure that miserable January day in *Pete's Eats*. "Chassis was okay, and they knocked the dents out of the front wing and the bonnet. I was able to sell it pretty much straight away, once they'd sorted out the undertray: got quite a decent price for it, considering. There was just the one thing, and those little Christmas trees you get in the filling stations sorted that out."

"What do you mean, Christmas trees?" I asked.

"Those piney air freshener things, you know," he said, sketching an isosceles triangle with his finger. "The inside stank something evil afterwards, worse than the tannery after market day. The blokes in the garage wanted to know had I been driving animals around? I told them something must have nested up in there, the night of the accident."

"I see," I said, staring at him as he gazed unconcernedly into his coffee mug. "And did you tell them what?"

"Not bloody likely," he said. "I'm useless with all those Welsh words still. I'd have needed old Hari there just to make myself understood, and what good would it have been, even then?"

THE BEAST OF BODALOG

Given the pride Welsh folk take in their country's magnificent national symbol – Y Ddraig Goch, the Red Dragon – it won't surprise anyone that Welsh mythology is steeped in dragon-lore. There is scarcely a cave or lake that wasn't at one time believed the refuge of some scaly, fire-breathing saurian. Wales can even argue that its dragon mythology has persisted into modern times, as was seen in Rhayader in the 1980s with the mysterious case of the Beast of Bodalog.

Rhayader is a small market town in Powys, mid-Wales, and for the most part is surrounded by hilly farmland. Not much of consequence has ever happened there, except during the autumn of 1988, when an unknown predator began stalking its livestock, and over a period of two months killed at least 35 sheep, in nearly all cases draining them of blood. The response among the local community was bewilderment. The usual rumours began to circulate: it was a big cat, or a crazed dog, or even a disturbed man. But the physical evidence suggested none of these possibilities. To begin with, the sheep carcasses had not been savaged or mutilated. In all cases, a single wound had proved fatal – a deep but unidentifiable bite delivered to each animal's breast, and it was through these relatively small vents that the unfortunate creatures' life fluids had then been sucked.

The farmers and local police had no clue what they were dealing with, and when university zoologists were called in, they too were bewildered, though it was one of these who made the disturbing suggestion the culprit might be some kind of gigantic snake.

No such creature is native to the British Isles of course – the UK's sole harmful species of snake is the Vipera berus, or adder, which is too small to attack a full-grown sheep – but in the tropics, similar damage to wildlife was known to be the work of certain breeds of large swampland serpent; for example pythons or anacondas. For some reason, the sheep carcasses were never checked for snake venom, even though the animals continued to die at an alarming rate, but when professional trackers were called in, the predator's trail was finally uncovered. It appeared as a broad, winding furrow, which had circled several of the decimated flocks before sweeping away along a serpentine path over the wild Welsh grasslands. When this was followed, it was found to end on the banks of the River Wye, as though the cold-blooded killer was emerging at night and slinking back beneath the surface, sated with blood, as the sun arose.

The local population was terrified, and the term 'Beast of Bodalog' – named after the local farm that had suffered most depredations – was born. The idea that the mysterious monster was a giant snake created a particular sense of horror, even though there was no indication that humans were at risk. The tabloid newspapers gave it much coverage, and all kinds of stories were aired, evoking memories of those ancient monsters coiling through the pantheon of Welsh mythology, the dragons, or 'wyrms' as they were known in Britain during the Dark Ages. However, more serious proposals were also put forward. Had some exotic species escaped from a zoo perhaps? Had some wealthy eccentric accidentally, or maybe deliberately, released an unusual pet that had outgrown its captivity? The River Wye itself was subject to investigation. It runs 134 miles from its headwaters in the Cambrian Mountains to the Severn Estuary just below Chepstow. The fifth largest river in Britain, it is rich in fish, invertebrates and birdlife, supports a range of diverse habitats and basically hosts its own ecosystem. If an apex predator were to find refuge in the Wye, it would have no shortage of food or concealment.

Of course, if the predator were of tropical origin, the Welsh climate would be a problem. Even a mild British winter would be too much for so large a cold-blooded beast, and indeed this may have been what happened. As the damp autumn of 1988 turned into a bitter winter, progressively fewer attacks were reported until at last they petered out altogether. Nothing similar has been reported in the district since, though for many years after 1988 the unknown monster became a bogey figure, stern mothers warning their wayward children not to stray too near the River Wye or the Beast of the Bodalog would snatch them.

The case remains a favourite among cryptozoologists, who have come up with various theories over the years. Some have suggested that an overlarge mink – a rare mutation of some sort – might have been responsible, while others favour an unknown sea-creature briefly making its way upstream. Perhaps understandably, the latter theory is not popular with the locals, mainly because it doesn't discount the likelihood the Beast may return. No-one in Rhayader welcomes that possibility.

THE DRUID'S REST
Reggie Oliver

U p till that day it had been the best of holidays: the sun had shone in the hills and valleys of North Wales. Then towards evening, as Sheila and Anne were passing Bala Lake, a light drizzle began to fall. There was a Youth Hostel nearby marked on the map so they turned their bicycles in that direction, but it proved to be full to capacity. The warden suggested they continue North East towards Corwen. At that point both girls, students at Bangor University on their first summer vacation, were disheartened, but Sheila made an effort not to show it. She was anxious to point out the melancholy beauty of the dark green Welsh hills under heavy cloud. It was Sheila who had proposed a cycling tour of Snowdonia and she felt responsible. They rode on and soon they were riding uphill with the lake at their back.

Some Frenchman had said that in every relationship there is usually one who loves and one who gives permission to be loved. Sheila reflected on this as they laboured upwards. It had always been her way to initiate a relationship. Was it fear that if she did nothing, then nothing would happen? Or was it simply a sign of her more forceful nature? The questions lingered in her mind for a moment and then she let them go. Whatever the answer she was happy with the state of affairs, and so, it would seem, was Anne. Sheila was not even troubling to speculate whether their relationship would extend beyond an intense friendship; she only knew that when she caught sight of that slight, slender figure, the dark eyes, the rather untidy black curly hair, cut short, but still resembling a mop, something inside her turned over. This was happiness, she told herself.

Anne may have been less outgoing than Sheila, but she had her own brand of toughness. One of the things that had first attracted Sheila was the way, in the English poetry seminars they both attended, she would voice her views without any regard to the general consensus. She liked certain poets, and disliked others and, as it happened, those likes and dislikes coincided thrillingly with Sheila's. They were keen on the Metaphysicals and the Georgians whom many of their contemporaries found either dull or impenetrable.

For a while they rode on not saying a word. The rain began to fall steadily, but it was still not a torrent. All the same, it was not pleasurable. They came to a T junction. A signpost indicated that

46

the way to the right led to Corwen which the Youth Hostel Warden had suggested. To the left, according to the sign, was a place called Capel Drudion and this was only two miles distant as opposed to Corwen's fifteen. The sky was darkening.

"Shall we try this Capel Drudion? We should get there quite soon," said Sheila.

"Okay," said Anne.

As usual Sheila had taken responsibility. It made her apprehensive: if things went wrong the friendship would be tested. But this was the way it should be, so they took the road to the left. It was deserted, unbothered by cars at this time of day. "Obviously, this is 'the road less travelled by,'" thought Sheila and smiled. She considered relaying her pleasantry to Anne, but decided it was not quite the moment. Frost was another of their mutual favourites: Frost and Edward Thomas.

They passed through a forest that oppressed them on either side and emerged to see, on a little bare rise the village of Capel Drudion, a few dim lights now cheering the gloom.

It was not impressive, but it would do. There were slate roofed houses and a grey, slate roofed chapel of indeterminate denomination and there was what looked like a main street in which they saw the welcome lights of a combined post office and general store still open. They parked their bicycles outside and entered. The woman behind the counter, severe looking and in late middle age, stared at the shorts they were wearing and their damp T-shirts, not so much in disapproval as surprise. Sheila and Anne bought bars of chocolate.

"Is there anywhere around here where we can get a meal and stay the night?" asked Sheila.

"Oh, no!" said the woman, shaking her head. The idea seemed alien to her, even offensive.

"What, nowhere? No B and B? Nothing?"

"Well, there's *The Druid's Rest*."

"What's that?"

"Well, it's like a hotel or like an inn."

"Okay. Where's that?"

"Just down the street on the right. You can't miss it. It's got this like sign outside. Inn sign. Of a druid, I suppose. Resting, see. But nobody goes there like."

"Why not?"

"Well the owner has it as a hotel, see, for tax purposes or some such, but he doesn't have guests."

"I've never heard of that before," said Anne, intrigued.

"Oh, it goes on in these parts. Mind you, I don't exactly know how it works. I think he bought the place to live in, and then maybe couldn't change the use. I don't know."

"'He' being the owner?"

"That's right. Mr Rhys-Griffiths. You don't see him about much, but he has a reputation."

"What sort of reputation?"

There was a pause. A look came into the woman's eyes which bore witness to the stirrings of humanity. She almost smiled.

"Mind you," she said. "If you were to go there, see, and say you wanted to stay there the night, he'd have to let you in. Because otherwise you could report him, see! To the tax authorities for misuse of premises." The last words were spoken with a sort of relish, that Welsh love of words for their own sake.

"Right, thanks very much. We'll bear that in mind, er …?"

"Mrs Pugh. The name's Mrs Pugh. And tell that old … Mr Rhys-Griffiths that I sent you, see. Mrs Pugh sent you." By now she was smiling almost broadly, but it was not a pleasant sight.

"Yes. Thank you, Mrs Pugh," said Sheila. When they were outside the shop, she said to Anne: "Well, shall we risk it?" It began to rain heavily.

Anne giggled. "I think we'd better," she said.

They found *The Druid's Rest* on the edge of the village a little set back from the road just before it plunged down into another Snowdonian fold in the landscape. An inn sign on a tall post stood beside the road. Paint had flaked off it but Sheila and Anne could just see in the fading light the likeness of a man in a white beard, vaguely accoutred in flowing robes, leaning against a rock, one side of his face cupped in his hand. The general impression was of dejection rather than rest.

It was a long, two storied building, half-timbered in black with the walls an off white colour. A dim light shone in the gabled wooden porch. By it Sheila could see that there was an old-fashioned metal bell-pull. She pulled it and heard the clangour it made within. She had not expected an immediate response and none came, but they knew someone was there because they had seen lights in an upper window. Sheila had now set her mind on *The Druid's Rest*. Her resolve was strengthened by the sight of Anne shivering in the porch and the rain now coming down in sheets.

Just after Sheila's third ring the two girls heard footsteps, or rather what sounded like the scrape of feet across a stone floor. An old woman opened the door. She was dressed in a wraparound floral pinafore of the kind that female cleaners used to wear when they were called 'charwomen'. Her face was heavily powdered and a gash of deep red lipstick accentuated the thinness of her lips. She looked at Sheila and Anne with undisguised hatred.

"Who are you? What do you want?"

"We want to spend the night here. We're soaked to the skin," said Sheila, subtly insinuating her foot over the threshold so that the old woman could not shut the door in their faces.

"We know you don't often have guests at your hotel," said Anne, her smile friendly and charming, "but Mrs Pugh at the Post Office thought you might make an exception."

"Mrs Pugh," whispered the old woman as if uttering a malediction. She did not move but she took note of Sheila's foot in the door. Something stirred behind her, large and pale.

A man, huge in every direction, had appeared in the hallway. He wore faun coloured clothes and his white-blond hair was long enough to curl over his collar. His beard was of a similar colour but was not long and patriarchal like the druid on the sign but irregular and stubbled. He might have been in his sixties, younger at any rate than the old lady in the pinafore.

"What is it, Cookie?" he said. The voice boomed. It had a theatrical intonation and a strong Welsh accent.

"Mrs Pugh told them to come here," said the woman called Cookie.

"Mrs Pugh? What's it got to do with Mrs Pugh?"

"Are you Mr Rhys-Griffiths?" asked Sheila.

"What's it got to do with you?" said the man. "Why have you come?"

"I'm afraid we're closed," added Cookie trying to shut the door on Sheila's foot.

"All we want is to shelter here until the rain stops," said Sheila addressing the man over Cookie's head. "You are the landlord, I presume. It is your legal obligation to offer hospitality in such circumstances. We have money; we can pay you."

Sheila knew of no such 'legal obligation'. It was a bluff, but she had nothing to lose and her youthful pleasure in this bizarre situation gave her confidence. There was a silence. Cookie looked at Mr Rhys-Griffiths and he slowly nodded.

"You'd better come in," she said.

While Sheila and Anne wheeled their bicycles into the hall and put down their rucksacks Cookie and Mr Rhys-Griffiths watched them, having withdrawn a little. Aware of being scrutinised Sheila tried to dissipate her self-consciousness by being effusively grateful. Anne, less ill at ease, undid her rucksack and took out a pink hand towel with which she proceeded to dry her hair, smiling at her hosts as she did so. Sheila was astonished and delighted at her friend's coolness.

"Look," said Anne. "I know it's bloody cheeky, but could we have something to eat? We're absolutely starving as well as wet through."

Without looking at her Mr Rhys-Griffiths said: "See to that, Cookie. I will show them the premises." Cookie retreated without a word. "This way, young ladies," said Mr Rhys-Griffiths.

Rhys-Griffiths pointed towards a doorway to their left and led them through. They entered an almost lightless space in which their guide's pale bulk could be seen wandering about muttering to himself until a single bulb was switched on.

They found themselves in a bar with Rhys-Griffiths behind the counter staring at them with his grey watery eyes. Above and around him on shelves were arrayed glasses and bottled beers and reversed bottles with optics attached, all like a proper bar, except that the bottles were dusty and some of the labels announced brands of alcoholic beverage that had ceased trading long ago. There was a row small fruit juice bottles whose contents had separated into a species of mud surmounted by murky water. The dark tables and chairs had been kept polished, but everything behind the bar was covered with a thin film of dust. Rhys-Griffiths seemed to blend with these surroundings which indicated not so much decay as a kind of stasis, a void in which nothing occurred.

"Ah, yes," said Rhys-Griffiths. "This is the bar, you see. Yes. It's all here, you know. We don't much use it, but it's all ready. Everything where it should be. You see that?"

He pointed to a large stuffed pike in a glass case above the empty fireplace. There it pretended to swim, suspended forever in its painted prison, a trophy, a mortal tribute to the angler's prowess.

"A salmon, you know. Yes. Caught by my grandfather in Bala Lake. Yes. Biggest salmon ever recorded. My grandfather: finest fisherman in Wales, you know. Yes. We have the cups to prove it of course ..."

He talked on, his voice a booming monotone, seeming never to raise or lower it, so that it sounded like a strange natural phenomenon, like a river turning over rocks or a murmur of animals penned in for the night. He talked of his ancestry and of himself, blending his narrations together in such a way that it was hard to tell at any given point whether he was talking about himself, his parents or more distant relations. Sheila and Anne, caught in this ambiguous web of words, eventually sat down at one of the tables, succumbing at last to the delayed feeling of exhaustion.

Almost immediately, without stemming the flow of his talk, Rhys-Griffiths turned the light off so they were again plunged into darkness. "Yes, well, I'll show you the lounge," he said and, lifting up a flap of the bar counter led the way out into the hall and across into another dark doorway. Sheila and Anne exchanged a glance – both could just about see each other's eyes gleaming – and followed him.

The room they now entered was furnished like a personal sitting room. Rhys-Griffiths switched on a lamp that stood on a grand piano.

"Yes, this is my personal sitting room. I do most of my ... My stuff in here, you know. Yes ... I'm a musician. You see ... Grand piano ... Won prizes ... Promising future. They said I was a coming Sir Malcolm Sargent ... Illness unfortunately ... Above the fireplace, portrait of an ancestor by Sir Joshua Reynolds." They saw a dim, uncleaned eighteenth century face staring blankly out at them from an elaborate gilded frame. "Yes. He was a famous musician. Most famous in Wales. Now these ... You see these?" He pointed to a row of carved wooden chairs standing against one wall: they were polished, throne-like, discreetly ugly. Most had the word *EISTEDDFOD* carved on their backs. "Bardic Thrones. Oh, yes. I won them. At the Eisteddfod, of course ..."

"What for?"

"Poetry. Singing. Music ... Oh, yes. All those. I won them all. Famous." Sheila noticed that several of them had dates carved on them, mostly from the 1890s. "Of course, my health now won't allow me to go out, but they would always welcome me with open arms. Mention my name. Rhys-Griffiths. Yes. Famous of course ..."

The words murmured on. Sheila and Anne were beginning to move from amusement to embarrassment. It was clear now that Mrs Pugh had been motivated by malice, not simply towards Rhys-Griffiths, but towards them. The two looked at each other and a moment of shameful complicity passed between them. They glanced round the room, looking for something that might help them escape from this tide of confused self-aggrandisement. In the meantime Rhys-Griffiths stood by the mantelpiece and talked on and on.

On the piano, besides the lamp, stood two silver framed photographs. Sheila, to distract herself from Rhys-Griffiths's talk began to study them. One was of a young man seated, if Sheila was not mistaken, at the very piano on which the image rested. The man had wavy blonde hair and a romantic faraway expression in which Sheila detected an element of pose. The face was almost handsome, but for the bluntness of the features and the slight lack of definition in the mouth. She recognised in the figure jabbering at the fireplace a ruined and elderly version of the would-be musical Adonis.

Her glance at the picture had not gone undetected.

51

"Ah, yes. Me you know. At the piano. I could have been a concert pianist. A coming Horowitz. Oh, yes ... They all said so ... Yes. But I was prevented ... Rare disease ... Oh, yes ..."

By this time Anne had moved over to the piano, but she was not so much arrested by his picture as by the other photograph on the piano. It showed a young woman, again rather artificially posed, obviously the work of a professional photographer. The head was tilted back and the dark eyes mirrored the distant gaze of the young Rhys-Griffiths, except that this looked more natural, perhaps sadder as a result. What struck Sheila was that the expression was so similar to one she had seen in Anne.

"Yes," said Rhys-Griffiths, "my daughter. I expect you've heard of her. Famous singer. Yes ... All over the world ... Brilliant ... They all know her."

"What is her name?"

"You'll have heard of her ... Yes ... Oh. Yes ... Very famous ... You see this?" he said, picking up a china shepherdess from the mantelpiece. "Meissen, you know. Original. Eighteenth Century. Very rare. They only made five of them. The other four are in museums, all over the world ... Oh, yes ..."

Sheila and Anne became aware that another presence had joined them. They turned round and saw that Cookie had entered the room.

"It's ready," she said with undisguised resentment.

"Ah, yes. There you are you see. Cookie ... Been with us for years ... Loyalty ... And so on ..." Rhys-Griffiths moved towards the door while Cookie stood to one side watching the two girls. Anne went first, followed by Sheila whose arm Cookie grabbed as she was passing.

"Yes?" said Sheila.

Cookie said nothing but shook her head. Ridiculous, thought Sheila. Why is she trying to frighten me? But her unease grew.

The dining room was at the back of the hotel, a large, long room with a row of floor length curtains ranging across the back wall. Rhys-Griffiths indicated them as they entered.

"Finest view in all Wales," he said. "Can't see it now, of course. Curtains. Hand woven, of course ..."

There were a dozen or so tables in the dining room, all of them laid out with gleaming cutlery, sparkling glassware and pristine white napery.

"Have to keep this going, you see. In case the inspectors come," said Rhys-Griffiths.

A table for three in the corner was set for them with food already on it. Rhys-Griffiths studied the arrangements for a moment.

"Ah, Cookie, aren't you joining us?" Cookie shook her head. She was looking at Sheila and Anne.

"Ah, Cookie! Been with me for a long time. Loyalty, you see! Incredible. Yes. Came as a nanny for our daughter and stayed. Well, well, sit down! Tuck in! Tuck in! Cookie, you can fetch the tea now." Cookie disappeared to get the tea.

The meal with which they had been provided was a ham salad with some cold boiled potatoes. On the table was a bottle of salad cream which Rhys-Griffiths shook and then poured liberally over the wilting lettuce and half tomato that had been supplied as a garnish. Sheila noticed that he had been given four slices of ham to their one each. She wanted to know about his life and would have asked him, but the flow of conversation from him came in a torrent, interrupted for the briefest of intervals by avid mouthfuls of ham salad. His conversation maintained the same tenor of vague but fantastic self-aggrandisement: "Top people consulted me ... I'm well known ... I have the finest ... It's universally acknowledged ... Some of these people couldn't manage your Aunt Fanny's back yard. They need to be told. I told them, but they wouldn't listen, and as a result you have the situation we're in now, you see."

It was as if Rhys-Griffiths were continuing a conversation with himself in their company. Cookie came in with the tea and when she put down the pot she looked at Sheila with a glance that seemed to say: "I told you so." Rhys-Griffiths barely noticed her, but before she was out of the dining room he said to Sheila and Anne.

"Now then, are you two sleeping together?"

The question's ambiguity struck them dumb. Sheila whose mind had dwelt on such ambiguities more than Anne's blushed, but in the dining room's dim light it was barely noticeable. Only the silence spoke.

"Cookie, you'd better get two rooms ready. Numbers three and five. Yes."

"I've already done it," said Cookie.

"Ah, there you are, you see. Cookie. Knows my mind. Separate bedrooms. Can't have you sleeping together. That's the sort of thing I don't allow ... Question of upbringing. Old fashioned high moral standards ... Oh, yes. I'm well known for it ..."

"We don't ..." Anne began.

"Ah, well, there we are ... We'll say no more ... You see this pepper pot? Georgian silver ... I happen to be an expert on Georgian silver. One of my areas of knowledge, you know. They consult me about it .... Sotheby's, Christie's, the British Museum: they all come to me ... I have a reputation ..."

The sponge pudding and custard that Cookie brought them when the main course had been consumed was curiously tasteless. Rhys-

Griffiths ate his rapidly while the words continued to pour from him. When his eating was finished, he said: "So, there we are ... Cookie's done us well, eh? Done us proud. I make sure of that, you see. You go and thank her. She'd appreciate that. Then you can settle the financial ... Whatever. Then you can go to bed. Separate bedrooms. Rooms three and five ... Rules of the house ... Well, there we are ..." And as he was leaving the dining room he switched off the light, leaving them with only the light from the passage to guide them out.

"Fucking hell!" said Anne under her breath.

"Eh? What was that?" said Rhys-Griffiths, his huge head silhouetted in the dining room doorway.

"Nothing!"

"Don't be too long. You need to change out of those wet shorts. Young girls in shorts ... You catch a chill ... Wouldn't want that ... The winds are high ... I know. I know all about chills. Doctors consult me ... Yes ..."

Sheila and Anne stayed in the half darkness of the dining room until they were sure that Rhys-Griffiths had gone, then Sheila reached over and took Anne's hand.

"I'm sorry I got you into this," she said.

"I agreed. Anyway, I think it's funny. And at least we've got somewhere to stay." There was a roar of thunder and for a brief moment the curtains of the dining room were faintly illumined from behind by a flash of lightning.

Still holding her hand Sheila said: "Let's go to our separate beds."

Anne giggled.

And still giggling, though suppressing the noise as far as they could, they picked up their rucksacks in the hall and made their way upstairs.

One dim bulb illuminated a long corridor at the top of the stairs. They crept along it looking for rooms three and five. The first door they came to had no number on it, the second a number nine which they eventually realised was a number six that had slipped down and become reversed.

The walls above the dado were papered in some dingy greenish flock and the pictures that hung there turned out to be pictures of Rhys-Griffiths. There were portraits in oils and drawings of him, none of them distinguished. There were also several framed photographs of him shaking hands with various dignitaries, including a mayor and, bizarrely, what looked like a Red Indian chief in buckskins and feathered head-dress. Several photos showed him standing among bearded men in long white gowns and head-dresses, evidently Welsh Eisteddfod functionaries in their druidic garb. In all these pictures he was looking outwards with that distant, unfocussed gaze and smiling complacently.

"Ah, yes. There, you see. Pictures of me on important occasions ... Portraits ... I've stopped having them done. It got too much ... But I have to have them up. Cookie likes them. Dusts them every day you see. Now then, are you two going to bed? Get some sleep ... Very important ... Oh, yes ..."

Standing at the end of the corridor and wearing a beige tartan paisley dressing gown was Rhys-Griffiths. He seemed more than ever like a dim amorphous creature of the sea in that faint light.

"Your rooms are there and there," he said, pointing to two doors on opposite sides of the corridor. "You'd better go in. Take your wet shorts off. Get some sleep, you see. I don't want to hear any talking. No. This house has a reputation. Yes. Very high ... I'm known for it ..." And still murmuring he left them. Anne stuck out her tongue at the retreating form, but Sheila had not found it funny.

"Which room do you want?" Sheila asked.

"Does it matter?"

"Probably not. I'll have this one, unless you want it ..."

"Don't be silly."

"I'm only saying ... Can I see yours?"

"You better not. You heard what the man said."

"What's it got to do with him?"

"This is so weird! Good night!" And they both went into their rooms.

Sheila's had one small window that faced onto the front of the hotel, from which, occasionally, a passing car could be heard amid the constant patter of the rain, and once, improbably, the roar of a motorcycle. There was a drabness about the room that was disheartening. It was not dirty and the bed linen was pristine if slightly damp, but the place had the desolate atmosphere of long disuse. Sheila kept trying to put her feelings down to fancy and the rather absurd events of the previous hour, but reason never rules in such circumstances. She had the sense that she was in a room that was despised and neglected and that she too in consequence was unworthy. It felt as if Anne, only across the passageway, was remote, had cut herself off from her forever, and that this night was the beginning of the end of their relationship.

That was absurd. Of course it was absurd; but then so was this place.

There was, naturally, no en suite shower and toilet, but there was a wash hand basin. Sheila turned on the hot tap to see what would happen. The tap shuddered and groaned for a moment then vomited a gush of rusty brown fluid. It was cold. Sheila gave up the idea of a wash and began to prepare methodically for bed.

The wallpaper was yellow with tiny sprays of flowers on it and there were no pictures except one. Sheila had not noticed it at first because it had been oddly sited in one corner of the room to one side of a giant mahogany wardrobe. It appeared to be a plaster bas relief of a man's face laid over crimson velvet, under glass and in an elaborate and vulgar gilded frame. The face was white and looked like a death mask, except that it could not have been. It was unmistakably the face of Mr Rhys-Griffiths. The complacent half smile and the slightly puckered closed eyes combined to give an impression of seraphic ecstasy. Now she knew it was there, she could not escape its presence, sublimely indifferent to her and yet, somehow, intrusive.

It was absurd to feel guilty about wearing socks in the cold damp bed, but she did. She had the sense that someone – she was not sure who – would disapprove. The rain had ceased and the place had become silent. That only seemed to increase her anxiety. She worried about Anne and what she must think of her for dragging her here. She worried about the emptiness of her life without her. She worried about .... The worries drifted into nonsense as sleep took hold of her, but they were still worries. A long period of confused half oblivion followed until, several hours later, she was awake again.

The silence was no longer there, but all the noises came from within the house. It was the hum and murmur of talk. Everything seemed to be talking, the walls, the chairs, even the wardrobe ... Wait a minute! Was this a dream? Yes. It was. She woke again, but still the murmur persisted. She had the odd feeling that she was inside something living and that the living thing was talking, but she could not understand the words. She picked up odd sentences as in a dream, but they kept trailing off into unrecollected rubbish. But she knew the voice of her host.

"Yes ... Oh, yes ... Well, known, you know ... I was the driver of the whole event ... The druids came and drew ... I drew them ... I was the druids' drawing and my music drew them...Through the hills, soft as silk ... And the trees that I ordered to fly through the night ... They all knew who I was, and I saw that the owls were on guard ... I am panjandrum ... I wasn't going to have any nonsense ...."

Sheila shook her head to stop this everlasting flow of rubbish. It was poisoning her brain, wrecking it like a drug. But her head felt soft and furry and she could not get it out. She could get out of bed and she did. She swayed when she stood and the room softly hummed around her. Deep in her woolly brain fear began to bang a drum and her heart followed suit. What was happening to her?

The dizziness subsided a little. She stopped swaying and took a deep breath. The room was stuffy. Perhaps the thing to do was to open the window, get some air. She tried to open the window but it was stuck fast: the gap between window and sill had been painted over with glossy cream paint to seal it shut. She needed a knife or something to crack it open. Outside the window it was as black as a sheet of crepe. Nothing shone. The next best thing was to try the door. Her hands, unaccountably sweaty, slipped on the handle, but at last the door was open and she was in the dim lit passage.

The air was as thick here as in her bedroom, thicker even, and the voice was louder, or at any rate more penetrating, so much so that it seemed to vibrate inside her head, so much so that the whole building seemed to shiver at the sound.

"Oh, yes ... Here I am ... I am the one ... I'm one and only ... I have everything here ... I'm everyone ... I'm well known, I'm here on my own and they all come for me, come to me ..."

A dim figure came out of the gloom at the end of the corridor. It was Rhys-Griffiths in his paisley dressing gown. Had he seen her? His eyes must have looked in her direction but there was no reaction. He began to move towards her, then for no reason he turned back and began to move in a circle.

"Yes ... Yes ... Yes ... Oh, yes," he seemed to say and this voice blended with the other voices which were all his. Sheila turned away from him to look for Anne's door, but for some reason she had forgotten which one it was. She started to run away from Rhys-Griffiths to where she believed the staircase to be. She reached the stairs, and there standing at the top of them was the great pale bulk of Rhys-Griffiths in his dressing gown. It was impossible! He could not have got here! She turned back and looked down the corridor, but the other Rhys-Griffiths was gone.

She moved quickly away down the corridor but could hear him breathing and whispering just behind her. She turned and found herself staring up at the face of Rhys-Griffiths gazing vacantly over her head. He swayed to and fro and she felt his paisley clad paunch bumping against her breasts. She gave a little scream and retreated.

"Yes ... Yes ... Yes ... Yes," the man was murmuring. "Young girls alone ... Young girls in shorts ... Cold feet ... Bare bottoms ... I don't allow that sort of thing ... Oh, no ... Oh, no ..." And he began to advance down the corridor towards her, his feet treading heavily, the whole world shaking as he came on. Sheila scrambled away from him in terror. She tried several doors in the corridor just to escape, but they were all locked, then one gave way and she stumbled in.

She was in Anne's room. It appeared to be a mirror image of her own. The bedside light was on and Anne was sitting up in bed, a frozen expression on her face. When she saw Sheila her eyes widened a little but she said nothing and did not move.

On one side of the bed a man with his back to Sheila was sitting, crouched over the bed. He wore a paisley dressing gown and the white hair on the back of his head was wild. One hand was stretched under the blanket and feeling towards Anne's legs. He was crooning to himself.

"Young girls on their own ... Shouldn't allow that sort of thing ... Wet shorts ... Wet shirts ... Take them off ... I don't allow it ... I'm known for it. Wouldn't have my own daughter ... Couldn't have her ... I have healing powers ... Healing hands ... I'm well known for it ... Oh, yes ... Oh, yes ..."

Sheila saw the hand move under the blanket like a creature with a life of its own. Anne gasped with pain.

Sheila screamed: "Get out, you fucking pervert! Get the fuck out of here!"

Rhys-Griffiths looked around in shock, overbalanced in his chair. And fell over. He did not get up but started to crawl towards the door, still murmuring.

"Oh, yes ... I'm well known for it ... I knew what was best for her, but she wouldn't let me ... I'm the one ... I'm the one ... I'm the only one ..."

"Come on," said Sheila. "Quickly! We're getting out of here. Come on! We're not staying a moment longer in this shit hole."

Anne seemed at first to be in a kind of trance, but she responded eventually, though rather mechanically to Sheila's urgings. When she was dressed they went into Sheila's room while she dressed and packed. Nothing was said and the place was silent again. It appeared to be deserted.

Nobody stopped them as they crept down stairs with their ruck sacks took their bicycles from the hall, unbolted the door and crept out into the fresh air.

The sky was clear and full of stars. On the tarmac road pools stood in silent witness to the rain that had gone. They looked east and saw the faint streaks of a green dawn rising over the hills of Snowdonia. Without speaking they mounted their bicycles and set off on the road towards that morning.

After about five miles of silent riding Anne suddenly skidded to a halt at the bottom of a small incline. Sheila stopped too.

"Are you all right, Anne?" she said.

Anne blinked. "Yes. Yes ... I think so ... Well ..." Suddenly she turned and stared wild-eyed at her friend. "Christ! Where have I been?"

"You've just been in someone else's Hell," said Sheila.

Anne's dark eyes filled with tears. "Nor am I out of it," she said.

Sheila recognised the quotation and thought it a little melodramatic. As far as she was concerned they had escaped, with their wits and their lives intact. That was it. It was only when they reached Corwen that Sheila began to realise Anne might be a very different sort of person.

NIGHT OF THE BLOODY APE

*C*arew Castle sits on a rocky bluff above the Carew inlet, the tidal estuary of Milford Haven on West Wales's dramatic Pembroke coast.

It is an ominous structure, born of violence. The present castle was completed in the year 1100 to reinforce the Norman occupation of Pembrokeshire, though an Iron Age fortress had controlled the estuary from the same spot previously and had seen many battles. It was modified and strengthened during the 12th and 13th centuries in order to hold down the rebellious population, but like many of the great Welsh castles still remaining, it is these days regarded as a magnificent piece of period architecture and a prized money-spinner for local businesses.

The castle is now a ruin and is managed by Cadw, the historic environment department of the Welsh Government, but it was inhabited until the late 17th century, and strangely it is this latter, more sedate era rather than the turbulent Middle Ages, from whence the most gruesome of its legends comes to us.

The wealthy landowner and adventurer Sir Roland Rhys occupied the castle in the mid-17th century. Though well regarded for his knowledge and intellect, Sir Roland, who was rumoured to have made his fortune as a pirate, was also famous for his foul temper and aggressive possessiveness. When he returned from one of his many trips abroad with a new pet, a Barbary ape, which he had rescued from the wreckage of a Spanish galleon, it didn't delight those who knew him as much as frighten them, especially when they heard the name he had given it: Satan.

The ape, which was most likely a mandrill, a large, powerful species, came to adore its new master, and even to reflect his moods. When Sir Roland was content, the ape was content – even playful. But when he was angry, which was often, it would prowl the gloomy castle, snarling or screaming at anyone it encountered. Several servants left, citing terror of the ape as the reason. One said she'd feared she was inches from death – the beast had cornered her in a vault and had only spared her because Sir Roland, with apparent ill-grace, had called it away.

One particularly stormy night, when Sir Roland learned that his ne'er-do-well son had eloped with the daughter of a Flemish merchant, his fury knew no bounds. The situation worsened when the girl's father, whose name was Horowitz, arrived at Carew Castle, demanding restitution. Sir Roland was so enraged that he unleashed the ape upon him. It took to the task with gusto, and though Horowitz managed to fight the animal off, he suffered terrible injuries in the process. Even then it pursued him through the castle, and only a brave servant, who enclosed him in a side-chamber, saved his life.

As they hid there in the darkness, Horowitz and the servant listened in disbelief as the deranged duo, the ape and its master, shrieked and roared while searching the castle. Horowitz, it was said, crossed himself, praying earnestly that Sir Roland and his monster should meet the evil fate they deserved. In the morning, when all was quiet, the nervous servant ventured out to look around – he found his master in an upper room that was completely drenched with his blood.

He had been torn limb from limb, but of the ape called Satan there was no trace.

Fearing it was still somewhere in the lowering old structure, waiting to leap out on its next victim, the staff abandoned Carew Castle, never to return.

Even today, no-one is able to say what happened to the baleful creature. Popular myth tells how at night it still prowls the darkened ruin, hunting down the unwary. Ghost-watch societies also say the ape is present, but as a spirit – they claim to have heard its shrieks and the sound of its clawed feet gambolling along overhead floors that no longer exist. Perhaps it's no surprise that, to date, no record exists of any person, ghost-watcher or not, who has found the courage to spend a night in the castle alone.

SWALLOWING A DIRTY SEED
Simon Clark

C ould you spare us some food?"

"Food?"

"We haven't eaten all day. We were camping up the valley."

"We lost the rucksack with our supplies," the man added.

It was five in the afternoon. Despite the new electric oven causing the main's fuses to blow every forty minutes, I'd cooked my first proper meal in the cottage. A leg of Welsh lamb in rosemary; to accompany that, fresh vegetables and an apple and walnut stuffing of which I was particularly proud. The oven had behaved itself, on the whole, nothing had burnt, or emerged raw. And I'd poured myself a glass of crisp white wine, so chilled the glass immediately turned all frosty. That's when I heard the knock on the door. The cottage, tucked away deep in a Welsh valley, was miles from the nearest village and, at first, I thought it must be the man from the garage returning my car a day early.

Instead, there on the doorstep, looking as if they'd just hiked back from the Antarctic, stood a man and woman in their early twenties. Both were exhausted. Dark rings underscored their strangely glittery eyes; the man leaned forward, one elbow against the doorframe to support his weight. He was slightly built with dark curly hair. He wore a pale brown corduroy jacket and jeans; the girl wore a black suede jacket and matching black trousers. If anything, she looked physically stronger than the man. Statuesque would be a fair description to suit her. She'd tied her long blonde hair back into a pony tail; her brown eyes fixed on me without a hint of shyness. Both wore trainers. For campers they were pretty poorly equipped. I saw no signs of tents or sleeping bags.

"We can pay," the girl prompted. She unzipped a pocket on her jacket and pulled out about two pounds in loose change. The man leaned forwards, trying not to look to obvious, but I could see he was drawing the aromas of roasting lamb through his nostrils, as if he hoped to be nourished on the scents alone.

I smiled. Heck. I could afford to play the good Samaritan now I'd finally managed to sell my apartment in Manchester and set aside six months rental on this, my wilderness retreat.

"Come on in," I said warmly. "I'm just about to eat anyway. Roast lamb okay? No, put the money back in your pocket. The pair of you look as if you could do with a drink. White wine?"

"God, yes." The man sounded shocked by my generosity. "Brilliant. Thanks."

"Thank you very much, Mr?" The girl held out her hand.

"Stephen Carter." I shook her hand.

"My name is Dianne Johnson."

Her grip was firm, even vigorous. By contrast, the man lightly held my fingers when I shook hands with him. He said his was Ashley May. I could easily have imagined he was a young Church of England vicar who'd embarked on a camping holiday only to find the weather or the girl, or both, were more than he could cope with.

"Pretty lousy weather for camping," I said, pouring the wine. "This is the driest day we've had in a week."

"That's Wales in April." The girl made polite conversation. "We thought it might be warmer."

"I came here for the light," Ashley said in a small voice. "Here in April you get good light."

"Good light?"

The girl explained quickly. "Ashley's a landscape painter. He's been commissioned by a gallery in Bangor to paint three landscapes. They'll print a limited edition."

"For the tourists." Ashley shook his head mournfully and drained the glass of wine in one. "It would have paid the rent, too."

Would have paid the rent? He sounded as if some catastrophe had obliterated all hope of his life continuing.

"Here, Ashley," I told him. "Let me fill your glass. Top up, Dianna?"

"Please … lovely wine."

They drank as if they needed it. Hell, they gulped it as if they depended on its restorative power. Both were trembling as they raised the glasses to their lips.

They've just had one heck of shock, I realized, surprised by the sudden insight. Yes, they've come through something terrible. But in a quiet Welsh valley what could have that devastating effect on their nerves?

Now they were trying to pretend they were tired campers; forcing themselves to make polite conversation; struggling to be nonchalant; yet it seemed to me that at any moment their self-control would shatter and they would run screaming down the hillside all the way to Criccieth.

I served them huge platefuls of lamb and vegetables. They ate every scrap. I offered seconds; they hungrily accepted.

When they had finished, Dianne glanced at Ashley in a way that asked a question. He nodded. Then Dianne turned to me.

"I don't like to ask this," she began. "You've been so generous. But would you mind driving us to the nearest town?"

"Normally, I'd be delighted to oblige. But my car's at the garage."

"Then may we telephone for a taxi?"

"I'm terribly sorry. I'm still waiting to be connected. You see, I've only just moved in. Unfortunately, it's impossible to get a signal on mobile phones, too. It's beautiful here, but remote; that's the trade off, I guess."

"Is it far to town? Could we walk there before it gets dark?"

"I'm sorry to have to keep being so negative. But there's not a chance I'm afraid. It would be a two hour walk. Of course, there are no streetlights out here."

Ashley glanced out of the window. The expression on his face made me shiver. He looked scared out of his wits.

"God ... it's nearly dark now. *Dianne?"*

"Don't worry, Ashley. You won't be like him. I mean, there's no sign of anything?"

"Nothing's changed outwardly. *But I can feel it."*

"Ah, sorry to intrude,' I said awkwardly. "Might I ask, are you in any trouble?"

Dianne glared at me. "Trouble? We're not on the run from the police, or anything like that."

"Sorry. I didn't mean to imply that. It's just both of you seem ... unnerved."

"We're fine," she insisted firmly.

Ashley shot her a startled look as if she'd just told the lie of the century.

"We lost our tents, that's all." Dianne attempted to be matter-of-fact, as if they faced a minor glitch in their plans. "You wouldn't allow us to sleep here tonight?"

"We're so tired," Ashley whispered. "The tents went yesterday. Everything did. Food, spare clothes, torches."

"Went?"

"Stolen." Dianne shrugged. "We'd gone for a walk. They had been taken by the time we got back."

Come on, Stephen, I told myself, you can't turn them out on a day like this. Well ... evening would be a better description now. It was falling dark early as rain clouds avalanched over the Welsh hill-tops. Already lights from cottages on distant hillsides twinkled like stars.

I smiled. "No problem. I've got a single bed in the spare bedroom. Someone will have to make do with the sofa I'm afraid."

64

"That's fine." Ashley yawned. "I could sleep like a baby on that stone floor. Just as long as I don't have to spend another night outside."

"I've switched on the immersion heater," I told them. "So you can have hot baths."

"A bath." Dianne beamed her delight at Ashley. Her face was near child-like. "Would you be able to manage a hot bath?"

She seemed livelier for eating the meal – the wine and coffee would have helped, too. I found myself enjoying her company. After losing Anne I promised myself a moratorium on women for a while. But I had begun to wonder lately if I'd start to find myself lonely up here in the cottage – after all, it was slap bang deep in the heart of nowhere.

I finished eating a biscuit then said, "The water should be hot enough now. I've left out clean towels."

"You first, Ashley," she told him.

Meekly, he obeyed.

After he'd gone upstairs, I asked Dianne if she'd like a gin and tonic. She accepted gratefully. Her face had flushed now, and the smile seemed more genuine. I'd just unscrewed the top from the Gordon's and began to pour when, *bang!* The fuse blew again.

Instantly, the cottage lights went out. We were plunged into darkness.

The scream that followed turned my blood to ice. The shock caused me to hold my breath. Dimly, I realized that I was pouring gin over the table top. But that scream. It had been driven out of the man's mouth by sheer terror.

*

I slotted the ceramic fuse-holder back into the fuse box.

Click.

The lights came on, killing the darkness. The fridge shuddered into life.

I found my hands were still clammy with sweat. Ashley's terrible scream had disturbed me more than I could adequately describe. If a man realized he was about to have his throat cut, he'd probably scream in the same way – a violent outpouring of shock, despair and absolute horror. Ashley must have a clinical phobia of the dark.

Swiftly, I returned to the living room. All the lights had been switched on, as if to compensate for the three minutes or so of darkness earlier. The young man must have found his way downstairs somehow in the dark. Now he sat hunched and scared in the armchair, his fists clenched on his knees.

65

"Is he alright?"

Dianne looked up at me, her face pale. "Fine. You'll have the bath now Ashley?"

His eyes were wide and strangely glittery. "When the lights went out ... they moved. *Dianne, they moved ...*"

She shot me a glance as if to say, *Please don't listen to what he's saying. It means nothing.*

"In the dark," Ashley murmured as if he'd experienced some profound revelation, and now he finally understood a terrible truth. "*In the dark* ... Michael had said those words: 'in the dark.' "

I stood there. Cold shivers ran from head to foot. There was such a charge in that room. A charge of cold, blue fear.

*

I was in bed by eleven on that April night. The wind blew down the valley. It moaned around the chimney pots, drawing strange musical notes that sounded like a surreal composition for pan pipes – a song for souls lost in the darkness and achingly alone. The wind carried a flurry of hail to rattle against the windows. It clicked on the patio like so many scurrying insectile feet. In the next room slept Dianne Johnson. Ashley May occupied the sofa downstairs. As I came back from the bathroom I'd peeped over the banister down into the living room. All I could see of him beneath the blanket was an expanse of glistening forehead. He was sleeping with the table lamp burning brightly just inches from his face.

It's a terrible thing to be afraid of the dark. Especially to the extent of that young man.

Shaking my head, I'd gone to bed, then switched out the light. Burning out of the darkness were the red numerals of the clock radio. They read 11:04.

*

Disaster struck. I sat up blinking in the darkness; my heart pounded. I didn't know what had woken me. I didn't know what had happened.

But something had. I sensed it: an oppressive sense of dread bore down on me; a dead weight on my nerves. I checked the clock radio for the time. I saw nothing.

There was only the dark.

Then I sensed movement at the foot of the bed.

Hell. Someone was in here with me. An intruder moved through that all encompassing darkness.

Crash.

That was the chest of drawers at the foot of my bed being struck. A body thumped across my legs.

I thought: *You're being attacked! Fight back!*

I swung my fist.

Nothing. I'd swiped fresh air. But still that weight stopped me from moving my legs. At any moment hands would be at my throat.

Next I grabbed, instead of punching into the dark. My fingers closed round long hair.

"Please!"

"Dianne?"

"Please, help me."

"What's wrong?"

"It's Ashley… the lights went out."

My eyes snapped back in the direction of the clock radio. *Damn it, Stephen! You forget to switch off the immersion heater: now it's only gone and blown the fuse again.*

"It's okay," I told her. "I've got a torch … there …"

Dianne's face suddenly appeared in the blaze of torchlight. Her hair was wild; a deep, deep dread lanced through her brown eyes. Panting, she said, "The light went out. Now I can't find Ashley."

"You can't find him?"

"He's gone. Like Michael."

"Michael? Who's Michael?"

"He was on the camping trip with us. He went first, but … look, please. Can we just try and find Ashley? I'll tell you everything when I know he's safe."

My head was spinning. I remembered Ashley's terrified scream when the light went out earlier in the evening. He had a phobia of the dark. At least that's what I surmised. Had that phobia driven him to run wildly from the cottage?

If he had, I might not be able to find him. I still didn't know the area at all well. Beyond the cottage garden and the orchard there were woods and fields running for miles in the direction of the Lleyn Peninsula. You could hide entire armies out there.

"Dianne. You checked all the rooms?"

"I tried. I found a box of matches. As far as I could see he's not in the cottage. Then the matches ran out; that's when I decided to find you."

"Damn."

"God, I'm sorry … I'm sorry."

"Don't worry. We'll find him. Take this torch: I've a spare in the kitchen."

First I replaced the blown fuse with the standby ceramic fuse holder. Lights suddenly blazed. The fridge gave that wobbly shudder as the unit fired up again.

I pulled on my boots, and slipped a wax jacket over my pyjamas. Dianna had already dressed. She followed me outside and we walked across the lawn calling his name.

"Ashley? *Ashley?*"

Torch lights splashed across grass being blasted into flurries of ripples by the wind. The discordant pan pipe notes shrilled as the wind caught the chimneys – that serenade for lost souls was as dismal as ever.

"Ashley?"

We followed the garden wall until it reached the gate.

"Where does that lead?" called Dianne above the storm winds.

"The orchard," I said, following her as she hurried through the gate.

Currents of cold air whistled through the branches of the apple trees. I watched as Dianna walked slowly along the lines of fruit trees, carefully shining the torch into the whipping mass of branches. Did she expect to find her friend clinging to a trunk, monkey-like, his face twisted into a mask of terror?

After an hour searching the wood and surrounding fields we returned to the orchard. Again, Dianne shone the light into the fruit trees. I followed suit. Half-expecting to glimpse Ashley's frightened face peering out from the mass of branches; eyes wide with panic.

Suddenly, she asked, "In the orchard – how many trees are there?"

That was such a bizarrely inappropriate question in the circumstances that I floundered. "I ... I don't know ... actually, it's the first time I've been in ..."

She suddenly turned and walked back to the cottage.

Once inside, she quickly slipped off her jacket. "Stephen. I want to tell you something." She spoke briskly. "It's too late for Ashley. We'll never find him."

"This fear of the dark. Has it happened before?"

"It's nothing to do with being afraid of the dark. Sit down please." She sat down and patted the sofa cushion beside her.

I sat down, puzzled. Earlier she'd seemed so concerned for her friend; now she appeared to dismiss him from her thoughts.

I said, "I think it's best if I walk down to the farm and phone for help."

"No."

"We should call the police. Ashley might be hurt."

"No. Please listen to what I have to say first. It's too late for Ashley. It might also be too late for me."

"For you? Look, just give me half an hour. I can run down to the farm at ..."

"Please, Stephen." She squeezed my hand. "I want to – no – I *need* to tell you what happened to us."

The pan pipe notes boomed down the chimney. That mournful song for lost souls was becoming increasingly desperate.

"Listen. I was camping with Ashley and our friend Michael. We'd all been to college together. It was still a tradition we'd go on holiday as a threesome. All entirely platonic. This year, Ashley had been given the commission to paint the landscapes. His first real opportunity to earn money as an artist. And he really was a talented man. I've never seen such delicate brushwork. Anyway, the three of us decided to go camping in North Wales." She gave a little smile. "I imagine you noticed we weren't very well equipped – or experienced. So, there we were. Camping miles from anywhere. Ashley painted. Michael and I explored the valley. The weather was awful. Every morning you'd see the cloud come racing across the sky. We had hail, rain, even snow. The wind kept blowing out the stove. The sleeping bags were damp. The bread went all mouldy." She sighed. "On the Monday afternoon the three of us went for a walk. And there, deep in the forest, Michael found an apple tree. Just one, growing in the middle of all these huge oak trees. He was really delighted with the find. He picked one of the apples and ..."

"Just wait a minute," I said, puzzled. "This is April. You wouldn't have fruit on an apple tree at this time of year."

"This had. Even though the tree didn't have any leaves yet. The apples were red – red as strawberries. If I close my eyes, I can see them now as they hung from the bare branches like big red globes. Michael picked one from a branch. Then he cut slices with his penknife and we all ate a piece." She frowned as she remembered. "They were very sweet, but they had a sort of perfume flavour to them. You know, like the taste of Earl Grey tea. It was only as I was eating that I noticed the apple didn't have a core with pips. Instead, it was simply apple flesh all the way through. Then, do you know what I found?"

I shook my head. I wasn't going to like the outcome of what she was telling me.

She tilted her head to one side, her eyes far away. "I found the seeds. They were just under the skin of the apple. And they were white and soft; just like tomato seeds."

"Just under the skin? Then it can't have been an apple."

She shrugged; one of helpless despair rather any suggestion of being uncaring at her plight. "It looked like an apple."

"These apples. They had something to do with what happened to Michael and Ashley?"

"Yes." She pushed her long hair back from her face. "We all swallowed the seeds." Suddenly, she lifted her sweatshirt to show me her exposed midriff. "You can feel them under my skin."

"Your skin? Feel what under your skin?" It was as if a series of electric shocks had just tingled across my own skin. "Diane, what can you feel?"

"Touch." She grasped my hand and pressed my fingers against her stomach. "Hot, isn't it? Michael and Ashley started like that and …" She gave that despairing shrug again. "And now you can feel them growing under my skin."

I stared at her, my eyes wide.

"You can feel the roots," she said.

I could feel nothing but skin and firm stomach muscle beneath.

"Dianne," I began as calmly as I could. "Don't you think …"

"And there," she interrupted, and pointed to a dark growth on her side, just above the hip. "That's where one of the buds is already forcing its way through. It doesn't hurt. But I'm conscious of them – all those buds – pressing out through my flesh. It makes it very sensitive. All the time, I'm aware of my clothes against my skin. To slow down the growth I should take off my clothes and sit beneath bright lights. That seems the only way to retard it. In the darkness they grow. And then it is at an explosive rate. That's why Ashley was so afraid of the dark. And that's why Ashley disappeared when the lights failed. He would have felt the branches bursting through his skin; the pricking of the roots. They'd have been worming outwards through the soles of his feet. He would have felt an overwhelming compulsion to run from the house. A need for deep, fertile earth …"

"Dianne …"

"Tomorrow, if you count the trees in the orchard, you'll find there will be one more than yesterday."

"Dianne. I think I really do need to make a phone call. Will you be all right here by yourself?"

She's mentally ill.

The revelation had, perhaps, been too long in coming. But I realized the truth now. She and Ashley had absconded from a hospital somewhere. No, probably it wasn't even as dramatic as a midnight scramble through a psychiatric ward window. No, this so-called Care in the Community policy, which places the burden of care for people suffering mental illness on the patients themselves. They're expected to go home and tend to their own psychosis or neurosis or whatever malady ails them. Perhaps for some reason, she and Ashley had stopped taking their medication.

"Stephen, why don't you believe me? Look at my stomach. You can see the bud there, breaking through the skin, growing."

70

"It's not a tree bud. It's a mole; just a mole. Now …"

"Touch it."

"No."

"You're afraid, aren't you, Stephen?"

"No."

"Press your finger against it."

"Dianne …"

"Press hard, Stephen."

"Dianne, please …"

"Press. You can hear the bud casing crack."

"It's a mole."

"Just a mole?"

"Yes."

"Here, watch closely, Stephen."

"A mole."

"Watch. As I scratch the top off it."

"Dianne, don't …"

"When I scratch the top off you'll see a green leaf all curled up tight as a parcel inside."

"Dianna, stop it!" I gripped her fists in my hands, held them hard. "Don't hurt yourself – *please*."

"Okay, Stephen." She gazed up at me, meek as a scolded child. "I'm sorry. But I just wanted so much that you believe me."

I met that brown-eyed gaze. Her eyes seemed so calm now. As if she'd accepted a terrible calamity would overtake her. But it's okay, she seemed to be thinking. I'm ready for it now. I won't resist the inevitable.

"Look," I said gently. "Will you be alright here by yourself?"

"You're going to telephone the police, aren't you?"

"Yes … not because I think you're mad." It's true, I told that white lie, but my motives were good. "We need to find Ashley. He'll die of exposure out there on a night like this."

She gave a sad sigh. "He doesn't feel the cold now. Neither does Michael."

"Stay in here. Keep the door locked and the lights on." I checked the wall clock. "It's just past three o' clock now. I'll be back by four."

"Don't worry about me. I'll be alright." Her voice possessed a whispery quality and despite my aversion to the comparison I couldn't help but be reminded of a breeze rustling leaves on a tree. "I'll sit by the table lamp."

"Good girl."

"Stephen."

"Yes?"

She looked up into my eyes. Lightly she rubbed her bare stomach with one hand. "Will you do something for me? A special favour?"

"Whatever I can, yes."

"I'm frightened, so please … will … will you kiss me?"

*

I ran along the track. The torchlight flashed against the tractor ruts, then against the steep banking at either side, illuminating bushes and grass. The wind blew hard. Brambles would whip out horizontally across the track. Sometimes they lashed against my wax jacket with a crack. By this time, I was panting hard; the thump of my boots hitting the ground transmitted juddering shocks up into my neck.

Briefly, I stopped to zip up the jacket. The gales repeatedly caught it, causing it to balloon around my body.

Then I ran on. Above me, trees creaked and groaned in the storm winds. The skin on my back, rubbed by the heavy winter jacket, began to chafe. I wore nothing but pyjamas beneath it.

What a night, I thought in astonishment. Just think of the e-mail you can send to big Jim back at the office. Maybe in a few days I'd look back on all this in amusement. But I couldn't now. Although those two strangers had only walked into my life just hours ago, I was deeply worried about them. I hadn't wanted to leave the girl alone in the cottage. But what options did I have? If I waited until daylight Ashley would surely have died of hypothermia out there in this gale. But would Dianne be alright? Perhaps I should have hidden the knives? Then I would have needed to hide the screwdrivers and aspirin, too. But I didn't have time to do everything. Maybe the girl was only delusional, not suicidal.

Her manner had changed, too. She seemed somehow elated after I left her. That morbid air of resignation had gone.

Perhaps it was the kiss?

She'd asked me to kiss her. Poor kid, at that moment that was all I could give her. Anyway, I'd left her listening to music on the radio; she'd appeared calm enough.

Ahead, I saw the outline of the farmhouse through the darkness. The early-to-rise farmer was already up. I could see him moving about in the kitchen. At least I wouldn't have to stand there hammering at the door. I crossed the yard and knocked.

*

I arranged to meet the police back at the cottage. I ran back up the lane home. Sweat streamed down my chest. All I wanted was to get out of the sweat-soaked pyjamas and ease my body into a hot, steaming bath.

I took the short cut over the wall, raced through the orchard; the branches of the trees rattled in the wind; then I pushed through the gate into the cottage garden.

I stopped dead.

Damn.

I don't believe it, I thought, heart sinking; I don't damn well believe it. It's only gone and done it again!

The cottage lights were out. The fuse had blown.

Darkness.

I dashed across the lawn. The torchlight illuminated the grass being ripped this way and that by the gale blasting down the valley. The cottage door slammed open-shut-open-shut.

I all but flung myself through the doorway into the cottage. Then I stood there, hauling in lungful after lungful of cold air. Just a second of shining the torch around the room revealed it was deserted. And within a few moments I'd checked every other room in the cottage. All deserted. All silent. For all the world, I could have been in a tomb.

Back downstairs I went, to play the torch over the furniture, the table with the bottle of gin and two empty glasses, the empty sofa with the discarded blankets where Ashley had slept. Storm winds blew the branches of a tree to tap against the room window pane. In here, the only thing to be disturbed was a single chair – tipped onto its back as if someone had rushed by it in a frantic rush to escape the house.

She'd gone.

The emotion took me by surprise, yet I felt a sudden loss. I'd really liked Dianne. I remembered the way she'd asked me to kiss her. Her brown eyes, so gentle and trusting. Her hair, the way the wind had mussed it into a light froth that poured around her shoulders. She'd kissed me so passionately. Her hands had gripped my head as she held my mouth to hers.

That kiss.

Suddenly, I shivered. Quickly, I rubbed the back of my hand across my mouth as if to clean dirt from my lips. But it was too late.

Far, far too late.

I shivered again. Points of ice crawled across my stomach. When she kissed me it had felt as if she'd transferred something from her mouth to mine with her tongue. I must have imagined it, surely?

But no. It had felt as small as a seed. When she stopped kissing me and moved her head back I'd felt for it with my tongue. There was nothing there. I couldn't have swallowed it, could I? Was that the reason I couldn't find it? Because it had already slipped down my throat into my stomach? That small seed-like particle that I had felt slide between my cheek and gum, before it had vanished into my gullet.

Perspiration irritated my skin. Quickly, I unzipped my wax jacket and rubbed my stomach. God, I needed a bath. A red hot bath.

The kiss began to trouble me. I shouldn't have agreed to kiss her. Suddenly I wished I could turn back the clock, then when she asked, I'd firmly say, "No. I won't kiss you." As simple as that.

But it's too late. Much too late.

My skin felt acutely sensitive. I rubbed my stomach and my chest. The breeze blew the branches to tap against the glass again. Those damn branches … Tap, tap, tapping …

I grew uneasy.

No, I didn't.

I became frightened.

Because I knew no tree grew so close to the cottage that its branches could touch the glass.

Holding the torch in front of me, I walked outside, swinging the light to my left.

Tap, tap, tap …

And there, the tree.

Its slender trunk, rooted deeply into the edge of the lawn; its branches swayed to and fro like the limbs of a graceful dancer. And the branches kept tap, tap tapping at the glass.

As if it strived to attract my attention.

There had been no tree there yesterday. I was certain of that. Fear prickled through me. I looked back at the house. No, I wasn't going back there. I couldn't bear to hear those branches at the glass. Tap, tap tapping …

The wind blew; it caught the chimney pots and the pan pipe notes boomed loud and madly discordant.

With a shiver, I zipped up my wax jacket. There was no alternative. I would have to –

No –

This couldn't be happening …

At that moment the torch died on me. The bulb went from glowing an incandescent white, to yellow, to orange …

– to red …

– to dull red …

– then to nothing … I slapped the torch into the palm of my hand.

My skin itched. A dreadful prickling that ran over my hips, my stomach, the base of my back. A crawling, burning itching. And all I could hear were those cold gusts, the mad pan pipe music, the rattle of branches against the window pane.

"The torch is dead," I told myself as calmly as I could, even though the shiver running through my body had become a deep tremble that would not stop; a tremble that intensified until my teeth clacked together like dry bones being shaken hard in a sack. Savagely, I threw the torch into the grass – the bloody thing had betrayed me.

"It doesn't matter, Stephen," I panted. "It doesn't matter one little bit. Because it's going to be light in an hour."

Better still, the police would be here soon. I'd wait for them in the lane.

I found my way to the wall in the darkness. Then by sense of touch I reached the gate to the orchard.

Cross the orchard, Stephen; then wait in the lane.

Soon you'll see the lights of the police car as it brings a couple of down-to-earth Welsh coppers up to the cottage. Everything will be alright then. You'll be safe.

The orchard seemed packed tight with trees. There seemed to be barely a gap to scramble through. I groped my way forwards with grim determination. Branches snagged my jacket, pricked my face; twigs caught my hair.

Storm winds whipped through the trees with a howl, like they were wild animals, ferociously savaging the branches of a pear tree there, clawing at the grass here, before pawing hungrily at my coat.

Dear God. I wished I could see. The darkness was total. A black fog pressed against my eyes. I didn't even see the branches that gouged my face.

I was growing tired now. I could hardly move. My skin itched. I thought of that kiss. Now I was convinced that Dianne had transferred something into my mouth. I couldn't stop myself imagining this picture: *There's Dianne – beautiful Dianne – she opens her mouth. It is packed with seeds. Like when you slice open a melon. Seeds! Hundreds of seeds, all neatly packed, all so tightly packed. There instead of teeth she has a row of white, gleaming seeds.*

"Stephen. Shut out the picture." My head spun. A dizzying vertigo tugged at me. "Shut that picture out." Then I found myself whispering, "The seed … I've swallowed it. I'm sure I've swallowed the damned seed."

Must be nearly at the lane. Nearly there, got to be. The police car will be here any minute … I forged on through the orchard. Fruit trees tugged at me. They were everywhere, blocking my path, scratching my face, pulling my hair, brambles tried to trip me.

Then I was free of them. Away along the lane I could make out the lights of the police car coming up the track – that pulse of blue light illuminated the roadside hedges. I tried to run toward the wall that separated the orchard from the lane. I made it to within five paces.

Then I stopped.

I was too exhausted to move another step. The police car approached. I held up my hands to flag it down.

They drove past, not seeing me.

I tried to lower my arms. I couldn't. For some reason I'd frozen in that position. My face, too, had seized into some kind of fixed mask as I'd shouted. I couldn't move my feet. I could not move at all.

I was rooted to the spot.

*

"Mum!"

"What is it? What's wrong?"

"Mum, come and look at this!"

"Joel, I thought we were making a snowman up on the lawn."

"I wanted to play in the orchard."

"Keep your coat fastened up, it's freezing. And be a good boy or we won't go to the café for lunch."

"But I wanted to show you this."

"Oh, very well, Joel. What have you found?"

"That apple tree over there near the wall. The one by itself. There's a coat stuck up in the tree."

"Ugh, probably belonged to a tramp."

"It's a wax jacket like Dad's – and someone's pushed the branches through the sleeves like arms."

"Don't touch it, it'll be dirty. Now come back and finish the snowman with me."

"But Mum!"

"But Mum what?"

"There's still apples on the tree. Can I eat one?"

"Certainly not. They'll give you stomach ache. Now, come with me."

The two walked back hand-in-hand through the snow. Joel felt in his pocket where he'd put the apple he'd picked. He'd eat it later when he was in his room. A moment later, mother and son had reached the snowman. Next to it, grew a slender apple tree. The breeze blew. Gently, it tapped a branch against the window pane of the cottage.

As if it were cold and lonely.
And it wanted to come inside.

THE DEVIL MADE HIM DO IT

Gruesome murders allegedly inspired by the Devil are not just an aberration of modern times, though there have been some classic examples in recent decades.

In 1974 in the United States, 23-year-old Long Islander Ronald DeFeo Jr. shot his family dead while they slept in their beds, afterwards claiming dark forces had compelled him to the deed. In Yorkshire, between 1975 and 1980, lorry driver Peter Sutcliffe ritually murdered 13 women. On arrest, he told investigators a voice from a sepulchre had instructed him to commit the grisly acts. Regardless of how we 21st century sophisticates view these garbled explanations – seeing them as pathetic excuses, or a sign of mental illness – we may be surprised to learn that a similar level of skepticism was in force during more credulous ages.

A ghoulish example in Welsh history dates to 1756, when a man called Edward Morgan, who had no known criminal past, was to spend Christmas at the house of his married cousin, Rees Morgan, at Llanfabon in the Rhondda. By all accounts, Edward Morgan was a jovial man and pleasant company. And yet, on the night of Christmas Day, a very different personality emerged. After an enjoyable festive banquet, Morgan retired to his bed, apparently sated and content. But in the early hours of the morning, a young apprentice in the house awoke to find Morgan standing alongside him, armed with a knife. Without warning, Morgan attacked, hacking at his victim viciously. Though badly wounded, the apprentice escaped. Morgan made no attempt to pursue him, or even to run away. Instead, he went outside to the yard, sharpened his knife on a whetstone, and re-entered the house, where, one by one, he assailed his hosts and their daughter as they slept, stabbing them and cutting their throats. He then set fire to the premises and left.

Of course, the apprentice was already raising hue and cry, and it wasn't long before Morgan was captured. He had full recollection of his gory deeds, but was at a loss to explain them other than to say he'd been woken by a terrible voice commanding him to kill. When brought before the justices, he maintained this remarkable tale, insisting he had briefly been enthralled to Lucifer.

It was undoubtedly a mystery. The culprit had made no attempt to loot the house, and no sexual interference with any of the victims was reported. What other motive could he have had, and why did persist with the crimes when he knew full well there was a surviving witness? But the claim that Morgan was possessed was treated with contempt, which is unusual given that only 21 years had elapsed since the Witchcraft Act had decriminalised the practice of black magic. The 18th century was the Age of Enlightenment, and science was slowly replacing superstition. Even so, it must still have taken a hardheaded judge to disregard Morgan's story altogether.

A secondary mystery connected to the tale concerns Morgan's fate.

According to the Newgate Calendar, he was sentenced to be 'hanged in chains'.

Just that ... 'hanged in chains'.

The normal outcome for convicted murderers in that era was hanging by the neck, and then either dissection or the gibbet. But in most legal records this was actually specified. That Morgan was simply ordered to be 'hanged in chains' implies he was to be put on the gibbet alive, his eventual death to result from thirst, starvation or exposure. It is difficult to establish whether or not this occurred. No such punishment existed on the statute book, but it had happened in medieval times, and as late as 1817, Patrick Devan, leader of an activist group in Ireland accused of burning a family alive in their home at Wildgoose Lodge, was allegedly gibbeted alive.

Was this to be the Llanfabon murderer's fate? Was his brutal crime deemed so heinous that only an extreme punishment would suffice? We will never know for sure, but whatever sentence was passed, it was fulfilled. The only record in existence states simply that at Glamorgan on April 6th 1757, Edward Morgan was 'hanged in chains'.

THE FACE
Thana Niveau

Pistyll Rhaeadr and Wrexham steeple,
Snowdon's mountain without its people,
Overton yew trees, St Winefride's well,
Llangollen bridge and Gresford bells.

'The Seven Wonders of Wales' (anon.)

Harrie paged through the latest batch of digital photos, tagging her friends and family when prompted by the software. It was funny how the computer sometimes mixed people up. True, Owain and Gareth looked a lot alike. As brothers, they ought to. But surely she looked nothing like *her* brother. Gwilym was much taller, with longer, darker hair. She was short and blonde.

IS THIS GWILYM? the pop-up window asked.

Harrie shook her head and ticked "no". Then she entered her own name. *ANGHARAD*. She was the only 'A' in there so all she had to do was type the first letter for her full name to appear.

She'd gone through all the pics from their hike through Snowdonia and then the Berwyn Mountains in September. Most of the landscape photos didn't have people in them to tag but she and Owain always took a few pictures of each other, and Gareth when he came along.

Gareth was slightly younger than Owain but he'd seen and done some incredible things in his twenty-four years. He was a thrill seeker who'd started climbing the local mountains as a kid and progressed to extreme sports as soon as he was old enough to defy his and Owain's overprotective parents. He'd been skydiving, whitewater canoeing and he'd even gone swimming with great white sharks in South Africa. More than anything he loved climbing and he talked about someday going to the Himalayas. Owain didn't share his brother's lust for adventure but he and Harrie benefited from it, as he was always a great subject for dramatic photos.

"No, that's not Owain," Harrie chuckled, correcting the computer when it misidentified the bloke abseiling down a slate wall.

She was quite proud of some of the shots she'd taken of Snowdon shrouded in fog and there was one particularly striking image of a hawk cutting down through the mist like an arrow. Just a happy accident, really. She never could have captured that if she'd tried. The hawk was lightning-fast and after a sharp piercing cry it snatched a mouse from the ground. It soared back up into the sky, only to drop its prey a few seconds later. The mouse fell like a stone but the photo showed only a tiny grey blur. A shame, but at least she had the first shot.

After that there was a beautifully atmospheric series of castles too, but if she was honest, Owain's shots were better than hers. He had a great eye for interesting architectural details and features most people probably didn't even notice. He'd won a prize when he was a teenager for a photo of Llangollen Bridge and it had been used in a 'Beautiful Wales' ad campaign. His parents had it framed in the front room. Harrie hoped that someday one of her pics might garner some acclaim too. A great photo was ten percent skill and ninety percent luck. Well, maybe she'd enter the hawk photo in the next competition.

It was always fun retracing their steps this way. All the Seven Wonders were there, along with several other sights that hadn't made the rhyme. Then, from the old East Llangynog silver mine to craggy Craig y Mwn, the images led up to their favourite place of all to photograph: the stunning waterfall Pistyll Rhaeadr.

In full flood it was an awesome sight, plunging over the cliff in three cascades to the valley below. That was how Owain and Gareth liked it – a raging torrent, mighty and ferocious, thundering down the rock face and threatening to sweep away the fairy bridge – the natural stone arch that spanned the rushing water. But Harrie liked it best when the river was low. When there hadn't been much rain the water would spill gently over the rocks like silk, delicate and ghostly.

She tagged two photos of Gareth and Owain standing together at the base of the falls, their faces showing clear disappointment that the water wasn't more exciting. Harrie softened the focus in some of the images, blurring the movement of the water to make it look even more ethereal, like a mystical wedding veil. Owain wouldn't approve. He didn't like Photoshopped images. He was a purist, he said, and he preferred purely natural shots. Harrie suspected he was just lazy when it came to processing.

In her opinion, no photo was ever complete straight off the camera. Just as every face, however lovely, needed makeup, so every image needed adjusting. She almost always tweaked the contrast to make her shots a little more dramatic and sometimes she played with coloured filters for an otherworldly effect. And whereas Owain wasn't bothered by evidence of the modern world, Harrie always cloned out unsightly fences and telephone poles and stray tourists. "Middle Earth pics," Owain teasingly called them, although he had let her erase a litter bin from one of his castle shots.

She paged through some more pictures, surprised at how many she had taken. Owain probably had even more, since her memory card had run out that day and she'd forgotten to bring a spare.

WHO IS THIS?

Harrie blinked at the screen. It was a detail of the top of the falls, and the area highlighted by the box showed nothing but water.

"No one I know," she said with a laugh and closed the window. But the programme flagged the next photo as well with the same question.

She peered at the box, trying to see whatever the computer was seeing. But she couldn't make out a face anywhere in the swirling currents and frothy spray.

"Sorry, but no," she said, moving on.

A few shots later the computer prompted her again. This time she felt a little unnerved. Surely the pattern of the water was different in every picture, so how could it keep zeroing in on the exact same spot? Sometimes a clutch of shadows or branches might form the elements of a rudimentary face and confuse the software but this was different. The tagging box was in the same place every time. The computer was adamant that there was a face there.

Too intrigued to ignore it, she dragged one of the photos into the editing suite to try and isolate the face. She played with the brightness and the contrast, hoping to tease out any rocks behind the water that could be responsible for the confusion. There was nothing. But the more she stared at it, the more she started to think she could see a pair of eyes. Maybe it was like those holographic images that were so popular in the '90s.

You had to let your eyes go out of focus to see the 3D picture buried inside the pattern.

She tried that. She relaxed her eyes and the waterfall went blurry as she tried to look beneath the swarming pixels. And then she saw it. The face.

It looked wrong. Like some kind of alien, all sharp lines and angles. A long gash for a mouth. And what she'd taken for eyes were two bright smears, as though it –whatever *it* might be – were blind. Or seeing through a different kind of eyes. Staring.

Harrie shuddered and looked away. Her eyes immediately refocused and when she turned back to the computer she expected the face to have vanished. But it was still there. She couldn't un-see it now. In fact, it was so obvious that she wondered why she'd never seen it before.

That evening she showed the sequence to Owain. "Do you see anything strange?" she asked.

He studied the pictures and she imagined he was probably looking for some evidence of Photoshopping, like a fairy she might have superimposed onto the background.

"No," he said after a while. "Nothing at all. Why? What have you done to it?"

"I haven't done anything. It's something that's there in the picture. Look closer. Cross your eyes."

He frowned, looking puzzled, but he did it. After a few seconds she heard a sharp intake of breath.

"What the …?"

"You see it?"

"That's weird!"

Harrie felt inexplicable relief. A part of her had been worried that he wouldn't see the face at all, that she'd only seen it herself because the computer had put the idea in her mind. She didn't like the thought she was that suggestible.

"So what causes that, then?" Owain mused, enlarging the area with the mouse.

"I don't know. I wouldn't have seen it at all if the computer hadn't flagged it up. It's creepy, huh?"

"Yeah. I wonder if anyone else has noticed it?"

Harrie ousted him from her chair and navigated to the web browser. She typed 'Pistyll Rhaeadr' and 'face' into the search engine and the first hit was a blog called *Rhaeadr Wyneb*. It was Welsh for 'Waterfall Face'. And it was filled with photographs showing the same thing Harrie and Owain had seen. Everything from professional high-res photos to grainy mobile phone pics, but every image showed the same staring face, the same blind eyes.

"That is seriously creepy," Owain said, exchanging a haunted look with her.

They'd been up there hundreds of times, separately and together, ever since they were kids. How was it possible they'd never seen the face before?

Gareth was less impressed when they showed him the photos and the blog. "Underlying rock formation" was his predictable response. That had been Harrie's first thought as well, and it certainly made sense. The fact that they couldn't see what was forming the strange features didn't matter. It was there under the water. It had to be.

"Nature's full of weird stuff," Gareth assured them. "You ought to come climbing with me sometime. I'll show you some proper weirdness!"

"No thanks," Harrie laughed. "I'm happy to keep a respectful distance. My camera can take all the risks for me."

Owain likewise refused the offer. "I don't mind a bit of hill-walking but mountaineering is too much like hard work."

"Please yourselves," Gareth said. "But you don't know what you're missing."

*

Winter came early, a biting, snarling thing that kept Harrie and Owain huddling indoors. They promised to brave the mountains again once it snowed, however. Nothing transformed a landscape like snow and ice. Winter was a horrible season to live through but a spectacular one to photograph. And picturesque snowscapes were easy to sell.

Owain's phone jolted them awake one bitterly cold morning. It was Gareth.

"Bloody hell, mate," Owain grumbled. "What time is it?" He flailed sleepily at the bedside clock but only succeeded in knocking it to the floor.

Harrie cried out as he turned the lamp on, flooding the room with unwelcome light. She buried her head under the pillow as she listened to the one-sided conversation.

"Snow? Yeah, we know. It's not going to melt before noon, is it? Can't you let us …"

There was a pause. Harrie could hear the tinny voice on the other end of the line but only a few words came through: ice, frozen, climb.

Whatever Gareth was saying was clearly interesting because Owain sat up, fully alert. "Absolutely! Yeah. Of course, mate. We'll be right over."

"We will?" Harrie mumbled from beneath the warm refuge of the duvet.

Owain cruelly whipped it away and she hissed like a vampire exposed to sunlight.

"The waterfall's frozen solid!"

It took a few seconds for the words to penetrate her sleepy brain but once they did she was wide awake. "Seriously?"

Owain was already out of bed and getting dressed. "Gareth wants to climb it. It's a once-in-a-lifetime photo op. But we've got to get there before anyone else does."

Harrie scrambled out of bed and began pulling on layers of winter clothes. It was dark outside and probably still would be when they got to Pistyll Rhaeadr. She made sure she had both memory cards this time.

*

The frozen waterfall was a breathtaking sight, absolutely magical. The sun was just coming up, tinting the sky with delicate pink and gold as they arrived at the base of the falls. In places the ice was thick and blue and frozen solidly to the cliff face, resembling diminutive glaciers. In others it hung suspended in long jagged shards like the fangs of some crystal monster.

"Incredible," Harrie breathed.

She'd never seen anything like it in her life. Of course they'd experienced Pistyll Rhaeadr in snow before, and it was an exquisite sight. The spray from the falls gathered in the trees like glass ornaments, turning the surrounding area into a crystalline wonderland. But for the entire river and the waterfall itself to freeze solid … She could almost believe that the fairies had been responsible. It was so still and silent the whole world might be holding its breath.

Gareth gazed up at the columns of ice, his eyes shining with excitement. "I've only ever climbed one frozen waterfall," he told Harrie, "when Owain and I were in Norway. I never dreamed the one in my own back garden would look like this."

The two lower cascades looked challenging enough but the top one – the tallest – looked positively daunting. The entire waterfall was around two hundred and forty feet tall and more than half of that height was the top cascade. While some of the ice was attached to the rock, the majority of it hung free, a single giant icicle about twenty feet wide. It was thinner where it connected to the pool below, just a thread really. Harrie saw several chunks of ice scattered nearby from where it must have broken. Her stomach fluttered.

She hated to ask such a boring question but it came out anyway. "Is it safe?"

Gareth smiled at her. "Oh yes. It's just like climbing rock."

Harrie had never climbed either rock or ice in her life but even she knew that couldn't be true. Doubtless he was just trying to placate her so she wouldn't fret. Not that she could have talked him out of it anyway. Gareth was nothing if not tenacious.

"You're worried about that thin patch, aren't you? Well, don't be. If it breaks I'll fall all of ten feet, but if it holds I'll know the rest is strong enough."

"He'll be fine," Owain said lightly, shouldering the rucksack with his camera equipment. "I'll head up to the top and meet you when you get there. Harrie, why don't you follow him up the side as far as you're comfortable going?"

She nodded, happy with the plan. Owain knew her so well. She didn't have a great head for heights and had never even been to the top of the falls. She much preferred the perspective of looking *up* at majestic sights. The path wasn't that steep and there were plenty of little plateaus where she could stop and take pictures, but she had no desire to go much further than about halfway up.

Owain crossed the iron bridge at the bottom and set out along the footpath. Harrie watched until he disappeared into the woodlands. While Gareth sorted out his gear she took a few shots of the pristine ice. It was bizarre to be looking at a waterfall without the accompanying sound of rushing water. It wasn't entirely silent, though. Occasionally the ice would creak and groan, as though the mountain were mumbling in its sleep.

Gareth strapped crampons onto his climbing boots, equipping his feet with vicious spikes for what he called "front-pointing". In each hand he carried an ice axe, the pick end hooked downward at a slight angle. He chopped into the ice at the base of the falls to show Harrie how they worked and when she saw how well they stuck she felt a little more secure. But only a little.

"Cool," he said. "I'm off!"

Good luck, Harrie thought but didn't say.

Gareth swung one axe into the ice and then kicked the spikes of one foot in, pulling himself up a few inches. He swung the other axe and followed with the opposite foot. It looked like a slow and laborious process and she could already hear him panting with the effort. How long would it take him to reach the top?

He scaled the two lower cascades in just under an hour, leaving behind a trail of rope looped through ice screws. Harrie busied herself with pictures of the snowscape around her and the occasional shot of Gareth as she made her own way up alongside the column of ice. As he'd said it would, the thin ice held and he was soon onto the wide part of the main cascade. Harrie got used to the sound of his measured chops and after a while she stopped jumping every time he dislodged a brittle chunk of ice. She'd had to bite back a scream the first time an icicle had come loose and crashed to the frozen water below.

"Hey down there!"

She looked up, shielding her eyes from the glare of the white sun. A tiny silhouette stood at the top of the falls, waving to her. She waved back and then took a few shots of Owain up there, standing on the frozen river as though it were solid ground.

"Too bad we don't have ice skates," she called up to him.

When she passed the fairy bridge she considered staying put, but the scenery was just too magnificent. Besides, Gareth was already well into his assault on the final cascade and she'd dawdled so much she wasn't even level with him yet. For once she felt a twinge of competition with Owain. He would get some great vertiginous shots

86

of Gareth from high above but Harrie was in a better position for the kind of 'right there in the moment' images that graced the covers of adventure magazines. She was perfectly safe on the snow-covered hill; Gareth was the one taking all the risks. She told herself she could go higher.

Gareth chopped, kicked and hauled himself up, inch by slow, agonising inch. From her vantage point down below he looked like some strange insect-human hybrid, crawling up the icicle with long mantis arms. She raised her camera and zoomed in, just in time to capture him shearing off a long shard of ice with one axe. He ducked as it fell past, just missing him, and she watched it shatter like glass against the mirrored surface of the pool beneath.

If Gareth was worried he showed no sign of it. He was calm and cool, pausing to catch his breath before anchoring himself with a length of rope and continuing on up. Harrie released the breath she'd been holding and looked up towards the top of the falls. And froze. The face was watching her.

She'd forgotten all about it in the excitement over the snow but the sudden unwelcome idea came to her that she'd been *made* to forget.

Stop it, she told herself. What had Gareth said? Underlying rock formation. That's all it was.

Nature's full of weird stuff.

It was indeed. And those blind, staring eyes were among the weirdest. But how could she be seeing it now? She'd only seen it in photos, like everyone else who had contributed pictures to the blog they'd found. Nobody had ever seen the face in person, as it were.

Was it her imagination or had it got even colder? The ice seemed sharper and more brittle, hanging like knives in the trees. Harrie felt the deep chill penetrate to her bones. Her gloved hands trembled on the camera as she realised that Gareth was heading straight towards the face. She tried to tell herself there was no reason this should disturb her, that she was only worried about the stability of the ice and projecting irrational fears onto a convenient scapegoat – in this case an imagined presence.

She turned away and hiked a little higher up the path. Best just to focus on taking pictures. That was why they were here. Gareth knew what he was doing and he knew more about the mountains and waterfalls than she could ever hope to. So did Owain, for that matter. She looked up at the top of the cascade and there he was, lying on his belly, camera aimed down at his brother. She thought of her hawk photo and the one of the little grey blur that followed. Her stomach swooped.

She shook her head to banish the vision that was trying to form in her mind. Owain had shown her the ice screws Gareth used to anchor himself up there, the rope to fasten to them. He wasn't going to fall.

Teeth.

The word came into her mind as a whispered picture: sharp glistening fangs, frayed nylon rope, a death plunge.

What the hell was wrong with her? The world was so still and quiet she could hear Owain's camera clicking away some hundred feet above. There was nothing scuttling around up there with him, least of all something that would eat through rope.

Harrie pushed herself up the path, her boots sinking deep into the crisp snow. Her legs were quivering with the effort and she could only imagine how Gareth must feel. How could he keep at it? She'd have been exhausted after the first little cascade.

It's waiting for him.

"Nothing's waiting for anyone," she growled. It was just her fear of heights, intensifying the further she went. She was already higher than she'd ever climbed up the path before. No wonder her mind was feeding her little snacks of panic. She was determined now to make it all the way to the top, to prove to herself that there was nothing to fear, either from the height or from a nonexistent apparition behind the ice.

When at last she drew level with where the face was, she took a deep, frigid breath and looked straight at it. There was nothing there. Nothing but frozen water.

She looked up at Owain and waved. He gave a whoop and called down to her.

"I can't believe how high you've come! Are you scared?"

"No," she lied.

"Brave girl!"

She was delighted to have made him proud of her. Gareth was probably too winded to add anything to the conversation and that was okay. She didn't want him to lose his focus. He was two thirds of the way up the ice now. Just below the face.

There is no face.

As if in response, the ice creaked and there was a splintering sound far down below. The bottom of the pillar had broken away. The waterfall hung freely now, an enormous dangling icicle.

This time Gareth didn't look so calm. He stared for a long time at the place where the ice had come away and Harrie saw that his next axe placement was gentler than previous efforts. He tapped gingerly at the ice above him, testing it before letting the pick sink in. He quickly twisted in another ice screw and looped his rope through it, tugging it and seeming satisfied that it was secure. He was soaked through, covered in chipped ice and snow. Harrie didn't like the thought that he was being consumed by it.

She told herself angrily not to fret and she focused on her own task, zooming in for close-ups, zooming out for context. She turned the camera sideways to capture the whole length of the ice in portrait mode. Gareth was just a speck on the expanse of deep blue crystal. Insignificant to the fearsome majesty of nature.

As he continued doggedly on his way Harrie told herself that the ice sounded no different up here than it had at the base. It still groaned and creaked but it was only her imagination that made it sound like a voice. It was just rocks and water, that was all.

Gareth was right underneath the face now, just where the mouth would be. And now that he was so close to it she could see the strange features again. They emerged from the jagged pattern like something rising from a deep lake. The eyes seemed to shine beneath the ice, burning with malevolent white heat.

Gareth's axe was poised to strike the dark blur of the mouth but something made him hesitate. He stared up at the shadow, his eyes widening at whatever he saw there. The ice cracked. His hand wavered.

Harrie opened her mouth to call his name, to tell him to move away, that it wasn't safe. But the words froze in her throat. All she could do was watch helplessly as the shadowy mouth grew wider. The ice was splitting.

Gareth tried to scramble away to the side, kicking his feet in as he inched away from the unstable area, but it was already starting to crumble. Several shards broke away and seemed to fall forever before they smashed into the glassy pool below. Harrie felt the vibration from the impact all the way up on the hill and a little cry escaped her as she saw the waterfall tremble and sway.

Her stomach plunged as Gareth lost his footing. He hung by one arm, legs kicking wildly as he searched for the ice with his feet. A clump of snow fell from directly above him, knocking his axe loose. He fell several feet before the rope jerked him to a stop. Dazed, he hung there, swinging back and forth for several seconds, his face bloodied from where he'd struck the ice. He looked like a bug caught in a spider's web. At last he steadied himself against the ice and began to haul himself back up.

High above she could faintly hear Owain calling out and she might have heard Gareth say he was okay. But the sounds coming from the ice were too loud. Now there was no question about it. It was a voice.

And as she stared at the face behind the waterfall, the mouth gaped even wider, revealing rows of jagged crystal teeth. Greenish water oozed from between them like drool and the air steamed as if with hot breath. There was a hiss as the liquid slithered over the ice, melting it.

Gareth only had time to look up and see what was happening before the ice cracked and split and the waterfall broke away, snapping like a toothpick. He didn't make a sound as the huge mass of ice fell, carrying him all the way to the bottom, to the unyielding surface of the frozen pool. The impact shattered the silence and set the ice jingling on all the surrounding trees.

Like bells, Harrie thought crazily. *Or laughter.*

Owain was screaming his brother's name over and over but even his maddened cries couldn't drown out the sound of the ice. It grated together like teeth. Harrie turned her eyes to the terrible face and there was no mistaking it this time. It was smiling.

HOOF-BEATS IN THE MIST

For such a scenic realm, the mountainous lands of North Wales, particularly the rugged summits of Snowdonia, boast a plethora of strange, eerie and frightening tales, and in myth are populated by an astonishing array of evil and mischievous creatures.

The so-called bogey beasts of old Britain take many gruesome forms, but there are common trends from one region to the next. For example, animals are often impersonated, but usually in devilish and distorted fashion. Dogs, cats, cows, goats and even hares are among the most common. But in Wales, in addition to all these, there is the Ceffyl Dwr, a very mysterious entity whose activities are best illustrated by an incident allegedly dating from the 1960s, when a lone hiker staggered into a hotel at the foot of Mount Snowdon and gave a chilling account of an experience that had almost knocked him dead with fright.

It was early winter, and the hiker in question had known he was taking a chance venturing into the peaks alone with frost in the air and ice on the lakes and rivers. That first afternoon he'd persisted up to high ground despite perishing cold and an ominously dense fog. But he only really became concerned when he heard the sound of slow hoof-beats in the mist – as though a rider was close at his rear, though such a figure never revealed itself, even when he called back to it hoping to find company in this drear place. Unnerved, but also lost in the frozen vapour, he found himself stumbling along scant, rocky trails, constantly on the verge of plunging over precipices. Yet always those hooves clumped in his wake, growing steadily louder. As full darkness came, the hiker entered a deep gully, where he took refuge in a semi-derelict bothy (a stone shelter erected for the use of travellers), only for a night of sheer terror to follow.

While the hiker shivered in the icy darkness, outside the hooves constantly circled his sanctuary, and just before dawn they launched an attack, thudding several times into the walls and door, which the hiker had braced with planks and joists. These braces held, but the trapped man was then subjected to a succession of deafening equine shrieks, which only diminished after several minutes, along with a dwindling rumble of departing hooves. It was only much later in the day, around noon, when the hiker, half dead with cold and fear, staggered down the mountainside to safety. The locals in the pub taproom, whom he related the story to, took him *entirely seriously. Apparently, the exact same thing had happened to another lone wanderer only one week earlier.*

In short, the Ceffyl Dwr is a demonic horse native to the Welsh ridges. Folklorists are vague about its origins, but classify it alongside the Kelpie of Scotland and the Tatterfoal of northern England – an ancient, malevolent being who exists purely to torment and destroy man, and who to bring this about, adopts the beguiling and familiar form of a loyal and trusted beast.

DON'T LEAVE ME DOWN HERE
Steve Lockley

When Dai Evans first heard the rumble he knew only too well what it meant. He pressed an ear to the tunnel wall, listening to the sound of rushing water not too far away. It would only be a matter of time before it found a way through some weakness in the rock.

"We need to get out of here lads," he said, trying to maintain a measure of calm. The tunnel they were in was little more than four feet high and they would all have to crawl on hands and knees to get out of there.

But they needed to do it quickly while they still had the time. In an instant the pressure could be too great and the rock wall could give way filling the tunnel with a rushing torrent of water. The river through the valley was already full to bursting and more water was coming down from the mountains.

"We're with you Dai," Johnny Davies replied followed by a chorus of agreement from four other voices, including young Huw, still in his first week underground, still a little wet behind the ears. The light from Dai's helmet lamp picked him out in the darkness and he could see the fear in the boy's eyes.

Barely seventeen and digging in the dark so deep underground while others were still filling their heads with knowledge. Dai had always vowed that no son of his would follow him down the pit; he could follow any trade or profession but not this. But Dai had not been blessed with a son and now it was too late to put that right. Retirement beckoned and it couldn't come a day too soon. For the other men it was still about paying the mortgage and putting food on the table for their families, and they knew that they were lucky to still have a working mine in the valley even if it only kept a few men in jobs.

But for Dai it was about making it to the day when he could draw his pension and take what he was due.

They had barely gathered their things together and started the short crawl to where they would join the main tunnel when the loudest of rumbles filled the air. Rocks crashed and the sound of running water came too close, gushing up from the main drift, into their narrow space under pressure and washing up the sides of the tunnel before being sucked down again. It would be suicidal to attempt to fight against a torrent like this and Dai knew it. They may be working in a drift mine with its main tunnel cut straight into the side of the mountain with its myriad offshoots, like the one they were working in, but that didn't mean that the risk of collapsing tunnels was any less. That main tunnel led straight out onto the mountainside eventually and was the only way out of there.

"Run," demanded Huw. "We've got to get out of here."

There was no mistaking the panic in the youth's voice, but Dai knew there was no point in trying to fight their way through the torrent. The seam they were working rose up from the main drift that dug its way into the mountain, and for the time being at least they were safe enough there. If they had to try to get back through a flooded tunnel, even if the water was moving quickly, it would be better when it was not carrying fallen rocks with it.

"Wait," he said, and all the men apart from Huw stopped in their tracks. They all saw him as the man in charge. There was no given hierarchy as far as the bosses were concerned but they all looked to him for leadership, even the men with more than twenty years underground.

The youth took no notice of the warning and tried to push past but the space was too narrow. Hands reached out in the darkness to hold him back as headlamps moved around, wildly casting shadows of the men, making it look like there were many more bodies there than there really was.

"We can't just stay here," Huw said again, fighting against hands that were holding him back.

"That's exactly what we have to do," Dai said.

"I can get through. I'm the youngest, the smallest, the fittest. If there's a gap I'll be able to get through and get help."

"We have to wait," Dai repeated more firmly. "They'll know soon enough that we're in trouble."

He knew that it was a lie but he told it as convincingly as he could. They were the only ones working the seam and if no-one had heard the rock fall there was every chance that no-one would raise the alarm until the end of the shift. No-one else was working so far into the mountain; no-one else was cut off from the outside world. They would need help if they were going to get out of there again

It could be four hours before anyone knew there was a problem and another before they would be able to do much about it. They had to wait and hope the water level would not rise and that it was just trapped water that had fallen through, not an underground river that would keep pouring in until every last crevice was filled.

Huw skulked back up their narrow passageway with the others following behind. Dai knew they would be better moving to the slightly elevated section of the workings if they were going to wait it out. Lanterns strung along the main tunnel had cast a weak light into the section the men had been working in before the rock fall, but even that was suddenly extinguished by the torrent, leaving them with only the helmet lamps and the dull glow of the safety lamp. Most mines had replaced these old style lanterns with other methods of detecting the presence of inflammable gases, but not this one. Even though the design had gone through many changes and innovations, Dai still called it 'a Davy lamp'. He suspected that Huw would call it 'old school' or something like that, but it had saved countless lives regardless of the age of the technology and in places like this it still was. Dai checked the flame to make sure that it had not changed colour knowing there was a chance, no matter how slight, that a pocket of gas had been released by the collapsing roof.

There would have been a time when every miner would have had one but now the six of them shared a single lamp; more cost cutting.

"Take care of this," Dai said handing it over to the youth. He hoped it might help take his mind off things for a few minutes, at least while they waited to see how things played out. Huw looked at it as if it was some kind of alien object then reached out to take it.

"You know what you're looking for?" Dai asked.

"Of course," Huw said. "The colour of the flame changing."

That was good enough for Dai. He had no interest in testing the youth on what colour he was looking for. This wasn't about him keeping out a close eye for signs of Methane, it was about giving him something to concentrate on other than the water rushing close by. The youth pushed himself further back into the workings and settled.

"We should turn off some of the headlamps," Johnny Davies said in a voice soft enough that Huw would not be able to hear. "Save the battery just in case we're down here for a while."

"Good idea," Dai said even though he knew that there was more than enough power in the battery packs to last a whole shift. "The last thing we want is to be down here with no light at all." A quick glance in the direction of the far end of the tunnel revealed that Dai was concentrating on the safety lamp, oblivious to what the rest of them were doing.

"Anyone been caught in anything like this before?" Johnny asked. The movement of headlamps confirmed it was not a completely new experience for at least a couple of them.

"We just have to hope that it doesn't last for too long," Dai said softly. "There's only so much air in here, and if the water rises and starts to fill this section we could be in real trouble."

"That's if we don't all drown," a voice said. Dai thought it was Glyn Williams but he could not be sure. It was certainly one of the men who had turned his light off. Dai felt the urge to silence him but he knew that he was only saying what they were all thinking.

Those who had worked underground long enough had all been involved in close calls or had heard the stories about men who had been trapped behind a rock fall. The stories of those who had died in accidents lived far longer in the memory than those about men who had been rescued, even the ones that had made the national news at the time.

"How long do you reckon we've got Dai?" Johnny asked, directing his lamp towards the water still rushing past them. It seemed to have eased a little, but not enough for them to try to make their way through.

What it did mean was that the fallen rock had not sealed off the tunnel completely. Dai hoped that was going to prove to be a good thing though he knew they would never be able to fight against the force of water while it ran this quickly.

"Who knows? Maybe a few hours, maybe a lot longer. We have to make sure that we keep the boy calm though. The last thing we want is for him to panic." He gave Huw another quick look but he did not seem to have moved a muscle.

"It's not the first time this has happened and it won't be the last. Not until this place is closed down for good," Glyn said.

"Leave it Glyn," said Dai. "This isn't the time."

Dai knew that this was likely to mean the end of the mine. It was already close to being worked out and this seam had already been closed down once as being uneconomical.

The chances were that the company that owned the mine would not be keen to spend the money needed to make the place safe to work in again. Better to seal it off and sell the land off if they could.

"Of course it's the right time," Johnny hissed. "What else should we talk about? The weather? The football? What we're having for dinner? No, none of those because we both know that we might not see any of them again. We might not even see the sun again."

"Easy Johnny," a voice said. "Don't spook the kid."

Bodies shuffled in the near darkness as first one then another settled down into positions that were more comfortable. Backs were eased and stretched in a silence filled only with the sound of running water.

"Twenty years or more since the last one," Johnny said.

Dai didn't want to listen but he was talking softly so that Huw could not hear him. Even in the darkness it was clear that the others had huddled in a little closer to hear what he had to say. Although they know that this was not going to be a good story they would rather hear about the misery of others than think about what lay ahead for themselves.

"What happened?"

"Did they get out?"

The questions came thick and fast when Johnny did not dive straight into his story, but Dai knew more about what had happened that day than any of the others could have heard about. He could still hear the last voice calling to him in the darkness, and knew that he would never forget it. There had been times when he had woken in the night hearing the boy calling his name.

"One of the seams flooded," Johnny began.

"A fall like this one?" someone asked.

"No, much deeper down than this. A blast opened up the rock and water started to come in."

"It was this seam," Dai said.

"What?" Johnny asked.

"It was this one," Dai said firmly. "If you are going to tell the story then at least get the facts straight."

"But I heard it was the number two seam."

"This used to be number two, back in the day. Everything was renumbered when the mine was re-opened. A fresh start, new ideas, new safety measures. That didn't last long though, did it? Lots of promises they never stuck to. Plenty of hot air but it's happened again."

"So what happened last time?" someone asked.

Dai said nothing. He was not the one telling the story but he would put Johnny straight if he was getting it wrong. He owed the boy that much.

"Where you working here then Dai?" Johnny asked. "You've never mentioned it before."

"Yes I was here," Dai replied. He didn't want to talk about it, he had never wanted to. For months after it had happened he had clammed up, retreating into his own world and shutting everything and everyone else out of it. Even now he didn't want to talk about it despite the yeas that had gone by.

"Come on Dai."

"There's not much to tell," he said. What he really meant was that he wasn't going to tell them, at least not everything. There were things that had happened back then that he would take to his grave, but he was only too aware that this could be it.

"What happened?"

"How many were down here?"

"Did everyone get out?"

"How long were they down here?"

The questions bombarded him, the voices jumbled in the dark until he could not be sure who was asking what. But there seemed to more voices than there were men sitting there.

97

It was a trick, an echo, but it was confusing him a little until all he could hear was the sound of the boy from all those years ago. It hadn't been his fault then and he knew that their being trapped now was not his fault either. But that didn't stop him from feeling guilty. He could have done more; he *should* have done more.

Don't leave me down here.

"Who said that?" Dai asked. "We aren't leaving anyone down here."

He had heard the voice, soft but pleading, just as he had every night in his dreams since the day it had happened.

"Said what?"

Dai looked at the faces he could see in what little light there was, but none of them seemed to have any idea what he was talking about.

"Didn't you hear it?"

"You must be hearing things Dai," Huw said. "Now stop messing about and tell us what happened last time."

Was his mind playing tricks on him? He felt a shiver run up his spine and his mouth felt dry. He heard the sound of metal striking stone.

"What was that?" His heart started to race.

"Are you okay Dai?" a voice asked, but it was caught up in the rapid beating of a hammer fall, the rush of water and the banging of his own heart. He tried to shake the sound from his head but it would not leave him.

Don't leave me down here.

He clamped his hands over his ears to try to keep out the voice but he knew that it was calling to him.

Don't leave me down here.

"Dai?"

He moved his hands away, glad the voice had gone and that the only sound remaining was that of the water still moving not far away. It was starting to slow at least a little but there was every chance it was just a case of his mind playing tricks on him; wishful thinking.

"You okay?"

"Sorry," he said. "I'm okay."

"You sure?"

"Of course." He felt that he should keep talking. Perhaps that was the way to keep the voice at bay.

They were all still waiting to hear what had happened all that time ago.

After keeping it to himself for so long he knew that it was about time he broke the silence.

There were only a handful of people able to hear the story, and he knew only too well that they may not have the opportunity to tell anyone else. Maybe the story would die there with them, but he owed it to the boy's memory to tell the others what had happened.

"There was an explosion," he began. "We were struggling to hit our quotas to get any kind of bonus and we were working longer and harder than any of us were really able to. We were exhausted."

There were a few murmurs of understanding from the others. They would all have heard stories about the danger of working underground; the risk of a single blow hitting rocks that were holding up the ceiling above them; the fear of a spark igniting the Firedamp and causing an explosion that could be fatal, or even the simple concern that the ventilation might fail. It was a life far more dangerous than anyone who had not been touched by its effects could possibly understand. He had listened to his wife tell him more times than he could remember that she worried every time she heard there was any kind of incident, fearing that he might have been hurt, or worse, that more than once she had joined the group of wives who had gathered at the gates of the pit, waiting for news. When her fears had come true, and he had been among the group of men trapped underground, it had broken her and it destroyed their marriage when he had insisted on returning to work. Then all he had been left with was work, the pub, and an empty house.

"Anyway. There was a rock fall. Maybe the explosion came before the fall, maybe it all came together, I'm not sure. It all happened so fast. A couple of the men tried to get out while the rocks were still falling but they got caught as the roof caved in and the water came flooding through. One of them got crushed in the fall, the other was washed away."

"How many of you were there?"

"That left four of us. Two of the guys had been working down here for longer than me, and there was one lad who was only in his first week. He was a big strong lad, probably too big for working in small spaces like this." The others glanced across at the youth who was still tending the safety lamp, finding escape from their danger by concentrating on the flame. In so many ways he reminded Dai of the boy who had been trapped in this place the last time.

He had not realised the similarity until the situation had brought all those memories flooding back like a tidal wave. Now he was hearing his voice in every moment of silence, the memory haunting him at every turn.

"How long were you down here?"

"Two days." It was a fact, no more or less than that. Two days that had seemed like a lifetime. Two days where they had started as friends – before the complaints and the blame had come to the surface, only to be vented and the air eventually cleared; two days, at the end of which, when the rescue finally came, they had emerged as friends and comrades again who had come through their ordeal together.

All except one of them. The one they had left behind.

Don't leave me down here.

"Two days?" The whispers were almost of disbelief – not from doubt that he was telling the truth but that they had been trapped for so long. No food and probably very little water between them. He knew it was what they had to be thinking.

"Two days," he repeated.

"What happened when the rescue team got through?"

"They made a hole big enough to crawl through, but even that was unstable. They wanted to just make sure that there was food, water and air getting through to us while they secured the roof and could clear more of the debris away."

"That makes sense."

"Now it makes sense, but not back then. There was nothing we wanted more than to feel fresh air on our faces. We all know that there have been miners all over the world who have survived underground for much longer than that, even since then. We couldn't get out of there fast enough."

"I'm sure we would all feel the same."

"Of course we would. And when the rescue team gets to us we will want the same again, but we have to wait until everyone is sure that it's safe to get out."

"So what happened?"

"We couldn't wait. The two older guys got out first and that just left me and the kid behind. I heard the rescuers on the other side, counting us out as the first two scrambled through. One. Two. Then there was a rumble and we knew there wasn't going to be much time before there was another rock fall."

"But you managed to get out."

"They had just called out three when the rumble came again. This time louder, closer."

Don't leave me down here.

"The youth tried to follow me through but he was too big. The rescuers reached in to try to pull him through but it was too late. The rocks came down on top of him. He was still calling to us when we were pulled back in case any more of the roof came down and killed us all."

Don't leave me down here.

"You couldn't have saved him Dai."

"That doesn't make it any easier. I should have made him wait, I should have stayed on the other side with him until they had put an extra prop in. I should have done more."

"I'm sure you did everything you could."

He knew they meant it but that didn't mean it was true. At the very least they should have let the boy out first and made sure he was safe. He was responsible for him. He had promised the boy's mother he would look out for him and he had let her down as much as he had let the boy down. He wasn't going to let it happen again, no matter what happened.

The other men felt silent and Dai wondered what they were really thinking. Perhaps they thought he was a coward for having let the boy die. It was what he thought, what he had always thought.

A headlamp flickered and went out. It should have lasted longer but in that moment he caught the glimpse of a face in the near dark, a face in the rock that shifted and moved, its mouth opening wide and calling to him. He didn't need to hear the sound, didn't need to watch the lips move, to know what the face was calling.

"I can hear something," one of the men said, breaking the moment of silence that had descended on them. Dai wondered for a moment if he had heard the voice as well, but then came the unmistakeable sound of metal against rock.

"They're coming for us!" the youth said looking up from the glow of his lamp. Headlights were turned on and flashed in his direction. He raised a hand to cover his eyes from the sudden brightness

Don't leave me down here

"The water's slowed down," someone called and Dai tried to scramble across to take a look for himself. It was true. The flow had fallen and was draining away to the lower depths of the mine. His spirits lifted in an instant and he felt the urge to call out to the rescue team to let them know that they were alive.

"Come on," he said. "Let's see if we can shift some of the fall from this side. The sooner it's done, the sooner we can get out of here."

"But what if there's another fall?" the boy said, his earlier bravado tempered with fear.

"There won't be another fall," Dai said. He knew that there was still the chance that more rocks would come falling down on top of them but he could not let the boy know that. He had to keep him positive, make him feel that there was every hope that they would be out of there before long.

"Why don't you stay there for a while and keep an eye on that lamp for us," Dai said. The others had started to clamber out of the cramped space and into the drift. He heard the splash of water as boots stepped in and they started wading towards the fall.

"You won't leave me down here will you?" the boy pleaded.

Dai felt his answer catch in his throat as he tried to get the words out. "Of course we won't leave you down here."

He stepped into the steady flow of water that washed through the tunnel. It tugged against his legs but offered little more than token resistance as he waded towards the beam of headlamps ahead of him. He turned on his own lamp and followed, giving a last glance back at the boy couched over the Davy lamp, so absorbed in the flame, no doubt desperate to blot everything else out.

Dai pushed his way through the water, fighting against the pull of the current that caught at his legs, trying to tug him down into the depths just like the men who had died down there all those years ago. The sound of the hammering from the other side was growing louder, echoing along the tunnel as he grew closer. The other men were already clawing at fallen rocks and pulling them free. The knowledge that someone was clearing the way from the other side spurred them on and filling them with an energy that had seemed to have been slipping away, along with their hope.

"Come on Dai!" they urged.

They worked quickly and efficiently, breaking stone, pulling it clear, and splashing out of the way when debris fell away faster than they had anticipated.

"We should have got started on this sooner," one of them said.

"The water was coming too fast," said Dai. "You wouldn't have stood a chance."

"Shhh."

Dai was not sure which one of them had said it; he wondered if it had even been one of the others who had made the sound, or if it was simply inside his head. He paused just as the others did to hear the sound of another voice calling to them, then more than one voice, shouting to be heard through the rock.

"They're almost through," Dai said. "Best get a move on."

"Get the boy!"

"If I'm not back in time, don't let them give up until all four of us are out. All four of us. Make them count us out."

"Don't worry, Dai, no-one's going to get left behind."

Dai started back along the tunnel; he didn't need to be told twice. There was no way he was going to let him down. He had failed last time but he was not going to let this one down. This boy was going to get out of here and live the life he was supposed to, not have it snuffed out before his time.

"Time to go," he called when he was sure that he was within earshot.

Don't leave me down here.

"Don't worry," he said. "No-one's leaving you down here."

He knew that he had said this before, maybe more than once, but he had to give his reassurance.

"Who are you talking to, Dai?" Huw asked. Dai hadn't even seen him clamber out from where he had been waiting. He emerged with the safety lamp, holding it out in front of him like some picture of Florence Nightingale moving from bed to bed.

"Almost through," he said, ignoring the question.

Don't leave me down here.

Dai ignored the voice, helping the boy and his lamp past him, making sure he kept moving. He was only too aware that there was still more than enough danger to contend with. It was impossible to tell how much rock above them was being held in place by the blockage that had fallen into the tunnel. If the rescue team were confident it was safe for them to get through, there might not be time to hesitate.

"Keep moving," Dai said, one hand on the youth's back, determined he was not going to miss the opportunity to get out if there was only a narrow window of opportunity.

"Come on, Dai, we're going through now," one of the others shouted

Dai splashed through the water, trying to run with his head bowed, his headlamp waving wildly.

He felt the pain in his chest and the burning in his lungs as he struggled to keep his breath. From somewhere above came a sound like thunder; the shifting and rumbling of rock and earth in danger of crashing down upon them.

"Move!" he shouted, even though they were both moving as quickly as they could.

Don't leave me down here

"No-one's getting left down here," he managed in little more than a whisper, without knowing if he was talking to the boy in front of him or the guilt he had carried with him.

A headlamp flashed back in their direction revealing one figure crouched beside the blockage that had now been cleared sufficiently for someone to crawl through, and a pair of boots disappearing out of sight.

"One." The voice came from the other side of the debris, muffled but loud enough to reassure him. The youth came to a halt as they reached the slew of discarded rocks and rubble, cleared away to give them enough room to make their escape. The second figure kneeled down, and pushed his head into the opening.

"It's too small," Huw said, looking away from the escaping figure. Dai saw the fear in his eyes, the panic no more than a heartbeat away.

"Don't worry, it'll be fine. Put your arms in front of you and they'll pull you through." He was doing his best to reassure him, but Dai had no idea of how much he believed it. He wasn't even sure he believed it himself.

"Two."

"Your turn," Dai said. "Best not keep them waiting.

"You should go through first Dai. You'll be quicker than me."

"Not a chance, you're the young fit one. Get yourself in there."

Huw offered him the safety lamp as if it was the most precious thing in the world. There was no longer any need for it but there was no need to tell him that. That flame had been the youth's lifetime, the one thing that had kept him from panicking while they had been trapped. Dai watched as the boy kneeled down and reached into the narrow aperture. It was going to be a tight fit but he was going to get through somehow. He had to. Dai placed the lamp down on the rubble, clear of the slow but steady flow of water that now almost covered his boots.

The youth scrambled onto the opening, his boots pushing against loose rocks as he struggled to find purchase. Dai bent down to place his hands to take hold of them, offering himself as something to push against. He strained to stay still, his own boots sliding in the sludge and grit, but he pushed with every ounce of strength he could muster.

Don't leave me down here.

He pushed again and the youth moved, shifting no more than an inch but then another and another until the pressure reduced and the boots were pulled out of view. Dai squatted down to watch, to make sure that the boy was pulled free before he started after him.

"Three."

Don't leave me down here.

Dai knew that he would never be able to get the voice out of his head, no matter how hard he tried, no matter how long he lived. It's going to be alright. He tried to convince himself while he waited for the moment to make his exit. There was another rumble from above and voices from the other side of the opening called out to him.

"Wait a sec."

The opening was so inviting and yet he knew he should wait. The men on the other side had a better idea of what was going on than he did and he had to trust their judgement.

Don't leave me down here.

Air moved and brushed against his face before another rumble. More voices on the other side, the sound changing to one of disguised panic. "Move, move, move."

Another shower of dust and grit fell on his face. He coughed it away and scrambled into the narrow opening. He cried out as a rock fell on his leg but he kept moving, kicking himself free.

"Four," came the voice on the other side. "Let's go."

But they hadn't got him. More rocks fell to the sound of more rushing water. He pulled back from the opening just in time to avoid the rock fall and just in time he slid back into the tunnel where they had waited for the rescue, and wondered if they would come back once they realised. Words formed on his lips and came out in no more than a whisper. "Don't leave me down here."

THE WEREWOLF OF CLWYD

I t should be no surprise to anyone that the age of the werewolves coincided with the age of the witches – the 15th, 16th and 17th centuries.

In purely mythological terms, the two were inextricably linked. In the minds of Europe's largely uneducated population, werewolfism was brought about either through a pact with the Devil, by the application of magical salves provided by sorcerers, or by the donning of wolf-shirts or wolf-belts created during Satanic rites. This was also that period of history when science had not yet arrived but the Reformation in Europe had swept away much Church authority, and more importantly Church ritual, thus weakening the belief that miraculous powers could be invoked against the forces of darkness, and placing the onus of responsibility firmly on the local communities who felt threatened.

The werewolf trials of continental Europe were one result of this, countless men – and it was mainly men – accused of transforming themselves into beasts and unleashing devilish violence against their neighbours, usually women and children. On several occasions – Gilles Garnier in France (1573), Henry Gardinn in the Netherlands (1605), and Peter Stumpp in Germany (1589) – there had been a string of bloody murders and even acts of cannibalism, suggesting the suspects were actually serial killers, a concept beyond human imagination at the time. Whether these criminals deserved to be broken on the wheel or burned at the stake (or both, in the case of Stumpp) is open to debate, but that was often the outcome.

By contrast, Britain's legal documents of this period are virtually werewolf-free. There are almost no recorded werewolf trials in the annals of the British Isles, presumably because wolves had been exterminated from these islands during the Middle Ages and held no terror, either real or mythical, for rural society. But later on, in the relatively enlightened days of the late 18th century, there was a series of bewildering incidents in Clwyd, in Northeast Wales, which led to a large scale werewolf scare.

The first attack came in the year 1790, when a stagecoach travelling the wooded road between Denbigh and Wrexham was accosted by an enormous, hairy beast, described by the coachman as approaching on all-fours but then rearing up on two legs. Snarling hideously, it killed one of the horses on the spot, apparently tearing the poor beast limb from limb, before gambolling away into the darkness.

The following January, during heavy snow, a farmer in the district was found by a neighbour cowering inside his cottage, wielding a pitchfork. When he calmed himself sufficiently to talk, he told his neighbour that the previous night he and his dog had followed the tracks of a large wolf, only to be set upon by a hulking, hairy brute, which tore the dog's throat out and then pursued the farmer all the way back to his cottage, whereupon it rose on two feet and walked around the exterior, pounding on the door and gazing through the window with blue, moon-like eyes. The farmer and his neighbour searched the farm by daylight, and were appalled to find, first the butchered dog, and then meadows and fields covered with slaughtered livestock, sheep and cattle lying in pools of their own gore.

A full-on werewolf hunt ensued, advertised in exactly those terms in pamphlets of the time. It was organised by the local vicar, with soldiers participating alongside hundreds of civilians armed with staves, pikes and muskets. Maybe this succeeded in frightening the culprit away, because nobody was captured or even accused, and no further attacks were reported in that district. However, a sequel to the baffling case may have followed several years later, just over the English border near Bickerton, in Cheshire, when two tramps were found dead in a forest, their throats torn and bodies hideously mutilated. Neither of those slayings was ever solved.

These are the known and established facts. Other pieces of gossip from the time whose authenticity is less certain concern the search for a missing Clwyd girl, which allegedly located only her collar bone, and the murder of a local hermit by a band of villagers, who, convinced he was the wolf, tied him to a tree and burned him to death.

As stated, none of these latter tales can be verified, their antecedents lost in the mists of history. But don't get too cozy with the idea that all this happened a long, long time ago. As recently as 1992, several newspapers described a 'bear-like being' seen roaming the woods of Northeast Wales on two legs, and not long afterwards, a farmer reported that several of his sheep had been viciously torn to shreds.

Make of that what you will.

MATILDA OF THE NIGHT
Stephen Volk

*O*nly *a little dwt, I was. Four or five, see. Remember it like it was yesterday. Anyway, this day I run into our front room – the posh room, playin' like – not allowed to but I did sort of thing, and these three people looked round, all in a row on the settee, they were. All looking identical. Like a family. Man, woman, child. Just looking at me. All dressed all in black. All tight and polite, like, with their knees together. Give me the creeps, they did. Duw, aye! I was out of there like a blummin' shot ...*

The quarter-inch tape ran through the Revox. The machine sat so that its turning reels faced the rows of semi-lit young faces.

Well, I told my mam after, and she said, "Don't be daft. There's nobody like that been in here. Nobody's been in that room for a twelvemonth!" And I said, "Mam, I saw them!" But she wasn't 'aving it. Marched me in and showed me. Wasn't nobody there, course there wasn't. But, true as I'm sittin' here, this is it – a week later my father dropped dead of a heart attack. Bang! Out like a light. Down by the Co-op. Out like a light! ...

Ivan Rees switched it off with a twist of his hand, killing the old man's rasping, heavily-accented voice.

"Phantom funeral guests." The illumination stuttered into being. The ranks of students blinked as if awakened from slumber, which possibly they had been. "I got that from a retired collier in Pontypridd. Variation of the typical 'spectral funeral', also known as *toili*, or *teulu* in north Cardigan, probably from the dialectical pronunciations of the word for 'family'; or *anghladd*, unburied; in Montgomeryshire, *Drychiolaeth*."

Rees jabbed a button on the keyboard of his MacBook Air linked up to the overhead projector. An old woodcut of a house with a bird sitting on the roof appeared on the screen behind him.

"Other Welsh omens of death include the Corpse Candle or *Canwyll Corph* – lights appearing over the house of the soon to be deceased, or predicting the route of the funeral procession – and the *Deryn Corph*, or 'Death Bird', as you see here flapping its wings against the window of a sick person, often in the form of a screech owl ..."

He brought up an engraving of witches with those birds, in one of Goya's *Caprichos*.

"The word *strega* in Italy refers to both 'owl' and 'witch' – an association that goes back to the mythology surrounding Lilith, Adam's first wife, who became a creature of darkness and child stealer in Hebrew folklore, basically for answering back her husband. Interestingly, in China they call the owl 'the bird who snatches the soul'. The cross-cultural connections are fascinating."

The Edvard Munch woodcut fell over him now – a vampiric owl-death-woman.

"Then there's the *Cyhyraeth* or 'death sound'. A dismal, mournful groaning said to be made by a crying spirit. Which is nothing in comparison to the dread prediction of the banshee in Ireland. Here in Wales we have effectively her sister, the *Gwrach-y-Rhibyn*..."

To the audience's surprise Marilyn Monroe appeared on the screen in titillating close-up, from *Some Like It Hot*.

"No, she doesn't look like Marilyn Monroe." Chuckles. "In fact there's still a saying in parts of Wales if somebody's – aesthetically challenged: '*Y mae mor salw a Gwrach-y-Rhibyn*' – 'She's as ugly as the *Gwrach-y-Rhibyn*'."

More chuckles. His PowerPoint threw up another Goya print – a ghastly crone with monstrous visage and bat-like appendages.

"For the record, she's a hideous hag with long, matted hair, long black teeth, one grey eye and one black eye, a nose so hooked it meets her chin, withered arms, a crooked back and leathery wings. In other words, the sort of female that doesn't even get a shag after closing time on a Friday night in Newport city centre ... Oh, I don't know."

Laughter, more full-bodied this time.

"Anyway you wouldn't want to see what she *really* looks like, since anyone who sees her face or hears her blood-curdling cry, dies. There's an etymological similarity here with a witch called *Yr Hen Wrach*, who lived on an island in a large bog inland from Borth, Cardigan, described as seven feet tall, thin, with yellow skin and a huge head covered in jet black hair. This fearsome harridan was said to creep into houses and blow sickness into people's faces, thus causing illness. So another portent of death, of sorts, in another guise ..."

Hans Baldung Grien's *The Bewitched Groom* showed a witch leering through a window at a dead man.

"Literally, for the non-Welsh-speakers amongst you, *Gwrach-y-Rhibyn* means 'Hag of the Dribble' or 'Hag of the Mist' – connecting her to all sorts of stories of the lamia/swan maiden type we looked at on the Gower and Glamorgan coast. Sometimes she's called *Mallt-y-Nos* or 'Matilda of the Night', who rides the night sky alongside the Devil himself and his Hell hounds …"

Bottom and Tatania in a scene from *A Midsummer Night's Dream* superimposed themselves over Rees, rendering his plain denim jacket and jeans exotic, melodramatic. As he walked to and fro they decorated his skin like multicoloured, shifting tattoos.

"Marie Trevellyan groups her in the category of the *Tylwyth Teg* or Fairy Folk also known as *Bendith y Mamau*, Mother's Blessing. In times past they've been spotted at local markets in Haverfordwest, Milford, Laugharne and Fishguard. Some sources say that, come mid-Victorian times, they were driven out by Nonconformists and temperance, but the truth is belief in them persisted until only a generation or so ago. I clearly remember my own grandmother blaming them for things going missing round the house. Neither goblin nor ghost, they supposedly had human midwives and feared iron, hence the lucky horseshoe – which as we know is always the right way up because if you hang it upside down, all the good luck runs out. According to John Rhys in Celtic Folk Lore, the *Gwrach* may have been a goddess of the pagan Celts, like the quasi-divine hag of Ireland. Indeed, in *The Golden Bough*, Fraser says the *Gwrach-y-Rhibyn* is the name given to the last sheaf of corn cut at the culmination of the harvest ritual. Yes? At the back? Lad in the Cardiff City shirt?"

A hand was in the air.

"Isn't there a theory that what we call the 'Fairy Folk' might have been real?" The speaker was undeterred by sniggers. "Several writers suggest there was once a pygmy race on these islands, called the Cor – as in Korrigan, 'she-dwarf' – driven underground by invaders. What I mean is, bones have been found in caves, haven't they? Of short people. Ugly compared to human beings. With magical beliefs. Certain evidence they buried their dead, worshipped the moon, had rituals and some kind of social life …"

"Unlike most people in this room," said Rees.

Groans.

"No, yeah. I mean, seriously," said the boy. "We just call them Neanderthals."

"Oh, I know what you *mean*. I *do* know what you mean. Stan Gooch eat your heart out. And the ginger haired amongst you beware of your large big toe. They walk amongst us!"

More laughter. The boy blushed slightly and shuffled in his seat.

"Yes, there's the theory that these imaginary creatures might be the faint memories of another, long lost indigenous species – the Bronze Age replaced by iron," said Rees. "But as I've said before, it's not the folklorist's job to explain the inexplicable. That's not our business – our job is to record, analyse and classify. The reality or not of what we examine is irrelevant." He took the spool from the Revox and held it up. "Our work – your mission, if you choose to accept it – is ecology. It's incumbent on us to save this rich resource from being lost. Our stories are ourselves. We mustn't let them die."

He hoped what he said was going in. He tried to discern a glimmer of interest in their dull, placid faces, in their *incuriosity*, but was sure all they cared about was passing the module. Level one (CQFW level four): ten credits.

He killed the PowerPoint, closed the laptop. "Okay, go home. Start thinking about your essays. Next week we'll be talking about the Devil's hoofprints and changelings."

*

He saw Glyn at the foot of the steps, leaning back against a stone plinth outside the University building, flicking through a copy of *GQ*. Rees could not see for the life of him, and never could, why a perfectly intelligent man would buy such superficial drivel, but he knew better than to let it turn into an argument. Glyn had his childish, boorish side, which for some inexplicable reason he liked to cultivate. Rees supposed it was that macho aspect of gayness that had become all too blatant since he himself was growing up. Men beefing themselves up in the gym in an attempt to contradict the cliché of mincing effeminacy. Glyn certainly fitted into that category, biceps and pecs bulging ridiculously in a T-shirt several sizes too tight – but had just become another cliché altogether. He'd been immensely more attractive twelve years ago when they'd met, before all this nonsense, before the steroids, but Rees had given up on telling him that. How could he tell his partner that looking like a He-Man doll was bordering on the disgusting? Once, Glyn had said he wanted that: wanted to look disgusting, wanted people to stop in the street and point at him and say he looked monstrous, grotesque. Rees found he couldn't battle such absence of logic, so had long since given up trying.

"Doctor Rees? Doctor Rees?"

The voice came from behind him. Young. Breathless. Female.

Glyn stood up straight and put the *GQ* under one arm.

"You've got a groupie."

Rees turned.

"Can I have a quick word, please?" The girl facing him was about nineteen. He knew exactly what Glyn was thinking. *Scarf. Anorak. Bless. Mouse woman. And that hair. Poor thing. Why doesn't she do something about herself?* "My name's Katrina." *Scottish accent. Sexy. But would a little make-up kill you, love?*

111

"I'm doing your class as part of my MA in Welsh and Celtic Studies. I'm hoping to go into teaching."

"I'm, er… running rather late, as a matter of fact."

"It's – it's about the *Gwrach-y-Rhibyn*."

"Oh. As I say, if you want to discuss it in more detail we can do that in the next session ..."

"No, no. You don't understand. You see, it's quite a, well, coincidence. Do you believe in coincidences? I'd heard the name before. I thought 'God'. I didn't think it was real. I thought it was a made-up word."

"It's not. It's really quite well documented." Rees looked at his watch.

"No, this isn't documented. This is from an old lady. An old lady who's dying."

Dying.

Rees turned to face her.

Dying?

"You can talk about it next week, love," said Glyn. "I'm sure he'll be all ears." He tugged Rees's arm but Rees wasn't budging.

"Hold on, hold on. What old woman? Where?"

"In the nursing home where I work. Shifts. Bit of extra income to support me through college, while I'm doing my –"

"Yes, yes. I get that. What did she say, exactly?"

"She kept talking about her, this *Gwrach-y-Rhibyn* thing. Well, I didn't know what it was. I just thought it was gibberish. A lot of them are in a world of their own, they just ramble and the best thing is to let them get on with it, sort of thing. But she kept saying it. 'She's coming, she's coming!' and getting really, really upset about it. Inconsolable, at times. And one night I heard her crying, and I went upstairs to her bedroom, and she said to me, 'She's been. She's *been*!' All mad-looking. And that night an old man had died – Captain Birdseye we used to call him, lovely old bloke. And the thing is, there's *no way* she could have known. She couldn't have heard. She lives in a completely different part of the building. And nobody else knew until they found him the next morning. But *she* knew. She knew that this *Gwrach-y-Rhibyn* thing had come to get him. And she was right."

*

It was called *Morfa*, which even his rudimentary knowledge of his native tongue told him meant 'marsh' or 'fen'. The building was one of those vast Victorian piles on the way out of Porthcawl, formerly a grand hotel, now, with sad inevitability, a residential home for the elderly, overlooking the sweep of the appropriately-named Rest Bay. Rees had been on several holidays to the resort as a child, and remembered being confused between the local funfair, Coney Beach, and the Coney Island mentioned in American movies, in the same way he thought Dirk Bogarde and Humphrey Bogart were the same person. Strange how the embarrassment of those things came back to him now, along with memories of freezing sea and damp sand.

As he got out of his Citroën, and hoisted the Nagra out of the back, he could hear the dim strains of a karaoke version of *I Could Be So Lucky* increasing in volume as he stepped into the reception area. In the Day Room he could glimpse a middle-aged woman in a sequinned dress singing into a hefty microphone with the verve of a cruise ship entertainer. A podgy, greasy-haired boy sat manning the playback machine with his back to her while she belted it out. Geriatrics in arm chairs watched with loose jaws and gummy, bewildered mouths. One old dear was doing the twist in decrepit slow motion.

"Hello. My name is Doctor Ivan Rees," he said to the pretty if overweight girl behind the desk. "I'm from Cardiff University." He didn't usually have recourse to the title 'Doctor', but in this instance he thought it might be helpful to oil the wheels of accessibility. Luckily, he didn't need to explain in laborious detail that he was Associate Lecturer in the School of Celtic Studies, M. Litt (Oxford), Ph.D. (Columbia University, Bethesda, Maryland), M.A. University of Wales (Aberystwyth), or why he was there, because she was already saying she'd had a conversation with the Staff Nurse, who'd told Rees on the phone she had no objection to his visit as long as the resident in question didn't. Which was a hurdle far simpler to cross than Rees had imagined.

The pretty if overweight girl, whose name was Tina Griffiths, led him straight upstairs. "Katrina told me about you."

"Did she? Good. I hope."

"I don't know that you'll get what you want, though. They get very confused. They can't remember the word for 'telephone' or what they said five minutes ago, but they can remember years ago like it was yesterday."

"That's what I'm interested in."

He had a sense of anticipation he hadn't felt in a long time, and it had been as if Glyn resented it. Rees hadn't been able to concentrate much on the French film about persecuted monks they went to see immediately after meeting Katrina, and when Glyn tried to discuss the movie afterwards, Rees could hardly focus on what he was saying. When they got home he hadn't thought he was doing anything wrong by going straight to his bookshelves and taking down Giraldus Cambrensis' *Itinerary Through Wales*, Nennius's

History of the Britons, Walter Map's *De nugis curialium,* Rev. J. Ceredig Davies's *Folk-Lore of West and Mid-Wales* and T. Gwynn Jones's *Welsh Folklore and Folk-Custom* of 1930. Glyn hadn't seemed in the least bit interested that in the next half hour he'd had it confirmed that there was no record of the *Gwrach-y-Rhibyn* that wasn't at least a hundred years old, and even then quoted from the usual suspects. No doubt about it. This was the first genuine first-hand experience of a death portent in over a century. This was gold dust.

At 2 a.m., after tossing and turning, Glyn had stood naked at the bedroom door and asked him to come to bed. By the time Rees had registered what he had said, and turned from his computer screen, there was nobody there.

*

"She'll tire very easily."

"Of course."

"Mrs Llewellyn gives the illusion she's strong as an ox. She isn't." Tina escorted Rees along a corridor and through a fire door. "She has so much cancer in her, you could virtually scratch her skin and see it. Like one of those lottery cards." The girl rapped the door they came to, and Rees asked if she'd heard the woman talk about the *Gwrach-y-Rhibyn* as Katrina had. "All that morphine if you ask me. Or whatever it is in the pills they're giving her to stop the pain." She raised her voice. "Bronwen? It's only me, love. Tina. Orright if we come in? Are you decent?" She turned to Rees with wink and a whisper. "Scares easily, see. Lot of them do. Got to be careful."

Entering the room, Rees's first impression was the heat belting out of the four-bar electric fire. It hit him like a wave, then he remembered how old people felt the cold. The second thing was the smell, a sickly perfume odour used to cover something worse. Third was the sight of Bronwen Llewellyn lifting her body from the armchair facing the window. A small woman with thinning ginger hair, extraordinarily piercing blue eyes – had she had her cataracts done or did she need to? – and rounded nostrils that put Rees in mind of a bullock. A frail bullock.

He extended his hand. She walked straight between them and shut the door, evidently to keep the heat in. She pressed it. Opened it. Shut it again. Opened. Shut. Walked back between them to the sash window overlooking the grounds. Checked the catch. Locked. Unlocked. Locked. Unlocked. Rees could tell that Tina knew unless they broke the cycle this could go on all day.

"Bronwen, sweetheart. This is Doctor Rees from the University. D'you remember? The one who wrote you that nice letter?"

"I'm not dull."

"Bronwen likes to make sure the doors and windows are shut tight, don't you, Bronwen, love?"

"Because that's how she gets in. Through *cracks*."

Tina looked at Rees. The music downstairs had changed to a spirited rendition of *Stand By Your Man*.

"Okay. I'll leave you to it, then."

The girl was barely gone before Bronwen picked up a quilted draught-excluder in the form of a snake and rammed it against the bottom of the door with the toe of her slippers.

"And mirrors. She looks at you from *mirrors*."

Rees looked around and saw that the mirrors in the room were hooded by supermarket carrier bags or tea cloths held in place with drawing pins. He forced a friendly smile.

"Your room looks nice."

"This isn't my room. The things are mine, but it's not my room." Bronwen Llewellyn had an unmistakable Valleys lilt, sing-songy but not unintelligible. She'd record well. That was important, and a relief.

"Well, the things are nice. What are the labels for?" He'd noticed there were coloured Post-It notes on most of the objects. Royal Doulton figurines, a glass swan, an oval frame with a Pre-Raphaelite print in it – *The Lady of Shalott*. Even the bedside lamp and chest of drawers.

"That's who they go to when I pop off. No arguments. Organised, I am, see. Red is Jean. Green is Dilys. Blue is Mavis. Yellow is Oxfam."

*

She lifted her swollen ankles onto the foot stool as Rees sat on the bed, the Nagra beside him, setting up the microphone on the small table at her elbow. He could have used his iPhone to record her, as his students now did, but he'd become accustomed to recording on quarter-inch. Not so much that he resisted new technology, but this was the technology he'd known and relied upon for over twenty years. Perhaps he himself was superstitious in that regard. Old habits being only one step removed, perhaps, from magical thinking. Soon this tape would join the others, hundreds, meticulously labelled by subject and location on his study shelves, dated, indexed and cross-referenced – the sound files themselves copied and saved as MP3 files in that ether tantamount to a supernatural realm called Dropbox. He'd considered her use of the Post-It notes absurd and morbid, but it occurred to him now that he himself was guilty of labelling objects for people who might look at the artefacts long after his demise, just as much as she was.

"Here, am I going to sound Welshy? Last time I heard myself on one of them things, Crikey Moses! Welsh, be damned? I used to think I sounded like Princess Margaret!"

"It's painless, I promise." He blew into the mic. "One, two, one, two." The red needle wagged like a warning finger.

"Rees? That's a Welsh name, that is. You don't sound Welsh. English, you sound."

"Lost a bit of it going to uni, I expect."

"Glad to get rid of it, I expect," she said, with no apparent disdain.

He laughed. Truth is, she was right. He couldn't wait to get away and talk like normal people. To lose his past in RP and anonymity. To reinvent himself.

"You want to read this first." She produced something hidden down the side of the chair. An exercise book, pink for a little girl, with cartoon horses and fairies and bunnies on the cover. She thrust it at him forcefully. He felt obliged to take it, opening it to find the first page full of a list of names and dates written in a terribly shaky copperplate hand. Old-school education never goes away, he thought. Even if the faculty to hold a pen does.

"You know what that is?" Bronwen was confident he could not answer. "That's the name of everybody who's died. Here, I mean. In this place." She pointed to the floor with a finger bulging at the joints with arthritis. "Since I come here, anyway. Everybody who's heard her and seen her."

"You mean – I'm sorry. They *told* you they'd seen her? The *Gwrach-y-Rhibyn*?"

"Don't be *soft*! How can they tell me when they're dead? Nobody can *tell* you. Not once they've seen her."

"No, of course not."

"Once they *see* her, that's it. You can't get away from it, you can't get out of it. That's that. And I'll be *oocht* when she comes for me, too. And that'll be soon. Don't you worry."

He saw a cloudiness come over her eyes and thought it a kind of bewilderment. He thought of her cataracts again. Then saw the shudder of her lower lip with its aura of downy hairs, and a tremor in the hand that gripped the rim of the arm of the chair, and realised that it was fear.

"Can you – can you say that again, please? For the tape?"

He switched it on, and before he could ident the recording with his own voice, stating the day, time and full name of the subject, she spoke again, staring at a space above the fireplace as if she was alone in the room.

116

"They're dead. Just like I'll be dead, once I've seen the *Gwrach-y-Rhibyn*. Once she comes calling for me." She blinked and with an unstable, jerky movement turned to look at him, almost as if seeing him for the first time. Then he saw a little girl eager to please. "Was that all right?"

He nodded. It was. It was perfect.

*

The spool turned, a stray thread curling a corkscrew admonition in the air.

The cold of the wind from the sea did not infiltrate the room but he could hear the slow fingertips of rain tapping the window panes.

"Fifteen kids, my Mam had. Can't remember them all. Names. Some of them didn't live, see. They didn't in them days."

"Where was this?"

"Troedyrhiw. She always believed in them. Put a saucer of milk out for them every Sunday, the *Tylwyth Teg*. 'Don't you aggravate them,' she'd say, 'or they'll have your guts for garters.'"

"Which one is Mary?"

Rees had the old photograph album on his lap. It felt like an alien artefact. Nobody had photograph albums these days. They just uploaded their jpegs and selfies onto FaceBook or Twitter.

"This one, bless her. Like a little doll, she was. Bronwen and May, it was. May and Bronwen …" The old woman began fiddling with the locket on a chain round her neck. "I used to torment her terrible. S'pose I was jealous, her being younger and getting all the fuss, like. We used to share a bed, and I used to tickle her till she wet herself. Wicked, I was." She opened it and showed it to Rees, but in her trembling hands the face he could make out was blurred and indistinct. "I used to tell her I could make her hair fall out by just staring at her, and she'd scream blue murder. Then one night I started telling her about the *Gwrach-y-Rhibyn*." She snapped the locket shut and let it drop onto her wrinkled, puckered chest. "I told her there was this witch outside the window who was so ugly that if anyone set eyes on her they'd die of fright, just like that."

Rees eased forward, elbows on knees, knitting his fingers together, but said nothing. He wanted this pure. Unspoiled.

"And she said, 'No there isn't, Bron. Don't be 'orrible. It's just the branches in the wind. I know it is!' And I said, 'Are you *sure*? Are you *sure* that's all it is?' And she said, 'Yes!' And I said, 'What if it's *not* branches though? What if it's her long, long *fingernails* tapping the window – tap, tap, tap …'"

The old woman gulped and sniffed.

"Well. She screamed the house down. I had to go and sleep in my Mam's bed, and my dad slept with May. I was awful. Even before that night I was a handful. And after that, well ..."

"What do you mean?"

Her face seemed to sag. Her hands made little folds in the knees of her dress and a frown of resistance, of conflict, of hurt, cut into her face.

"If you..."

"No, I'll tell you. You came here to ask and I'll tell you. The next morning, I rushed in to wake her, see. I jumped in bed and cuddled up to her and tickled her like I always did, havin' a bit of fun. But she didn't move. She was cold and white like one of them enamel plates we had in the kitchen. I said, 'Come on, May! Play! Play with me!' I tried to wake her but I couldn't. Nobody could." Her eyes fixed on the bars of the electric fire. They bulged and shone glassily, each reflecting a dot of light.

Rees found his throat dry as he listened.

"And I knew, sure as eggs, Matilda of the Night had got her. She came for my little sister all those years ago. And now she's coming for me ..."

Rees felt a faint draught on his cheek and knew that the door had opened behind him. He hadn't heard it doing so but was now certain that somebody was occupying the space directly behind his left shoulder. He turned round.

He saw the tray with the microwave plate cover sheltering a meal, and holding it in both hands, the overweight but pretty Tina Griffiths.

"There you are. Meat and mash. It's time Doctor Rees was making tracks."

Rees looked at his watch and saw that it was 6 p.m. – he'd lost all track of time. As the girl placed down the tray he also saw a plastic container with around fifteen assorted pills inside it. Her daily dose. For what? Angina? Heart? Diabetes? Anxiety? Cholesterol? Or all of the above?

"Did I order meat and mash?"

"Yes you did, love."

"I don't like meat and mash. I like fish."

"No, you ordered meat and mash. It's beef. Beef and gravy."

"Oh, I like beef. I just don't like meat." Bronwen noticed Rees unplugging his recording equipment, coiling a cable round his hand. "He – he doesn't want to go. Does he?" Her lip shuddered with agitation. "Do you? Hmm?"

"I think I have to," said Rees. "She's in charge here, I'm afraid."

"But what – what if she *comes*? The *Gwrach-y-Rhibyn*? What if she comes *tonight*? And you're not here? What *then*?" She was

118

becoming tearful, and this upset Rees but did not seem to bother Tina spectacularly. In fact she became clipped. Firm.

"Bronwen. Now. Doctor Rees can't stay, can he? He has to go home. He's just a visitor. You know the rules, my love."

"Why? You've broken the rules before. You know you have. When Cliff was bad, you let his wife stay. Well now *I'm* bad. What about me? I'm *dying*! And I want him to *stay*!" Her voice stuttered into sobs. "I want someone with me. I'm frightened, can't you see? None of you buggers care! Nobody does!" Tears glistened on her cheeks. "Only him! He's the only one who listens to me!"

"She's upset, look," said Rees, taking the strap from his shoulder. "I'll stay. It's no problem. I don't mind staying. Honestly."

He sat down and watched Tina sigh and mop the old woman's tears with a few sheets from the box of tissues on the coffee table. Then a few sheets more. And a few sheets after that, till the childlike sniffling had subsided.

*

Just after midnight a thin young man of African ethnicity popped his head round the door and asked Rees a second time if he wanted a filter coffee. This time he said yes, thank you. He was tired but he had no intention of sleeping. At 2 a.m., quiet settling on the house with an almost physical presence, he paced up and down for a few minutes to stretch his back, then sat on the stool next to Bronwen Llewellyn's flowery and be-cushioned armchair.

Tap. Tap. Tap.

All being recorded. Night. Branches on the far side of the curtains.

Tap. Tap. Tap.

He thought of Bronwen's sister, Mary. May.

Eyelids heavy, he thought of the May Bride and May tree cults mentioned in Graves's *The White Goddess* … the mythic significance of the horse and the hare …

May. Maybe. Might. Perhaps.

The old woman's lips were moving slightly and he could see her eyeballs revolving under her lids. She'd been like that for five hours but he hadn't switched off the tape except for putting on a new one. She was dreaming and he wondered what she dreamed. She was almost forming words, and he stood for almost an hour with the microphone an inch from her mouth in case she did.

*

119

Arriving home in Penarth, he found he was famished. He put on a slice of toast, booting up his computer as the toaster chirruped, and ate it standing up as he typed the details into his archive list, not sure if it was excitement, caffeine or tiredness making his hands visibly shake. Too exhausted to edit, he calculated he could get six or seven hours sleep before heading back to the nursing home. As it turned out, it was five o'clock in the afternoon when he woke inexplicably anxious about where he was for several seconds, and was helping himself to some brie and slices of apple with his leather jacket already on when Glyn arrived home from the Wetherspoon's in Cardiff Bay where he worked, the old Harry Ramsden's.

Glyn saw that Rees was dressed to leave and his face dropped. "Jesus Christ, you could've waited. I've got pasta. I was going to make meatballs." He dumped his carrier bag of shopping on the kitchen surface. "I don't know why I bother."

"The ingredients will keep till tomorrow."

"Oh, you'll be around tomorrow?"

"I don't know."

"Well, thanks."

"Look, I had no idea you were cooking. I'm going out. I have to go out. How could I know?"

"You'd know if you picked up the phone. You'd know if you spoke to me."

Rees looked at the ceiling and rolled his eyes. Glyn hated when he made him feel like a child. Rees was a year older than his father, but he didn't want him to *be* his father – far fucking from it, thank you very much.

"You still don't get it, do you?" Glyn threw a bag of tomatoes into the chiller of the refrigerator. "Where were you last night – *all* night? Did it cross your mind I might like to know? No. Did it even cross your mind I might be worried? No. Your mobile was switched off …"

"Yes. I was working."

"Why?"

"I had to be."

"Why?"

"Because I have to get this story. The whole story."

"Why?"

"For God's sake, because time is running out, if you must know. Because if I don't get it now, I'll never get it." Rees didn't want the food any more and left the chunk of cheese and apple core on the plate. He zipped up the case of the Nagra as Glyn made great theatrics of stocking the kitchen cabinets, banging doors ludicrously. "Look, I apologise if I didn't explain, but this is ridiculous, it really is. Why are you so angry?" Rees walked to the door, picking up his headphones en route.

"I'm angry," said Glyn, "because it never entered your head, did it? Well, did it?"

*

The overcooked lamb chops defeated her. She sawed at them with a knife then gave up, exhausted, chest heaving. He made weak tea from the jug kettle. As she sipped it he thought of those thin, sipping sounds appearing on his tape.

"Bronwen, when did you first hear about Matilda of the Night?"

"When did you first hear about Father Christmas?"

"I mean, was it from a relative? Do you have relations I could go and talk to?"

"All gone," she said. "You get old. Nobody left, see. Not much of you left either, in the brain box. You don't want to get old, I'm telling you."

Rees sniffed a laugh. "I am old."

"How old are you then?"

"Fifty-three."

"That's no age."

"Say that to my twenty-year-old students." He remembered Glyn was that age at the start of it. Teacher and pupil. The old, old story.

"Then they need their bloody heads examined. Parents still alive?"

"My dad died when I was seven."

"What about your mother?"

Rees shook his head. "Ten years ago. I was in America."

"You weren't there."

"Working. Studying. Same thing. Conference. Talking to complete strangers." He felt the warmth of the bars of the electric fire. He blinked his eyes. They were unaccountably dry. "I got a phone call in this dreadful hotel room. This Holiday Inn – you know, where all the rooms across the world are identical? There was no time to do anything. It had already happened. She was gone. The worst thing was hearing all that emotion in my sister's voice and being so far away." He realised he was playing with one of the day-glo Post-It notes and stuck it back where it was meant to be. "Do you want me to close the curtains?" Bronwen said nothing. He walked over and tugged them shut, then sat back down.

"Sometimes it's easier to be on your own," she said. "Then the people you love can't be taken away. And sometimes you keep yourself in a box, try to pretend it'll never hurt you again. But it does."

Rees told himself he didn't understand what she meant. But even as he tried to dismiss it, it made him feel raw, exposed, uncomfortable. He needed to get out for a minute.

"I'm just – just going to get some water. Is that all right? Do you – do you want some?"

Bronwen didn't nod. She stared glassy-eyed. Her hands supported her cup and saucer and thoughts and words seemed to have deserted her, or she had absconded to memory. He left the room with the tape spools turning and gently closed the door after him.

He walked to the water cooler at the end of the landing. The floorboards did not creak under his footsteps. He yanked a paper cup from the dispenser, half-filled it and took a gulp. He poured the residue into his cupped left hand and rubbed it over his face and the back of his neck, then rubbed his eyes too.

In a nearby room he could hear an elderly person moaning in their sleep. It almost sounded like weeping. He hoped they were dreaming and this wasn't the sound of their waking despair. When he was a child he had wondered long and hard why old people did not rage screaming and gnashing at the prospect of death, and he still could not completely understand why they didn't. The fact they might settle into a kind of numb acceptance only struck him as even more horrifying.

A large window overlooked the garden. The wind from the bay was considerable and in the semi-dark he could make out hydrangea bushes undulating and the branches of trees gesticulating mutely in pools of artificial light. He untied the ornate tassels of the curtains and dragged them tightly across to overlap each other.

"Is that the one with George Clooney?"

The nurses down in the reception area were talking about what movie they fancied seeing. He walked back, leaned over the banister and saw them eating Jaffa cakes below.

"Oh, is that with that comic off the telly? I can't stand him. He really does my head in, that bloke. I'm not kidding."

*

Rees opened the door to see her on her feet, swaying unsteadily, shoulders heaving.

"No, you can't! I'm not ready! Skin off! *Skin off, you bloody –!"* She was facing the window with an outstretched hand. Saw him now. "She's there! She's *out* there! I can *hear* her! I can hear her bloody *whassnames* flapping!"

122

"Sit down. Please sit down, Mrs Llewellyn. Just sit down and I'll take a look for you." He managed to settle her into her armchair, then opened the drapes to see what she had seen – except he didn't. "It's just the canvas come loose from one of those parasol-type things in the garden ..."

"No! It's her *wharracalls* – wings! It's Matilda! Matilda of the Night! She's out there with her long hair and, and long fingers and she's after me. She was perched on the windowsill. I *know* she was!"

"Shshsh. Honestly now. It's nothing." Rees bent down to pick up the cup and saucer, fallen from the arm of her chair but miraculously unbroken. As he stood up he felt Bronwen clinging to his sleeve, sobbing.

"You'll be there, won't you? When she comes back?"

"I don't know if I ..."

"When she does come for the last time, please! I promise I'll tell you everything. You'll have everything on your tape like you want it. I'll tell you everything I hear and everything I see, I promise. Just say you'll be with me." Fear shone in the old woman's eyes and Rees didn't feel able to look at it.

As gently as possible he peeled her fingers off him. He sat her down and knelt and placed his hands over hers, which were ice cold. He looked at her and could feel the warmth emanating from his skin but he couldn't feel hers getting any warmer, at all. This is the way it will go, he thought. The cold. The cold that cannot be warmed. Is this the way we all go? Grey and cold and separated and lost?

"I will. I promise," he said.

*

"She *wants* me to do it."

"But *you* want to do it, that's the point. You want her to die, don't you? You can't bloody wait."

"Rubbish."

"How is it rubbish? When she dies you'll have exactly what you want. You said so yourself. A recording of someone experiencing this – this 'death visitation', whatever the fuck that is."

"She's going to die, Glyn. Whether I'm there sat beside her or not. I can't stop it happening."

"No, but you can use it. For yourself. For your precious collection."

Rees sighed in exasperation. "This isn't for my 'collection'. Christ. It's more than that. How do I get through to you? Nobody has catalogued something like this – ever. This isn't some piddling article in *Folklore*. This could be my – my *Man Who Mistook his Wife for a Hat*. Something that gets me noticed, finally."

"Me. Exactly. You're a bloody vulture, Ivan. Haven't you got any feelings of – ?"

"Why should I not have feelings? Of course I have feelings. It doesn't mean I shouldn't do my job."

"And what's your job? To prey off this demented old biddy who – "

"So what do you want me to do? Abandon her? She's all I've got." Rees corrected himself. "*I'm* all *she's* got."

"Freudian slip."

"That's not true."

"It is true. It's more important than I am."

"Don't be preposterous."

"Preposterous, am I? If I'm preposterous, why are you with me? I'm serious, Ivan? Why? Because you don't seem to want to be with me or listen to me half the time. Do you actually *want* to be loved?"

That made Rees laugh out loud, and it shouldn't have, because it chilled him to the bone. "What's that supposed to mean?"

Glyn stared at him across the dining table. "What *do* you want, Ivan, eh? Because I'll be honest, I don't have a bloody clue."

Rees stood and scraped the residue of his tuna salad into the waste disposal. He could feel Glyn smouldering but didn't turn to face him and waited for him to leave the table. The chair rasped.

"Go. Go and watch her die, Ivan. Be there, if that's what matters to you so much. But if I matter to you, stay with me tonight instead of her."

*

She opened her eyes blearily, tortoise head sunk deep in the propped-up pillows.

"Thank you."

"For what?"

Still half in sleep, the truth comes easier than in wakefulness or daylight. But hesitant. "I'm not scared when you're here."

He pulled up the fold of the blanket under her mottled, stringy chin. "Go to sleep."

She already was.

*

A shadow hand crept across the wall and rested on his shoulder.

124

Rees shook awake with a gasp, the dream already doused. The Holiday Inn banished. The hare run to ground. Was it time to get up? Was he late for school? Mum?

"The Manager wants a word with you," said Katrina close to his ear.

"Now?"

"Now."

What time was it? How long had he slept? He remembered looking at his watch when it was 5 a.m. – what time was it now? Five past seven.

Nack-nack-nack-nack.

The tape spool was spinning, its tail flapping with a metronomic tic. He switched the machine off and lifted his coat from the back of a chair.

Blinking, he felt like a little boy summoned to the headmaster's study as he descended the stairs past a wizened monkey of an old gent hung on the elbow of an obese carer as if to cruelly emphasise the difference. But Penny Greatorex, revealed after a knock on the office door, did not look like a headmaster. She wore the hard superiority of an MBA, contrasting noxiously with a chunky cardigan depicting a timber wolf. The pleasantries were minimal. Katrina left them alone and soon he realised why.

"Dr Rees, I'm sure you're a very bright man but do you seriously think that talking about 'omens of death' is really appropriate to this kind of establishment?"

Instantly on the back foot, Rees told her how he'd explained fully to the Staff Nurse and she'd given permission for him to visit.

"She had no business to. Sara is only an RSN."

"Well, I'm sorry, but Mrs Llewellyn seems more than happy to …"

"That's as may be, but we are the ones legally responsible for her care. And I'm afraid the feedback from some of my staff is that her mental wellbeing has deteriorated since you began coming."

Rees stiffened. "It might seem like that, but truly, I'm not the cause of her increased anxiety at all. I'm merely listening to her."

"Well, perhaps indulging her in her dementia and paranoia isn't doing her a great deal of good, let me put it like that. I'm sure you'd put it differently, but that really isn't my concern. Our resident's welfare is. And in her current state she's a very emotionally vulnerable lady who doesn't require any additional stress in her life. So I'd appreciate if you would leave the premises, please."

"What?"

"Oh, come on. Apart from health and safety concerns and insurance concerns, can you imagine what her relatives – or her relatives' *lawyers* – would say about a complete stranger staying in

125

her room overnight? Can you *imagine* how embarrassing that would be if some accident happened?"

"She *has* no relatives." He laughed. "If you knew anything about her, you'd know that." He tried to stop his anger from rising.

"I'm not prepared to debate this, Dr Rees. I think you can see that."

"Yes, I can." Afraid of adding something he might regret, he turned on his heel.

"Where are you going?"

He thought that was obvious. "Upstairs, to say goodbye to her."

"I'm sorry. I don't think that's a good idea in the slightest."

"For God's sake. She'll be upset if she sees I'm gone without saying something." He looked at her in her timber wolf cardigan. "But you really don't give a shit, do you?"

"Yes," Penny Greatorex said, and her face showed a glimmer of hurt. "As a matter of fact I do. Very much so." But this was her domain – alpha of the pack – and she wanted him out of it. "Jérôme will bring down your equipment to your car. There's no point in waking her, is there? God knows, the day is long enough when you're their age." She didn't look up from the year planner, which was now getting her undivided attention.

*

Having loaded the Nagra, his shoulder bag and laptop into the back seat, Rees sat with his hands gripping the steering wheel for several minutes before finally turning the ignition key. The engine gave its tinny French snarl. He looked up at the landing window and half-saw a face with a crayon-squiggle of hair.

He turned the Citroën in a tight three-point turn and crawled to the automatic gates, which opened as if by hauled by ghostly hands. Pausing where the driveway met the road, which would take him home through Nottage, via the A48 and Culverhouse Cross, a route he infinitely preferred to the motorway, he adjusted the rear view mirror and saw his own eyes, sandpaper-dry from the kind of conflict he loathed and usually avoided, then sharply turned from their accusations.

He realised he didn't want to arrive back at the house while Glyn was there, and Glyn didn't normally leave for work till about eleven. He drove to the Museum of Welsh Life at Saint Fagan's, his old stomping ground once upon a time, but wasn't thinking. He should have known they weren't open until ten. He turned around in the car park and drove to the coast. He didn't really care where he was driving. He found himself at Llantwit Major, walking along the rocky beach where he and his father had caught crabs in a plastic bucket, the smell of bladderwrack and crushed limpets in his nostrils. Distant figures crouched and splashed. The cries of children easily entertained. Wind nice as a razor. Familiar wind, mind. He thought of rolled up sleeves and varicose veins.

His cheeks burned.

*

Glyn's Doc Marten boots were not by the front door. Rees slid off his trainers. The smell of burnt filter coffee stung his nostrils. He dropped the paper cone and its contents in the waste bin under the sink, swilling the black residue in the glass jug under the tap and poured it away, something he always did because his boyfriend didn't. It wasn't even an annoyance to Rees any more. He accepted it, in the way he hoped Glyn accepted the million and one ways his own habits were no doubt irritating. Tolerance. Habit. Acceptance. Wasn't that what having a relationship was about?

Openness?

He almost heard Glyn's voice saying it, and tightened. What if he didn't want to be open? What then? Why was he being forced into being something he wasn't? Why couldn't he just be who he was?

For the next few hours he sat immobile at the kitchen table and listened to the erratic rhythms her breathing.

He listened to her lips smacking, her occasional snort and snore and deep, long silences. His pen hovered over paper as she turned over in her slumber. As she wheezed and fretted and stretched under the starched nursing home sheets. (How many had died in those sheets?) His eyes closed as she coughed and mumbled and grunted. He was the sole and private audience to a symphony of moans. The aural hieroglyphics of her inner life.

Tap tap tap ...

Branches. Trees.

He frowned, leant forward. A thin, plaintive sobbing. Hardly audible. Reaching out to him, for comfort. Last night, yesterday, the past caught on tape.

Memory. Fear.

Rees paused it and sipped his glass of water. Glyn was normally home at five in the evening if he wasn't working evenings. Now it was six. Rees rang The Fig Tree to book a table for dinner. Their favourite place in Cardiff, and walking distance. *How many people, sir?*

"Two," he said.

Staring him in the face from the notice board was the old snapshot of Glyn and himself in Rhodes, uncannily tanned and exceptionally happy. There he was, in that rough old taverna, making a fool of himself. Deludedly happy for a passing, photographic instant. Drunk. Silly. Wasting his time. He never even liked the sun. What was he doing there? What was he pretending?

He suddenly felt completely exhausted, and remembered he'd only slept for an hour or two at the most. He went into the bedroom.

Fully dressed, he unbuttoned his collar and lay on one side of the double bed and curled his knees up, wrapping one arm under his knees. His eyes remained open because he was so overtired his stupid body was fighting it, churning up too many random and unwelcome thoughts. Like Bronwen in her room, crying, not knowing why that nice young man (young?) didn't come back when he said he would. *When he promised!* He imagined her ball-jointed paws feeling the empty place on the corner of her bed where the Nagra had sat. Her devastated expression – lost, lonely, discarded – as below at the desk two overweight nurses ate biscuits from a tin and discussed the latest Peter Andre programme. His throat felt blocked. He felt he was going to choke.

He sat up and took off his clothes. The heat was making him restless and adding to his woes. He dropped his socks and underpants on the carpet, picked up a wire coat hanger for his shirt and trousers and opened the cupboard door.

They were all gone. Glyn's jeans. Glyn's workman's jacket he got in Amsterdam. The linen shirt, the one Rees always told him to wear to dinner parties. The harem pants that had seen better days. *Only good enough for the bin.*

Rees stood back three faltering steps and could see that the suitcase on top of the wardrobe was gone too, and his stomach lurched.

The drawers with the folded T-shirts and sweaters he knew without looking would be empty. He wondered about the toothbrush. The shampoo that gave that orange and lemon scent to Glyn's hair he'd get a whiff of when he kissed his neck. The odour vividly came back to him. Smell. Sound. Touch.

He'd checked the land line for calls when he'd come in, always, but checked again. *You have no messages.* (That voice. Whose voice? Who was she? Was she alive? How did we know for sure?) Back in the bedroom he snatched up his i-Phone from the bedside table where it was plugged in to recharge, tapped in his four digit password, but could see instantly that the speech-bubble logo showed nothing. He scrolled sideways with his finger, pressed *Contacts*, then *All Contacts*. Thumbed down to 'G'. Tapped the name. Glyn's mobile number flashed up.

Rees stared at it. He could ring it. He knew he could. So what was stopping him? His innards felt like lead. An ache incapacitated him, physical and real. It was in control of him and he was at its mercy. He didn't know why.

He pressed the exit button, letting it die and placing it back down where his wristwatch lay.

*

The wall was bereft of wallpaper, plain concrete, with thin lines of water running down it. He was puzzled why nobody was panicking and thought he should tell them there was a leak somewhere above them before a disaster happened. He might get into serious trouble if he didn't mention it, and it worried him. Tina wore make-up. Her mascara was running, her head tilted slightly down. She was sobbing pitifully and he wanted to put his arms round her but before he could reach her she drew back the starched white sheet from the body on the slab. He was wondering why somebody didn't answer that bloody telephone as he saw it was Bronwen Llewellyn, mouth caved in without the benefit of teeth, eyes sky blue and dead as buttons, redness pooling and sticky at the back of her skull.

He woke, stabbed by reality. Not a gasp in him. The dark still had work to do. The sheet twined round one naked leg, he was alone, still.

"Hello." The throbbing iPhone now illuminating his cheek. "Yes?"

*

We leave the lights on. I don't know what she was doing up and about, but a lot of them go wandering, it's not that unusual. You can't lock them in like prisoners, can you? She must've had a hell of a bump. Tina said she was just lying there at the bottom of the stairs, groaning. Couple of minutes she had this massive bruise all up her thigh, turning purple, you could see it. God knows what she thought she was doing. She must've been out looking. Looking for someone ...

*

He saw a branch. He saw its knuckles. Its mossy fingernails.

*

Yes. The Royal Glam in Llantrisant. Aye, I just came on and they told me. Hell of a crack, they said. Going all in and out of consciousness, really confused and in pain. They didn'ae try moving

129

her till the paramedics got here. Sirens and everything. Yes, Penny
went with them. She just rang with the latest. Said they'd checked
for fractures and were putting her in for an MRI-type effort ...

*

Rees threw on clothes, grabbed his jacket and patted his pockets,
checking for his car keys. He reached the front door and swirled
back. Cursed at his jelly-mind, foggy from sleep, the urgency of
Katrina's voice having thrown him. He'd forgotten his priority
completely. He lifted the Nagra strap. Snatched a few boxes of
pristine quarter-inch still in their cellophane wrapper. Hit the light
switch.

It was what she wanted, he told himself. He was doing what
she'd asked for.

*

Drizzle barely more than a mist made his view of the night semi-
opaque through the thinly-speckled windscreen. He flipped the
wipers.

On. Off. On. Off. On. Off.

His headlight beams picked up the wraith of a shaggy pony
limping across the road through Llantristant Common, emerging
from fog and disappearing into it again like a heavy-hoofed
intoxication, a pagan acid flashback.

*

He blinked from the *GIG Cymru/NHS Wales* logo – *Bwrdd Iechyd
Cwm Taf Health Board* – following the arrow to the car park and
snatching a ticket at the barrier, before running through the
emptiness to the footbridge.

Main Entrance/Prif Fynedfa

A congregation of wheelchair-users lurked under the portico,
back-lit by the bilious strip-lighting of the interior, the side of them
facing him in shadow. The figures seemed to have gathered as if in
ritual formation around an ash tray on a stainless steel plinth. He
saw their dappled skin and heard their damaged lungs crackling as
they gnawed at their cigarettes.

To his left a grille covered the shop. A little boy was crying and
plucking at the slats, and Rees imagined the mother was in the
nearby toilet with the occupant of the empty buggy he now passed.
The information desk to the left was unmanned – no one in sight –
so he kept walking, lured towards a central atrium. The floors were

colour-coded, he now saw – lines painted in red, blue and green running through the building like arteries, directing people obediently to their shuffling appointments with Surgical Assessment, with Anaesthesia, with Supported Recovery, with death. This was where it happened. This was where it always ended. This was the building built for it. The shininess and disinfectant not so much fighting E-coli or MRSA but fragility, despair and the fucking inevitable.

He looked at the overhanging signage and found 'Critical Care (ICU)' – the arrow pointed right.

South Wing/Adain y De

He took to the stairs three at a time because the lift was taking an age. He didn't strictly know she was in Intensive Care. She might be in a general ward, or A&E. She might even be on her way home with cuts and bruises for all he knew, but somehow he believed his instinct was right. He felt bad when he saw that the reason the lift was delayed was a gurney with an old man lying on it fighting for breath.

Ahead of him down the corridor he saw Penny Greatorex with her mobile to her ear, and he paused, nose to a window while she passed. Not that he needed to – she was far too involved in her call to notice him. Who was she ringing? The home, or *her* home? *Darling, sorry I'm late, but one of the old ladies is very inconveniently dying.* Outside the window a coarse expanse of green plastic flapped like a sail, tethered to scaffolding poles. Once she'd got in the lift, he hurried down the corridor through the double doors from which she'd emerged.

"Bronwen Llewellyn. A patient called Bronwen Llewellyn?"

The dark-haired nurse baulked. "You'll have to ask on the ward."

"Which ward?"

"I'm sorry, I can't tell you that."

"Oh, for God's sake."

Seeing his obvious agitation, she pointed. "That one. Sixteen."

His palm shoved the heavy door. It didn't give. He looked through the glass, shielding his eyes. Pressed the intercom next to the entry phone. It squawked. He asked if he could see a patient, please, giving Bronwen's name. The intercom went dead, cut off like the last crackling message of a Spitfire pilot.

Through the window a nurse with fat arms approached the door, opened it half way but blocked his entry with her bulk. He tried to read in her eyes what she knew, but it was impossible.

"The nursing home informed me. I know this is … but I came here as …"

"Are you a relative, sir?"

He could not think of an alternative. "Yes."

"Siân? *Diolch yn fawr i chi.*" The voice came from behind her. She stepped back, letting the door open, and Rees saw a skinny, blond man with a stethoscope curling out of his pocket finish writing something on a clip board. The chap was in his twenties and not conventionally handsome – usually a euphemism, but in this case true. "Mr Llewellyn?"

"Yes."

"Your mam's been in the wars, poor thing. Have you come far?"

"Quite a way."

"Well, you're here now. That's what matters, eh? We put her in a room to herself. To give her a bit of peace."

*

In a way he was prepared for it, in a way it hit him like a ton of bricks. He expected the hospital bed, the clouding oxygen mask, the drip, the white patches on her chest connected to the ECG flickering its digital data. What he didn't except was to see that vital bundle, that sprightly calf, looking like a punctured bag. Nostrils flaring under the plastic, hissing cone. Wrinkled lips pouting and twitching. Eyelids struggling to so much as flicker. Eyes – black eyes from the fall – themselves hooded, failing, pooped. The massive lump at her temple, hideously discoloured and embossed with a dozen stitches like the work of some brutal staple-gun. Worst of all, the cruel harshness of the venflon needle rammed into that snappable forearm with its sagging skin lined like bark, the cotton wool absorbing an ooze of dark blood. He wondered how many times they'd gone for a vein and missed. He thought of her yelp and recoil and tears, and the platitudes that would have come back at her. It made him shudder.

"I know," said the doctor, or registrar as he called himself, whose name was Sand. (*Dr Sand* – it sounded like a comic book hero – or villain.) "She's getting her sleep, and that's a good thing after what she's been through. The fact she hasn't broken anything is a miracle, but a bash on the skull isn't funny for anybody – especially at her age. It looks worse than it is, with all the inflammation, but that will go down. Our worry is the impact on her system, something like this. We have to keep an eye on a head injury, in case there's any sort of bleeding in the skull, any haemorrhaging, any swelling. So far so good, but the next twenty-four hours is the crucial time. We can't take anything for granted. I'm sure you understand."

Rees looked at the blue-black bruising muddied around the crook of her elbow. His mouth was desert dry. He clacked as he swallowed.

"Is she going to die?"

"I've told you all I can. So far she's been a brave old thing, love her."

"Just tell me the truth. Please. What are the chances of her pulling through?"

"I really can't give you chances, Mr Llewellyn. All we can do is keep an eye on her and hope for the best. I'm sorry."

"How long have I got?"

Dr Sand paused at the door. "You can stay as long as you like."

*

He sat beside the bed. Did not pick up her hand as he felt, peculiarly, he might break her. Or that his gesture might be some kind of imposition, one she didn't want or need. Old people tended to have very clear boundaries of privacy and didn't like them abused. This is what he told himself.

Wach, the breathing in the oxygen mask said. *Wachch... Waaccchhh... Waacher... Wachch-ur...*

"*Wrach-y-wribyn... nuh ... wraaach ...*"

Her eyes, stuck with a rheumy, Galapagos glue, opened. A leaden cloud having moved across the sky of them.

"Tilda ... Muh ... Muh ..."

Rees didn't need to struggle to make out the words.

She turned a groggy inch to him, struggling to focus.

"Put it on ..." Throat caked with suffering. "Put it on."

Her arm lifted, bone, skin. He followed the line of her quavering finger. It led to the Nagra he'd placed on the chair next to the door.

*

The lick of leader made a rhythmic tick and tock. In a quite mesmerising way if you let it be, one spool blossomed with tape as the other slowly diminished. Luckily he had a collection of little plastic clamps and one of these held the microphone to a metal rib of the bed head, coiled with gaffer tape. It was important to position it as close to her mouth as possible to get a clean recording.

"Uh ... Matilda ... I ... Aye ... shush ... shush..."

"Bronwen? Bronwen? I'm here. I'm here, look. What do you want to tell me?"

"I want to tell you ..." Her feather-light fingers tugged the oxygen mask to one side, the elastic cutting a scar-line into her cheek. Its hissing became louder. "I want to tell you you're a good boy."

Where was that coming from? Was that the pain killers talking? He fought a smile.

"Bronwen, do you remember our arrangement?" He reached between his legs and brought his chair round, closer.

"Arr – arrange …?" The mask, skewiff, twisted, added to her look of helpless puzzlement. Resembling a dislodged red nose, it made her stray hair look like a clownish wig.

"Yes, our arrangement. What you'd tell me? If I came? D'you remember?"

She lost all her strength at that point and her arm fell from the oxygen mask to the bed. Something about the brown paw of it frightened him, but he reached out to hold it.

The door opened. He retracted his hand like a thief.

"How's she going? Is she sleeping, still?" The camp voice and bleached hair betrayed the ICU nurse's sexuality. The plucked eyebrows and sun-bed tan added to Rees's impression he must be a drag queen on the quiet. "I've come to change her dressing." What dressing? Of course – her thigh. Katrina had said. The rainbow bruising. Maybe other damage he didn't know about. "Why don't you go and get a bite to eat for ten minutes? A coffee or something? But it's bloody dreadful, I warn you."

"Thanks," said Rees, easing himself to his feet.

"What's this palaver?" Drag Queen said as he peeled down the sheet, thumbing at the mic. Slim hips and slip-ons. "It's not interfering with our equipment, is it?"

"No, I cleared it with Dr Sand," Rees lied. "He said it's fine."

The ICU nurse looked at the Nagra, then at him. Rees wondered what he was thinking, but didn't really care. One thing he did know – if this was going to be a long night, he did need that coffee, and better to do it now whilst Bronwen was being properly supervised.

"Ten minutes," Rees said to her, imagining she could hear.

*

Ground Floor/Llawr Gwaelod

The hospital café was trying hard to be a Costa but towers of plates full of chips and rejected pasties destroyed any illusion. The server clearly spent more on piercings than on personal hygiene, and the wipe of a ubiquitous cloth saturated with toxic spray only moved around the grease on the formica tabletops.

Rees tried to concentrate on the sounds around him while his Americano cooled: the squidge of doors swinging open and closed, the squeak of nurses' rubber soles and trolley wheels on highly-polished floors. The sounds alone gave him a sense of place. Other than that, he could have been anywhere: an airport, shopping mall. They anchored him.

He'd left the spools turning. Let it record everything, just in case. The odd word, the odd sound – it might mean everything later, when he played the reels back in the hermetic comfort of his own home. *Home.* He wondered what that meant now, and thought of the house in darkness, empty.

He dug out his phone. Messages? None. He looked at the back of his hand, the blue rivers running under the pink surface. He remembered an old trick a friend used to do, plucking the skin on the back of your hand and counting to ten. The longer your skin stayed pinched before becoming soft again, the older your skin was. He remembered when he did it, in his twenties, he was only fractionally a one. The last time he did it he reached four.

He looked up, aware of being watched even before doing so. The gaze came from three people seated on a lime green sofa. Man, woman, child. Dressed formally, in black, as if they'd come from a funeral. They weren't looking at each other. They were looking at him.

*

Through the corridor window, the sheeting that strait-jacketed the scaffolding outside sucked in and breathed out like the building's lungs. Its green glistened with rain.

Rees pressed the ICU intercom again and waited, rubbing the mysterious but nonetheless physical tension in his neck. He heard some whispering and light, conspiratorial chuckling behind him – his first thought being that he was being laughed at, ridiculed, humiliated. Memories of the school yard. He turned, and through an open door into the ward opposite he could see two nurses stripping a bed. They stopped laughing abruptly when they saw him, frozen until the door re-opened.

He hadn't registered the notice board before. This time he did. The thumb-tacked greeting cards written by young hands, thanking the nurses for being lovely to nanny or grampa. Saying, praying, these votive offerings, that they were glad to have them back. That they didn't want their last memory to be of them sitting in that terrible bed, yellowing and shrinking, accursed by medical bafflement. Young, unblemished faces, smooth cheeks. It seemed an act of abuse to expose them to it. And there they were – the trite pictures of dogs, cats, cuddly bunnies. Or was it a hare?

He stopped dead. Katrina stood with a semi-wet raincoat over her arm, nodding to a nurse. He felt his stomach knot at the thought

135

of what she was being told, but when he caught her eyes and she gave the flicker of a smile by way of greeting he knew it wasn't what he feared. As the nurse hung up her coat, Katrina took a tissue and wiped the rain from her hair and face.

*

He sat with elbows on knees staring at the old woman, tube trailing from the oxygen mask clamped like a vicious sucker over her puckered maw, lips forming invisible syllables, the occasional fearful gulp or gasp as if to remind them, or herself, that she was still there.

He could not hear the rain on the roof. They were isolated from it. The bastion of medicine and pharmaceuticals protected him here, he was not sure from what – he supposed, from nature. From night.

Muh ... tild ...

"I remember when I was about seven," said Katrina, "or maybe six, asking my mum, 'Mum, what's death?' And she said – she'd answer anything, my mum – 'Och, you get a wee taste of it every time you go to sleep, hen. That's all it is. A big, long sleep.' I didn't close my eyes for a month."

Katrina wanted him to smile but Rees didn't respond, so she filled the silence.

"Hey. She's had a good innings. When it comes, it comes, eh?" She saw him look at the floor and misinterpreted his lack of communication. "It wasn't me who went to Penny, by the way."

"It doesn't matter."

"You didn't think …?"

"I didn't think anything. I don't think anything. Let's just leave it, can we?"

"You know all that stuff about the *Gwrach-y-Rhibyn*? I think she was just lonely. I think she'd say anything for a bit of company."

"And in the end," said Rees, "who's she got in the world? Just you and me."

"And her son." Katrina saw Rees's features jolt as he tried to make sense of what she'd said. "She never mentioned him? Kai?"

"No. What the hell? Why didn't *you* mention it?"

"I didn't think it was important. To you, I mean. Anyway, he lives in Spain. According to her, they couldn't wait to put her in a nursing home and they were off. 'Course, old people can be very one-sided about things like that. Maybe the guy had no choice. Maybe he lost his job, ran out of cash. Had to downsize. He had a family. Kids."

"She has grandchildren?"

136

"Oh, yeah. Four. She gets photos, letters. I tried to get her to do a Skype but she wasn't having it. It was always: 'It's up to him.' She's proud, our Bronwen – and a bit pig-headed and a bit of a well, pain in the arse, too, at times. They get like that. You can't tell fact from fiction."

"In your vast experience," murmured Rees, pretending it was not for her ears.

"Well. Sorry. I'm sorry you didn't know. Anyway, what time is it?" Katrina looked at her watch. "They phoned and e-mailed him as soon as it happened. The fall, I mean. His contact numbers were on file in case of emergencies. Obviously. He should be landing at Heathrow soon, if his flight isn't delayed. I hope to Christ he makes it in time."

"In time?"

His spoken thought didn't need elaboration. He voiced it only to be cruel to her, because she was being cruel to him by saying this. He didn't really know why. Katrina stood, and he was only dimly listening now.

"Penny's gone off to collect him. I think it's all the old girl has ever wanted, really, deep down. For him to be with her at the end. Isn't that all any of us want in the end? To not be alone?"

Rees's eyes were fixed on the old woman. He heard a sharp intake of breath, saw her jaw glove-puppetting behind the plastic hiss, the tendons stretching in her neck. "What can you hear, Bronwen, love? What can you see?" He circled the bed and lifted the microphone from the sheet to rest on her undulating chest. Held it there with the flat of his hand. "Bronwen?"

"Nnn … She'll be here, now just … Buh, above, above us, she is, sh, she is, now just … Blummy toes scratchin' the flamin' roof, can you *hear* them? Scra-scratchity scratch-scratch … Flamin' … nggghff … puh." The vowels drifted – consonants becoming stutters and starts and mute spits, lips contorting in some dream-life, eyes only briefly alert and cognisant and he could tell it was burdensome, a torture. She sagged, thorax lifting the black bar of the mic with the each mucus-filled rattle.

"What did she say?" He looked over at Katrina but a shrug was the most the girl could offer.

Now Bronwen's mouth flexed like a sphincter. A newborn mute and writhing for first breath. Until which, pain. Just pain.

Rees felt a wave of nausea, a scent-memory of grease and acidic coffee courtesy of the cafeteria.

Chu-kak! Chu-kak! Chu-kak! Chu-kak!

The sound – a sudden feathery slashing – startled him, tugged his chin to see the tape on the Nagra had run out and the loose tail was flailing, whipping circles, ablur. He'd seen this a thousand times before. Stupid that it had made him jump, something so innocuous and banal.

He walked to the machine.

"I better ring her," said Katrina, getting up. "See if he's touched down. They don't allow you to make phone calls in here. I better go outside. I'll be back in a minute."

Rees said nothing. She probably thought she'd got on his nerves and needed to give him a bit of space. She hadn't. Not really. It was all petty. Pointless. She was a decent sort. There was nothing wrong with her. He didn't like putting down people the way Glyn did. She was ordinary. She was not a deep thinker, or snappy dresser, but that wasn't a crime. She cared. That was why she'd come, after all. And that said a lot. And for some strange reason, now, he wanted to acknowledge this to her in some way that wasn't condescending or trite, but she was gone.

*

He turned the tape recorder off, took the delicate stray end between his thumb and forefinger of one hand and pulled out a length of it, enough to insert it carefully into the gap between the heads, then curled the free end back round the empty spool. He switched to 'Rewind' for a few seconds and put on his headphones. He wanted to know what she had said – or tried to say.

He pressed 'Stop' then 'Play'.

" – can you hear, Bronwen, love? What can you see?"

The sharp intake. Disembodied now, though he knew it was from the person lying behind him. Not clearer in meaning but more ambiguous. Fright? Surprise? Discomfort?

"Bronwen?"

Rees listened to the muffled, shuffling sound as, a ghost on tape, some audio doppelganger, he had lifted the microphone from the surface of the hospital bed and placed it – pop, *numb* – on her hollow chest.

"Nnn ... She'll be here, now just ..."

A laugh somewhere. Why had he not heard it? Faint. Several walls away. A cackle at a dirty joke, it sounded like, then stifled in a snigger by the hand of a nurse realising ICU was no place for such hilarity – or was it a patient's relative attacked by a short, savage burst of hysteria?

"Buh, above, above us, she is, sh, she is, now just ..."

Then – the other noise ... Something. What was it? Even fainter ...

"Blummy toes scratchin' the flamin' roof, can you hear them? Scra-scratchity scratch-scratch ... Flamin' ... nggghff ... puh."

138

For once he wished Bronwen would shut up. It was a background drone, lifting high then dropping low …

He stopped the tape and rewound it again. Turned up the volume.

Pressed 'Play' again.

" – *scratchin' the flamin' roof, can you hear them? Scra-scratchity scratch-scratch … Flamin' … nggghff … puh.*"

Of course … An ambulance. *Ambiwlans.* The siren and its Doppler effect, growing louder as it pulls in to A&E on the far side of the building. Not a cry at all. Not a *bird-like cry* or screech. Not a *drawn-out* screech at all …

He saw it, bright green and luminous yellow, flapping? Why did he think, *flapping*?

"What did she say?"

His own voice in the Sennheisers, hooking him.

He wound it back. Rewind. Stop. Play.

Ambulance/Ambiwlans

Too far. Earlier than the first time. Katrina's voice.

" – *should be landing at Heathrow soon, if his flight isn't delayed. I hope to Christ he makes it in time."*

"In time?"

His own voice. Bitter. Old. Cruel. More like his father's.

In the pause it rose again. The siren. *But it wasn't there before –* it most definitely wasn't *there* before, the wailing. The shift from high pitch to low – almost musical. The cawing ululation … How could it be *earlier* this time? How could it be *growing*? Getting *louder* even now, as he listened?

"– all the old girl has ever wanted, really, deep down. For him to be with her at the end. Isn't that all any of us want in the end? To not be alone?"

*

His back to Bronwen Llewellyn, Rees switched off the Nagra and tugged away his head set as if it was on fire, her words – in reality now – suddenly sharp in his ears, as sharp as was possible from behind the oxygen mask:

"*Gutter* she's hanging from now … *cowing* looking in at us … knows, see, she does … it's her job, see … *swining* thing, she is…"

Without turning he grabbed another tape box and let it fall to his feet, sprung open on the floor, clear plastic fluttering after it. He tried with feverish fingers to lace up a new reel, yanking out a yard of the white leader. He fed it past the recording heads and made a loop, knotting it onto the empty spool before pressing 'Record' and

139

'Play' simultaneously. He realised he was panting and held his breath.

"Bronwell Llewellyn. Royal Glamorgan Hospital. Tape four. Time … Time …" It became a question – "Time?" – not even for the tape any more, and it was always for the tape. *Always.* Because the tape would outlast him – wouldn't it? Though now he seemed its servant. The tape asked him for more but he couldn't give it. Not a fact, not a confessional, nothing. The most he could give in the abject silence was his fear.

Knowing he must, he turned to face the bed.

Katrina sat with her back to him. She was facing the old woman, slightly bent forward, forearms on thighs, wearing her Dorothy Perkins raincoat. He could see in harrowing clarity dark, mercury rivulets beading down it, lines chasing each other.

"You were quick," he said, forcing a lightness into it that stuck in his throat.

Katrina did not reply. Nor did she turn.

She extended a hand to rest gently on Bronwen's and it was not the hand he last remembered as Katrina's. Of course he had not examined it, not had occasion or need to, but Katrina's had been soft and white, and now the skin was – what? – brown, if not grey, and he was sure if anything her fingers had been rather dainty, but these? These were too long, surely – far too long, and the knuckles too many … The most appalling thing of all was he now saw that the figure's back was hunched quite notably, the head sinking low to its chest as the hand with palpable urgency squeezed and shook the old woman's.

Almost paralysed, yet feeling the sac of his testes prickle and tighten, Rees knew that the object was to wake her and that Bronwen knew this with unique and horrible certainty. He could see that she had her eyes so tightly shut that her entire face was a route map of wrinkles pointing at a central point. Her lower lip shook in her non-babble, shining with rogue spittle as the oxygen mask misted in bursts. She resisted. She *resisted.* Weak as she was, enfeebled as she was, mute as she was, she was defying the night with every ounce of her embattled being. But the night was relentless. It persisted. It was waiting, predator at the water hole, with its filthy, lank, coal-black hair for her to give in, as it knew she must.

It was waiting with immoral, sickening patience for her to open her eyes.

"No," Rees said, voice his own again, not his father's, not on tape, not artificial or an electromagnetic reproduction but alarming real. Knowing that more than almost anything he'd had in life, or wanted in life, he wanted Bronwen's eyes to stay closed.

"Not her," he breathed. "Not yet."

In bemusement or arrogance the hunched figure did not respond, and knowing what he had to do – seeing past it the flickering eyelids that tried so hard to keep shut – Rees grabbed its shoulder and yanked it round to face him, tearing its gaze from its victim.

Two swishing curtains of long, thickly-matted hair fell either side of its Geronimo cheeks, the face framed by them hard to reconcile as human. It filled his vision, riddled with warts, Neanderthal brow sloping above a bony ridge overhanging holes dug into putty. In the same instant the lips of a jutting jaw, ancient and simian, pulled back from a mouth with frightening elasticity to display gums blackened and rotten as it emitted a sound he failed to define even as it consumed him.

Strangely, he remembered seeing a programme about the making of a monster movie of the fifties which showed the roar of a dinosaur ravaging New York created by the amalgamation of recordings of a bear, an elephant and a howler monkey. His brain tried to deduce, to codify, oddly, some similar recipe for what was assaulting his ears, but the task defeated him. Even in that grasping moment of lucidity, on another level, he understood completely that he was lost in the all-encompassing trap of it. There was no escape but to succumb, and the burden of resistance was shockingly easy to divest. He let it bathe him, that strange manufacture of the vast, insouciant yawn of a lion, the manic glee of a chimpanzee and the plaintive top C of a mezzo-soprano singing La Cieca's aria from *La Gioconda* – the first opera he had seen that had made him weep. It – all of it – rose, transporting and yet holding him like a claw.

Perhaps he found beauty in that sound because he knew that if he was hearing it, Bronwen was not.

And even as the noise coursed through him, he knew that the only scream they'd hear on the tape would be his own, torn from him now as a crippling fire exploded in his chest, fissures of agony snaking down one arm. Pain choked him as he tried to blot out the inhuman howl of the *Gwrach-y-Rhibyn* with his own. But he was doubled, quartered, falling, fallen, as the polished floor raced to hit his splayed hand then, as it twisted, his forehead.

*

Hiroshima whited him back to the world. Faces? Faces he didn't know. Demons. Saviours. Making him afraid. Fishermen hauling him back from drowning. But drowning felt best.

*

Two hundred joules. Stand back please!

*

The kick again. Cold. Shirt ripped open. Paddles descending.

*

Not responding. Nothing happening. One more time. Stand back please! Stand back!

*

"She's coming for me," he could hear somewhere in the room. "She came for him, and next she'll come for me." And he knew Katrina, upside-down Katrina, returning now from outside, would comfort the old woman in her madness.

He didn't care. What mattered was that she was safe. That she had time. Time enough to see her son. Time to make a difference. And the light was bright. And he didn't mind that, either. He didn't mind anything very much at all.

And the last thing he listened to was his own voice in his own head.

"To the folklorist, nothing must die. There is life every time a mouth opens to tell a story."

Now I am a story, he thought.

Tell me.

THE GOBLIN STONE

There are enigmatic standing stones the length of Britain; on lone moors, the ridges of desolate hills, or deep in tangled forests. Some are carved with eerie glyphs, others eroded by the passing millennia – but all possess an undeniable presence and power.

Whether they represent a truly esoteric past is still a source of debate. Most are Neolithic in origin, and whether they once served as tribal meeting places, the focal points for lurid religious rites or perhaps had more mundane purposes – were they distance-markers, or used as tethering posts for animals, for instance? – without exception they are wreathed in legend and superstition. And Carreg-y-Bwci, near Lampeter in Ceredigion, Southwest Wales, has more than its fair share of both.

In appearance, Carreg-y-Bwci is less impressive now than it was in former days; once a soaring a monolith, it long ago toppled over and now lies flat in the midst of a circular embankment. Despite its recumbent posture, the stone still looks vaguely phallic, perhaps explaining why it has long enjoyed a ritualistic aura, which New Agers and other sensation seekers have found enticing. But local folk, primarily the farmers in the district, are less enthused. Because Carreg-y-Bwci is Welsh for 'the Goblin Stone', a title it has earned over centuries of mysterious happenings there, all apparently connected to the presence of unknown but menacing entities.

In 1940, it was reported that at least three men had died at the scene in separate incidents, after attempting to move or break up the stone for building materials. Investigators theorised they had been struck by lightning bolts, having been caught in electrical storms on high, exposed ground – but the less skeptical responded that three lightning strikes all in the same spot was itself suspicious. In the 1950s, another farm-worker claimed to have been driven from the hillside by a weird, localised lightning storm. Others have reported odd visions at the stone – indefinable shapes circling it in the darkness, or glimpses of bizarre alien landscapes – while yet more have described curious, inexplicable sounds: whispers, chuckles, shrieks.

The most dramatic incident supposedly occurred in the early 17th century, at a period when the Goblin Stone was actively shunned by the local community. A lad who was new to the area became lost and made camp next to the stone, intending to spend *only one night in its shelter – but his next few hours were filled with horrific torments as half-seen beings, "diminutive in stature and fiendish of feature", persistently assaulted him, physically restraining him when he tried to flee. The following morning he was found wandering, dazed and incoherent, his whole body covered with mysterious bruises.*

Despite recent attempts to promote the stone as part of a misidentified Roman ruin (which would clearly be too prosaic an explanation for many), Carreg-y-Bwci remains a popular attraction on the folklore trail, a status undimmed – in fact enhanced – by continued modern-day reports of strange phenomena in its vicinity.

THE SOUND OF THE SEA
Paul Lewis

Alll his life Richard had loved the sound of the sea. He could hear it now as he stood at the kitchen window, gazing down anxiously at the woman at the edge of the water.

Beyond the peninsular there was only the restless Atlantic. A gale whipped white horses into a fury and sent them galloping towards the shore. Foam swirled around the rocks on which Caitlin perched. She looked as graceful as a seabird and just as fragile, and she was far too exposed for his liking.

As if aware of his anxiety she twisted around, only to turn away again sharply. There was a flash of light over her shoulder as she whipped out the rod, casting a spinner into the sea.

A memory surfaced, unbidden. Weymouth in summertime. Alison, then eleven, hair long, teeth imprisoned behind braces. She had seen a small rod in a gift shop window and had nagged for it until he'd given in. Michelle, bored, had returned to their rented cottage.

Father and daughter had spent a damp windswept afternoon huddled together on the beach, casting out, reeling in, catching nothing, until their fingers were numb with cold. The fish they ate that night was bought wrapped in paper with chips.

Richard blinked and shoved the memory aside. It took him a moment to realise Caitlin had vanished from the rocks.

"Shit," he said as his heart gave a kick. He leant forward until his face was close enough to the window for his breath to mist the glass. There was only the turbulent grey and white of the sea.

"Shit," he repeated and hurried outside. The gale harassed him with all of its force. He stuck his hands in his pockets and started along the path, body hunched against the cold.

The cottages were on a grassy bank overlooking the sea, the path continuing at a gentle incline to steep steps leading down to the beach. He had no sooner set off than Caitlin appeared at the top of the steps, a brace of silvery fish held in one hand. Mackerel he guessed from the look of them.

"*Hello*," she greeted in her warm Welsh honey voice. "Bit of a wild afternoon to be going on one of your walks, isn't it? And there's you without so much as a jacket to keep you warm."

"I was just getting some air." He could hardly admit the truth and, besides, he would have been of little use if she had fallen in. There were treacherous currents below the surface, she had once mentioned. People had been swept away to their deaths. Not something Richard, a weak and nervous swimmer, wanted to hear.

They walked back to the cottages. Caitlin slowed when they reached his kitchen door. "Don't you ever get bored?"

He shook his head. "Not really."

"I didn't mean to be rude," she added hastily. "It's just that, well, I don't get many guests, mainly hikers and cyclists and they only stay a night or two. I mean, it's not very comfortable, is it?"

"It's fine," he said. The holiday let was basic, little more than a converted outhouse but it suited his needs. He hadn't been looking for comfort. He hadn't been looking for anything other than a place to rest his head. Somehow, though, one night had become two nights and before he knew it he'd been there for a week with no great urge to move on. "I'm enjoying the peace and quiet."

"Well, if you're sure." she said.

"I'm positive."

"Good." She turned to leave, then raised the fish and asked, "Do you want one of these?"

Richard laughed. "Thanks but I wouldn't know where to start."

"Never been fishing?"

"No," he said, thinking of Weymouth. "Never."

"You should come with me. It'll make a change from all that walking. I'll be out again tomorrow, if you're interested."

"Sure," he said, feeling it would be politer to cry off with an excuse in the morning rather than turn her down there and then.

"Right you are. See you tomorrow."

"*Hwyl fawr*." Goodbye. He liked the way she smiled when he used one of the Welsh phrases he'd picked up. She must have been close to his age, fifty or thereabouts, but that smile took years off her.

He went inside and sat on the sofa in front of the fire with the Lee Child he'd left there that morning. He had to hold it almost at arm's length to read. With his mind elsewhere his eyes slid across the words as though they were greased. The cottage, already small, seemed to shrink. He put the book down, feeling unsettled, like he had an itch he couldn't reach to scratch.

He put on his coat and went outside, not bothering to lock the door. The wind was no less fierce and every bit as chilly.

A mellow light flickered through Caitlin's window. There was only ever candlelight, as though she lived in a different world to his, a different time too. He'd once heard candles referred to as God's light. Maybe it was a religious thing with her.

A short walk led him into the village of Swn Y Môr, though maybe village was pushing it. There was no pub and no shop, just a narrow road with a terrace of old houses on one side and a sea wall

146

of matching grey stone on the other. Time-worn steps led down to a jetty that pointed seaward like a stubby finger.

While the village was drab, its setting more than compensated.

The coastline here was a place of wild but undeniable beauty, Sŵn Y Môr nestling in a dramatic curve of cliffs that marched away until they were lost in the distance. Too buffeted and cold to admire the view that afternoon, Richard made himself push on. He walked at a clip so he could keep warm and so he could be back before dusk. Clouds dimmed the sky, threatening rain; another reason not to dawdle.

Looking to sea he noticed a boat, made into a bathtub toy by distance. It was heading for the jetty, pitching and yawing wildly through the swell. Whoever had taken it out was either brave or mad.

As usual the village was deserted. Richard usually hurried past the houses, for the simple if ludicrous reason that they gave him the creeps. The postcard charm they owned from a distance did not stand up to closer scrutiny. They were squat, as though crushed by the shadows of the cliffs overlooking them. With no front gardens they abutted directly onto the road so it was possible to see the rotting wooden window frames and the dust that speckled the glass.

No smoke spiralled from their chimneys, no voices could be heard from behind those grimy windows. There was nothing but the gusting wind and the tide pounding the beach and the sea wall.

An irrational idea came to him; that none of the houses was lived in, that the village had been abandoned like a Welsh St Kilda. The thought made him shiver, even if the most likely reason there was nobody around was because everyone was off at work. With no large industry anywhere close and the nearest town miles away, it would be dark when they left and dark when they got home again.

That would also explain the noticeable absence of cars.

As if to prove his theory he crossed the road to the nearest house so he could look through the window. Though the light was fading he could make out a table, a wooden dresser and a chair on which a pale garment of some kind had been draped. Richard got closer still until his nose was almost touching the pane.

While there were no nets or curtains, dappled smears of dust obscured the glass almost as effectively. Finding a clear patch he peered in and realised that what he'd thought was a garment draped on the chair was the naked body of someone incredibly old.

He stumbled back, telling himself that he couldn't have seen what he thought he had seen; an emaciated woman, the deflated bladders of her breasts sagging against starkly prominent ribs. Her legs had been parted, a blackness between them as though stained by the shadows edging the room. Her head had appeared to turn

147

until she was looking straight at him.

Richard wiped a hand across his mouth. His heart pounded in double time. He felt sick yet had to fight a simultaneous urge to laugh, certain that if he looked through the window again he would see nothing but an empty room. There had been no old woman, just a phantom of light and dark given life by his own state of mind.

He tugged his jacket collar up and hurried on, determined to reach the end of the village before the rain came. Despite the wind that challenged his every step it did not take long. The road simply ended. Beyond it was the cliff face, part of which had sheared away, dumping a shapeless mound of earth and rock onto the beach. From the weathering of the exposed cliff and the tall grass that carpeted the debris, the landslip had plainly occurred a long time ago.

He stared at nothing for a little while, lost in thought. When he turned to make his way back he saw the boat had tied up alongside the jetty, where four men were putting crates into neat stacks. He had an impression of dark hair and beards but they were too far away for him to see with any clarity. They in turn paid him no heed at all.

Another man of perhaps sixty stood at the roadside, smoke escaping from a cigarette stuck to his lip. From beneath his dark knitted cap he squinted at the steep hill that was the only way in and out of the village. As Richard walked by the man nodded and called, "*Mae 'n rhaid taw ti yw 'r boi sy 'n aros yn tŷ Caitlin.*"

The incomprehension must have been clear on Richard's face for the man, who he guessed to be the boat's skipper, spoke again in English. "I said, you must be the fellow staying in Caitlin's place." His tone was neither friendly nor unfriendly while the expression on his tanned and deeply lined face was one of open curiosity.

"I'm renting the cottage, yes." Richard gestured at the boat. "You did well. I thought there were no fish left to catch."

"Don't you believe it, *bach. Mae 'r môr yn rhoi i ni.*"

Before Richard could ask what that meant, he heard an engine and turned to see a white van creeping down the hill.

"Here we go," the man said, two fingers in his mouth shaping a whistle to his crew. Each man hoisted three crates, leaving a solitary crate on the jetty. They carried their load towards the road with such little effort they might as well have been carrying folded linen.

Richard left them to it. The van passed him and pulled up by the wall. Glancing back he saw the driver get out and open the rear doors. He wondered how much the skipper and crew would be paid for the catch and whether it had been worth risking their lives for.

That evening a storm roared in. Richard drank whisky and fell asleep on the sofa earlier than usual. When he woke just before dawn the storm had blown itself out. He had left the fire on all night, making the room unbearable, so he took his coffee outside.

Caitlin's place was in darkness but the village had stirred into life. Every window of every house was filled with candlelight.

The sky was clear and freckled with stars. Looking down Richard saw small shapes moving in the water. Rocks, he thought, assuming it was the tide creating an illusion of motion as it flowed around them.

But no, whatever they were, they were definitely moving. Some drifted out to sea, others glided along the shoreline. All were soon beyond his sight. Surely they couldn't have been people swimming, he thought, not at that hour and not in water that must have been close to freezing. He stood there for several minutes, shivering, waiting to catch sight of anyone making their way up the beach.

When no one appeared he told himself it must have been seals he had seen.

*

He watched her for a while until he was confident enough to try but he got it hopelessly wrong and she laughed and held him by the arms so she could guide his movements. They stood on the same outcropping she had fished from yesterday, only now the nature of the sea was entirely different. It had lost its wild fury, the incoming tide caressing rather than attacking the shore.

"Like this," Caitlin said, standing close enough for her hips to brush his, almost breathing the words into his ear in those melodic Welsh tones. "That's right … now *flick* the rod over your shoulder."

It worked. The spinner flew straight out a satisfying distance before splashing into the water.

"Now reel in. Steady, not too fast."

He wasn't expecting to catch anything but then again he hadn't expected to be there at all. Yet after just a few turns of the reel the line tautened and he felt a rush of excitement at the realisation that, despite his ineptitude, he had only gone and caught a bloody fish.

With Caitlin urging him on, he reeled in until the fish was close enough for him to raise the rod and lift it clear of the water.

"Mackerel," Caitlin said, deftly unhooking his catch and killing it by smacking its head hard against the rock.

Richard cast again, glad he had taken up her offer instead of contriving an excuse. The weather, cold and grey and windy all week long, had vastly improved. It remained cold but the wind was now more of a breeze and the sky more blue than grey.

He couldn't resist stealing glances at Caitlin, who had a distant look in her deep blue eyes and a half-smile on her lips. Her long hair was dark flecked with white, as though spun from a midwinter sky. She wore a grey skirt and matching woollen coat and plain sturdy boots. She appeared to him to be a part of the landscape while he, overdressed in his lurid North Face gear, felt apart from it.

He caught one more fish before the tide and the cold drove them home. They reached the cottages, where Caitlin said: "You'd be welcome to come round for dinner. Seeing as you caught it."

He agreed without hesitation.

The afternoon he spent on the cliff tops, following paths he had walked several times already, seeing something different in the view each time. From above, Sŵn Y Môr appeared as quaint as it did from afar, its grey and lifeless character disguised by distance. The boat was still tied to the jetty, which was odd given the sea was flat and calm. He wondered where the skipper and his crew could be, if not at sea. Certainly there was no one moving around the village, something he should have become used to by now but which he still found disquieting. Didn't anyone walk the dog or wash the windows? Probably not the latter, he thought.

The place was too strange for his liking. There were people around, the candles he'd seen early that morning testified to that, but they clearly did not want to make themselves known. Caitlin aside, the skipper was the only person he'd spoken to in a week. He could not shake off of a sense of the village itself wanting him gone.

At six that evening he knocked on Caitlin's door. Inside, the cottage looked just as he imagined it would. With no hallway the front door led directly into the living room, which had a large fireplace and wooden beams and a window with a sea view. The furniture was old but well cared for. On a table in the corner was an antique Singer sewing machine, made of black metal with painted floral designs. Richard's grandmother used to have one like it when he was small.

Next to the Singer, rather incongruously, was a Toshiba laptop.

Candles burned in holders. Through an open door he could see a kitchen dominated by a range as antiquated as the Singer. The air was warm from the open fire and rich with cooking smells.

"Anything I can do to help?" he asked.

"You could lift that sewing machine down. Careful, mind you. It's heavy. I usually leave it there and eat wherever I'm sitting."

Everything she served him was fresh, from the mackerel to the potatoes and carrots dug from her garden. There were greens she'd foraged along the shoreline, and which Richard had not tried before. Once he was done he saluted her with his glass. "That was superb."

She dipped her head. "*Diolch*."

"And you really didn't buy any of it?"

"Really."

"Where I'm from everyone relies on supermarkets. They

150

wouldn't know how to grow and forage stuff like you do. I wouldn't."

"You caught the fish."

"With your help. But, come on, you can't get lucky every time. What happens on days when you don't catch anything?"

She give him one of her little half smiles. "That never happens, Richard. *Mae'r môr yn rhoi i ni.*"

He recalled the skipper saying something similar. Richard did not have to ask what it meant, for Caitlin immediately translated. "'The sea provides'. And it does, Richard. We have everything we need."

He topped up their glasses. "I don't believe that's possible. Not in today's world. Sure, you can grow and catch or whatever, but you still use gas to cook on. And you have that laptop. And a Tesco."

A few days ago he'd noticed a supermarket delivery van pulling up outside her cottage. Clearly the locals saw no reason to make the long round trip to Aberystwyth should the sea ever fail to provide.

She reached out to touch his hand. "Conveniences. We move with the times but we could manage without them. We did in the old days. I don't recall life being any worse for being simpler."

For a moment it sounded as though she spoke from personal experience. Then he remembered Welsh, not English, was her first language. Some things were bound to get lost in translation.

"They don't call them the good old days for nothing," she said with a wink to make it clear she was teasing.

They finished the bottle of red he'd brought with him and started on one of Caitlin's. Richard learnt she made a living making traditional clothing that was sold in upmarket gift shops. The holiday let brought in some money, but not much. He was hardly surprised by that, remembering how he had almost driven past the tiny roadside sign advertising it while making his aimless way north.

In turn he told Caitlin a version of his life story. Divorced, no kids, deciding once he'd hit fifty to sell his car business in Bristol so he could do what he'd always wanted to do, which was travel while he was still young enough and healthy enough to enjoy it.

The rest of the story he kept to himself.

When they stood to gather up the dishes they were both a little unsteady on their feet. The wine had gone to his head and must have gone to hers too, for Caitlin reached out as if to steady herself. Then she was in his arms, her face turned up to his. They kissed for a long time, after which she took him to her bed without a word said.

Richard had no idea what time he woke afterwards. The room was in darkness. He could hear Caitlin's soft breathing beside him and eased out of bed so as not to disturb her. He opened the door to the living room to let in just enough light to find his clothes and then dressed and slipped quietly out into the cold night air.

*

"There used to be a chapel there, you know. Once upon a time."

Richard turned at the sound of her voice. He had got up with the dawn and taken an early walk through the village. Its inhabitants had remained typically reclusive, their houses as silent and forbidding as the cliffs. He had made his way to the end of the road with only the gulls for company. That was where Caitlin had called to him. He wondered if her being there then was coincidence or design.

"What happened to it?"

She nodded at the landslide. "That's what happened to it."

"Good God," he said, conscious of the irony. "Was anyone ...?"

"Killed? Yes." She slipped an arm through his and kissed him lightly on the cheek. There was no hint of the awkwardness he had feared between them after last night. "But it was a long time ago."

"Tell me about it," he said and led her along the rough ground where the road ended, and from there down to the beach.

The story she told was so tragic he was surprised it was not more widely known. Just before Christmas of 1897 the Welsh coast was pummelled by the worst storm in memory. It came from nowhere; when the fishing boats put out with the morning tide the sea was like a mirror. The pressure fell as the day wore on, until clouds blackened the sky and the sea grew heavy and wild.

A breeze became a strong wind that soon blew like a hurricane, turning the Atlantic against the land. Waves overran the wall and rained down onto the houses, blowing in windows and ripping tiles from the roofs. With the storm growing ever more ferocious, and with their homes flooded out, the desperate villagers sought shelter in the chapel. Built as it was of stone and stout Welsh wood they knew they would be safe there with their God to watch over them.

God, though, had His mind elsewhere that day and while the chapel was strong its foundations were not. It stood on a wide cliff ledge at the edge of the village. What the folk of Sŵn Y Môr had not known as they prayed behind those old stone walls was that the cliff had been weakened by centuries of exposure to extreme conditions.

No sooner had the storm waned than the ledge gave way.

"Nobody survived," Caitlin said sadly. The tide was out. They were making their way along the beach to the cottages, hand in hand, shingle shifting and scraping beneath their feet. "Some died directly in the fall, others were crushed when the chapel walls

152

collapsed on top of them. Those that were left drowned when the sea rushed in."

Richard glanced at her. She seemed upset, as if the events were of a more recent vintage than a century and then some ago.

"The fishing boats never returned," she said, so softly it was a struggle to hear her. "Only one failed to go out that day, because it had been taking on water. Its captain and crew should have lived because of that. Instead they drowned in the chapel ruins."

Richard stayed silent, aware there was a very good chance some of Caitlin's forebears had lost their lives that day. A long time ago, but history had a way of haunting you when it was personal.

They reached the top of the steps and rested awhile to catch their breath. Richard stared out at the calm Atlantic, thinking that while the sea might provide it also took whatever it wanted in return.

"It calls to you, doesn't it?" she said, out of nowhere.

"What does?"

"The sea. You feel at home when you're close to it."

"I like the sound of it," he said, remembering Weymouth and trying hard to forget. "Always have, I guess."

She leant in close and said, "It's not good to be alone for too long." Then it was her turn to lead him, first to her cottage and then to her bed. Soon after they were done Caitlin drifted off in his arms. He lay awake for a little while, listening to the whispering sea, until he too sank down into the endless depths of sleep.

*

Such was the pattern of the weeks that followed. They woke with the dawn and spent their days walking together, either along the cliff tops or, if the weather was bad, through the village and back along the beach. The village still felt abandoned but with Caitlin at his side its unnatural silence no longer bothered him. He thought he glimpsed occasional fleeting movements in the windows. He never saw the skipper again, though every now and then he did catch sight of the fishing boat, a smudge on the distant horizon.

Evenings they spent in her cottage, where he would read while she stitched her Welsh clothing, the little round glasses she wore perched on the end of her nose as she worked giving her the look of an old-fashioned teacher. They shared her bed every night.

He spent less time in his cottage and more time in hers until he was to all intents and purposes living there. The city became a memory, his old life began to feel like someone else's.

There were nights when she couldn't sleep, when she would work in the living room as quietly as she could. If he was awake he would hear the rapid thrumming of the sewing machine or the snip-

snipping of scissors. He never minded. To hear her was to know she was near, and that was all he wanted.

They fished too. Under her tutelage Richard was soon casting like an old hand and could tie some decent knots. They gathered mussels, foraged wild greens along the shoreline. One day Caitlin took off with a basket piled with food. When Richard asked where she was going she said, "To the village. Some of the older ones can't care for themselves. We look after our own here, see."

He remembered the fishing crew leaving a solitary crate on the jetty. Had that part of their catch been set aside for the same older ones? He remembered too the ancient, naked woman he'd imagined he'd seen through the window and felt his colour rise at the thought that he might not have imagined her after all.

"That's lovely," he said, partly because he thought it was but mostly to cover his embarrassment.

"So are you, *cariad*," she said, and kissed him.

Cariad. Like darling or sweetheart but more beautiful than either, like hearing a love song whenever she said it.

*

As December approached the weather closed in and they spent more time indoors than out. Richard left Swn Y Môr just the once, driving south to Aberystwyth to stock up with books. Caitlin had insisted there was no need, that it would be easier to order them online. He, though, worried the Saab might not start if he left it sitting idle too much longer, had wanted to take it for a decent run.

When he asked her to go with him she made out she couldn't because she had too much work to get done. While he had not noticed her being exceptionally busy he decided to let it go. Caitlin had been unusually quiet of late. He did not ask what was bothering her, feeling sure she would tell him when she was ready.

Between the winding Welsh roads and an unexpected snowfall the trip took longer than expected. It was dark by the time he returned. When he went inside her cottage it was as silent as only empty places can be. He put down the bag of books he'd brought in and hurried back outside, convinced something was wrong.

A full moon painted the world silver and made the cold air feel colder. Finding no immediate sign of her he stood by the steps and gazed at the Atlantic and the moon's gleaming twin it held captive.

Caitlin was waist deep in the water and moving further out. Even from afar he could tell she was naked, her skin turned pale and ghostly by the milky luminescence washing over her.

Before he could move or call to her, she arched her body and dived in, outstretched arms arrowed, legs kicking. She struck out, swimming with confident strokes, and for a moment it seemed to Richard in his distressed state that the sea had washed away her flesh so that all he could see was the dull glint of bone.

He blinked the vision away and rushed down the steps to the beach. There he waited, sick with worry, for her to come to her senses and get out of the water before the cold or the tide could take her. After what felt like an age she stood and waded to shore.

As she started making her way up the beach to the steps where he waited she saw him and cried out his name. He had worried she would be angry with him for watching over her, as if she was a child who could not be trusted to keep herself safe. Instead she ran to him and threw her arms around him and held her tight enough almost to hurt. Richard felt himself stained by patches of ice as water from her body soaked into his clothes.

"You came back to me," she said, sounding like she had trouble believing it. Her mouth tasted of salt when she kissed him.

Wrapping her in his coat he led her back to the cottage where he sat her in front of the fire and replaced the coat with a heavy woollen blanket. When he pressed a glass of scotch into her hands he was surprised by the warmth of her skin.

He sat down clumsily next to her, the strength deserting his legs as the enormity of what could easily have been sunk in. She rested her head on his shoulder and said again, as if worried he had not heard her the first time, "You came back to me."

He sighed, stroked her damp hair. "I was always going to."

There was a lull, then she said. "Come to bed."

Much later, in a voice made small by sadness, she said, "I couldn't live without you."

He shifted around on the bed so he could hold her and was dismayed to feel her tremble, as though she was only now feeling the cold she had not felt in the water. "And I couldn't live without you."

"But you will leave, one day. You can't stay here forever."

"Try and stop me."

"You can't stay, Richard. You have too much to lose."

"You're wrong," he said. "I have nothing left *to* lose."

That came out without him meaning to but he knew he would tell her the rest. The story spilled from him like water from a broken dam. He told her about his daughter, about the drugs that had killed her. An accidental overdose, the coroner had said, as if they should derive comfort from her lack of intent. And then one day Michelle left him too. He had a feeling she blamed him for their daughter's death, though he had no idea why. He'd been told she had remarried.

He was unaware he was crying until he felt Caitlin kiss the tears from his face. "Don't ever leave me," she whispered.

"I couldn't. Not now."

"You mean that?"

"Yes," he said. And he did, he meant it with all of his heart.

*

They came for him later that night while he slept. Before he properly understood what was happening, light on his eyes had broken his dreams and rough hands were rolling him onto his stomach.

His face was pressed into the pillow, muffling his cries of fear and outrage, and his hands were pinned behind his back. As hard as he fought he could not prevent his wrists being bound. His feet were free so he kicked and hit something soft. Before he could kick out again his legs were held fast and they were quickly tied too.

Shock dulled his brain. He could make no sense of this, could only think someone had broken into the cottage and that made him fear for Caitlin until he heard her say, "Careful, don't hurt him." The realisation she was a conspirator in whatever this was made him feel angry and betrayed and terrified all at once.

A hand reached under his chin to raise his head and a wad of cloth too bulky to swallow was pushed into his mouth. Something soft like a towel was placed over his eyes and knotted behind his head.

He was helpless to resist when they lifted him and carried into the living room. He heard the front door open and the air turned bitter. Outside, icy feathers brushed his face; it was snowing. He tried to break free, twisting his body violently, but the ties that bound him were too tight, the hands that held him too strong.

The sea was the only sound he heard as they took him into the village. Soon they descended a short flight of steps and he knew he was being taken to the jetty. There he was handed down to unseen others, who placed him in a sitting position with his back against a hard surface and his bound legs outstretched.

A gentle rocking; he was on a boat. Though he listened for voices he heard only water lapping the hull and waves shushing the beach. Then it became impossible to hear anything for the engine suddenly coughed into life and the boat started moving.

Richard tried to get up but the swaying of the deck and his own restricted movements outdid him. Panic set in when it occurred to him these people could do whatever they wanted and there was nobody who would be any the wiser. He had not told a soul where he was going. There had been no one to tell. He had long ago severed his ties with the past and all those who had ever known him.

156

He flinched as something touched his hair. The blindfold was lifted and there was Caitlin, crouching before him, an angel lit up in the darkness. Richard glanced around. The fishing boat was smaller than he recalled, coiled ropes and stacked lobster pots filling every available space on the deck. Light spilled from the cabin, showing the skipper stood at the wheel. Looking up, Richard saw gulls, pale as ghosts, drift in eerie silence across the starlit sky.

He tried asking Caitlin to take the gag from his mouth. Though he could say nothing intelligible around it she evidently understood. She shook her head, put a finger to her lips and nodded towards the slowly receding shore.

Richard turned his head until he could see what she wanted him to see; the houses of Sŵn Y Môr, indistinct faces watching from windows aglow with candlelight.

Movement closer by caught his attention and he saw perhaps a dozen people on the beach, striding into the sea. He found the sight profoundly disturbing and immediately looked away, sick with apprehension.

Caitlin sat down with him. Putting her arm around his shoulder she held him tight and leant in close so she could whisper into his ear. "Don't be afraid. Remember, *mae'r môr yn rhoi i ni.*"

She kissed him gently on his eyes. No sooner had she stepped away from him than the crewmen emerged from the shadows around the cabin where they had waited unseen.

Helpless with fright though he was, part of him remained stubbornly convinced this was not happening for real. It had to be a sick joke, a prank, a weird initiation rite of some kind. He was still thinking that when they lifted him up and dropped him over the side.

The water froze him. He had never felt such dreadful cold. It made him rigid with shock. When the sea closed over his head it sounded nothing like it did above the surface, there being nothing at all calming about the way it rumbled and gurgled and roared.

He felt an agonising pain in his ears and a weight on his chest that made him desperate to breathe but his mouth was still gagged and some survival instinct countered the urge to inhale.

Impulsively he kicked his legs but they would not move and through the numbness in his head he dimly recalled his ankles were tied, his wrists bound too. The pressure increased as he sank deeper. He snorted water through his nose, letting in a swirling cold that rushed down his throat and into his lungs like an incoming tide. It froze his bones to the marrow. It turned his blood to ice.

As his vision dimmed he thought he glimpsed blurry figures moving through the water towards him, bone-thin hands reaching out to either embrace him or to hold him down.

That was the last thing he saw before the darkness came.

*

It was still dark when he emerged from the sea, onto the beach where Caitlin was waiting.

Behind her the villagers were silhouetted by candlelight as they stood in their open front doors, ready to welcome him into their homes now he was one of their own. The boat was tied up at the jetty.

The gag was gone from his mouth and the ties from his wrists and ankles so he could move and breathe freely. He went to her as she came to him. They met and embraced and kissed long and hard. Her mouth had the taste of the wild Atlantic and he drank of her deeply. Though as naked as the day he was born he felt warm.

"I knew you would come back to me, *cariad*," she said. "Listen."

He listened. And he understood.

The sound of the sea was his heartbeat.

A QUICK PINT AND A SLOW HANGING

Wales is rightly proud of its upland hostelries. There is many a climber and hiker, after a tough day tramping the Welsh hills, been glad of the warmth and hospitality extended to him or her as they ventured through the doors of The Cornmill at Llangollen, or The Tafarn Sinc in Pembrokeshire, or perhaps most famously of all, the Skirrid Mountain Inn, near Llanfihangel Crucorny in Gwent.

Renowned as one of the finest mountain pubs in the world, the Skirrid is famous for its good beer and congenial atmosphere. But it's also the case that people once gathered here for darker purposes. In fact, this pub's memories can still induce shudders in the modern age – and sometimes worse. Take an incident from the 2000s, when a thirsty mountaineer had to be assisted from the premises, insisting he was being throttled by an invisible ligature. In ordinary circumstances, an ambulance might have been called ... had the staff and locals not been all too familiar with these symptoms.

There was certainly no cause for alarm, because as with other occasions when this had occurred, once outside, the stricken climber was restored to immediate health.

To understand the roots of this, one must look far back into history, when the Skirrid provided food and ale for weary wayfarers but also doubled as a court of law. The earliest written record we have of this comes to us from the 12th century. The current Skirrid building was not then standing, though another house stood on the exact same site and served the same dual-purpose. It was here where, in 1110, one John Crowther was condemned to die for sheep rustling, taken to the inn's main stairwell and hoisted by the neck to one of the overarching beams.

As one might imagine, hanging was no quick death in those days. Slow strangulation was almost always the outcome; a terrible spectacle, which often resulted in onlookers hanging onto the condemned's legs in an effort to speed his or her demise. Despite this, the tradition of hanging felons at this indoor venue continued until midway through the 17th century. The modern day building is believed to have been constructed circa 1600, from which point the rate of executions appears to have accelerated to an amazing pace. An astonishing 182 are said to have occurred over the following 80 years.

Why so many is a question often asked.

The answer is simple: lots of offences in England and Wales carried the death penalty; it was not until 1823, well after the Skirrid's main stairway ceased to function as a gallows, when the death penalty was restricted by statute to the crimes of murder, treason and piracy. It is also possible that many of those executions at the Skirrid were military in nature. The Civil War of 1642-51 engulfed all the countries of Britain, including Wales, and barbarous treatment was often dealt to those taken captive. In addition, the infamous Bloody Assizes were held in 1685 in response to the Earl of Monmouth's ill-fated rebellion against James II. Many of those rebels taken prisoner – 144 is a conservative estimate – met their fate at the end of a rope, and it is possible the Skirrid was witness to a significant number of these. The Western Circuit Court – the main judicial power behind the Assizes – covered South Wales as well as West England. But stories that Judge Jeffreys himself presided at the Skirrid are deemed unlikely. Lord Chief Justice George Jeffreys, the notorious 'Hanging Judge', is said to haunt countless locations across Southwest Britain, but his spirit was specifically placed at the Skirrid by Living TV's Most Haunted team in 2003. Despite this, and though Jeffreys was a Welshman, there is no factual account of him ever being present there.

Not that eerie evidence doesn't abound at the Skirrid.

For one thing, there are livid rope burns on the stout beam above the main stairwell, and these are believed to be genuine reminders that condemned men once swung from it. In addition, numerous hauntings have been recorded. At least two female ghosts are believed to walk the premises, one of those belonging to a local woman lying in a nearby churchyard. Numerous vigils and séances have yielded mysterious results, including one transmitted live on radio during the 1990s. And then there are the many visitors who popped in for a quick pint, only to later report – or is 'imagine' a better word? – the chilling sensation of an invisible halter slowly tightening around their necks.

THE FLOW
Tim Lebbon

In many ways, Ruth had never really left. But when she heard about the village being revealed again after six straight years of drought, she knew she had to go back. To see the only place where she had ever belonged. To relive that time when she had become her true self.

To make sure.

*

She stood high on the hillside and looked down on the distant remains. She'd prepared herself for the emotions this moment might stir within her, but when the time came she was surprised, because she felt nothing. Not sadness or joy, not fear or delight. Perhaps she was too far away to really see.

She moved down the hillside, looking for somewhere to sit for a while. She found a small stone memorial, one of six that had been built around the valley using stones from the old demolished chapel, and sat on the ground beside it. Someone had left a small bunch of flowers there recently. Though the petals were shrivelling and turning brown, they were still pretty. There was a card attached with scrawled writing fading to the elements, but she didn't bother reading it.

From high up, the view across the valley brought back so many memories. She'd spent over twenty years of her life in the little village, most of them happy, the last few much less so, and she'd walked these hillsides many times before. She knew them well. Knew the sweeps and slopes, the streams and small ravines. The places to hide.

"Bloody hell," she said softly, sighing into her cupped hands. It was getting chilly up here, even though the summer was not yet over, and the drought had sucked all but the final few pools of water from what was once a great reservoir. They said it would fill again, given time. They said it was an unusual occurrence, and one which the village's exiled residents should not take advantage of to visit their old homes. It was dangerous, there were sinkholes and quicksands, the walls still standing would become unstable once they started drying out. But there were those who'd already vowed to return, and some who said they were looking for lost things. One old residents' association had promised to remove any remaining structures and rebuild them higher on the hillside, tributes to the drowned village and those who had been forced to move from there. The local news even suggested there were those searching for a legendary hoard of jewellery that had been left behind.

People would be digging.

And that was why Ruth had to come. She could not allow anyone to go digging. Not after three decades of water had worked at the ground, washing it away here, burying it deeper there. Moving stuff around. Nothing was certain now that the tides of time had receded. After all these years had passed she had a whole new life to protect—a job as business manager of a large building firm, a husband, three great kids. She had respect in her London neighbourhood two hundred miles away. She was growing through her middle age gracefully, and disgrace had no place in her life.

Most of all, she could not let her nightmare become real.

She shivered, but it was little to do with the chill. Standing, leaning back against the stone memorial, she accidentally kicked the bunch of flowers so that it fell over. Petals scattered, and a waft of sweet decay touched her nose.

Mud, must, dampness, the rich smell of muck upturned, her dream is all this, so much more tactile and sensory than is usual in a dream. Many times she wakes and looks around her bedroom, searching for a trace of mud on the sheets or damp footprints on the pale carpet. She laughs at herself afterwards, but for a few seconds after surfacing she is struggling to surface at all. Gerald's hands are clawed around her shoulders, pulling her back down into the nightmare. She has the sense of a rapid, liquid movement beneath him, washing away his rot, flowing. His eyes are starting to open, bloodshot yellow orbs in the dark brown silt, rolling in their sockets as his face breaks surface and his mouth spews a deluge of foul muck. He cannot speak, but that says it all.

And then he rises, and this is when she wakes.

"Fuck's sake!" she said, angry at herself. The dreams never usually bothered her that much anymore, and they were so irregular that she easily forgot about them. Thinking about them now, here in the sunlight of a late Welsh afternoon, was just foolish. She was no fool. "Just concentrate, Ruth!" She shrugged the small rucksack higher on her shoulders and started down into the valley.

The walk down the hillside was surprisingly nostalgic, and while to begin with she did not recognise exact locations, she knew where she was. The lie of the land was familiar, its weight around her, the shape of the sky and the carved ridges separating them. It was as if she'd heaved on an old coat from decades ago and found that it still fitted.

She came across the copse of trees where she'd played with her

162

friends when she was very young. They'd built a tree house, and though the structure itself was long gone, she was amazed to see a trace of decayed nails in the old oak's trunk. She stared at these scars for a while, actually remembering tall, dreamy Gareth banging them in with a hammer he'd borrowed from his father. They'd had a picnic that same day – cheese sandwiches, lemonade, bitter apples scrumped from Mrs Machen's garden – then later they'd raced back down the lane into the village. The lane was gone now, overgrown and subsumed into the deep hedgerow between fields. She wondered whether Gareth was gone as well. He and his family had left the village several years before it was flooded to make the new reservoir, having no part in the lengthy legal processes, disputes, and demonstrations, and she hadn't heard of him since. He could be anywhere. Maybe he was dead.

Further down the hillside was a place that inspired a more complex mix of feelings. The old barn had been a ruin even thirty years before, and it was here that she and Gerald had first made love. She had been nineteen, him a couple of years older. He'd brought a blanket and a bottle of cider, and under the blazing sun of a day very like today they had their first experience of each other. At the time it had been nice. It had hurt at first, but she had gone back to the village smiling and happy. It had become Their Place, and they'd ventured there another half-dozen times that summer to make love, becoming more and more daring in their explorations.

The complexity of her feelings were because she only associated this place with good times. Gerald had only ever been loving and gentle here, nice to her, not violent and evil. That had all come later.

"Bastard," she breathed, looking through a tangle of brambles and ferns at what was left of the barn. Only one wall still stood, and it was held up by the undergrowth surrounding it. "You bastard." Ruth was surprised to find tears blurring her vision and she angrily wiped them away.

As she walked further downhill she knew what was to come, but she tried to keep her eyes down, seeing only what was close by. Another field, an overgrown hedge where she had to trample ferns to find the stile, a woodland she could not remember being there, and then she emerged from beneath the shadows of trees and saw the full devastation before her.

The valley was gone, and it took her breath away. In its place was the remnant of the vast reservoir. Thirty feet ahead of her and slightly downhill, the dried reservoir bed began. It stretched right across the valley in every direction, a monochrome splash of nothing upon the rich green palette of the countryside. It was as if someone had come to paint this scene and had yet to finish, leaving only the background tone ready for colours of life, the final scenes, to be painted in. A reservoir, perhaps. Or a village.

Even this close it was all but camouflaged by the layers of silt. It had dried in the sun to a pale grey, though darker patches across the valley floor showed where water was still present. It was the ghost of the place where she had been born and brought up, and which even after so long she still thought of as home.

Despite everything that had happened here, it was still where she belonged.

Ruth started to cry. This time she did not wipe away the tears because they were for all the right reasons. Not Gerald, but everyone and everything else that village had been. Her parents, owners of the small shop for almost fifty years before she and Gerald had taken it over. Her friends, forging a life for themselves in that small community of fifty houses, a school, a chapel, and a corner store. The people whose ancestors had built the village, and whose descendants would only hear about the place on long-forgotten documentaries or obscure YouTube videos. And the village itself, a disorganised collection of buildings that had grown around the small, cheerful stream and the pond that it birthed. Such a happy place now made sad. Sadder still now that it was no longer only in her memory.

With the landscape so altered, it took her a while to figure out where the old shop had stood. It took a little while longer to make out where the coal shed had been.

She hefted the rucksack, heard the clank of metal tools inside, and took her first step out into the grey.

*

Ruth stood in the space where she used to live and looked around at what was left. There was more than elsewhere. The shop that had been in her family for generations was no longer recognisable, but the layout was still familiar to her. The end wall had fallen, but front and rear walls still stood, and the top third of the fireplace was visible in the other end wall above the silt. There were even the stubs of shelf brackets still evident between stone joints, though the counter behind which she'd stood for several years had rotted to nothing. The doorway behind the counter, leading into the rest of the house, was half an arch.

Silt filled the room, feet deep. It clung to everything, painting it greyer than the vaguest of memories.

Gerald had proposed to her in this room, one evening when she was tidying the shop and locking up for her parents. He had first punched her here, too, close to the doorway. The first *real* punch.

She crouched and ducked through the half-arch, and then she

was in the room where she had killed him.

The staircase was gone. The hallway was misshapen, one wall bowed inward to such an extent that she crept carefully back out, certain that it would fall at any moment. She retreated from the remains of the house, and only then did she see the drift of smoothed silt piled against the other side of the wall.

She stared into that space and remembered what she had done.

He has her pushed against the hardwood staircase, bannisters pressing uncomfortably against her back, the stench of booze about him, hair greasy and stringy where it hangs over his once-handsome face, and it's all so unfair. Not in this house. This should always have been her happy place. In a way that's what upsets her more – that he can hurt her here, where her parents were always so kind, where memories were always so fine. He's marring those memories, and she hates him for it. That, and other things.

"You never would," he says, stumbling forward. His confidence is his downfall. She does not lower the knife, and his clumsy strike fails to turn it aside.

Ruth gasped and raised a hand to her mouth as she remembered. Seeing the place brought the memory fresher than ever before, with every smell and sight, every sound of flowing blood and dying breaths.

She sobbed, once, and then gathered herself and stood straight once again. It had been a long time ago. The guilt was a faded thing, mellowed by time in the manner of grief. She had never doubted that she'd done the right thing, but for years afterwards she had beat herself up about it, in those long quiet times when she was on her own. He'd cast his evil shadow over her even after his death – in guilt, and fear of being found out – and she hated the fucker even more for that.

Now she was here to make sure it remained history.

The coal bunker was close to the back of the house, and the small, heavy stone structure had withstood much of what had been thrown against it. The level of silt inside seemed lower than elsewhere, as if the ground itself had sunk away beneath the weight.

Sunk into a void, she thought with a shiver. As she shrugged the rucksack from her back, she had the sudden sense that someone was watching her.

She stood up straight and looked around. Everything had changed without her noticing. It was suddenly quieter, more still, the landscape holding its breath. Even the sunlight seemed flatter than before, a memory of heat. She felt eyes upon her – skin tingling, hairs on the back of her neck standing on end.

"Hello?" she said, but not too loud. Shouting seemed out of place here, as if the remains of the village were sacred.

If there was someone there, they were intentionally hiding away.

Ruth turned a full circle, seeing no one. But she did see the village as it had been in memory – the heavy bank of trees and bushes at the bottom of her garden, the several houses surrounding hers, the pub, the church spire that had been demolished before the valley was flooded. Some of the bodies in the graveyard had been disinterred and buried elsewhere, others remained where they had rested for a century or more. The gravestones had all been removed and a layer of gravel and concrete poured over the graves, but nothing could hide the fact that hundreds still lay there.

Hundreds, plus one more that must never be known.

She pieced together the segmented spade, stepped into the roofless coal bunker, and pressed the blade against the dried silt. That first cut into the muddy ground shocked her rigid as –

– the blade opens his skin and slips inside, smooth, meeting little resistance against his hated flesh. Gerald gasps and his eyes go wide. He lashes out at her. She pulls out the knife, shocked at what has happened, terrified at what she has done, and before she can drop it he lunges closer to her, impaling himself again. The metal whispers against flesh, warmth flows across her hand, her husband's expression shifts from shock to pain. "Ow. Ouch!"

She almost laughs.

He slumps a little, tugging the knife and her hand down with him, his clothes lifting so that she can see the pouting, leaking wounds and the blade still clasped tight between his ribs –

– the spade opened the soil in a fine, dry smile. She pulled back a little, staring at the wound she'd placed in the land. It pouted.

And someone *was* watching her, she could feel it across very inch of exposed skin, a creeping awareness that she had felt before but never questioned. Sixth sense, some people called it, but she'd never felt the need to put a name to what she knew.

"Who are you?" she shouted. "Where are you?" Her voice echoed across the barren, monotone landscape, the sound flat as if the greyness had stolen its life.

"Ruth Games," a voice said. She jumped, dropped the spade and turned around, and a man was standing thirty metres from her.

Gerald, it's Gerald, and his eyes will be filled with mud!

But that was ridiculous. She barked a nervous laugh and raised a hand in greeting.

He must have emerged from behind the stone wall standing there, the last remnant of one of the three Franklee Cottages that had once stood along the lane from her home and shop. The wall was clotted with dried mud and shrivelled water plants, and several holes in its upper reach held the rotten remains of roof timbers. "Ruth Games, it really is you."

"Gareth?" she breathed. He seemed taller than he'd ever been, gaunter, and his rich hair had mostly fallen away, those few fine strands remaining grey as the landscape around them.

He smiled. It should have illuminated his face, but somehow it avoided his eyes.

"It's so good to see you," he said.

"It's been ..."

"Over thirty years." His smile faded a little, still touching his lips. "Thirty-five? You're looking good."

"For my age," she said, berating herself. Was she really slipping into flirt mode? Here, now? She'd always held a torch for Gareth, even though they'd never been more than teenaged friends. She had often wondered how different her life might have been if she'd tried to turn that torch into a blaze.

"It's strange being back," he said. He walked closer, limping slightly. She was shocked that this slight weakness in him upset her. "Especially as it all looks so familiar."

"Really?" she asked.

"Well ..." He looked around some more, never focussing on one thing for more than a second or two. Even her. "Well, after so long away I can still see things ... still remember ..."

"I found where we built the treehouse."

"Oh, that old thing." Gareth's gaze flickered left and right, and every now and then he looked down at his empty hands.

"Why did you come?" Ruth asked. It suddenly seemed like a very important question.

"I'm looking for something."

"Me too," she said. They stood in silence for a while, surrounded by the washed-out remains of the place they'd both once called home. They had a shared history, and in this ruined village where time was blurred it felt so recent. He'd been tall and effortlessly graceful, a twinkle in his eye that all the village girls liked, imbued with a deep-set kindness that Ruth's mother had once called beautiful.

"Well ..." this older version of Gareth said. "I'll keep looking. Others will be here soon, so they reckon. People digging. I want to find it before them."

"Me too," she whispered. She was going to ask what he sought, and why, and what he'd been doing for all those years. But suddenly three decades felt like nothing. It was their time in the village that mattered, back then where they were mere kids, and now, when she was here to protect the memory of her past and however much future she had left.

He smiled, turned, started walking away. But she called him back.

"Gareth!" He turned around again. "This evening, will you sit on the hillside with me? We can watch the sun go down on the village, reminisce. I have wine and some food in my car, and I was going to camp. Just like the old days. Will you?"

"Of course," he said.

She watched him disappear eventually behind hills of dried mud and tumbled walls, and when she started digging again, she no longer felt eyes on her.

It must have been him.

*

Evening fell quickly in the valley. She was deep, but not deep enough. Her husband and children thought she was in Nottingham at a conference, and what would they think of her now? Digging in filth, seeking a corpse, moving herself closer to a secret that was hers alone? She was sweating, uncomfortable, hungry and thirsty, and knew that she needed to rest. There was a heavy sleeping bag in her rucksack, and the green hillside had never been so inviting.

She was covered in dust, as grey and timeless as the village she had returned to.

But she decided to keep digging. With every three spadefuls she removed from the hole, two more slipped back in when the sides collapsed. The fine, dusty silt was still damp this far down, but also fragile and wont to slump at the slightest disturbance.

They'll dig, she thought. *They'll come to see what they can find, tourists and historians and old residents of the village*. While she was living there, no one had reason to go excavating her garden. Under fifty feet of water, her secret should always have been safe. But now the novelty hunters would come, and the history seekers. She could not risk them finding Gerald down there after all this time, did not want to consider the uproar and the gossip that would ensue. It had been hanging over her forever.

She'd told everyone that Gerald had run away with a student from Cardiff. Those who knew him well had no trouble believing that of him, and those who did not – some of her family, friends, people from other villages – only felt sorry for her. Ruth played the part of the betrayed wife for a while, but then the plans to abandon the village and flood the valley came, and everyone had more important things to think about. Not at all sure she'd got away with it, she shovelled coal, but never let it get so low that she saw the compacted earth floor of the bunker, beneath which lay his shallow grave.

And sometimes she had those dreams.

His foul mouth that had kissed and bitten her, rotten teeth,

168

*peeling skin over mummified flesh, the flow of water somewhere
deep beneath him, and the soft, susurrant shhhh as he pushed up
from below and grit slipped away from his face, his nose, his open
eyes ... and they had always been open, even in his grave. Open,
and searching for her.*

"Damn it." She kicked a pile of soil and watched it disintegrate,
hearing no whispers.

One more time she pressed the spade in, moving soil, searching
for her murdered husband before anyone else came and found him.
But she went no deeper.

The lush green hillsides called to her. She went, crying, trying to
convince herself it was because she had grit in her eye.

*

She walked back uphill to where she'd parked her car, taking a head
torch from her rucksack for the last scramble up the steep slope. The
back seat of the BMW was tempting, but something about sleeping
out under the stars attracted her.

There was Gareth, too. She didn't like the idea of him sitting
down there waiting for her. She didn't want to disappoint. Hopefully
by this time tomorrow she would be on her way home to her
normal, safe, secure life, but for now he was her link to a past she
enjoyed remembering. A past before Gerald.

I don't know him anymore, she thought, thinking of Gareth's
thinning, grey hair and the limp. But though that was true, their old
friendship still hung between them. Besides, she could look after
herself.

By the time she walked downhill again it was dark, the
landscape lit by star and moonlight, her torch splashing her route.
She paused several times and turned it off, and the reflection of
moonlight from the vast expanse of dried reservoir bed was eerie. It
was a silvery colour, dusty, dead. She imagined shapes walking
there at night, and she was suddenly pleased that she would have
some company.

Gareth called her over when he saw the torch, and she found
him standing close to the copse of trees she had visited earlier. He
was smiling.

"I found it too," he said, pointing up into the canopy.

"You hammered your thumb," she said. "It might have been the
only time I heard you swear."

"Fucking hurt." He sounded so sad.

"I have a bottle of wine," she said. "No tent, but you can have
my sleeping mat. I'll just use the sleeping bag. That okay?"

"If that's okay with you, Ruth."

They sat close together, and Gareth spent half an hour building a small fire. They chatted about old times – friends they'd had, incidents, people from the village. Only after a while did their questions and comments involve anything later than the day Gareth and his family had left the village. Initially they didn't even talk about the compulsory purchase of houses and businesses and the construction of the reservoir. There was no need, because it was not part of a history that linked them.

They passed the bottle back and forth. It grew cold, and they both slipped on warmer clothing. At last their talk brought them closer to the present.

"I hear you married Gerald?"

"Huh. Yeah."

"Nice bloke."

"He was a prick."

"Oh. So what happened?"

"He ran off with a student from Cardiff." It sounded so false, so ridiculous, that she thought Gareth would laugh in her face. But he said nothing. He stared out over the silvery valley. Something seemed to haunt him, shadowing his features and stealing the life from his eyes.

"What is it?" Ruth asked. "What's bothering you so much?"

"This place," he said. "It's just ... weird. When we left I never thought I'd see it again. And when I heard about the reservoir drying up and the old place resurfacing, I thought it'd be an opportunity. But I wish I hadn't come back."

"Why?"

"It's not the place it used to be." He shrugged. He was stating the obvious.

But later, as Ruth huddled in the sleeping bag and tried to get to sleep, she began to think that he spoke a much deeper truth.

*

She knew that she was dreaming ...

Gerald stalked from beneath the trees, laughing, cursing, spitting soil from his mouth. He was wearing the clothes she'd buried him in, his body withered and leathery, eyes rolling in their sockets.

"Stupid bitch," he said, the words he'd spewed on her time and again. "Look at you. *Look* at you!" He raised his hand and pointed the knife at her. She'd left it buried in his gut, but now it was in his hand, blade still keen after all these years.

She was trapped in her slapping bag, unable to move, stand, run. She rolled like a butterfly constrained inside its chrysalis. Perhaps with the knife Gerald would free her.

170

She screamed, because it was so unfair.

It was the first time she had dreamed of him out of the ground. She *knew* that she was dreaming.

But still ...

*

She snapped awake, breathing hard, listening for her screams echoing across the landscape. Birds sang. A gentle breeze muttered between the trees.

She struggled quickly from the sleeping bag and looked around, but she was alone on the hillside. Gareth was gone. He'd left her a note rolled in the neck of the empty wine bottle, written on an envelope.

Ruth

I'm going home. I realise I won't find what I'm looking for here. Maybe you won't either. Think about it before you go back down there, won't you? I don't like that place anymore. It's not where we used to live and had those great times.

Thanks for remembering them with me. Take care.

Gareth

x

She felt sad. She did as Gareth had suggested and thought about it.

Then she packed her stuff and walked back down towards the old village.

*

She saw them from far away. They were the only splash of colour on the landscape. Dread filled her as she approached, but her feet took her rapidly closer, puffing up clouds of dust as she drew nearer to her old, fallen home.

There were maybe eight or nine people gathered there. Others were walking around the rest of the village, and Ruth wished that she'd finished her work yesterday. It would be so much harder today. Digging, retrieving, hiding the remains ...

Some of them turned to watch her approach. One shape lifted a hand and waved, and for a moment she thought it was Gareth. But this man was much older, shorter, and his other hand clasped an old woman's arm. She seemed ready to drop.

They were gathered around the dangerously leaning wall at the back of her old house.

Her heart hammered. *Turn and go*, she thought. *Get the hell out. Get away.*

Twenty metres from them she slowed, not wishing to approach the house.

"What is it?" she asked. But none of them answered, because moments later she saw.

The shape was huddled on top of the wall, exposed for the world to see. The skeleton sat – clothes rotted to scraps, dark hide visible here and there, shreds of dirty hair stuck to its browned skull – as if it had just finished watching the sunrise. It was hunched down, but not so low that she could not see both of its arms bent inwards, both hands resting around the wood-handled knife protruding from its belly.

"Oh, my God," she whispered. "My God."

"Quite," the old man said.

The slope of silt dried against the wall showed a mess of thin scratch marks, trails perhaps put there by loose skeletal digits. No shoe or footprints. No sign that anyone alive had placed the remains on view.

It seemed to be grinning at her. Staring right at her. *Look at you!*

Ruth turned away. She was going to walk, but she started to stagger. She did not want to attract attention, but she started to run. Out of the village, up the slope to the point where grey turned to green, still she felt those hollowed eyes watching her go, and heard that hate-filled voice mocking her every step of the way.

She fled her past. But eventually it would catch up.

DOPPELGANGER

One of the scariest hauntings on record anywhere – though technically it might not even be correct to classify it as a haunting – occurred in South Wales in the 17th century. It first came to light in the 1690s, in a series of scholarly letters apparently written 20 years earlier, and it concerns a family called Bowen, who lived in a comfortable house but as part of a remote community known as Llanellan, on the Gower peninsula.

The head of the family, Lieutenant-Colonel Bowen, a former officer in Oliver Cromwell's New Model Army and a hero of many battles during the Civil War, was having difficulty adjusting to peacetime. Since retiring, he'd become a loutish and debauched man, who eventually separated from his God-fearing wife and went to live in Ireland, where he apparently drank and whored to his heart's delight. But it was during his absence when the Bowen family's real problems at Llanellan began.

The first disturbances suggested poltergeist activity: banging doors, knocked over furniture, thrown ornaments. But then, to Mrs Bowen's disbelief, her husband mysteriously reappeared one night in her private chamber, apparently from nowhere, and demanded the right to bed her. The shocked woman knew her real husband was still overseas. Sensing a terrible presence, she denied the strange visitor her favours and it flew into a ghastly rage, screaming and smashing valuables. It only left – in fact vanished – when she prayed, leaving a scent of sulphur behind it.

But this wasn't the end of the menacing doppelganger.

From here on, it continued to appear, interrupting the family and their servants when they were working, eating or at prayer. Sometimes it was charming, at others threatening and full of base suggestions. On one occasion it was found awaiting Mrs Bowen in her bed, and allegedly stank like a carcass. Even when it wasn't present there were further poltergeist incidents, including violent assaults, which left family members badly bruised, and disembodied voices shouting in unknown languages.

Even the real Colonel Bowen was witness to these bizarre events. When his wife begged him to return home, the manifestations increased – he watched in disbelief as his own devilish twin cavorted around the house. It was the colonel who finally removed his family from this terror, taking them all back to Ireland with him, leaving the mansion to fall into ruin.

Folklorists are at a loss to explain this story. They note that prayer appeared to hold the foul thing at bay, but did not exorcise it. They point out that Llanellan occupied a wild, bleak spot on the Burry Estuary, which was often thought to be the abode of fairies. But they acknowledge there are no answers to be found here.

It remains a mystery today, but as a curious footnote to the tale, several years after the Bowen family left Llanellan, a shipwreck on the nearby coast saw several victims of the Bubonic plague washed ashore, the subsequent outbreak decimating the district. All the time this happened, the Bowen family, happily reunited as a result of the 'doppelganger' torment, were living safely in Ireland.

THE OFFSPRING
Steve Jordan

You have one new message: *Kelly – meet me in the Skerries as soon as you get this. I really need to talk."*

His voice was so full of tension, she barely recognised it as Delwyn's.

Kelly ran through the wind and rain, pulling her skirt down with one hand and her hood over her hair with the other, into the shelter of the *Skerries*. It was a popular student pub not far from the Bangor University campus. The interior, all varnished wood panelling, hosted a well-stocked, well-kept bar, new padded stools, a widescreen TV for the rugby and a small stage for local bands and quiz nights. In the warmer months the place boomed, but the wide windows on every side meant the mood indoors was often determined by the weather. On a day when it was pissing it down, the bar was bleak. All the homely browns of the varnished wood looked washed out and grey.

Kelly found Delwyn at the back, near the stairs up to the games room, sitting in one of the old armchairs as far away from the rest of the patrons as possible (two old men and a dog – quite busy for a Tuesday afternoon). He sat with his back hunched and his head hanging down like monk at prayer. When she approached, he looked up at her with wide, bloodshot eyes.

"Sit down," he said, scratching behind his ears as his knees jiggled nervously.

"What's the matter?" Kelly asked him. "You look shattered."

"I haven't slept," he said, avoiding eye contact.

They sat in an uneasy silence for a couple of seconds.

"And?"

He just stared at his knees, fidgeting. She'd never seen him like this. Despite their totally different backgrounds, they became friends during their first year in the student halls of residence. Kelly could pin it to one night in particular when they played *Streets of Rage* on Delwyn's *SEGA Megadrive* until four in the morning while the rest of the block was at *Bar One* getting shit faced and/or chlamydia. It didn't matter that he was a straight-talking rugby player and she was an animal biology student obsessed with RPG games – they just gelled.

"Did you go to Llanberis?"

He nodded.

"I read that the village has been getting pretty run down and depressing recently," she said, trying to coax him into engaging with her.

"Listen, you know a lot about animals, right?" he said.

She couldn't help but roll her eyes. "I study animal physiology, biology and habitats, yes."

"There's no way that … you don't get like, big stuff out there? Like, *big* animals out there?"

"What do you mean? There are no elephants in Snowdonia. Or Welsh dragons, for that matter."

"What about in the lake?"

"Artic charr, most famously. Nothing the size of a bus though as far as I'm aware."

He extended his right hand out front of him and held it straight. When they both saw how badly it was shaking, he pulled it back in embarrassment.

"What's going on, Delwyn?"

"I saw something."

"What did you see?"

He winced. "I don't know."

"Describe it to me."

"It was dark. I was walking near the lake. My uncle was doing my head in – I just needed to get out of the house. He kept insisting I stay inside. I wish I'd listened."

He looked like he could cry.

"Describe what you saw."

"I wouldn't know where to start. You wouldn't believe me. It was dark. It was so *big*."

He stood suddenly and let out a long, frustrated sigh.

"I can't do this," he said. "Just forget it. Forget I said anything. I don't really know what I saw. It was dark ... It was dark."

"Just try and calm down."

He paced, rubbing his eyes.

"I've got to go," he said, and walked straight out without turning back.

Kelly sat still, taking in what had just happened.

"Are you drinkin'?" She looked up to see the landlord looming over her with crossed arms. "If you're not drinkin' you'll have to leave."

She considered chasing Delwyn, but she wasn't sure she had the patience. It seemed far more tempting to take a trip to Llanberis herself.

"I'll take a bottle of Coke. To go."

*

176

She had to turn *Slayer* off so she could concentrate on her driving. The rain was getting dangerous, like nothing she had ever seen outside TV documentaries. Water fell onto the windshield like it was being fired from a Tommy gun. It wasn't a long drive, but already she was desperate to get to Llanberis. She relished the thought of heading straight into *Pete's Eats* just off the High Street and settling with a nice hot mug of coffee, as long as it took for the weather to calm.

When she saw the lake, she knew she wasn't far. Llyn Padarn shivered in time with the bullets of rain. On the opposite side, the Llyn Padarn railway track sat unused, dominated by mountainous terrain that was just visible through the mist of movement.

Despite the interminable wet grey, and the bleakness of the abandoned picnic tables and child's swings by the lakeside, Llyn Padarn was a beautiful sight. If anything, the weather only complemented its whimsical beauty. Llanberis was Snowdonia at its most picturesque – a living water-colour in every direction. It was easy to understand why landscapes like these had conjured such vivid images in Welsh folklore for centuries. As a visitor, Kelly felt like she was suddenly part of something fantastical.

The sight was so captivating that it took Kelly a moment to notice just how empty the lake was. It was raining the last time she visited with Delwyn, but the lake had still teemed with row-boats and kayaks. They'd visited together occasionally since Kelly's first trip while studying marine biology for a module in her first year. Ever since then, keeping tabs on the lake's ecosystem had become a hobby of sorts.

Llyn Padarn, one of the deepest lakes in Wales, was made a site of 'Special Scientific Interest' after it was discovered to be home to a big, red-bellied species of fish that had survived the Ice Age – the Arctic charr. Over recent years, the population of the species had been dwindling. Nutrients from raw sewage that found its way into the lake had caused a toxic algal bloom, harming the local ecosystem. Last year, the sewage network was re-routed and juvenile charr had been released into the lake to try and aid spawning. However, rather fascinatingly, the decline had continued. Perhaps whatever Delwyn had seen held the answer. If she could only see it herself, maybe get a picture of it, Kelly knew it could make her final year dissertation really shine. Hell, it would make her *famous*.

The blanket of water ahead of the car wriggled in waves, until it revealed something blocking her path.

She slammed the brakes of her Yaris so hard, her eyes felt as though they would launch out of their sockets. The car continued to skid forward. She wrenched the wheel left and right clumsily as adrenaline muddled her thinking. It was pure luck that she stopped just short of the massive tree that blocked the A4086 both ways.

She sat rigid and steadied her breathing until she was calm enough to process her surroundings. She looked around and checked her mirrors – there were no other cars coming in either direction.

Exiting the car and throwing her hood up, Kelly ran over to inspect the damage. The tree had stood beside a small, water-logged children's play area next to the lake. The tree's roots were still firmly in the ground. A couple of feet up, something had split the wood with such horrific force that it sent the tree's spine tumbling over the road. Branches lay snapped and bent either side.

Thunder cracked above her and faded quickly. There was no lightning.

As she stepped back toward the car, something floating in the lake caught her eye. At first she thought it was just a bin bag with air trapped inside it, but after shielding her eyes from the rain, she could see the faint outline of a man lying face down in the water, limbs submerged.

A strange helplessness overcame her. She couldn't swim to save her life, let alone someone else's. She ran towards the shoreline and called out, before realising that lifeless bodies rarely answered. She turned back to the road, hoping for a car to emerge through the rain that she could flag down and call for help. When none came, she checked her mobile. No reception.

She looked back to the lake – the shape in the water had vanished. She blinked a few times and squinted at the area where she thought she'd seen it. There was nothing. Uncertainly, she tried to assure herself it must have been her imagination – she'd come here expecting to see something and had been spooked by the thunder, perhaps. Abruptly, she turned from the lake and began to run toward the village. She badly needed that mug of coffee now.

*

The afternoon was ageing quickly. The ceaseless grey around her was turning darker by the minute.

She banged on the red-painted wooden door again, hard as she could, desperate to get out of the stinking weather. *Pete's Eats* was the third place she had tried, but even her favourite eatery in the village was closed. The same was true up and down the entire High Street. She'd read a story in Bangor's local paper about the closure of the lakeside railway and the village's sudden decline in recent months, but she would never have guessed the extent to which everything had shut down. She'd seen the recession hit worn out seaside towns off-season, transforming high streets into rows of empty husks, but Llanberis? The place was gorgeous, how could any amount of bad weather or poor trade deter people from coming here? The village was in total hibernation. Almost, at least – some deranged soul had gone to the trouble of scrawling something in red spray paint on the wall of the white-painted house across the street. *Llamhigyn y Dwr*, it said, next to a badly-drawn bat symbol.

The pubs, the cafés, the shops – all closed. The hotels looked like haunted mansions and even the church doors were bolted tight. There were no cars in the road – none in the twenty minutes since she'd parked. There were no tourists, not even the middle-aged bearded men in rambling gear looking to tackle the breathtaking plains, and those fools loved some insane weather; it made the walk more of a challenge. Occasionally she saw someone walk hurriedly down the street only to disappear. If she passed them, their eyes did not meet hers.

Out of sheer frustration, she ran out into the crossroads between the High Street and Goodman Street. She looked in every direction, waiting for a car – anything.

Nothing moved but the rain.

She was startled by a short burst of a siren. A police car had stopped in front of her.

She ran to the driver's window as it opened.

"Are you alright there?" asked a young, local uniformed policeman from the driver's seat. An older, bearded, scrawny looking man in a tie and raincoat sat next to him.

"I don't suppose you can tell me where I can get a tea around here?" Kelly asked.

"Everywhere is shut at this time, best go home if I were you," the young one said, before his attention drifted past her. "Look, sir."

He pointed to the graffiti bat symbol across the road. The older one shook his head like a disappointed headmaster, and then regarded Kelly warily.

"May I ask what business you have in Llanberis, madam? Not exactly tourist season," he said.

"I don't see how that's any business of yours," Kelly said, instinctively apprehensive.

"Well, from your accent I'm guessing you're a student," he said with a knowing smile. "Just go home and stay well away from the lakeside. The whole place is out of bounds."

"Why?"

He hesitated.

"Lake might be toxic," he said, his smile fading. "Best not to take any chances."

"I'll be sure to," Kelly lied. "Thanks for the warning."

*

The rain had calmed to a gentle spitting by the time she was ready to meet her contact. She continued on toward the National Slate Museum – a fairly nondescript-looking set of grey buildings that she'd never been inside.

The mysteries of slate didn't really interest her. The railway that stopped there, on the other hand, was a different story.

She approached the small station to see *Bedwyr* resting along the track waiting for her, an old locomotive with three small carriages behind it. Caradog, dressed in his worn out trench coat and railwayman's cap, stood beside the grand machine.

"Aye," he called, and waved her forward.

"Caradog."

"Hello young miss," he said, characteristically upbeat. "Good to see you again. How do I find you this winter's eve?"

"Wet-through and cold, but ready to go. Thanks for agreeing to this."

"No problem. Any excuse to give the old girl a test, keep her parts going. *Bedwyr* here will take you up to Pen-y-Lynn and back again, the loop set up so we'll be back without a problem," he said with real relish. "She moved up here from Bala Lake a couple year back. Only locomotive here now since we had to close. I just couldn't bring myself to sell her."

"Seems like everything's closed around here," Kelly said with sympathy. "When I visited last with Delwyn … when was that, six months ago?"

"Aye."

"Well, then the place was bustling. Okay the weather was better then but … the village is deserted. What's happened?"

His expression turned absent and cold.

"A lot of people have been moving away. I expect you know all about the fish numbers dropping."

"Yes."

"Well, recently the livestock in the farmland has been disappearing overnight. Started just after *Calan Gaeaf*. The farmers tried barbed wire and electrified fences, to try and deter whatever was killing their livelihood. It just carried on mind. The fences were untouched, but the cull continued. A few days later, a fisherman disappeared. A few more since. They just vanished. What's better, I ask you? Moving away or vanishing into thin air?"

The memory of the body in the lake reared its ugly head.

"Didn't mean to scare you, love," Caradog said, apologetically. "Thought you would know."

"You're saying that livestock and fishermen have been disappearing?"

"Aye. Near Llyn Padarn, north and south. Some crazy man, the police reckon," he said scoffing.

"What do you think it is?"

"Who am I, Kojak?" he joked, but his eyes betrayed fear. "So, what's this all about? Seems like a strange thing for someone to want to ride the old railway in pitch darkness."

"I want to try and get as much of a view of the lake as I can, as quick as I can."

"In the dark?"

"You let me worry about that. It's for a module I'm researching. Nocturnal mating habits," she lied. "Plus I want to see if there's any evidence of sewage still being dumped in the lake. Police told me it was toxic."

Caradog shrugged. "Heard stupider things I suppose."

Kelly could believe that, most of them from his own mouth.

"Did you ever see any strange wildlife out here?" she asked.

"No," he said instantly, and a little sharply.

"Delwyn was here recently. Saw something that scared him half to death."

"Sorry to hear that."

"Seen anything strange at all?"

"Goo."

"What?"

"I keep seeing piles of goo around the place. Mostly in the fields around the lake, occasionally hanging in bushes. Like, this kind of see-through gunk stuff. Weird, isn't it?"

"Could you be any more specific?"

"Not really. Slipped on some and nearly broke my bloody arse. Do you think it's anything to do with that sewage you're after?"

"Not unless the sludge has grown legs and gone for a walk about," Kelly said, with all the sarcasm she could muster. Caradog gave a dry laugh.

"Shall we get going?" he said.

"Just one more question, do you know what *Llamhigyn y Dwr* means? Am I saying that right?"

"Seen it too have you? Bloody kids, scaring people. It means Water Leaper. Tiny things they are in the stories, sort of like a frog with bat-wings. Tiny. Nonsense superstition, is all. Now, I really must insist we get going. Do you want to ride up with me or in your own personal carriage, my lady?"

He did a little bow like a dame at a pageant.

"I'll take this carriage," she said, climbing aboard halfway down the train. She was anxious to avoid distractions, especially

Caradog's tedious ramblings. She needed to give the lake her full attention.

"Just make sure you stay in it. If you hear anything, give me a shout."

"Hear anything?"

Caradog looked up at the sky, like he was cowering from it. "You'll know it if you hear it."

*

The rain ceased, and moonlight prevailed.

The rail track stretched all the way across the lake's northern shore and, as she'd hoped, it gave her a great view of the lake. She set her camera to night vision and took a look through the scope – it was crystal clear. If something came out of the water, if anything happened, she'd see it and capture its image in a second. If it was dangerous, the train kept her constantly on the move.

The lake remained still.

Nothing unusual happened as they reached the northernmost part of the lake near the Pen-y-Llyn bridge, and turned back.

Her mind wandered as thoughts of her imagined 'Biologist Extraordinaire' fame dissipated into nothing. She considered what the police had said, and wondered what truth there was to the reports of the sewage being re-routed last year. Perhaps the organic pollutants in sewage had led to a genetic mutation. But not in any known wildlife; something 'other', something that had nestled in the incredible cold of the lake's depths until it was recently forced out into the open as the fish it fed on declined. Caradog said this 'Water Leaper' of myth was tiny. Perhaps things had changed.

Suddenly, she was wide awake again. She checked her watch. It was nearly nine. Across the lake, she could see the village – still silent. Perhaps only two or three lights were on in the houses.

Thunder clapped above. No rain came.

Then it clapped again, further south. The sound was moving.

And again, but louder and more distinct. It wasn't thunder at all – sounded more like a sail catching a strong wind over and over, or the flapping of giant dragon's wings.

Kelly stood in the carriage and peered through the glassless passenger window. She readied the camera for a killer shot. She extended the scope out of the window, and watched the night-vision screen as she tilted it up at the sky directly above her.

There was a load solid thud – like a *splat* – against the carriage roof above her, so strong that the carriage shook and her concentration slipped, along with the camera from her fingers.

"No!"

She made a desperate lunge for it, even touched it for a moment with the tips of her fingers, before it fell from her grasp, hit the rocky bank beside the train and bounced into the lake. She watched it floating there, until the train sped away and it was out of sight.

She slammed her fist on the chair next to her before willing herself calm. A wasted day in the pissing rain – and just what the hell had hit the carriage?

The thud sounded as if something wet had landed. An image of a half-eaten body hitting the roof flashed through her mind... then something slid off the roof and dropped past the window.

It was a large, thick lump of transparent goo. It drooled down the edge of the carriage like spit from the mouth of a bulldog. Kelly stood rigid and wide eyed, watching the dense, disgusting liquid pour from above her.

"What the hell *is* that?"

"You say something?" Caradog called back over the noise of the locomotive.

She willed herself from the safety of the middle of the carriage to the window opposite the drool. She stuck her neck above the window, and looked up.

Still nothing, and yet she could hear the strange flapping sound above her in the darkness of night.

Instinct told her that they needed to get back to the station quickly. Whatever was going on, she didn't want to be part of it anymore. She stepped over the small barricade onto the next carriage, making her way towards Caradog to ask him if their progress could be hastened. When she caught sight of him through the front carriage, she saw his face, mouthing silent prayers, captured in glistening-eyed terror.

Kelly threw her head out the carriage window and looked up again – and saw nothing her years of biological study could explain.

Its sheer size was the most frightening thing – to look up and see something so vast bearing down on them. Putrid sludge seeped from the sides of its wide, lipless mouth.

Two bulging, bile-coloured eyes looked down at her. It was a frog's face, drenched in slime and twisted by mutation. Flanking its emotionless features were thin, webbed wings, the membrane edged with razor-sharp spikes. Hanging below the legless body, almost touching the carriage she'd been in a moment before, was a lizard-like tail, tipped with the thick, venom-injecting barb of a scorpion.

"Get back inside!" Caradog screamed.

Kelly whipped herself back inside the carriage, and kept down low as she muffled her mouth with her hands, trying to force back the screams.

The wings flapped.

The creature retreated toward the mountains, then circled back again, its tail tensed and ready to strike.

It charged toward them. Its scorpion barb pierced the metal roof of the carriage with a horrible squeal, narrowly missing Kelly by inches. The metal creaked with a long, droning whine, and the carriage tipped over.

*

Kelly awoke to a throbbing pain in the back of her head. She opened her eyes to find herself lying on the carriage ceiling, surrounded by leaves and dirt. Her feet were submerged in water. She pushed her body up against the wall, lifting her boots out. She touched the back of her head, and pulled away fingers covered in blood. She could hear someone whimpering, and it took her a moment to realise it was her own voice.

Scrambling through the near window and out into the open, Kelly saw that the carriages and locomotive had been toppled.

"Caradog," she whispered.

Silence.

As she pushed herself to her feet, the pain intensified. Her vision blurred. She cradled her head, waiting for the pain to subside again before moving forward.

Bedwyr had fallen awkwardly and taken the worst of the impact. The chimney had been cracked, probably when it skidded down the bank and crashed into an outcrop of rocks on the shore of the lake.

On other side of the train, Kelly found Caradog. He was on the edge of the bank, lying on his back about four metres away from the crash. It was impossible to tell if he was alive or not. Kelly wasn't going to stick around to find out.

As she hurried away from the wreckage, her footsteps broke the silence and the lake suddenly stirred. From beneath the surface, giant bat wings shot out towards Caradog's prone body. The tips of the wings stabbed into the ground and pulled its drooling, slime-soaked frog face out into the open.

Kelly fell to her knees. She watched as the creature's stinging barb reared up behind it, coiling before shooting into Caradog's stomach. He made a choking noise that wasn't quite a scream. The stinger pulled away from his belly, leaving a gaping hole. Blood seeped from him.

His body contorted, and all at once, he began to disintegrate.

He was being pulled to pieces from the inside. His clothes were torn away; dark blood oozed from deep tears in the flesh beneath. Fighting and straining through the exposed organs and tissue were

184

tiny winged creatures. Hordes of them ripped the limbs and head from his torso, flopping onto the ground like slimy new-born calves.

As its offspring writhed and breathed fresh air, the creature's tongue shot from its mouth and licked up the torn and twisted remains, its blood-clogged slobber collecting at the lake's edge.

The offspring slid back toward the water, submerging beneath the blood. But the hulking creature stayed above, its body expanding as it took in air, its yellow eyes resting on Kelly.

She didn't even have a chance to scream.

PROPHECY OF FIRE

Thee is one particularly strange and eerie tale of old Wales that is unquestionably true. Though it had its origins in ancient myth, it evolved into a well-documented event in the Middle Ages and went on to have an all-too real and horrific outcome in London during the Reformation.

The Age of the Welsh Saints was a remarkable period of history, when men and women deemed to have been especially active in the path of Christ received astonishing levels of posthumous devotion. Throughout medieval Wales, there were processions and pilgrimages to hermitages and handsomely painted shrines, often in remote locations, where Masses and hymn services were held, and all sorts of relics and other treasures gathered. Many of these sacred personages – Pedrog, Tudwal, Brynach, Woolos and Gwladus, to name but a few – were practically unheard of in the wider realms of Britain, though there was one whose reputation had already travelled: St Derfel Gadarn, a monk of the late 6th century, who was also rumoured to have served as a knight at the table of King Arthur ('Gadarn' meaning 'the Strong').

Though a real person, who occupied the monastery at Llantwit, later founded a church at Llandderfel in Gwynedd, and finally died as Abbott of Ynys Enlli on Bardsey Island (his bones laid to rest among the 20,000 other monks who sleep there!), Derfel's origins are shrouded in unlikely legend. Not only was he reputedly a knight, who survived the cataclysmic battle of Camlan (where Arthur died) and only then turned to the religious life, he was also said to be a cousin of Hywel, the mythical King of Brittany.

Whether or not any of this has a basis in truth, St Derfel was massively respected across Wales and for some reason, possibly because of his former career in the military, was believed to have power to intercede for those condemned to Hell for committing mortal sins. Perhaps in this respect it is no surprise he was so popular, and this popularity only grew as the centuries rolled by. It helped that an amazing wooden image of Derfel – fully armoured and sitting astride a stag – was placed in the church at Llandderfel as a focus for veneration. Not only that, the statue was mechanical – parts of it actually moved, including the eyes, which blinked. This was not an attempted deception; everyone knew it was only a statue, but it must have been a wonder to the average medieval peasant. So miraculous was the image deemed to be that one Welsh prophecy held it would never be burned unless it "also burned down a forest".

And here the story takes a turn for the disturbing.

When the Reformation came to Britain, Thomas Cromwell sought to clamp down hard on those zealous Catholic enclaves "worshipful of gargoyles", in other words who knelt and prayed before statues. Even greater energy was put into this cause after the Pilgrimage of Grace in northern England, which in 1536 caused a real crisis for Henry VIII's government. Thus, in 1538, to the despair of the population of Llandderfel, the image of Derfel was hacked away from its mount and taken to London, where – "as a lesson to all credulous and treasonous fools" – it was to be ritually burned at Smithfield. At the same time, a certain Franciscan priest from Oxford, the official confessor of Queen Catherine of Aragon, was sentenced to death for refusing to deny papal supremacy in the Church. In addition to this, he refused to cast doubt on the heavenly powers invested in the image of Derfel, and so the Bishop of London decided – purely, it seems, for grotesquely theatrical reasons – to burn them both together at the same stake.

In a chilling fulfillment of the old Welsh prophecy, the name of the priest who perished in the flames on May 22nd that year, alongside the wooden statue of St Derfel, was Father John Forest.

DIALEDD
Bryn Fortey

The pale pink bathrobe she had been wearing when answering the door was crumpled on the hallway floor between two large and slightly ostentatious Japanese styled umbrella holders. "Take me, Peter," she demanded, pulling at his clothes. "Take me here! Take me now!"

"Take it easy," he muttered, kicking off his slip-on shoes while she kissed his neck, blew in his ear, then heaved his t-shirt up and over his head.

"No, not easy. I want it hard!"

Was she hot, or was she HOT! But someone had to keep their feet on the ground, even bare ones. "You're sure your husband is out for the day?"

"Of course I am."

He was now as naked as her.

"He thinks that silly office couldn't run without him. Never takes time off," she continued, pulling him down to the floor. "Makes do with a pub lunch so we can eat together in the evening."

The hallway boasted highly polished laminate flooring which, while fully admirable in itself, was not Peter's favourite surface for the sort of Sex Olympics Pauline obviously had in mind. "Wouldn't we be better in the bedroom?" he asked hopefully, but knew he was on a loser when she adopted her spoilt girl pout.

"For all Ben's size," she started, knowing full well he didn't like to be reminded how big her husband was, "he treats me like a piece of porcelain. He's so bloody gentle! So this time I want it rough and tough. I want you to take me here on this hard wooden floor, with no consideration whatsoever for my comfort or well-being. You comprehend, sweetie?"

"Sure." He didn't go quite so far as to shrug. "I guess ..."

"Sweetie Peetie ...?"

Knowing his liking for old blues singers, Pauline often called him after Peetie Wheatstraw, a bad-ass singer/pianist who called himself 'The Devil's Son-in-Law'. Usually when she wanted to get round him for something.

"Peetie ...?"

Well she was naked, he was naked, and the hall radiator was turned on. Also, it was what he was there for. Peter was a twenty-two year old self-styled Big City Playboy, Newport variety, working his way from a deprived childhood towards the better things in life. Pauline was a bored thirty-eight, married to businessman Ben who, yes, was called Big, because that was what he was.

When Pauline was played carefully, like an expert fisherman casting for a big catch, she could be a quite generous and understanding lady. Peter had left his car home this morning, with the intention of telling her how he could not afford the repairs needed for its MOT. So he pushed her roughly by the shoulders, forcing her flat on her back. "Okay," he drawled, reaching out and flicking both her nipples in turn. "You're my bitch girl, and don't you forget it."

"Ohhh, Peter," she moaned, and that was when the front door crashed open.

"I knew it! I just fuckin' knew it!" shouted an angry voice.

Pauline scrambled from him and scurried to the far side of the hall. Muttering that it wasn't her fault, between sobs, and pressing the knuckles of her left hand to her mouth.

Glancing over his shoulder from where he lay, Ben really did look big, and angry. Big, angry, and out for trouble. Peter started to crawl to where most of his clothes lay scattered, but Ben pinned him with a heavy foot to the centre of his back. Which hurt.

"Oh no, boyo," he hissed theatrically. "You're going nowhere."

Peter had had narrow squeaks before. Of course he had. Big City Playboys took their chances and knew the score, but he'd never been caught quite like this. Then Ben removed his foot so he rolled quickly onto his back, correctly guessing that a good kicking was on the menu.

The first swing landed on Peter's outer thigh and he twisted round to grab Ben's foot before he could kick a second time.

Ben pulled.

Peter hung on.

Ben pulled harder.

Peter let go.

Ben staggered back, losing his footing and shouting obscenities as he fell into the coat rack. Peter grabbed the nearest item of clothing and was up and running before he could recover. Through the front door, past Ben's car, out into the cold day and onto the roadway. Still as naked as the day he was born.

"Come back, you bastard!" he could hear Ben shouting.

"Good morning, ma'am," said Peter, passing an extremely surprised lady out walking her pet Pekinese.

He finally stopped when it seemed reasonable to assume he was not being chased, and when there was no-one near to take in his nakedness. Peter held up the one item of clothing he had managed to escape with. Pauline's pale pink bathrobe. Luckily she boasted a quite statuesque figure so, even though a little tight, he was able to double-knot the belt and successfully cover the physical embarrassment of total nudity. Though what it might be doing for his psychological wellbeing was another matter entirely.

A number of years back, when Newport was still only a town, all this would have been totally unthinkable. At least now, the freer attitudes of a cosmopolitan city meant that even exotic creeds and beliefs could be clasped in a metropolitan embrace. Peter knew he was a Big City Playboy but if anyone, seeing him like this, thought it possible he might be a Big City Gay Boy, well, he could live with that.

"Good morning," he said with a nod while passing a couple of elderly pensioners, feeling happy in their shared state of bonded citizenship.

"Poofter!" the old woman shouted at his fast receding pale pink back.

There were always exceptions, he thought sadly. It was at that moment a mobile phone in the bathrobe pocket started to ring. Boy, did he jump.

Peter stared at the shiny red mobile phone while the tinny ring-tones of a fifties pop hit did little to calm his startled sensibilities. He lifted it slowly to his ear.

"Okay, you slime-ball gigolo," thundered Ben's voice. "Pauline has put me in the picture, so I'm up to speed with how parasites like you prey on ladies of a certain age, and I've got all your details."

There was a pause, but Peter thought it best to remain silent.

"I've got your wallet in my hand," continued the angry husband. "I know your name, Peter Mark Cunningham, and your address. I even know your National Insurance Number. I've got you taped, buttoned down, in a hole with no way out. I'm not finished with you yet, Peter Mark Cunningham, not by a long way."

Peter slipped the phone back into the bathrobe's pocket. He was beginning to wonder whether or not this might be a good time to ditch the flat and move back in with his parents for a spell. Changing his address would therefore be no problem. Even changing his name would not be too much hassle. He wasn't too sure about his National Insurance Number though.

Parents: always there, ready to help. That little welcoming light shining in the window of their hearts. But maybe he had better not turn up dressed only in a woman's pale pink bathrobe. Not in the Pill area, Newport's old Dockland. Not with his workshy father still clinging to an old-time hard-man status that no longer had any meaning. Not with his mother almost permanently under the influence of antidepressants and cheap cider.

Maybe it wasn't such a good idea after all.

Up ahead maybe half a dozen ten to twelve year olds, who should have been in school, were loitering on a corner, sharing cigarettes.

"Hey! Look at 'im!"

"Why're you dressed like that, mister?"

"He's a nut, that's why."

"He's a tranny."

"No, trannies wear wigs and false boobs."

"Well he's half a tranny, and all nut."

"That's for sure."

Peter held his head high, quickening his pace to get passed and away from them. It was no way for a Big City Playboy to be spoken to, not by these youngsters nor Ben on the phone, but he kept his dignity intact. As much as circumstances would allow.

"Take no notice, babycake. The cheeky little devils give me a much worse time than that."

Peter had not noticed, till then, that he had company. The newcomer was slim, sleek and tidy. Not a hair out of place. Dressed a little flamboyant for Peter's taste, and with just a hint of – oh dear! – makeup.

"There is definitely something, hmmm, theatrical about you," the newcomer suggested.

Peter stopped and looked him straight in his delicately shadowed eyes. "There is a perfectly reasonable explanation for my current predicament," he told him, "and it in no way involves my sexual orientation."

"What a pity," the newcomer said. "You have such beautifully defined cheekbones."

"Look," said Peter, "as a citizen of the world, I defend your right to be whatever you want to be. This home of ours, this Gateway City to Wales, holds tolerance to its municipal bosom. All I ask is that you endorse the same privilege to me."

"Are you sure you're not gay?" he asked.

"Piss off!" responded Peter, turning sharply and striding away, other things now becoming more uppermost in his mind. He would soon reach Stow Hill, leaving these more residential streets behind. There would be the St Woolas Hospital and Cathedral to pass and then the steep fall down to the city centre. And all that meant people, lots of them, and him still dressed in a pale pink woman's bathrobe. Also there was the question of Big Ben lurking in the background.

In the short term he could still change his address, and name. Even see what could be done about his National Insurance Number. If things looked really bad he could even relocate to Cardiff.

Cardiff?

Well, maybe not.

Turning a corner which brought Stow Hill into sight, Peter was astounded to see that the main thoroughfare he was making for was completely filled with black men wearing tribal costume. All seemingly carrying short or long spears and shields. Some with ostrich feather headdresses, some without, but all moving towards the Newport city centre.

Whatever the occasion, some sort of festival he supposed, though not one he had heard about, it could be to his advantage. He could tag along with whatever the celebration was, drawing relatively little attention to himself.

Peter even allowed himself a smile as he hurried to join the throng. A gathering such as he had never seen before. He was still smiling when the long spear, the *assegai*, struck him in the chest. Peter was dead before he hit the pavement. His body gave a single spasm, the pale pink bathrobe turning dark red as the blood spread from his terrible wound.

Peter was not the first to die this day, and he would not be the last.

*

The Zulu hordes came pouring down Stow Hill in much the same way as the Chartists had in 1839, but this time there were no Redcoats with muskets waiting in the Westgate Hotel. There was no longer even a Westgate Hotel itself. Yet another retrogressive step which, according to Simon's grandmother, was further proof that Newport had been a really nice town turned into a rubbish city.

"Why are some of them wearing ostrich feathers?" asked Belinda.

"Chieftains," guessed Simon, saying it as if he really knew, gripping her elbow as a couple of a*ssegais* thudded into the boarded up former Burtons shop front. Guiding her quickly past the jewellers – she would only start looking at engagement rings – they ducked into Phones 4 U.

"What's going on?" he asked a cowering sales assistant.

"It's all over Wales," she replied, an hysterical edge to her voice. "Zulus everywhere. Invading! Killing! There's bound to be atrocities."

"Atrocities?" echoed Belinda, turning it into a question.

"What about resistance?" demanded Simon. "Has the army been mobilised?"

The salesgirl shook her head. "All the networks are down now," she explained. "No way to find out anymore."

Newport's only problems since becoming a City had been economical, but this was something else. A council meeting would surely be called. Even Cardiff Bay would be a hive of activity, realised Simon. He was sure the First Minister would be rallying the nation.

Outside the Zulus were milling around, killing any locals they came across. Chanting, shouting, waving their *assegais* and shaking their cowhide shields. Simon noticed that one word being repeated quite a lot was '*Dialedd*'. Strange that invading Zulus should be chanting the Welsh word for vengeance. Strange, and rather scary.

The three of them, Simon, Belinda and the salesgirl, crouched behind the counter while a sea of black bodies ebbed and flowed past the Phones 4 U shop front. Cries of fear, terror, and of hurt, intermingled with the shouts and chants of the African invaders.

Then the shop door burst open and a Zulu warrior charged in. Simon and Belinda held their breath and tried not to move, but it was too much for the salesgirl who jumped up and made a dash for the door.

With a triumphant whoop-like shout, the Zulu hit the girl across the head with the wooden shaft of his *ixwa*, a short stabbing *assegai* as opposed to the longer throwing variety. Dropping both his shield and weapon, he set about stripping the stunned girl, and himself.

"Ah ..." whispered Belinda quietly to herself. "Atrocities ..."

Rising, before Simon could stop her, she lifted a large display stand and crashed it down on the Zulu's head, probably killing him there and then. To make sure though, as the screaming girl disentangled herself from beneath her would-be-attacker, Belinda picked up his *ixwa* and plunged it into his back.

Simon looked at his girlfriend with a new and sudden respect. Up until now he had stayed with her because of Belinda's enthusiastic experimentation in the area of bedroom gymnastics. Maybe not the best basis for lifelong commitment, but the short term advantages added up.

It seemed quieter outside the shop now. The invaders seemingly working their way down Commercial Street. "What's going on, Simon?" asked Belinda.

"Well it might sound daft, but the only thing I can think of is that this is the Zulu Nation's revenge for Rorke's Drift."

"Rorke's what?"

"A Mission Station in Southern Africa where one hundred and fifty British and Colonial troops held out against three to four thousand Zulus in 1879."

"Eighteen seventy fucking nine!"

"I know." Simon shrugged. "But why else are they here, shouting vengeance in Welsh?"

"I saw it on the tele," broke in the salesgirl, now on her feet and dressing. "An old film with Michael Caine talking posh."

"That's right, and I'll bet all the Zulus have seen that film as well. The regiments concerned, though based at Brecon, were not primarily Welsh, recruiting heavily from the Birmingham area. The film wrongly named them the South Wales Borderers, which they weren't called until a couple of years later." Simon was in full lecture mode now. "Of the known nationalities comprising the 24th Regiment of Foot at the battle, forty-nine were English and thirty-two were Welsh. If they want true vengeance, maybe they would be better off invading Birmingham."

"For God's sake, Simon! People are being speared to death on the streets of Newport, and probably throughout the rest of Wales as well, and you're giving a bloody history lesson!"

Well someone had to evaluate cause and effect, thought Simon peevishly, but decided against making an issue of it. "It looks quiet out there now," he said instead. "Maybe we should make a dash for it."

"I'm not," said the Phones 4 U girl. "I'm going to hide in the back of the store until I know it really is safe to leave."

"Belinda?"

"I'm game."

You certainly are, my dear, you most certainly are, thought Simon as he gently opened the shop door. There were plenty of bodies, including a few Zulus, but mostly Newport residents. People who had been shopping or just passing through the city centre, totally unprepared for what fate had in store.

A dying teenager, calling for his mother, breathed his last as Belinda reached his side.

It seemed that the Zulu force had split into three at the bottom of Stow Hill. Some advancing up High Street, others along Commercial Street, and a third force by way of Bridge Street, which probably meant they had the Civic Centre by now.

Skinner Street looked untouched so Simon guided Belinda in that direction, turning into Dock Street. "I don't suppose they're still running," she said, nodding towards the Bus Station entrance.

Simon just shook his head. He could see smoke rising beyond some of the buildings and the sounds and clamour of fighting could be heard. "Maybe we should have stayed in the Phones 4 U shop," he muttered, worried that any corner turned might lead them into the conflict. "This way will only lead us into Commercial Street and they have definitely gone down there. Better go back and find somewhere to hide. We were stupid to come into the open."

With Simon holding her arm tightly, they started to retrace their steps. If they got out of this alive, he decided, he was going to propose. He knew it was what she wanted and though he had been dodging the issue up until now, he was seeing her in a different light. There was more to the girl than he had previously realised.

"I do love you, Belinda," he said as they hurried down Dock Street, but before she could reply a group of men came running from the Bus Station.

"What's happening?" called Simon.

"They're in there," panted a man in bus driver's uniform.

"Butchering people hiding in buses," said another. "With those bloody spears! Killing them!"

"Behind you!" shouted Belinda, grabbing hold of Simon.

Coming out behind the men were about a dozen chanting Zulu warriors. "*Dialedd! Dialedd!*" they repeated, time and again.

"Split up," called Simon, desperately hoping that it might confuse their attackers if they went in different directions. Instead it merely confused themselves as they bumped one into each other as panic took over.

Oh God! thought Simon, was this really it? Was the last thing he would ever hear going to be that single Welsh word? Hadn't they learnt any more of the language?

Belinda grabbed hold of Simon as a dark shadow suddenly covered the sun. "What's happening?" she asked, pointing.

The chasing Zulus had halted, looking up. "*Dabulamanzi kaMpande!*" exclaimed one, and they all threw themselves face down onto the ground.

Simon, Belinda and the others turned, slowly, to see what on earth could have spooked them in this way. Standing there, distant yet near, was the huge and monstrous figure of a Zulu warrior chieftain, an unbelievable sixty metres up into the sky. It towered, probably over the whole of Wales, and Simon had recognised the name. Prince Dadulamanzi, the rashly aggressive half-brother of the Zulu King, had led the failed attack on the Rorke's Drift Station. But that was in 1879!

This can't be happening, he thought wildly. But if it was a vision or a dream, it was one they were all sharing.

"*KILL DIMOND Y RHAI SY'N DAL I WRITHWYNEBU,*" boomed the huge Zulu in a voice that carried far.

"Kill only those who still oppose," said Simon in a quick translation from the Welsh.

"*YN CYNNIG CAETHIWED I'R GWEDDILL,*" continued the apparition.

"Offer servitude to the rest," muttered Simon.

"What's going on?" asked Belinda. "I don't understand!"

"*DIALEDD YN FY!*" declared the new conqueror.

"Vengeance is mine," whispered Simon, dropping to his knees and pulling Belinda with him.

The new First Minister waved his gigantic *assegai* up into the clouds. "*DABULAMANZI KAMPANDE,*" he declared, for all to hear, "*TYWYSOG CYMRU!*"

"Prince of Wales," repeated Simon in English, as he bowed his head to the pavement.

The other men followed his lead. Belinda too, crying quietly with a mixture of anger, fear and the frustration of not knowing what was to come.

Oh we're fucked now, thought Simon bitterly. Well and truly, shafted to the hilt.

THE DARK HEART OF MAGNIFICENCE

Plas Mawr at Conwy, in North Wales, is one of the most magnificently preserved Tudor townhouses in the whole of the United Kingdom. First constructed in 1585 by Robert Wynne, a local MP and County Sheriff, it was regarded as an extravagant masterpiece at the time, and it still stands today in much the same condition, complete with many original features.

However, there is a dark and disturbing story at the heart of Plas Mawr's history. It concerns the occupancy of the house by an 18th century family whose name has been lost to antiquity. According to the story, the head of the household, an officer in the army, was dispatched with his regiment to serve on the Duke of Marlborough's campaigns against the French during the War of the Spanish Succession (1701-1714). As the war dragged on, stories reached Britain that terrible battles were being fought, and that a colossal death-toll was mounting. The strain on the family at Plas Mawr, who had received no word of their loved one, became intense. The missing soldier's wife was ailing badly by the time news arrived that her husband had returned from the war safely and was headed for home.

In her eagerness to see him as he approached, she ran up a dark stair to the top of the house with her youngest son in her arms – only to trip and fall a considerable distance. The pair were later found by servants at the foot of the staircase, both severely injured. A certain Doctor Dic was called. All we know for certain about this practitioner is that he was young and inexperienced – and unfortunate, because when he first saw his two patients laid out in the Lantern Room, they were already dead. At this inopportune moment, the master of the house returned, a scarred and dangerous veteran, roaring for his family.

Young Doctor Dic was so frightened that he attempted to escape by climbing up the chimney, only to become trapped in the maze of dark, airless shafts, most of which were clogged with soot and other filth.

The returned soldier, beside himself with grief, searched the house, intent on killing the doctor who had failed his wife and son, but never finding him. In fact no-one found Doctor Dic ever again.

The luckless practitioner was wedged into his secret hidey hole, and there he either suffocated or starved to death. His rotting bones are still lodged in place somewhere behind the mansion's heavy stone walls. But is it his ghost that now roams the house at night, *opening doors and banging cupboards as though searching endlessly for something he can never find? Or is it the spirit of the deranged husband, still seeking vengeance for the deaths of his wife and child?*

THE RISING TIDE
Priya Sharma

E verything's wide at Newgale; the beach, the sky, but it's
water that draws me. The sea goes on for miles.

The rising tide comes in, chasing and baiting. I scream at
it, but it doesn't help. I still feel dead. The crash of the waves
swallows up the sound.

I wander. Further up the beach are surfers who look as sleek as
seals, dressed in neoprene as they brave the breakers. How free they
must feel.

A figure walks towards me. A girl, with a dog that turns in
circles around her. The animal crouches, belly to the ground,
waiting for her to hurl the ball she's carrying. When she does the
dog's off like a shot, making ripples and splashes on the water
glistening on the sand.

Closer, and I see the girl more clearly. The sight of her shocks
me to a stop. Her black hair streams out behind her in the wind. The
girl's mouthing something. I think it's my name. Her dog bounds up
to me, sniffing and licking, keen to be acquainted.

"Get down, you brute." She catches the dog's collar and hauls
him back. "I'm so sorry."

I try to speak but my throat is tight. I'm choking on emotions
that I can't swallow.

"Jessica?" The word comes out, faint and strangled.

It's not Jessica. There's no way it could be her. Not here. Not
now. This isn't a teenager but a woman with straight, brunette hair,
not Jessica's lively black curls.

"Are you okay?" The woman puts the dog on its leash. "Can I
do anything to help you?"

I shake my head, tear stricken and mute. She lingers for a
moment, looking awkward and uncertain, and I have to turn my
back on her to make her go away.

*

"Have a seat."

My GP ushered me in. Pictures of children that I presumed were
hers hung over her desk. There was the overwhelming odour of air
freshener as if she'd sprayed away her last patient.

I explained why I'd come. She passed me a box of tissues when
I started to cry.

"It sounds like a terrible situation for everyone." Her vague tone made me think that, having listened to my tale, she'd already apportioned blame. "What's your mood like?"

She asked me the standard questions relating to my malady; poor sleep, inability to eat, mounting anxiety and loss of pleasure.

"Any thoughts of suicide?" She clutched the string of bright beads around her neck.

"No," I lied.

I'd thought about getting on a train and running away. I'd thought about throwing myself under one.

"Could you fill this in for me?" It was a formal depression questionnaire. The modern NHS requires that everything be quantified, even misery.

She totted up my score.

"Right, I think we should start antidepressants." She was brisk. The use of 'we' gave the process an illusion of democracy.

"Yes."

"Citalopram, twenty milligrams a day," she said.

Citalopram, a drug to keep my serotonin circulating. To bathe my brain in this happy chemical and make me well again. Or functional, at least.

"Do you need to see a counsellor?"

I shake my head.

"I'll write you a sick note."

"I can't go off sick."

"Nonsense. You're not well enough to work."

"I can manage."

"It's not just about you." She uncapped her pen. "It's about patient safety too. You need a clear head."

Patient safety. That stung, as it revealed what she, and everyone else, must have really thought of me.

*

Arosfa's the name of the hut that stands on the top of Treffgarne hill, near Lion's Rock, within sight of a cluster of houses and church that comprise the village.

Arosfa. An apt name given by my father. It means 'remain here'. That's all I want. To stay here and never have to face the world again. It's all I have left of Dad. We'd come here at weekends. He'd shrug off his overalls and roam as if set free. We'd walk and talk all day. I'd go with Dad while he went about his real vocation; a cleansing or a healing ritual.

Now Arosfa's windows are dirty and the floor unswept. Dad would be upset to see it so neglected.

When I get back from Newgale, the door's ajar. I stand, listening, sure that I'd locked it before I left. There are no signs that it's been forced. I push the door open. No one's there but I have the feeling of being only seconds too late to see who was standing there.

Nothing. Nothing but the stained and faded curtains, made in exchange for Dad's shingle cure, which hang in the window. Dad's empty whisky bottles, thick with dust, line the shelves. Each one was payment for a divination or a charm. His books are swollen with damp but look undisturbed. Piles of my clothes are left where I dropped them. Dirty cups and plates are all over the place. I should clean up.

Then I see the wet patches that stain the floorboards, making them darker. Footprints. Not the outline of shoes but heels and toes, fainter along the arches where the curve lifts away. I put my foot alongside them. The intruder's feet are smaller than mine.

*

My mobile's flashing at me. I've got a missed call.

"Cariad? It's Tom." There's a pause. There's a hard edge to his voice, like he's daring me to be furious at him for his defiance. "I know you said not to call but we need to talk. About the girl. About us."

The last thing I want to do is talk.

"Let me know you're okay, even if you don't want to see me."

More silence.

"Let me help you. You don't have to go through this alone." His anger rises. "The thing is, I love you. And I think you love me."

I wish he'd said it before Jessica. I wish I'd said it back. Not just because I'm too ashamed to face him now but because depression's a dark hole where no light goes. Your dearest wish becomes as inconsequential as crumbs.

I don't deserve Tom.

"Cariad, please ..."

I turn off the phone, cutting him off mid sentence.

*

I had met Tom on the first day of my new job in the Casualty department of Bronglais General Hospital, Aberystwyth. It was a new speciality to me, a new hospital and a new town. My orientation session had been curtailed after half an hour due to the department being busier than normal so I had no idea where anything was or who to ask for what. The staff were a hard, sardonic lot.

"Maria, would you mind looking at this x-ray?" I asked. Dr Maria Callaghan, registrar, was our supervisor. "This bloke hurt his shoulder. I'm not sure if there's a hairline break of his ..."

"Posterior or anterior?"

"Sorry?"

"What did they teach you at medical school? The force of injury," she enunciated each word, "was it posteriorly or anteriorly?"

"Oh, anterior. Head on tackle."

She slapped the film onto a light box.

"No fracture. No dislocation."

Then she walked off.

I could feel the blotchy flush breaking out on my chest and face, the redness a beacon of upset, anger or embarrassment.

"Hey, don't let her get to you. I'm Ellen." Her badge said Nurse Practitioner. "Or, don't let her see when she does. If you need help, come and ask me."

If Maria was bad, the paramedics were worse. It takes a certain sort to survive the forefront of the frontline.

"We need you in our ambulance, now." A paramedic stopped me in the corridor. "I can't tell whether this guy's dead or not."

He ran out to his domain, parked in the ambulance bay. I followed thinking how badly hurt is this man, that they're not bringing him inside? Were they expecting me to perform heroics, such as a chest drain or tracheostomy?

We got into the back of the ambulance.

"What do you think, love? Will he make it?" The paramedic roared with laughter.

The man on the trolley stared at me with a blank eye. The other side of his head was a nebulous hole full of crushed eye, shards of skull and macerated brain.

The door opened and a second paramedic addressed us.

"Piss off, Glynn. Let her alone."

I should've told Glynn to piss off myself but my mouth was too dry. Not that I was squeamish but it was surreal. I'd never seen a human head so decimated.

Glynn got out, still giggling, and the other man climbed in and closed the door.

"Sorry about him. I'm Tom." I must have looked particularly stupid because he asked if I knew how to verify a death. "I mean, you might as well do it now that you're here."

I nodded. Of course I did, but before Casualty I'd worked on a ward for the elderly where death occurred in bed or on the toilet.

"What happened to him?"

"Tyre blew out and he hit a tree at high speed. Poor lad didn't stand a chance."

Tom was tall. He stood back, not crowding me like Glynn had.

I checked the body, a pointless exercise to formalise the obvious. No heartbeat, no breath sounds, no pain response, the lone pupil fixed and dilated. Rest in peace.

"What's the C stand for Dr Evans?" Tom asked when I handed the form back to him.

"Cariad." Meaning darling, dearest.

"And are you?"

"What?"

"Beloved."

I scowled at him. It was only later that I realised he was flirting with me.

*

I reinforce Arosfa's door with bolts from a shop in Haverfordwest. When I wake the next morning the light's mean and thin, unable to reach the corners of the room. The crows caw from the trees.

I get up and brush my teeth at the sink, not bothering to clear it of dirty dishes. I use bottled water as what's coming from the tap is brackish. I should get the electricity reconnected. It would be better than camping lanterns and torches.

I sit outside on the stone bench, wearing a jumper and coat over my pyjamas. The foil strip crackles as I pop out an antidepressant. I wonder what Dad would say about it as I swallow the pill.

Physician, heal thyself.

I remember lying on the camp bed in the dark. I was sixteen. Across Arosfa there was silence instead of Dad's breathing from the depth of dreaming. I looked at my watch. The luminous hands told me it was two in the morning.

"Dad?"

He was outside. There was no light pollution to nullify the night and hide the stars.

"Why are you up, Cariad?" Dad took off his jacket and put it around me. He took a slug from his bottle of whisky. "Are you okay, chick?"

"Yes."

He touched the curve of my cheek where there was a bruise.

"Are you going to tell me then?"

"You've heard it all already."

"Yes, I've heard it from everyone. Just not you. Cariad, you're not one for scrapping. What made you go at that girl like that?"

"I hate her."

"I don't recall bringing you up to hate people. It's bad to wish ill on others. The universe will send it back to you, ten fold."

I scowled.

"What did she say to get you so riled?"

"She said …" I struggled to say it. "She said that you were a piss artist that sold crap and empty promises."

"I've had worse said about me." I shot an angry look at him as he laughed. "I'm sorry." He nudged me. "Think about it. She didn't say that, Cariad. Emily Appleton's never had an original thought in her life. That's her dad talking. We've always agreed to ignore stuff like this. Why did you get so upset?"

"I just did."

He took a deep breath. I'd never spoken to him in that tone before.

"Cariad," he said slowly, "I think that you got so upset because you think she's right." Dad was wily. "It's okay, you know. Don't cry. This is how life works. You've got to find your own way."

"I'm not rejecting you." I wiped my face.

"When did you get so wise?" He laughed. "Will you promise me something?"

"What?"

"Keep a door open here, for possibilities." He tapped my forehead. "Don't close your mind to the idea that beneath what we know there's a whole world that we can only guess at. There are things in life that we know that we don't understand. The real danger is the stuff in the blind spot that we don't even know exists."

"That's a riddle."

"It's the long way of saying that what you don't know about is what bites you in the butt."

*

"Sorry to keep you waiting."

I'd been seeing my GP for four months. I felt like she was sick of me. Or maybe I was sick of her. Or sick of still feeling the same.

"How are you?"

She was an expert in communication, having had special training. She knew exactly how to tell me that she didn't have much time without saying it aloud. Her gaze kept darting to her computer screen.

"Improved." I cut things short, knowing it was what she wanted to hear.

"Are you less tearful than last time?"

"Yes." That was true. I'd gone beyond crying.

"Are you sleeping?"

I nodded. I slept through afternoons, having spent the night lying awake. Two in the morning was the hardest time. The drowning hour where misery was at its deepest.

"Any idea when the inquest will be?"

"Not yet."

The thought was terrifying. I didn't want to face the family's anger and the Coroner's inquisition.

"Cariad," her face softened, "I'm not trying to rush you back to work but the longer you're off, the harder going back will be. When do you think you'll be ready to get back in the saddle?"

This from a woman who looked like she'd never fallen off the horse.

"Soon. Just not yet. I need a bit more time."

Before I hadn't wanted time off. Now I couldn't face going back.

"What will you do with yourself?"

"I'll go to my Dad's." I didn't mention that Dad was dead.

"Where's that?"

"Near Haverfordwest."

I wanted to be away. To leave Aberystwyth and drive along the blue of Cardigan Bay, past the painted houses of Aberaeron. I knew I was nearly at the Landsker line and home when I reached the Preseli Hills, whose blue stone made the inexplicable two hundred and fifty mile journey to the Salisbury Plain for the building of Stonehenge. The beautiful Preselis, whose hollows fill up with sun by day and at night the mist pours itself onto the road.

My GP's nails were bare but elegantly shaped, at the end of tapered fingers. I looked at her hands as she signed the sick note because I couldn't bear to look her in the face.

*

I sat beside Maria at the workstation, both of us writing in patients' records. She broke the silence. "You get upset easily, don't you Cariad?"

Any opportunity to undermine me.

"Do I?"

I tried not to sound defensive but I was strung out from self-doubt, stretched thin as an onion skin by the line of patients that never seemed to lessen. Sometimes I felt there was a whole wave of them about to crash down on me. Their fear made me fraught, as did their anger at being kept waiting. Waiting to be seen, waiting for test results, waiting for another doctor to come when a senior's opinion was needed.

"Yes, you should watch that," Maria continued. "Being too emotional is how you make mistakes. And you'll do no good trying to be everyone's friend. The nurses all tell me how caring you are, which is all very well, but it's only part of the job."

There was me, thinking it was the very essence of our vocation.

"Cariad, I'm not saying this to be hurtful. I'm trying to be supportive." Like all good bullies she knew how to couch her comments so as to avoid reprisal.

"Hello, my beauties." Glynn tapped the desk, the oily rag of a man eager for attention. "Which one of you is taking me out later?"

Tom hung back. We shared a smile that contained all that had passed between us. When I looked away, Maria was staring at me, unhappy with what she'd seen.

*

The cliffs at Newgale are covered in sporadic patches of gorse, some of it bearing yellow blooms. When gorse goes out of flower, love goes out of fashion. Another piece of Dad's wisdom. The cliff face is spotted with pink thrift and white sea campion. The rock itself is layers of different coloured stripes, marking time's strata. This is what we are. Layers of history, one event laid down upon another. We are less consequential than sediment.

The tide has carved out caves. We imagine that we can do what stone can't; that we can hold back the rising tide and remain whole and unaffected. So much for my grandiose plans of helping people. I can't even help myself.

I squat in one of the caves. It smells of rocks and salt. I've come armed with one of Dad's empty whisky bottles. I half fill it with pebbles and then say her name over and over, Jessica, Jessica, into the bottle's mouth. I pray her in and then screw the cap on. I'm not sure if I've recalled it as Dad taught me. This was his legacy, this knowledge that's so at odds with everything else about me. I wish I'd listened more when Dad talked.

The match flares in the cave's cold shade and I hold a candle in the flame, letting wax drip around the bottle top to seal it.

I'll contain Jessica this way. I wade out into the cold water. The tide dragging at my thighs threatens to drag me down. I've not got a good throwing arm but I cast the bottle out as far as I can. It lands with a splash and then it's gone.

*

I'd been working at Bronglais General for five months when I first met Jessica.

Saturdays were the worst. Inebriated brawlers and the hopeless attempting suicide were heaped upon victims of heart attacks and strokes. They threatened to overwhelm me. No matter how much I studied, I never knew enough. No matter how hard I worked, I couldn't keep up.

The girl in the cubicle was wrapped in a blanket. Her dark curls were stiff with brine. The woman that fussed over her was striking too. Like the girl, she had a beaked nose and black eyes but her hair was unruly and streaked with grey. She was taller, scrawnier, and her long black coat flapped around her as she moved.

"Hello Jessica." I read her name from the casualty card. "I'm Dr Evans. Are you Jessica's mum?"

The tall woman nodded. She hovered over me in a mix of anxiety and threat that I read as 'Look after my girl'.

"What happened to you, Jessica?"

"I nearly drowned."

"How?"

"My dog went into the water. We were on the beach." She smiled, rueful. "I went in after him and we got caught in a big wave."

"She was lucky," her mother's mouth became a thin line. "A group of lads were body boarding and one of them was close enough to reach her."

"How long were you in the water?"

"I don't know. It felt like forever."

"I'll bet. Did you black out at all?"

"No."

"Good. You must've been terrified."

Her mother started to cry. I envied Jessica that maternal love.

"I'm okay, Mum. Don't fuss."

I checked Jessica's chart. Her pulse and blood pressure were normal and she wasn't hypothermic.

"Come on, Jessica. Let's check you out."

She looked at me with admiring shyness, hesitating as if she wanted to say something. I paused, encouraging her to speak.

"I'm going into lower sixth in September. I want to study Medicine when I finish."

"Then we might work together one day. What do you think about that?"

I put my stethoscope to Jessica's chest and listened to the steady *lub-dub* of her heart as her atria and ventricles contracted in turn. Her lungs inflated normally, a healthy pair of bellows.

"Everything seems fine," I said. "How's the dog?"

"Damn the dog," her mother spat. "Leave the bloody thing to drown next time."

"He swam to shore in the end. Mum's friend took him to the vet."

The curtain twitched.

"Excuse me." Ellen pulled me from the cubicle. "Maria wants everyone in the resus bay now. There's been a pile up."

"One second," I told Ellen and went back in. "Sorry about that. Your chest x-ray is normal, Jessica. I think you're okay to go home. If you feel short of breath or get chest pains, a cough or fever, then we need to see you again."

I remember thinking, at that moment, that I'd hit my stride. My confidence was growing. I was finally playing my part.

"Are you sure?" her mother asked. "The vet's keeping the dog in for observation."

To which I replied, "Don't worry, Jessica will be fine."

*

Painful thoughts. They gnaw.

Everything's magnified by the unflinching lens of two am, my every defect, fuck up and misstep that obliterates any modest successes.

Then, of course, there's the one act that negates everything. Even when I close my eyes, it's there.

I get up, sliding from my sleeping bag. When I put my feet down, they land in a cold puddle on the floor. I'll check that the roof's sound in the morning. Not that it matters. Damp permeates everything. It's in the walls. It's gathered on the window. Everything smells dank.

When I go outside the night's murky. A gusty wind makes the low mist twist and swirl around me. It softens and blurs the lights of the houses. I need to pee but can't bear the idea of going to the *ty-dach*, the little house. The toilet drops into the neglected septic tank that's now rank. I don't want to be alone in there. Ivy has insinuated itself through the wall panels and crept up the inside. I walk out into the middle of the field instead.

Wet grass brushes my legs as I squat and relieve myself. Steam rises. A chill goes up my back which makes me feel exposed. There's a dense fog, blowing in fast over the hill. I'm vulnerable, unable to run and overcome by the idea that I'm going to die out here, knickers around my ankles, urine running down my leg.

I glance over my shoulder, wondering at the fullness of my bladder. The fog eddies and whirls in the wind, making shapes too fleeting for me to focus on.

My stream slows to a trickle. I hear something behind me, higher pitched than the hoot of an owl. I look back again, pulling up my pyjama bottoms. A black shadow is in the fog's depths. Something's coming out of the night.

It's taking shape, pulling itself together from pieces of darkness. It looks like a long legged figure with straggly hair. A raven of a woman. Her long coat flaps around her. She's covering the ground between us in great strides.

It's the *Gwrach-y-Rhibyn*. The Hag in the Mist. She's a death omen.

I run. As I near Arosfa I hear a shriek and I stumble. My mistake is looking back. The hag's in flight, her coat transformed into great wings. I try and scramble to my feet but my trembling legs collapse and because of this she passes over me with a shrill scream of frustration that her clawed hands are empty.

She's circling but it's enough time for me to get to Arosfa. I slam the door behind me, lock it and throw the bolts. The hag hits the door with a thud. I upturn the table and put it against the door and then sit on the opposite side of the room. I can hear a strange fluttering sound, as if she's hovering outside.

How long the night is. The wind picks up, rattling the roof. The hag taunts me. Just when I think she's gone, there's a sudden slapping sound against the door or one of the walls, followed by a flap, flap, flap as she prowls around Arosfa, trying to get in. I drag the bed to the centre of the room and sit with my legs drawn up and my arms wrapped around them.

Around dawn the wind drops and everything's quiet. I think the hag's gone. I doze off for an hour and then wake with puffy, swollen eyes. I pull the curtains and the clarity of the morning light mocks me, as does the torn black bin liner lying on Arosfa's step when I open the door.

*

Jessica was rushed in the night after I saw her. Glynn pushed the trolley. Tom worked on her as they went.

"Bleep the crash team. Now."

Jessica's skin was white, her lips cyanosis blue. The rhythms of resuscitation failed to rouse her. I stood trembling instead of piling in and helping. I couldn't even muster the basic primer for survival. The ABC of airway, breathing and circulation.

Her mother stood by, her gangly limbs impotent as they hung by her side. We looked at one another.

"What's happened to Jessica?"

"She said she couldn't breathe. By the time the ambulance arrived, she'd collapsed."

209

More doctors and nurses ran in, answering the call. Ellen pulled the curtain across the bay so that Jessica's mother wouldn't have to witness the indignities required to save a life.

"We need to help Jessica now," Ellen spoke to her mum. "Go with Jamie and he'll get you a cup of tea. I'll come and get you when there's news."

"I want to stay."

"Let them help her." Jamie put an arm around her, gentle and insistent. He was the best member of staff at calming relatives and breaking bad news. "We'll only be around the corner when she needs you."

There were enough people with Jessica, I told myself. I'd just be in the way.

Maria found me later, in the staff toilets. She stood beside me as I washed my hands, removing smudged mascara with her little finger. She watched me in the mirror.

"You saw her yesterday, didn't you?" She didn't need to explain who she was talking about.

"Yes. How is she?"

"It doesn't look good. She went into the sea, right?"

"She was fine yesterday. Her chest x-ray was normal. I don't understand."

"Secondary drowning." She uncapped her lipstick and applied the coral bullet to her mouth. It was as though she was suddenly talking under water. I had to concentrate on the movements of her lips. I must've looked blank because she started to explain. "The surfactant that keeps the lungs open gets stripped off the lungs by sea water. Drowning follows within twenty-four hours."

Maria didn't need to tell me. I'd read about it, briefly. Without surfactant, her lungs had collapsed and she'd starved of oxygen. So Jessica had drowned on dry land.

"What were her blood gases like?" Maria tied her hair up in a knot. "That's the crucial bit."

Blood gases. A special measurement to check the gas profile in the blood. As soon as she said it I knew the yawning truth was that I hadn't done it. I didn't know I should have. Like my dad said, the most dangerous kind of ignorance isn't what we know that we don't know but what we have no inkling of.

Which is a long way of saying that what you don't know about is what bites you in the butt.

*

210

I wake from fitful sleep with a start. It's dark. The mattress is sodden with water that's level with the bed. I turn on my camping lantern but it doesn't reveal where the water's coming in.

This isn't a leak. It's pouring down all four walls, flooding in faster than it can drain out.

I wade through water up to my thighs, lighting the lanterns as I go. I unlock the door but the top bolt won't budge. It looks clogged with decades of rust, not shiny and clean as it had been when fitted only a few days ago. I get down, soaking myself, trying to force the bottom bolt but this is stuck too. I shoulder the door in frustration but all I get for my efforts is a jarring pain from shoulder to elbow.

I try and smash the window over the sink with a chair but it's reinforced with wire mesh. Sodden, I haul myself up onto the narrow draining board which creaks under my weight. I try and kick the glass out, not caring about my bare feet, without success.

Stop. Be calm. I find my mobile by the bed but it's too wet to summon help. What else? Preserve the light, move the lanterns to higher places to keep them dry. My waterproof torch is in my bag. I put its loop around my wrist. The empty kettle floats. Plastic beakers and melamine plates bob past me. I'm flotsam and jetsam too. The room's filling up fast. I have to tread water.

Outside there's a frenzied barking. I shout, a waterlogged sound, hoping some nocturnal dog walker will hear me, but no.

The lanterns are submerged one by one. They glow momentarily making a ball of watery light, then they flicker and go out. Darkness magnifies the water's sound, the rush that's filling Arosfa up.

I turn on the torch. The white arc swings about, illuminating choppy water and the pale face in the corner.

Water's treacherous. It's brought Jessica to me. She's been baptised and now she's reborn. Her hair's plastered to her scalp. Her lips are dusky, her skin translucent and mottled from being submerged too long. Her neck and shoulders are bare. She glows, as if lit from within. Jessica opens her mouth and pebbles fall out. The bottle that I cast into the sea floats between us. The bottle top has been smashed off. Red wax still clings to the broken bottle's neck.

Jessica dips beneath the surface.

Fear's energising. I scream and thrash. Water slops into my mouth, drowning my shout. I taste brine, brine up here on Treffgarne hill.

There's churning, as if deep, vast undercurrents are about to pull me down. I feel a sharp tug at my pyjama leg. I kick out. Then Jessica yanks me down. I lose the torch in a panic. The beam of shrinking light descends.

Jessica's hand is clamped around my ankle as we follow the light into the depths. I might as well be out at open sea. Just when I think my chest will explode, she lets me go. I break the surface as if catapulted up, gasping and coughing. Waves buffet me about.

It's not mercy on Jessica's part. She's toying with me. This time I can feel her full weight, both arms around my calves like a clinging child. For someone so slight she's like a plummeting anchor taking me to the ocean floor.

This time we go further into the inky water. It doesn't make sense; we're too deep to be within Arosfa. It must be oxygen deprivation making me disorientated. I start to panic and struggle even more, desperate to inhale, even if it's just saltwater.

Jessica grants me another reprieve. Air has never seemed so sweet. I surface with aching lungs but all I can manage are shallow breaths. Not that there's much air left, only a few inches between the water level and the roof. I have to tip my head back to keep my mouth and nose clear.

It's not over though. Jessica comes up in front of me. I take a deep breath and tip my head so that I can keep her in sight. Her eyes are empty, like everything's been poured out of her. Her arms slide around me, like a lover's, her legs twine about mine. She's a dead weight. We sink like a stone.

The sea is vast. I'm weary of the struggle. I want to give in but the fear is physiological, my cells fighting to save themselves. The pain is surprising.

Then it comes. I have to gasp. I'm stunned as cold water floods my lungs, freezing me from within. Bubbles escape from my nose and mouth. Stars explode at the periphery of my vision.

Jessica releases me, which makes me sad because it's now that I want someone to hold me. I drift.

Being lost brings me a contrary clarity. My life returns to me. Mum, when she was still alive. It was dusk and I was in the garden of the cottage at Molleston, watching her as she stood at the sink. She looked up and saw me, giving me a broad smile.

I remember the afternoon sun sliding around a classroom. The algebraic symbols scrawled on the board finally rearranged themselves from a jumble into something I understood. In that moment I had the joy of intuition, of a knowledge as complex as my father's, and it thrilled me because it was mine.

I remember kissing Tom in a darkened room that was washed by the light of a mute television. Kissing him until my mouth felt bruised and swollen.

And Jessica's sweet, trusting smile.

The last bubbles escape into blackness.

Down at Newgale beach the sea is wide and the tide carries on rising.

THE HAG LANDS

One of many strange contradictions in the folklore of old Britain is the seriousness with which mythical terrors were regarded by rural societies who at the same time had to deal with everyday real-life horror. If anything, almost no distinction was drawn between the two. Bad things happened, whether by the hand of man, the whim of nature, or the will of mysterious unknown entities – it was all the same to remote communities.

For example, in the mid 16th century, a notorious band of outlaws called the Red Bandits of Mawddwy terrorised Meirionnydd. They raped, robbed and murdered with impunity, so dangerous that in 1555 one of those on their tail, the Sheriff of Dolgellau, also fell victim to them. Of course, the sheriff's death was an exception to the rule, and ultimately, as with violent crime today, the majority of the bandits' victims were harmless innocents who wanted only to lead peaceful lives. And yet for all this, the rural population of old Wales, particularly in the wild mountain districts, was far more frightened of the so-called Gwyllion, a hag-like fairy who existed solely to torment and abuse its human neighbours.

It's easy these days to scoff at such things. A preponderance of children's books has created an image in our mind's eye of the fairy as a diminutive, happy-go-lucky sprite, usually female, always pretty and dainty, often equipped with butterfly wings. The very word, 'fairy', has the ring of Enid Blyton about it. But not so the original term, 'faerie', whose curious 'old world' spelling seems to hint at a more sinister being.

The Gwyllion, or the 'Old Woman of the Mountain', is a good example of this.

Long known about in obscure Welsh legend, the Gwyllion was brought to the attention of a wider public by the writings of a Pontypool minister of the early 18th century, the Rev. Edward Jones, otherwise known as 'Prophet Jones' both for his frequent premonitions and his alleged dealings with otherworldly folk. According to Jones, the Gwyllion inhabited Wales's inner mountain regions, and would appear as hideous crones in long, tattered robes, usually to waylay lone travellers.

The most traditional version of the legend is embodied in the 17th century story of Robert Williams, a farmer of Crickhowel, who was making a long journey on foot, and had lost his way in the

Black Mountain range on the border between Carmarthenshire and Powys (what is now the Brecon Beacons National Park). It was early evening and a mist was falling. Williams was fearful of being marooned overnight, and so when he saw a woman tramping the path ahead of him – "a stolid countrywoman wearing a four-cornered hat" – he called out to her, and when she failed to slow down, hurried to catch up. Somehow or other, even when he ran, the woman contrived to stay ahead. The mist grew thicker, and thinking that if nothing else the woman might lead him to safety, Williams continued to follow – but a few minutes later found he had blundered from the path into a deep bog. As he struggled to free himself, a devilish cackling echoed along the road. He only survived the ordeal with strenuous efforts, and had no good thing to say about the Gwyllion afterwards.

An even more frightening tale is dated to around the same period, and features one John ap John of Cwm Celyn, who was also travelling alone in the Brecon mountains, on his way to Caerleon Fair. When he heard a voice from behind hailing him by his own name, he became concerned – nobody knew him in these parts. He hurried on, but the voice continued to call him, drawing steadily closer and ever more inhuman. At length, fearful he was about to be overhauled, John ap John lay face-down and refused to look up while something indescribable shrieked and cackled and danced all around him, clumping the ground with lumpish feet. Only after hours of this torture, did the Gwyllion leave him be. When he finally arrived at a friendly village, he was a gibbering wreck, swearing he would never again travel the Welsh byways alone.

Amazingly enough, such tales have persisted into relatively modern times. Some of them date from as recently as the 1960s. All could be apocryphal, or even a tissue of lies depending on how one wishes to view them, but the Welsh word 'gwyll' is often used to imply 'darkness and doom', and those matters are real enough whatever form they take. On the basis there is rarely smoke without fire, perhaps it's a wise policy never to be too dismissive of ancient tales, particularly in the hag-ridden wastes of the Welsh mountains.

214

APPLE OF THEIR EYES
Gary Fry

"If you're not careful, you'll start looking like an apple, mate."

"What do you … mean?" Smith replied, struggling to hold back another attack of acid reflux.

Jenkins, the student with whom he'd foolishly agreed to holiday this spring, tapped Smith's almost empty pint glass with one hand. "The gut-rot, pal. Bleeding cider. Christ, I don't know how you can stomach the stuff."

The hotel bar, a half-dead place on the outskirts of Llangefni, resounded with their inebriated bickering. After travelling yesterday from Yorkshire for a week's break on Anglesey, they'd planned to study during the days and get hammered in the evenings. But in the event, they'd just got hammered today. Well, what the hell; they were in their first year of a physics degree at Leeds and had plenty of time to muck around. During the next few years, there'd be alcohol, lectures, parties, studies, alcohol, debate, alcohol, and maybe even the odd girl if they were lucky …

Little chance of that here! Smith glanced around, at aged couples seated in alcoves nursing pints; at the bored-looking barmaid with heavy jowls; at his own reflection in the mirror beyond the row of optics. But there must be something wrong with the glass; it had clearly warped and made him bulge, as if he was suffering a mild hallucination. Then again, he had drunk ten pints of cider today, a feat to which his mate had just alluded.

"Quit whining, fella," Smith replied, but sucked in his rotund belly anyway. He was nineteen. Christ, what would he look like at forty? But he refused to think about that, and then completed his riposte. "It's like being out with a *bird*, for Christ's sake."

Jenkins smiled, an exhausted expression. It put Smith momentarily in mind of his late-father, the way the old sod had always treated him with sadistically amused indifference. In truth, it made him feel mad.

"Oh, bugger off to bed, if you can't take the pace," Smith went on, the booze in his blood inspiring little more than mean-spiritedness. He took another slurp of his apple-infused poison, letting it rattle around in his brain.

Jenkins got up from his bar stool, slumped across the beer lounge, reached the door leading up to their rooms, and turned to speak. "See you tomorrow, pal. Maybe by then you'll be a better frame of mind."

"Yeah, whatever." Smith swivelled back to his drink and lifted the glass, watching the off-yellow liquid swirl at the bottom. "Some bleeding fun you turned out to be."

Then there was just himself and a bunch of elderly folk, Anglesey's answer to nightclub ravers. Why had he and Jenkins decided to come here, anyway? His friend was from Bangor, of course, just a few miles from the Menai Strait. But that wasn't the main reason for choosing the island. The key thing was that they both liked quiet; they were intellectuals inspired by nature, history, tradition. And few places were more stimulating and downright mysterious than this small Welsh territory. They'd planned to visit Holyhead Mountain with its Roman watchtower; the medieval castle at Beaumaris; and the eighteenth Century copper mines in Almwich. And to *drink*, of course. Hell, what was the point of being nineteen if you couldn't lash your liver from time to time?

Smith returned to his pint, fumbling in one pocket for change. The first installment of his Student Loan was almost gone, and there were months before the next. He couldn't afford to blow much more on beer, not when he had so many nights to fill during summer. He supposed he could go home to Bradford and sponge off his mum for a while, but what fun was that? No, when it came to women, he needed a real ...

"Hello there," said a voice from behind, but after twisting on the stool and making the pub writhe in a drunken blur, Smith noticed who'd spoken.

It was a girl, about his age, and boasting the most amazing eyes he'd ever seen. He'd heard some people – poets, maybe; folk he'd read as a kid, even though his dad had made fun of that – describe such eyes as almond-shaped, but that wasn't Smith's first impression. In truth, he believed they resembled apple pips, the way they broadened around the iris and tapered to a neat point on either side. She wasn't even wearing makeup to enhance this characteristic. Otherwise, she was just a decent-looking young woman: fair flesh, a pretty smile, and – from what he could observe in his peripheral vision – a slender body. Her jacket certainly bulged in the right places. Smith felt his own body thrill to the unexpected sight.

"Oh, *hi*," he replied, only now getting his vision back under control. He sensed cider sloshing in his skull, compromising his words, his thoughts, his actions. But then he added, "Are you a ... local?"

"Local-ish," she explained, those eyes narrowing as the smile underscoring them stepped up its campaign. But the damage was already done: even without so much alcohol inside him, Smith reckoned he'd have been smitten.

They got talking and he bought her a drink – a cider just like his own refreshed pint – and half-an-hour later they were seated in an alcove recently vacated by two living corpses who'd gone home to read, talk politics or something equally unexciting.

"How do you stand it round here?" Smith asked, having realised that the girl's accent was authentically Welsh, suggesting that she was almost certainly a native of Anglesey. "I mean, I know the … island has its charms, but I'm not sure I could … survive on only Romans ruins and … rumours of druids."

The girl's smile grew broader, those eyes – as green as apples, Smith noticed in the beer lounge's warm light – flashing like patches of liquid.

"I get by," she said, and took another deep slurp of cider. She indicated her glass by tapping its rim with one pointed fingernail. "The drink helps."

He sniggered, only half-ashamed of his own frequent recourse to alcohol. Well, he'd had a rough childhood and there were things he still had to get straight in his mind. After taking another needful gulp, he said, "Amen to that … er … hey, that's a point. You haven't even told me … your name yet."

"You haven't asked."

"I'm asking now," Smith went on, leaning towards the woman and again sucking in his voluminous gut. *You'll start looking like an apple*, he heard his friend Jenkins's voice say in his head, but then told that to bugger off. In his drunken condition, this phrase had tugged at a buried memory and one Smith could live without, especially as he was on the verge of pulling some considerable local talent.

The woman smiled, her unusual eyes never failing to beguile him. But instead of revealing her name and consenting to the intimacy he'd hoped to establish, she lifted her almost empty glass. "Shall we get another drink?"

That was promising; she wanted more of his company. He quickly gathered the glasses from the table and rose to make for the bar. Student Loan be-damned! *This* was worth the investment.

At that moment, the woman laid one cool hand on his arm. He glanced down at the appendage, noticing thin patches of webbing stretched between the fingers … But then he realised this was just his vision, distorted by booze.

"Not here," she added, and her voice was alluring, like the noise sea-sirens were reputed to make. "The cider's vulgar. But I can take you somewhere for a *real* drink. And you have to believe me when I tell you that it's out of this world."

Did she mean her home? Was she old enough to have her own place, with no stuffy mother or – worse – a punitive father around?

Whatever the truth was, Smith decided to accept the invitation. How could he do anything else when a girl with such incredible eyes looked at him like that?

After bidding good night to the briefly reanimated barmaid, they were outside, heading across a starlit car park. There was only one vehicle in the shale lot – the girl's judging by the way she removed a key from one denim pocket and activated its electric locks.

"Are you okay to drive?" Smith asked, moving with the inertia of a pinball to the small hatchback's passenger side. If the girl, unobserved by him or Jenkins, had been in the pub before approaching Smith, she'd surely had another drink earlier, putting her over the legal limit. But maybe that didn't matter in such a godforsaken place as Anglesey. Maybe the chances of getting into any trouble were as remote as its tin-pot capital.

"Don't worry about me," the girl said, belting herself inside the car, just as Smith struggled to do. He had to pull the strap hard to clear his voluminous belly. Then the girl finished. "I know exactly what I'm doing."

Something worried him about this comment, but then the notion was gone, swept downstream on a toxic tide. As the car ducked and dodged its way through an almost deserted Llangefni, Smith found his mind rushing back to his studies in Leeds, to a foundation course on classical physics. He had a mock exam next month about Newtonian principles, about human enquiry back when the universe had been knowable, before all this quantum theoretical rot had ruined everything. Then Smith remembered drowning …

But he quickly pushed aside *that* particular memory. He looked around the interior of the car, reorienting himself to his circumstances. Maybe the cider had made him nod for a second, threatening to induce the dreams he often used it to keep at bay. There was now a heady stench of apples in the car, and he wondered whether he'd belched. Surely if this was the girl's perfume, he'd have smelled it back in the pub.

His fair chauffeur was talking, steering her robust vehicle along a country lane. The cosmos illuminated land around them, which consisted of fields, trees and hedges. That was all Anglesey was in Smith's experience: fields, trees and hedges. His and Jenkins's arrival by bus yesterday had hardly inspired awe. But perhaps the girl could change that now.

"Some argue that Anglesey is in fact Avalon, whose name is derived from the Welsh word *Afallach*, which means 'rich in apples'."

As soon as she said "apples", Smith sensed that heady aroma step up its assault. Now he had the bizarre notion that it was coming from the girl's mouth, as if she'd drunk even more cider today than

218

he had. When she spoke again, the smell only seemed to grow stronger.

"In Roman times, the place was indeed known for apple production. The historical chronicler Geoffrey of Monmouth called it '*Insule Ponorum*' – in other words, 'The island of the apples.' "

All this information threatened to bring Smith's violently repressed memory back to the surface of his reeling mind. The alcohol had dug deep in his psyche, and this woman – perhaps unwittingly, even though Smith couldn't be certain about anything right now – was tugging at the recollection. With so much brilliant starlight around the vehicle, the landscape took on a spectral hue, like raw bone licked clean by an ancient lake.

"What I'm getting at here, my friend, is that Anglesey has a reputation for fine apples," his new acquaintance said. "And we all know what apples, liquidised and fermented, are the principal ingredients of, don't we?"

She sounded like a parent instructing a child. Nevertheless, Smith immediately supplied the information.

"Cider," he said with another harsh burp.

The girl grinned, those apple-pip eyes more bewitching than ever. Her hands seemed to be wrapped around the steering wheel with far more flesh than there should be.

Then she said, "Not just *any* cider, mate. I'm talking about the *finest* cider you or anyone else will ever drink. That's where we're headed now. To the village where I live, in which we'll find what's believed to be the oldest tree on the island."

"An … apple tree?" Smith enquired with the intuitive acumen he knew would eventually gain him a second-class degree. Then the world appeared to swim again, taking on colours and shapes that were frankly impossible. Meanwhile, his driver babbled on about her beloved Anglesey – there was much material about the Roman, the druids, and once, rather alarmingly, something about human sacrifices – but by this time, he was unable to remain attentive. The memory he'd been trying to avoid had finally returned to bedevil him.

He'd been young, about six or seven years old, and had arranged a Halloween party at his modest Bradford terraced home. His mum – overprotective, a tad neurotic – had prepared a bowl of water in the back garden and dropped apples inside for Smith and his friends to play a game of bobbing. The idea was to hold your hands behind your back, stoop over the bowl and remove apples with your teeth. Smith had been very bad at it; the fruit, floating on the water, had continued to evade his bite. But that was when his dad – mean-spirited, drunk from festive beverages – had offered swift advice.

He'd pushed his son's head directly into the bowl and held it there until he was unable to breathe.

All Smith could remember, as the world went dark and mysterious, was his dad saying, "You have to wedge them against the bottom and then sink your teeth in, lad!" Smith had had little choice on this occasion, because the apple he'd targeted was hard against his mouth, its flesh collapsing with the pressure weighing on the back of his head. Then he'd heard his mum intervene, telling his dad in her ineffectual way to leave the boy alone. And finally, maybe a minute after he'd been assaulted, Smith was allowed to stand again, shaking water from his face, choking and gasping, watching his friends gaze on with unblinking stares. Then Smith had run back inside his home and locked himself in his bedroom, the victim of a latest example of paternal brutality.

Why had his dad done that to him? What had Smith ever done to deserve such cruel treatment? It certainly hadn't stopped there. During the next four years, before his mother had finally divorced the man and moved away with her only child, his dad had continued to mistreat him, both physically and verbally. It simply hadn't made sense, and Smith now realised he'd been struggling to reconcile himself to this illogical behaviour for well over a decade.

No wonder he preferred the orderly world of Newtonian physics, in which the universe was mechanistic and ultimately knowable. An apple falls from a tree and there's a perfectly rational explanation; it doesn't just occur without reason.

An apple ...

The thought brought Smith back to his present circumstances, where an attractive girl beside him steered her car into a small village.

Most of the houses they passed were squat and bore thatched roofs, each almost secretive in appearance. There were no streetlamps hereabouts, which implied that the locale mightn't even be served by modern utilities. Smith had heard of such places out in the wilds of the British Isles, where heat was generated by old-fashioned devices and cooking was conducted over real flame.

At that moment, an image of human sacrifice – a man being burned alive inside a giant wicker man – came to Smith's mind, but he shoved this aside, just as he had all that pitiable business concerning his dad. Smith was a grown man now and could look after himself. And when the vehicle pulled up outside a building that resembled a pub, with stark red light burning at one thickly curtained window, he decided to take control of his situation.

Turning as the girl tugged on her handbrake and killed the engine, he said, "What exactly is going on here?"

By now, a little of his drunkenness had left and he could speak without hindrance. Nevertheless, his first sight of his companion was alarming: red light from the nearby pub window seemed to bleed into her face, making it look as if she'd been skinned alive. But then the image settled and he saw the girl for what she was, just a harmless Welshwoman with a penchant for sharing her culture with strangers.

"Follow me," she said, and got out of the car, slamming the door after her.

Smith did as he'd been bidden. Once outside, he noticed that the girl was pointing, away from the pub and across a deserted village square. He tracked the direction of her finger and saw, suffused in shadow and as large as any university building, a gnarled tree, its limbs plentiful and in leafy bloom. There were small objects dangling from each branch – circular objects the size of human fists. Smith knew immediately that these were apples.

Beyond the tree, at a moonlit distance, a small body of water rippled and glistened … but then his attention was drawn back to what the girl was saying.

"That's the tree that offers the fruit to make such a splendid drink. Honestly, you'll have never tasted anything like it. Come inside and let's fix you up with a pint."

He didn't care for the way she kept talking about others in the village. He'd hoped to be offered this mythical beverage in only her company. But as she'd started pacing for the pub – the entrance had a board flapping above it, which read *The Newborough* and had a sketch of apples at its core – he could only follow, intrigued by the drink to which she'd effusively alluded.

Inside, the pub was low lit. About twenty people sat in alcoves and on bar stools, enjoying glasses full of what looked like standard public house fare: beer, short-and-mixes, the occasional soft drink. On the ceiling in the middle of the lounge was a large lamp, casting red light like a weird astral body, giving the place an otherworldly atmosphere. And of course that was when Smith noticed the drinkers' eyes.

Just like the girl's who'd brought him here, all were shaped like apple pips, oval at the centre and tapered at the corners. Otherwise these people looked conventional, dressed in the casual garments one might expect in any local drinking den. But those eyes … and the grins that, as each member of the ensemble turned slowly his way, suffused every pale face …

That was when the girl – Christ, he still hadn't acquired her name – spoke again.

"I've brought along a guest to taste the … fine stuff."

Smith disliked the way she'd hesitated; it had reminded of old horror movies in which the most threatening events were always hammed up. Nevertheless, as the small crowd parted to allow access to the bar, the girl nudged him forwards with one hand against his back – a hand that felt considerably larger than it should.

That was just faltering drunkenness playing tricks on his psyche. Another drink would sort out such nonsense. As he moved forwards, amid the grinning mob with tapered eyes, he tried reassuring himself that small gene pools, uncorrupted by migration, often shared physical characteristics. There was the Nordic bone-structure of northeast people, the ginger hair of Scots, and the fair flesh of the Irish. But Smith struggled to pursue this line of reasoning, because that was when he spotted a number of pictures on the walls.

Most made reference to apples in some way – great piles in orchards or loaded on old-fashioned trailers – but what was *this* one about? At first the sketch reminded Smith of his earlier reflections on Newton, how an apple had fallen from a tree and offered the great scientist insight about gravity. But was this an apple? Embedded in the ground to its halfway point, as if dropped with great force, it had certainly fallen from somewhere. But there was nothing obvious for it to have come from, just a vast sea of stars. A tree standing beside it offered spatial context; the silvery ball of matter must be about twenty yards in diameter.

This was only a drawing, of course; Smith could see its pencilled shading even in the murky light. But what should he make of the next picture in the row? This one, closer to the bar, showed the same large, silvery ball, but on this occasion a tiny worm appeared to have emerged from it, wriggling slowly away. That put Smith in mind of other fears he'd had as a child, how he'd often imagined that, after biting into a piece of fruit, they'd be a maggot lurking at the centre, eager to get inside him. It would lay eggs in his belly, filling him with its offspring, which would eventually burst out in a shower of gore. He'd been very impressionable, unease caused by his punitive dad hardly helping to keep his imagination at bay.

As if his memories had come to vivid life, a third picture displayed many more worms, with that giant silver ball situated way behind them. Again, the spatial context was revealing, because although most of the worms were as small as the first, one of them – presumably the first, grown bigger since its emergence from that ball – was nearly as big as another tree. The landscape around these entities looked like the one Smith had observed yesterday while travelling across Anglesey with Jenkins. But during that coach trip, he certainly hadn't spotted anything so … otherworldly.

222

The largest wormlike creature was a mass of writhing, slimy flesh. The artist had done a good job of capturing the thing's bulky body, its flattened head, its mouthful of razor-sharp teeth. It was limbless yet deeply threatening, appearing to leak droplets of a greenish substance which hissed visibly as they struck the ground. But the most powerful aspect was something Smith's floundering mind should have noticed first: the thing's large, bulbous eyes were the shape of apple pips.

Fear assaulted him deep in his gut. By now, he'd been encouraged to approach the bar, that outsized hand still hard against his back. In his peripheral vision, he sensed many other people – each proud of their acolyte, the imperious girl with whom Smith had arrived – gather around him, closing off any chance of retreat. Then a figure appeared from behind the bar, a burly man with thickset arms and a beard as dense as a forest.

"Give him a pint of the … pure stuff," the girl said from behind Smith, and any physical attraction he'd felt towards her disappeared when he recalled those familiar eyes, the ones shared by all his latest drinking companions … and perhaps something far worse.

Rather than access the pumps in front of him, the barman narrowed his eyes and turned away. He unlocked a door at the rear of the bar, entered an unseen room, moved around with a regular chink of glass, and finally reappeared. Now he carried an unmarked bottle, green and dripping beads of dew, rather like the creature in the final drawing on the wall. He paced forwards, removed a pint glass from a shelf above the bar, levered off the bottle's cap with a metal device that resembled an apple corer, and poured out the beverage.

It hit the glass with a hissing sound, filling the base and then rising, a sediment-ridden liquid. It was clearly cider, but a cider of which Smith had never previously been aware. It was nothing like the mass-produced, chemical-enhanced crap he knocked back in the Student Union bar. This looked like the real deal, the way the drink's ancient inventors had intended it. Perhaps the recipe had remained a village secret for centuries; maybe the ingredients could only be acquired from a unique source: that tree in the square outside.

But what did that silver ball mean, and all those other weird sketches by some deranged local artist? Did the cider made here possess hallucinogenic properties and were such visions a product of its impact?

Smith turned, examining his eager attendants, including the girl who'd picked him up in Llangefni. Their eyes looked freakish, like the multiple orbs of a single entity filling the lounge from wall to wall. There seemed to be far too much flesh on display, as if every onlooker had … expanded somehow, their bodies betraying their true identities.

But Smith found it hard to keep on looking. The drink had been set down on the bar behind him, a thump of glass against wood. He twisted back, his perceptions swimming, and then, with unwitting fortitude, he reached out to grasp the offering. He heard his dad's voice in his mind, calling him a "spineless wuss" and more besides. Then he lifted the pint to his mouth, muttered, "*Oh, bugger off, you old bastard,*" and took a gulp from the glass, the liquid filling his head with its pungent scent.

The girl hadn't exaggerated; the cider was impossibly delicious. Smith could detect ripe apples in there, but it wasn't sickly. The brew was tempered by an underlying bitterness that just failed to become unpalatable. The combination of both sweet and sour was delicately balanced and yet triumphant. Smith now felt like a god consuming nectar. The wild sensations with which the taste filled his body threatened to render inadequate everything he'd drink again.

By the time he'd sunk half the glass, his surroundings started swaying, but he no longer cared about such trivialities. He thought this must be what taking strong drugs was like, a sudden diminishment of all previous concerns. The solid uprights of the bar began lurching and bending, but Smith continued to drink, reducing the pint of cider to a quarter of its content. He couldn't help himself. It was like the plea of a beautiful girl or a cry for help from a child. Nature had equipped the body with certain receptive devices, and by overruling them you ceased to be human. Smith had become a mass of nerve endings, of sensory delights. He wanted the experience to go on. He wondered how he'd ever summon enough resolve to leave this mysterious village on an island he'd found dull until now.

"Is he ready yet?" a voice said from behind, and Smith realised it hadn't been the girl who'd spoken. But if she'd been addressed by this man's question, didn't that imply complicity? She hadn't had chance to explain to her peers her motive for bringing Smith here. Had she – *they* – plotted all this?

"By the time we get him there, he'll be ripe enough," said another voice, a female this time, but much older than the village's youthful agent, its sly abductor, its nefarious honey-trap.

As Smith drained the last of the mind-blowing beverage, hands were laid upon him – again, each felt overburdened by flesh – and he was turned away from the bar … to confront a terror beyond even his most savage dreams.

The villagers had *changed*. Although their eyes remained the same unusual shape (*like apple pips*, a treacherous voice in Smith's head announced), their skin had become loose and slimy in appearance. It had also assumed a reddish texture, the low lamp overhead making each look as if they'd been peeled alive. They'd retained their limbs, a semblance of humanity even interbreeding had failed to eradicate, but every other element had been stripped away. Their teeth were like slivers of ice.

Maybe the cider made him experience such things; yes, that was the only explanation, a Newtonian one, in which the world, however bizarre it could appear, never ceased making rational sense. Smith must simply wait until the alcohol wore off. But how was that possible when all his companions now took hold of his plump body (*like an apple*, his fellow student Jenkins said in Smith's memory) and lifted him high to frogmarch out of the pub, into the cool night?

As the territory around him lurched and churned, Smith sensed himself being conveyed across a flat surface and then into a field that felt soft beneath his ruthless conveyers. It was as if he was strapped to the back of solitary creature, one with many spindly legs and arms. Laid on his back, Smith saw the upper reaches of the tree he'd spotted earlier, cutting across his range of vision. Its branches were heavy with fruit, each a glistening orb of green and red.

How much time had passed since his arrival in the village? It was difficult to tell; his mind was all a-whirl. Stars and the wicked hook of a moon wheeled around until eventually the procession stopped and he was lowered to the ground.

Thank God, he thought, his relief palpable, despite the booze still rioting inside him. Back on his feet, the world grew no less stable and then he lost his balance. Moments later, realising he'd been helped on his way by a number of misshapen hands on his back, he plunged into a body of water, a large pond near a shadowy stretch of woodland. The scent of apples was intoxicating; he wondered whether the liquid in which he now floundered was gallons of squeezed juice.

"*Hey!*" he protested, trying hard to eliminate things he'd heard the girl say while driving. One disturbing recollection involved the word "sacrifice", but he refused to allow that to stop him protesting. "Okay, everyone, you've had your fun. Now just get me out of here."

"This isn't *fun*," said the girl, who seemed likely to remain forever nameless in Smith's mind. She'd come to the edge of the pond, which, in Smith's shaky estimation, might be twenty yards in diameter. Coupled with so many trees nearby, something about this dimension resounded in memory. *A bowl-shaped hole in the ground*, he thought frantically. *What could have caused such a thing?*

But now someone else was speaking.

"Every year the Old One must be fed," said this man, stepping out of a crowd whose members were no less hideous in appearance than he presently appeared. Like all the others, including the girl, he still boasted odd-shaped eyes, his flesh was too baggy on slipshod bones, and he looked like he'd been peeled to the sinew. "It secures our crops and livelihoods."

Jesus, this was getting like a tawdry horror film, Smith thought. He turned to observe the woodland on the far side of the pond in which he bobbed like a plump, ripe apple.

And then froze.

Something was moving through it, quickly his way.

Christ, how big would anything have to be to make trees creak and groan like that? By now, the giddy chatter among the crowd behind Smith had lapsed into awed silence. Stars filling the sky gazed on with alien indifference.

"*It's coming,*" someone whispered, maybe even the girl, but now Smith's mind was filled with only one stark recollection: his dad thrusting his head into a bowl full of water.

"*Come on, let's have you,*" he hissed, gazing at the woodland, which had appeared only as small, single trees in the pictures on the pub's walls. Maybe what the recent speaker had meant was that a creature from another planet, after landing in a spacecraft and growing large enough to inseminate local people, had a positive effect on vegetation, the way worms were supposed to enrich common gardens.

But none of that mattered now; Smith had given up trying to be reasonable, logical, Newtonian. He'd finally entered the realm of irrational.

"Why does an apple fall from a tree?" he shouted, his voice firm and yet fearful. "Why do some fathers abuse innocent children? Why do decent people get subjected to *this* kind of stuff?"

Nobody answered from behind … but up ahead a massive breakage of trees, its source concealed by a tenuous barrier of foliage, hinted at an imminent response. There were audible lashings of slime, like lava bubbling up from some restless volcano. Briefly, Smith thought he saw something pale in there, its moonlit flesh writhing like the tender skin of fruit.

"Because," he cried, picturing his dad's face in his mind, "that's just the way things are and we must all live with it."

As more trees were felled by a mighty force approaching, Smith wondered how deep the pond was in which his bloated body floated, thanks to his kicking legs. He only hoped that when the *thing* finally appeared, displaying its weird-shaped eyes and teeth like apple corers, he'd drown before it pushed him right to the bottom and took a good solid bite.

226

BENEATH THE SEA OF WRECKS

Do water monsters exist?

It's an age-old question for cryptozoologists. There are umpteen reasons why they should not, and yet fearsome, lake-dwelling entities continue to be reported in every corner of the world. Wales is no different, though the rumoured presence of Welsh aquatic beasts can largely be put down to the rich depth of folklore in the region. Dragons and serpents abound in Celtic mythology, so much of which is centred on the springs, rivers and lakes of ancient Cymru. The terrifying Afanc, for example, was a notorious medieval horror, a ferocious monster that allegedly swam up the River Conwy, depopulating the surrounding meadows of cattle and sheep, not to mention the occasional shepherd, and which required an army of peasants to snare it, drag it uphill, and finally dump it in Lake Glas-Lyn on the lower slopes of Mount Snowdon, where it supposedly still lives.

However, unlike Scotland and Ireland, most of Wales's water monsters are said to live offshore. The country's extensive, jagged coastline has long been rumoured the haunt of underwater giants. Sightings date until relatively recently. In 1882, a number of witnesses attested to watching an unidentified sea monster from Llandudno Pier. Dinosaur-like creatures were reported in Barmouth bay in 1937 and 1975, and on one occasion enormous webbed footprints were photographed along the beach there.

And yet none of these stories compare with the terror that struck the frigate, Robert Ellis, off the coast of Anglesey in 1805. This portion of the Irish Sea, which incorporates Colwyn Bay and the Menai Strait, has always had an eerie reputation. In ancient times, when St Patrick was said to have banished all serpents from Ireland, several of their larger brethren supposedly made the Irish Sea their home, but, fearing the saint's wrath, would stay closer to the shores of Britain, particularly favouring the sea off North Wales. In the decades after World War Two, this stretch of water was referred to as the 'Sea of Wrecks' thanks to the preponderance of strange disappearances and maritime disasters occurring in its vicinity.

Even so, it is not possible to imagine the crew of the Robert Ellis ever expecting the events of October 1805. The vessel wasn't far north of the Anglesey coast, when a large V-wash was sighted approaching from behind. Initially, the crew assumed it was a whale, but when the object drew closer, they were astounded by the *sight of an archetypical sea serpent: a slender but immensely long reptilian creature, maybe 100 feet from nose to tail. Apparently it thrashed its way aboard through the tiller hole, causing chaos on the upper deck, before winding itself around the central mast. There was much damage to navigational equipment and the ship was knocked off course. The crew attacked the beast with axes and oars. In retaliation, it snapped and slashed at them, but caused no casualties. Eventually, defeated, it loosened itself from the mast and slithered back overboard. According to several written testimonies, the creature continued to follow the Robert Ellis for two days, looking for a chance to come aboard again.*

This story brings to mind the accounts of crewmen on board the HMS Daedalus in 1845, which was allegedly pursued through the Atlantic by a colossal serpent. A similar tale was told by a group of naturalists, who sighted a plesiosaur-necked monster off the coast of Brazil in 1905. None of these are ancient tales, so it would perhaps be unwise to simply disregard them. One theory concerning the Anglesey serpent is that it was an unusually large conger eel. Another suggested an oarfish, which species has been recorded as reaching lengths of 56 feet.

Whatever the true explanation, there seems no doubt this incident occurred. That said, no one died or was injured. One perhaps doesn't need to get too jumpy, but all the same it might pay to exercise a little caution the next time you are navigating the Sea of Wrecks.

LEARNING THE LANGUAGE
John Llewellyn Probert

My name is Richard Lewis Morgan. I am Welsh. And there is something horribly wrong with me.

Right now, I'm about two thirds of the way up Skirrid Fawr, or the Holy Mountain as it's known to many of the residents of the nearby town of Abergavenny. My girlfriend Natasha is just a little bit ahead of me – she's already out from under the tree cover and making her way across the long, bare, open summit of the mountain to the white stone marker at the end. I've taken this opportunity to take a breather and go over as much of all of what's happened as I can remember. My mother always told me if something is bothering you a lot, then you should think about it, say it out loud even. Things always seem more manageable if you say them out loud

Natasha will not be coming back down the mountain.

Actually, writing that has made what I have to do a little easier. The knife in my pocket is made of stainless steel and I've owned it since I was a boy. I'm the only one to have ever used it, except for the time Reverend Watkins borrowed it once to get the hymn book cupboard open in Llantryso Church. It's the only thing I have that my father gave me. Apart from my destiny, of course.

Some people call this place the Holy Mountain because when Christ was crucified God struck it in his anger, cracking the mountain in two. You can still see the fissure today, overgrown with brambles and ferns and dotted with sheep who don't mind venturing into what some presumably believe is a divine rift. Why God should have aimed his wrath at Wales rather than at Jerusalem, or Rome, no-one has ever been able to explain to me. It's also claimed that once, when the Devil strode across Wales, his foot came to rest on this place and thus broke off a fragment of the rock. I like that story better, but then I would. While I have never seen much evidence of God at work in this country, I know that this is a land of ancient power and even more ancient beings. My mother and father knew it, too. After all, that was how I came to learn of them in the first place.

If I move on a little I can just see Natasha ahead of me, her white jacket bobbing along the mountain top. She'll be at the marker in a bit. It was put there many years ago by the Welsh National Trust. It's what they call a triangulation or 'trig' point, to allow you to orientate yourself with other mountains in the area. Far fewer people know that it is no coincidence these triangulation points are where they are; that they are markers of the deep seated power of each mountain; that a sacrifice to the spirit of a mountain must be made at the site of the marker. In blood.

She's nearly there, and there's no-one else around. I didn't expect there to be this early on a Tuesday morning.

Time to get moving, I think.

*

I have already mentioned going to church in my childhood and you might therefore be forgiven for thinking that my family were Christians. Until I reached a certain age I had assumed that myself. We went every Sunday, my mother, my father, and I.

I should have suspected something was wrong when I learned that my school-friends' church attendances differed from my own in one significant way. They always went to the same one, whereas my parents did their best to attend a different church every Sunday. There were so many in the area around Abergavenny that it easily took us several months to get round them all. Each Sunday the routine would be the same. Father would tell us where we were going and mother would pack a small picnic if we were going to be driving for more than an hour. We were always the first to arrive and my parents would spend the time before the service making a careful examination of the graves before securing themselves a seat at the back just prior to the service beginning. Father would be jotting things down in a small black notebook right up to the point where the vicar took his place at the front, and again afterwards before leaving the building. Each vicar, and each congregation, was always very welcoming towards my parents, presumably because they always told them they were thinking of moving to the area, and that it was important to them to see what the local church was like. If I asked if we were really moving house once we were in the car afterwards, my mother would give me a look, and ask me if I really wanted to leave that lovely house of ours?

Seeing as I've brought it up, this is as good a time as any to describe 'that lovely house of ours'. Accessed via a tiny country lane on the outskirts of town, the house where I grew up was the Victorian vicarage to the now derelict and desanctified church that adjoined it. I loved that old house, even though the sun never quite seemed to reach it, even though we often needed to have the electric lights on throughout the day, and even though for much of the year it was so cold there that I would wake to a crust of ice coating the inside of my bedroom window. It was my childhood home and I regarded it with the same affection that my parents did.

230

I was fortunate, I suppose, in having parents who did not need to go out to work. We were by no means well off, but I always had reasonable clothes to go to school in, and my considerable academic achievements at such a young age had already served to ostracise me from my peers. Unfashionable clothing had merely served to cement my reputation as 'odd' – something I was quite happy to encourage.

Thus it was that I was out of the house more than my parents were. My father spent most of the daylight hours in his study, a vast book-lined room in which he would lock himself for hours engrossed in whichever volume he had taken down from the woodworm-ridden shelves.

One day, my father chanced to leave his study door open and I, being a curious child who had never been told to stay out of it, found myself examining the heavy tome he himself must have been reading before being called to the telephone. I could read at least as well as any boy my age, and it was with a mixture of confusion and fascination that I tried to read the peculiar combinations of consonants, the arrangements of vowels and letters into words that were as unpronounceable as they were unreadable.

I was in the process of turning the page when I became aware of a presence behind me. My father had returned. He did not seem unhappy with my gentle handling of the page, and so I asked him.

"Is this Welsh?"

He appeared to ponder my question for a moment before replying.

"It is," he said. "But a more ancient and darker Welsh than most who now call this land home would be aware ever existed."

"Can you read it?"

A smile. "Some," my father said. "And just a little more every day."

"Is it what you're looking for in the churches?"

The smile broadened but no answer was forthcoming. "I think your mother is looking for you," he said. "You'd better go to her."

My mother hadn't been looking for me at all, and when I returned to my father's study the door was once again locked.

*

I never learned to speak modern Welsh. My parents were among the many residents of the country who were unable to converse in their native tongue and so it was never an issue in our household.

The dark Welsh, however, the ancient and almost forgotten language my father had shown me in what turned out to be a quite unique volume, was another matter altogether. My education began

231

one morning over breakfast, with my father scribbling a few letters on the back of the envelope that had housed yet another final demand for the electricity bill.

He passed the creased paper over to me. "How do you think that should sound?" he asked.

I frowned. To me it just looked like a random collection of letters that didn't belong together. But I did my best, producing something that made me sound as if I could use a powerful decongestant.

"Try again," said my father, "but try making the sound in your throat, rather than your nose."

I did as I was told.

"That's better." My father was obviously pleased, and my mother flashed me an encouraging smile as she cleared the plates away.

By the end of the week I had mastered a number of new 'words' and was able to move onto my first guttural and awkwardly pronounced sentence. I remember that Saturday afternoon well, as I was made to repeat the five words over and over until I could recite the sequence of noises perfectly, and without the aid of the volume from which my father had transcribed them.

"Good," he said, eventually satisfied. "Now when we go to church tomorrow, I want you to say those words under your breath once the vicar steps into the pulpit. Very quietly, mind. No-one else must hear them. Not even your mother and me. Do you understand?"

I nodded. "Why?"

His response made no sense to me at the time. "Because the ones we want to get in touch with need to be called in the right way," he said. "They won't listen to us, but they might listen to you."

"Who are they?" I wanted to know. "Are they friends?"

"We hope they will be," said my mother, resting proud hands on my shoulders. "We hope they will be very good friends indeed."

"But how will they be able to hear if I'm so quiet?"

I could see my father had to suppress a chuckle at this. "Because they have very special ears," he replied. "Ears that can only hear certain special words."

"Are they Welsh?"

Both my parents nodded in a way that suggested pride in their child who had taken a great leap forward.

"They are," said my father. "The purest Welsh there is. From the times when England did not even exist, not as anyone knows it now."

232

"Is Wales older than England, then?" My parents were in a rare revelatory mood and my twelve year old self was keen to exploit it.

My father seemed to be considering something for a moment and then, prompted by a nod from my mother, he spoke again.

"Wales is not just older than England, my son," he said. "There are some who believe it to be the place where life first sprang from on this planet. To be born Welsh is to be born not just privileged, but to be born into an ancestry that leads back to a time before man, before the mammals that led to the development of man."

"Before dinosaurs?"

My mother nodded. "Failed experiments of those who first came here," she said. "They cast them out to other parts of the world, where they eventually died and gave rise to fossil fragments – the only evidence of their passing."

A bit like the chat your parents try to have with you about the birds and the bees, this was all rather hard to believe.

"We did about dinosaurs in school," I said. My parents nodded. "And evolution." They nodded again. "And the Bible." Here they frowned and shook their heads.

"Throughout millennia people have tried to come up with explanations for who we are, where we came from, and where we might go after this life," my father said. "None of it is true. The truth is in the volumes in my study, and I have so much yet to decipher, so much that I need help understanding."

"You can help us," my mother explained. "You are able to say the words, and you are just young enough that your voice should be in the right frequency to reach them."

"But why in a church?" I wanted to know.

"People feel they are closer to God in a church," said my father. "In Wales, they are closer to the ancient beings that slumber beneath the Earth. It is easier for Them to hear you in such places."

"And the gravestones?" My parents exchanged looks. "You're always looking for what's written on them," I said.

"It is not what's written on them that's important," my mother said, "but the way in which they have been arranged. These, too, are markers of the receptivity of one of the Ancients to our communications."

"And we believe we have found the one where we may best be heard." My father's eyes were glittering with triumph, even though he had received little in the way of confirmation that he was on the right track.

"And we're going to go there?" I asked.

"We are," said my father.

"On Sunday," said my mother.

"Tomorrow," they both said together.

You may be wondering why I was sat in St Peter's Church in the tiny parish of Llanwenarth Citra the next day. You may be wondering why I had not refused point blank to be involved in something that sounded at best ridiculous and at worst frankly dangerous. But I was twelve, I was shunned by school friends and had no-one other than my parents to talk to. When you are that age and that alone, it's very difficult not to go along with what you've been told to do.

So there I was, sitting at the back of this small church, in between parents who were convinced that when I made some strange noises something fantastic and unworldly was going to occur. Quite what it was they hadn't told me, and now I wonder if they had actually thought that far.

The congregation ceased its sullen rendition of *How Great Thou Art* and the packed congregation resumed their seats, as did we. Father had pointed out before the service began that with us present the congregation made up an odd number, which seemed to be of great significance to his mind. Now, as the vicar ascended the steps to the pulpit, my father prodded me, as if I needed reminding of my task.

Even at the last minute I hesitated, wondering if it might perhaps be better to face the wrath of my parents than whatever I might call forth from the depths of the planet.

But in the end, I did as I was told.

At first, nothing happened. The vicar, an elderly man with a few wisps of white hair crowning his otherwise gleaming bald head, continued to address his rather meagre flock with alternating words of condemnation and reassurance, the people before him nodding in agreement as he poured loathing on those whom he claimed were responsible for the general state of moral decay in the country.

Everyone assumed the rumble we heard was due to an encroaching electrical storm.

When the building began to rattle I imagine some must have thought they were to be witness to the first earthquake in Wales in a millennium. Perhaps others thought the wrath of God was about to be visited upon them.

Which, in a way, it was.

People only began to panic when the red fog descended.

It cloaked the building rapidly, covering the windows and turning the feeble daylight an unearthly shade of scarlet.

"Fear not, my brethren," said the priest in the most fearful voice I had ever heard. "If we are to be judged, let us not be afraid, for our hearts are pure and minds are –"

We never got to find out what the vicar thought our minds might be like, because at that point the stained glass exploded inward, and the red mist that had coalesced on its surface began to drip into the building, running down the white walls, pooling on the floor tiles and spreading towards the frightened crowd, who even now were retreating to the centre aisle in a bid to escape the creeping miasmic horror.

All eyes turned to the pulpit and widened in horror. The vicar, struck by numerous shards of splintered glass, was now slumped over his pulpit, his body a rainbow of glittering colours, the predominant of which was red.

My parents stood, horrified by what I, and by turns they, seemed to have caused. They turned for the door, only to find that others were already ahead of them. The middle aged robust-looking lady who opened the door found herself faced with more of the red fog, which billowed in and, like superheated acid, dissolved her flesh from her bones as it made contact.

"Send it back!" My father was squeezing my shoulder so hard it hurt. "Send it back now!"

"I don't know how!" I sobbed through tears. "You didn't teach me any other words."

"Backwards," said my mother. "Say them backwards."

"It was hard enough saying them forwards," said my father, his normal reserve gone. "How is he possibly going to be able to reverse the words of summoning?"

Personally I had no idea, but I was going to try. Amidst all the screaming and the stampeding, the desperation and the panic, I climbed onto a pew and tried hard to remember the final word my father had taught me. Then I reversed the letters.

I spoke the first word.

Nothing. Just the same screaming and madness and encroaching red death.

Never mind, there were four more words to go.

Carefully and methodically, I remembered each one, turned it around, and spoke it, using the same guttural whisper my father had showed me.

As the last croaking syllable left my lips, something happened, although it was not what I was expecting.

The world turned white.

At first I thought I had been blinded. Then, as my eyes began to adjust, I realised that I, and everything around me, was covered with ash. Tiny fragments of it floated through the air, coming to rest on the motionless bodies of those around me.

Including those of my parents.

I jumped down from the pew, stirring up a fine cloud of white powder as I did so, and waded through more of the stuff to where my parents' bodies were lying.

I reached out to touch my mother's ash-coated face, and the flesh beneath crumbled into yet more of the dust that surrounded me. I grabbed at her hand and it turned to nothing beneath my fingertips.

My father's body was the same, as was the body of everyone else in the church. A slight breeze blew through the broken windows, and reduced the shapes that still resembled human forms to powder. I took faltering steps towards the door, and made my way out into a world that I quickly realised was not my own at all.

The sky was not just the wrong colour – a strange admixture of red and gold peppered with orange pinpricks that I assumed must be stars, although a few of the large ones were obviously planets – it was the wrong shade as well, as if the sun that gave this realm light was much further away than the sun is from our earth.

The church was still there, standing behind me against this darkly glittering backdrop, and the graveyard was there, too. Now, however, the teetering stone markers resembled rotted teeth in the mouth of some vast and cankered beast, and I wondered if the leathery substance on which I was standing might be its tongue.

I took a step forward and the world shook, the ground yielding a little beneath me, as if perhaps I was walking on flesh rather than earth. A sound midway between an ambulance siren and a creature screaming in distress seared my ears, and I put my hands up to cover them.

But that was not the worst.

As I looked up to the heavens, at that vista so unnatural and so alien, the sky itself parted, splitting open lengthways, and an eye vaster than the entirety of creation regarded me with curiosity.

I could feel it probing my mind, filling it with knowledge, with experience beyond my years, as if it was preparing me for something. I suddenly felt older, much older.

I realised with terror a little later on that it was not just my mind it had changed.

*

"We thought we'd lost you, too."

The nurse had a lovely Welsh accent. The doctor with her was English and I instantly disliked him. Both of them looked at me as if

I was lucky to be alive, and when I glanced down to see most of my body covered in bandages I could see why. I would have asked them what had happened but it took several days before I was on a sufficiently low dose of morphine to let me form sentences.

In a word, Llanwenarth Church had exploded. The ongoing investigation had postulated a leaking gas main (didn't they always?) but nothing had been proven. The building had been destroyed and nearly everyone attending church that Sunday morning had been killed.

Everyone, that is, except me.

And even I was not who everyone thought I was.

I had mumbled my date of birth to both nurses and doctors to be rewarded with sympathetic looks and reassuring words.

"I'm sure you'll remember who you really are soon," one especially pretty nurse had said when I had insisted I'd been born just over twelve years ago.

"My dear fellow ..." the consultant had given me a stern look on his ward round a few days later, "... you seem to be an intelligent young chap so I'll be blunt with you. Who knows, it may serve to jolt you back into reality. However old you may think you are, by my reckoning you are at least twenty five, if not older than that. I'm sure your real date of birth will come back to you in good time, as will your real name and where you come from." He flipped through the case notes. "As for your address, our computer system has no record of a house being there. Nevertheless, I'm sure once you're up and about and out of here everything will start to come back."

"Up and about?" I croaked in a voice much deeper than the one that had quoted those unwieldy words in the church days – or was it years? – ago.

The consultant nodded. "Beneath those bandages is a whole collection of minor cuts and abrasions. A couple of your wounds needed suturing and there's a nasty burn on your right arm, which is why you were on the morphine, but that's healing nicely. There's really nothing to stop you from getting out of that bed and seeing if you can remember how to walk. In fact I insist on it."

I was wheeled from my bed to the Physiotherapy Department two floors down by a bored-looking porter who stopped to converse with one of the young female domestic staff. It turned out he was still very sorry about going off with someone else at the nightclub last Saturday and that if only she would give him another chance he would prove how faithful he could be.

This conversation was intended to be conducted out of my earshot, but somehow I seemed to have developed an extremely acute sense of hearing. More peculiar than this, however, was my realisation about halfway through what they were saying, that they had been talking in Welsh, a language that up until that moment had always been a complete mystery to me.

The porter returned, red-faced, and continued to push me towards the lifts. On the wall next to the push buttons was a list of all the floors and what was located on them, in English and Welsh.

I could understand both languages perfectly.

I was still shaking as I was wheeled into the Physiotherapy Department. The physiotherapist was stern, but I probably needed it. She thought my lack of coordination was because of shock which, in a way, it was. But it wasn't the result of physical trauma that caused me to totter and wobble along the walking bars, rather it was the shock of having discovered my new ability, as well as having to adapt to a body that was now several inches taller, hairier, and considerably better developed than the puny twelve year old one I seemed to have been relieved of by my experiences. It didn't take me long to get used to it, however, and before long I was considered physically fit for discharge.

The psychiatrist, however, wasn't so sure, and, after a month of counselling in an attempt to recover what she called my "lost years" I was eternally grateful to her for arranging my discharge to a halfway house close to the hospital. It was somewhere I could "mentally get back on my feet again" rather than being left to fend for myself, something that would inevitably have led me to living a hand-to-mouth existence on the streets of Abergavenny. Fortunately I did not have to remain within the confines of the building, and so, one sunny day shortly after I had arrived there, I made my way to where my parents' house should have been.

It was a walk of about two miles, and took me straight through Abergavenny town. As I walked, I noticed two very strange things. The road signs, all in Welsh as well as English, were now perfectly readable in both languages.

But the Welsh communicated something entirely different to me.

As I read the words, as I took in their meaning, I realised I was interpreting them as the Dark Welsh my father had introduced me to at my home in that increasingly distant never-land of the youth I seemed to have lost. The words spoke of a rising, of a return, of the sacrifices that must be made and of the locations at which they needed to take place. And most important of all they stressed the very special quality the victims had to possess. Not virgins like in the horror films, or babies like in the black magic novels my mother used to consume. Oh no, the sacrificial victims needed to bring about a reawakening of the Ancient Ones of this land only needed to possess one quality.

They had to be English.

Why have the Welsh always despised the English so? Harboured a hatred of that nation that always went beyond the friendly rivalry of a rugby match or simple neighbourly competition? Even when I was a child in school the teacher would make unpleasant jokes about the English, and the children who claimed that nationality would squirm in their seats, embarrassed and not understanding why they should come in for such vilification.

The Welsh have always hated the English, and now, perhaps for the first time in millennia, I had been shown the reason why.

You need to be made to hate something before you can be made to kill it. And if that hatred is ingrained over generations it just makes it all the easier to carry out your task when the powers that put that hatred there in the first place tell you it is finally time for them to return. The Welsh people were created by this land. Clad in the mud and dirt of the ancients, they rose full-formed from the hills and the rivers and the valleys. Fashioned by its elements and rooted in its history, the Welsh have always been here, and always will be. The English are from everywhere and nowhere. Nomads and vagabonds, they have dared to call a land their own that they really have very little claim to. At least, not in the way the Welsh can claim their heritage.

So let it be the English who suffer so that our land might truly live.

By the time I arrived at the site of my parents' house I was not surprised to find no trace of it. It wasn't needed anymore. For all I know it had never existed. The crumbled remains of the desanctified church were still there, although now something told me that were I to trace my steps back to Llanwenarth I would find ruins that were very similar.

It does not take much to disorientate a man and I, it seemed, had become the plaything, or perhaps more accurately, the Messiah, of the Ancient Gods of Wales. I walked back through the town, trying to ignore the road signs, trying to ignore the whispering voices in my head that were insisting, in the Dark Welsh of the ancients, that the first victim needed to be soon, that English blood needed to be spilled on the sacred Welsh soil of a nearby mountain to begin the cataclysmic chain of events that would change this land, and the world, forever.

As I stumbled back into the halfway house, my fingers pressed to my temples to try and shut out that infernal whispering, I almost cried out, screaming at the creatures in my head to stop, that there was no-one I could offer them, that there was no-one I knew who I could convince to come with me to their dread place of sacrifice.

There was a girl sitting in the front room, flicking through a magazine.

She had the weary, vaguely tarnished look of someone who has seen too much at too young an age. A bit like myself, actually. She looked up as I entered and gave me her best attempt at a smile.

"Hello," she said in an accent that sent a vortex of hot blood swirling through my veins. "I'm Natasha."

*

There isn't much left to say. Here I am, four days later, close to the Place of Sacrifice. Writing all this down has helped, I think, although I've just gone over it all again and I realise I'm finding it more and more difficult to determine how much of what I've written actually happened and how much is me trying to remember what happened and getting it wrong. There might be lots of things wrong, I think, but I also think I know how to make them right.

Natasha's reached the marker now. How white it looks, gleaming in the morning sunlight.

The Welsh sunlight.

The sunlight of my fathers, and their fathers, and of those who live beneath the mountain.

The English shall not have it, none of them.

Natasha will be the first. The first in a long line of glorious sacrifices to the spirits of this holy land on which only the Welsh are fit to tread.

Natasha will be the first, and then I shall look for others.

And if you are English, I will be looking for you.

SOURCES

All of these stories are original to *Terror Tales of Wales* with the exception of 'Old as the Hills' by Steve Duffy, which first appeared in *Ghosts & Scholars #33*, 2001, and 'Swallowing a Dirty Seed' by Simon Clark, which first appeared in *Midnight Never Comes*, 1997.

FUTURE TITLES

If you enjoyed *Terror Tales of Wales*, why not seek out the first five volumes in this series: *Terror Tales of the Lake District, Terror Tales of the Cotswolds, Terror Tales of East Anglia, Terror Tales of London*, and *Terror Tales of the Seaside* – available from most good online retailers, including Amazon, or order directly from http://www.grayfriarpress.com.

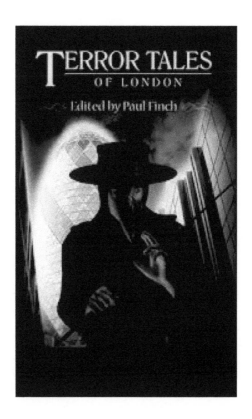

In addition, watch out for the next title in this series, *Terror Tales of Yorkshire*. Check regularly for updates with Gray Friar Press and on the editor's own webpage: http://paulfinch-writer.blogspot.co.uk/. Alternatively, follow him on Twitter: @paulfinchauthor.

Lightning Source UK Ltd.
Milton Keynes UK
UKHW010648050321
379837UK00002B/595